GHOSTS

NOEL HYND

ZEBRA BOOKS
KENSINGTON PUBLISHING CORP.

ZEBRA BOOKS are published by

Kensington Publishing Corp.
475 Park Avenue South
New York, NY 10016

Zebra and the Z logo Reg. U.S. Pat. & TM Off.

First Printing: November, 1993

Printed in the United States of America

Author's Note

What follows is, of course, a novel, so certain fictional liberties have been taken—specifically with some of the geographic locations on the island of Nantucket, as well as with the people of the island. Cort Street does not exist by that name, for example, nor do a pair of detectives-with-attitudes like Rodzienko and Gelman. The truth about haunted houses on the island, however, may be stranger than any novelist could imagine.

A note of very special thanks is also in order to Mrs. Virginia Hillger, for many favors over the years. Thanks, too, to whomever the woman in white was who drifted through our summer residence a few summers back and, in a spiritual sort of way, inspired this book.

—You could get lost delving into the other side of life.

St. Jude

Prologue

Rev. George Andrew Osaro glanced at his watch. It was five minutes past nine on the sweetly pleasant summer night of June 21. In the downstairs meeting hall of the Christ and Holy Trinity Lutheran Church on Nantucket Island, Massachusetts, Reverend Osaro moved the evening's symposium toward its conclusion.

"I think we just have time for our last three stories," he said, surveying his audience. "Why don't we proceed?"

On this evening, the minister sat on a stage at the front of the crowded hall. He was a short wiry man, half of European ancestry and half of Japanese. He had short dark hair, a clear fresh face and big round glasses that gave him an owlish look. He sat at the center of a long table, flanked by three panel participants on each side and glanced at two women and a man seated in chairs nearby. His left hand found his pipe, which had sat all evening on the table before him. His right hand found a tobacco pouch and as he spoke he deftly packed a briar with thumb and forefinger.

"Who wants to proceed? Mary?"

At the end of the table a woman named Mary Rovere nodded.

"Spiritual Nantucket" was the topic of the evening. "Ghosts on Our Island" was the subtitle. The latter defined the event more concisely than the former. On a stage before an audience were seven people who had, as Osaro might have explained it,

9

experienced the paranormal. Interacted with spirits. Or at least one spirit. Or, at the very least, they all thought they had.

George Osaro was a maverick like that. He used church space to stage an evening of fascinating creepiness, an extravaganza delving into a possible existence other than this one. And why not? Osaro had charged five dollars apiece to tourists and residents, had put ads in the local papers and had induced the radio stations on Cape Cod and Martha's Vineyard to mention it as a public service. After all, it was a church benefit. He had also put up posters on the supermarket bulletin boards and had now drawn one hundred sixteen paying customers. Osaro might have made an excellent advance man for a gubernatorial candidate.

So what if this was small-time show biz in a church hall? Reverend Osaro had painlessly netted in excess of five hundred dollars for his parish. Nantucket was an old island rattling with new money, distant generations and creaking houses. If the distant generations and creaking houses could induce the tourists and summer people to redistribute some of that new money into his church's coffers, was that such a crime?

Ghost.

A profanity in the minister's presence would pass unnoticed. An obscenity would breeze past him as well. But "ghost" was one word Osaro disdained.

Spiritual: This was the term Reverend Osaro preferred.

Ghosts, he argued, were shapeless white cartoon characters like Casper, or bad actors wearing white sheets in old Charlie Chan movies, or a double image on a television screen. Spirits, on the other hand, were those grand, buoyant, immeasurable, indefinable things that exist within all of us, only to be liberated after one's earthly demise. Sometimes they hung around for a while on their way "somewhere else." That was what the good minister said. And that's what this evening was about. Well, it was his theory, anyway, and it didn't strain his Christian orthodoxy all that much, either.

For that matter, his Christian beliefs were a large part of it. Osaro constantly endeavored to interpret the afterlife—and the many possible permutations of it—in terms of accepted church doctrine.

Yet here again was his penchant for packing an auditorium. The subtitle of the convocation: "Ghosts on Our Island." The term "ghost" was a bow in the direction of salesmanship. Osaro wanted people to know that if they came and dropped their five bucks into the collection box in the front hall, they could hear seven crackling good "ghost stories" directly from the people who had lived them.

"Ready, Mary?" George Osaro asked.

"Ready," she said.

Mary Rovere spoke of a house she and her husband had inherited four decades earlier. She was a plump woman with glasses, middle-aged and remorselessly middle brow. She was unfashionably coiffed and dowdily dressed. She had been an island summer resident for forty years, which was part of her story.

"I have to tell you," Mary said. "When it happened, I was absolutely terrified. Why wouldn't I be? I was looking at a man who I knew to be dead. Yet there he was. In my bedroom. Right in front of me." She drew a breath. "And he was trying to tell me something."

Then she backtracked. It began, she said, a flat thirty years earlier. She was sixteen years old at the time. She was sitting in the bedroom in the Nantucket house that her family still owned.

The house itself was a matter of contention.

"My grandfather was from Germany," she announced. "He was a very old-fashioned man named Heinreich Schumacher. He had come to America with a sister named Bettina around nineteen ten. They settled on Nantucket."

Osaro carefully lit his pipe and drew deeply upon it. A puffy white cloud enshrouded him. Mary drew a breath and eased into her tale.

"All his life, Grandpa was very distrustful of everyone, particularly in the new world. He had also had a very bitter falling out with Bettina. Eventually, she married and moved to Milwaukee. Their parents died in Germany, then the brother and

11

sister each claimed the other had cheated them. How or why, I don't know. I don't even know who was right. What I do know is that Grandpa, after he retired from the business of importing textiles, didn't want to be alone. My mother was his only child and was divorced. So Grandpa invited us to move into the house here on the island. Mother assumed he owned it outright. There was never a problem until soon after he died."

Death always has a way of complicating things. So it was in Grandfather Schumacher's case as well. First off, no one could locate the old man's will. And then there was the main event.

Bettina's side of the family hadn't communicated with Schumacher for decades, Mary said. When he died, the family was notified, but no one came to the funeral. Only then, after Grandpa was laid to rest, did they decide that they loved him. Or at least, the family's lawyers loved what they thought he might have left behind.

"When Grandpa passed away, his sister claimed that she and her brother had bought our house jointly in nineteen eleven. A trip to Town Hall actually bore out that part of her claim. Bettina had only allowed her brother to live in the house, argued their lawyers, out of the goodness of her heart. But now that Heinrich Schumacher was dead, some other arrangement would have to be made. The lawyers suggested that Mary's mother pay Bettina's family half of the fair market value of the house to settle the claim. That, or sell it, move out and split the proceeds.

"We didn't have the money for that. Mother was a bank teller. We barely had money for a lawyer."

Mrs. Rovere sipped from a glass of water.

"Grandpa had always said that he had bought out her share. But he had never produced a document," she continued. "The dispute grew nasty. So Bettina's family hired a local lawyer, filed suit against us and, over the course of several months, tried to evict us. Mother used to sit at the kitchen table and cry. It looked as though we were on our way out of our own home. 'Your grandpa would be rolling in his grave if he knew what was going on,' she used to say."

12

Mary drew a breath. As it turned out, she said, Grandpa was doing more than rolling.

"I was in bed reading one night when I was sixteen years old," she said. "This was in nineteen fifty-six. Uh oh," she said, laughing slightly. "I just gave away my age."

Some laughter went around the audience.

"It was late," she continued, "and my mother was asleep in the next room. I put down the book and I turned off the light. But this strange feeling came over me. I couldn't sleep. My eyes caught the glimmer of something in the room with me. Let me tell you. I nearly jumped out of my skin. In the darkness, I saw this bright figure materialize through a wall about six feet from me. Then it stopped before my bed. It was in the shape of a man. Then I realized: I was looking at Grandpa. I recognized this flat hat and big long topcoat that he always wore. He was standing there in the dark room looking at me. Somehow, I could see his eyes! Oh, I could *feel* him there! You know how you just *know* that there's someone in a room with you?" There were a few nods around the church meeting hall. "No doubt about it. I sat up real fast in bed and turned on the light. But nothing was there. He was gone."

Mary paused. She smiled ruefully.

"Now, I'm the first to tell you: Right away I tried to convince myself that I'd dreamed it. I told myself I had. But I finally fell asleep with the lamp on that night. I didn't want any more visitors."

Mrs. Rovere reached again for the glass of water that was on the panelists' table in front of her. She sipped, then continued.

"It happened again a week later. Same vision. Late at night. Coming through the same stretch of woodwork. I reached over, turned on the light, and everything was gone again. Yet the second time, it didn't unnerve me as much. Somehow I didn't sense any danger. Yet I also knew. Something important was unsettled. So it would happen again."

Reverend Osaro broke the mood a little by speaking. "Did you mention to your mother that this had happened?" he asked.

"No," Mary Rovere said. "I was afraid. Well, you know how it is. Mother was upset enough. And anyway, I didn't know if she would believe me."

"So it did appear again? This spirit?" Osaro asked.

"This was the third and final time," Mary said. "It was about a week later. And it coincided with the time when the fight between the two families was about to go to court. Lawyers and lawsuits . . ." She shook her head. "Very unpleasant stuff. I hated all of it."

"Everyone does," Osaro concurred.

"I don't really know how Grandpa communicated with me when he appeared the third time," Mary said. "I don't remember his lips moving. But I do remember him telling me something."

She drew a deep breath. "This time, I was half expecting him. So I rose. Sure enough, I opened my eyes and I saw him. He was dark, but sort of shining. He came right through the wall, just as he had the two previous times. He approached my bed. I remember I was sweating now because this was the first time he'd drawn so close. But then suddenly, everything seemed all right. It was my grandfather, after all. When I remembered how much we had loved each other I was completely over my fear. And he had something to tell me."

Somewhere in the very still meeting hall, someone coughed.

"Again, I reached for the light," Mary said, continuing. "He moved toward me very quickly. He was so close that his face was within a few feet of mine. I will never forget that view. It's still with me today."

Mary shook her head. "My grandfather's face. It seemed solid, yet I could see what was on the other side of it. I worked up the nerve to reach for the lamp. Not because I wanted to chase him away, but because I wanted to see him better. Then I felt his hand on mine. Oh, that hand! That touch! I would have recognized my grandfather's hand anywhere. But it was cold. Like snow is cold. And yet, he communicated to me that everything was all right. He was there to help Mom and me. So I moved my hand back to the bed and he released me.

14

"He stepped back. With a very theatrical motion, he opened this big long black coat that he must have worn for thirty years. It was black serge and I think it had come on his back from Germany. In any case," she laughed wanly, "he always wore it in his lifetime so why shouldn't he wear it in death?"

To Mary's left, Reverend Osaro smiled.

"He kept his eyes fixed on me. Then he pointed with his left hand. Very low. He was definitely indicating something. He pointed to the lower inside lining of the coat. His long index finger ran softly across the worn material. Then he straightened and, just as fast, vanished. I turned on the light and the room was still again.

"The next day, I told my mother the story. She insisted I had been dreaming, of course. Told me that my imagination must have been running wild. Things like that didn't happen."

Mary raised her eyebrows as if to suggest that she knew better.

" 'Well then, whatever happened to Grandpa's coat?' I asked her. And she told me. It was in the trunk of the car. It was boxed with several other things that were about to be thrown away. My mother felt that the old coat was so worn that no one would want it. She was probably right." Mary grinned. "But I had a different reaction. 'Let's go look at it,' I said."

They went out to the car, Mary said, and eventually located the tattered coat at the bottom of the least accessible box. But they pulled it out, fighting with the weight of other clothes upon the coat.

"My mother is here tonight," Mary said. "She'll tell you what happened if you don't believe me."

Mary pointed to an elderly woman in the third row. The woman smiled and nodded. Mary kept talking.

"The coat pockets were empty. I laid the coat out on the ground, then ran my hand across the lining to the part that Grandpa had indicated. Immediately, I felt something. I almost jumped when I found it. We took a pair of scissors and undid the stitching on the coat. There were all of Grandpa's important papers within the lining, right where he'd hidden them years ago. He'd worn the coat all the time because he was always carrying his papers with him." She paused. "Everything was right where he had indicated back when his vision had appeared before me."

Mary shrugged. At the rear of the church meeting hall, Timothy Brooks slipped quietly into the room. Brooks was a handsome, athletically built man in his late thirties, just above six feet tall, with dark blond hair, blue eyes and a square jaw. Unobtrusively, he sat down at a seat near the rear. Osaro, his friend, gave Brooks a very slight nod, imperceptibly to almost everyone else.

"Call it what you want," Mary concluded. "A dream. Clairvoyance. A spirit. What was found was his will. And with it there was a notarized document, all filled out and legally executed, that Bettina had signed in nineteen forty-nine. It was a bill of sale. Grandpa had bought his share of the house from her. Bettina's case was thrown out of court a week later."

Mary sighed.

"That's the way we inherited our home on this island," she said. "And that's my first and only experience with the supernatural. The house is up on Cliff Road and I won't tell you the exact location." She smiled. "As for Grandpa's coat, it's our family superstition. We've never discarded it. We keep it in the front hall hanging right there on an old wooden coat rack. 'In case Grandpa ever drops by again,' my Mother still says. "After all, there's not one bit of doubt in our family: Grandpa's watching over us. He even came back from the dead and gave us back our home."

There was an appreciative murmur in the hall, followed by polite applause. It was led by Reverend Osaro, who again glanced at his watch. He allowed a few questions from the audience. Then, holding his pipe in his hand, he introduced a man named Leon Kane. Kane was seated at the other end of the table and appeared to be in his seventies.

"Leon?" Osaro asked, "What have you got for us?"

Kane seemed almost embarrassed. His hair was white and thin, his face round, his voice gravelly. Reverend Osaro had talked him into taking part in the colloquium, but he still seemed ill at ease with it.

"I'll tell you something," he said, shaking his head, "two years ago if you had told me that I'd be sitting here talking about ghosts, I'd—"

"Spirits," the pastor corrected gently. "Let's call them what they are. They're living things, not dead. Same as you or I."

"Spirits. Ghosts. Whatever, Reverend," Leon Kane said a little cantankerously. "There's not a dime's worth of difference between them as far as I know." Kane thought about it, then turned to the smaller, younger man. "Hell, I *like* the word 'ghost'! What's the matter with it? That's what the hell my wife saw, so why can't I call it that?"

"As you prefer," Osaro said. The minister smiled indulgently. He did, after all, believe in freedom of thought. "Please go on," he said, apology in his tone.

"Where was I?" Kane asked.

Osaro helped him. " 'Two years ago, if anyone had told you—"

"Oh, right—that's it. Of course," Kane said. "Look, I'm a sane, sober guy. I'm a retired firefighter. Worked on the fire department in Providence for seventeen years, then I come here, was on the Nantucket Fire Department for another five. Retired nine years ago. Widowed two years ago, which is what I want to tell you about."

A hush slowly covered the hall.

Kane waited for a moment, as if to work up a final element of courage. Then he began.

"I was watching the Bruins play hockey one evening," he said. "My wife was in the kitchen cleaning up after dinner. It was about seven-thirty in the evening. I remember it real well. The Bruins were playing the Rangers at Madison Square Garden. November first, Nineteen-ninety. Cold night in the early fall. The game had just started. Anyway, I'm watching the television and I hear a man's voice in the kitchen with my wife."

Someone laughed very quietly at the notion of a strange man in the kitchen with the retired fireman's wife.

"I heard the man say, 'Laura, I've come for you.' Nothing more. Just that. But very clear. I heard them words. I looked toward the kitchen and I didn't see nothing. Nothing at all. It was one of them things that even after it happened, I couldn't even tell whether it really *had* happened." He glanced around to no one in particular. "Know what I mean?"

There were nods around the room. Most of the audience listened attentively, including Tim Brooks, still stationed toward the back.

"So finally I yelled out to the old girl, 'Laura?' That was my wife's name. Laura," Mr. Kane said. " 'Laura? You okay out there, honey?' No answer. So now I'm wondering: What the heck's going on? Well," he chuckled, "I started to get up. You know, pull my fat old self up out of the chair. Just then, Laura appeared at the kitchen door. Well, we'd been married for thirty-six years. And I'd never seen her so shaken. 'Honey?' I asked her. 'What is it?' She looked real frightened."

Kane paused, then went on. " 'I just saw my brother in the kitchen,' my wife said. She was talking about her brother Willie. Her only brother. Well, Willie had died in a car accident in Natick. Willie had been dead for six years."

Kane's wife came over and sat down on the ottoman near his chair. He put his hand on hers. She said she was terribly scared because she knew she hadn't imagined what she had seen. She had seen a ghost, she had said. That's what she had called it. A ghost. So Leon Kane continued to call it that, too, Reverend Osaro notwithstanding. In Leon Kane's explanation, Willie had been there one minute as solid as a stone barn. The next moment he had been gone.

"I would of talked her out of it," Leon Kane said, "I'm sure I would of. But I didn't 'cause *I* heard the voice, too. Clear as a bell. 'I've come for you, Laura.' Plain as day. Just like that. And know what? It was Willie's voice. I recognized it, too."

Two little waves went around the audience in the meeting hall. One of fascination. The other of discomfort. Kane gave the moment a long pause, and even Tim Brooks felt a hair or two rise on the back of his neck.

18

"I guess he had come for her," Kane said. "Came from wherever you come from after you're dead." He pursed his lips. "Next day, the very next *day*, my Laura had a stroke. By evening she was gone."

He ran his hand through his hair. It was clear that the story still caused him anguish. For a moment, thinking of his wife of thirty-six summers, something caught in his throat and he couldn't talk.

"But that's not even the end of the story," he added as he recovered. "See, we was redecorating the house, Laura and me, when she died. The next thing that we was going to do was get rid of this ugly old green carpet that we had in the den. Well, three days later I come home and the carpet was in a big heap on the floor. It had all been pulled up. I didn't know how it had got that way. I thought one of my daughters had done it. Or one of the grandchildren who were visiting. But, no. None of them fessed up to it. So I put the carpet back down. Sure enough, I found it pulled up again two days later. And then a third time after that."

Mr. Kane smiled. A ripple of laughter moved around the meeting hall. "So finally, hell, I got smart," he said. "I threw it out! I ordered a new one that Laura had liked but had never gotten around to buy. Had the carpet people rush the order. Well, sir. I brought the new one home and put it down myself. It's been there since. Never got disturbed." Again, he smiled ruefully. "Nothing happened again. What it seemed like," he concluded, "was that Laura was keeping an eye on me for a few days to see if I could make it through her passing all right. When she saw that I could carry on without her, she left. She went to wherever good souls go."

He shrugged.

"It's not scary," Leon Kane said. "It's comforting if you think about it real hard. See, deep down in my heart I know the person I love is out there somewhere. Waiting for me. I can't explain it. I just know that in the same way Laura's brother came for her, she kept her eye on me. And now she's out there in The Good Place waiting for me." His eyes were sparkling, though moist.

"I'm seventy-four years old," he said. "And you know what? I'm not scared of making that trip myself someday. Not scared at all." He smiled. "I keep hoping that someday I'll look up, see her, and know that it's my time and she's come to take me to Heaven with her." He tucked his lower lip into his teeth for a moment and held it. Then he turned toward Osaro. "That's it, Reverend. That's my story. That's all."

Applause followed. Then a few hands came aloft from those in the audience. Osaro cut off the questions.

"For reasons of time, I'd like to move to our final panelist," he said. "Maybe if some of you have questions or comments for Mr. Kane, he might be generous enough to stay for a few minutes afterward to speak with you."

Kane nodded to indicate he would.

"Otherwise," Reverend Osaro said, "I'd like to go directly to our final guest, Doctor Richard Friedman."

Osaro indicated a lean, angular man with short dark hair and glasses. The doctor looked like a doctor. He sat at the end of the table, next to Mary Rovere.

"Doctor Friedman is in private practice in Boston and has maintained a summer home here in Nantucket for the last ten years."

"Two different homes here in Nantucket," Dr. Friedman said, picking up the introduction. "That's part of the story. We were pretty much driven out of the first one. I'm afraid my tale is nowhere nearly as uplifting as my predecessor's."

He cleared his throat and his eyebrows furrowed unpleasantly.

"The house is on Milk Street," Dr. Friedman began. "It's not terribly old. It was built around nineteen hundred and was only inhabited by four owners before us. I've traced who they all were. I don't know of anything violent or terrible that ever happened at that address."

It started, the physician said, on a day shortly after they had moved in. His daughter, Rachel, had a bedroom adjoining the guest room on the second floor.

"She's a bright little girl," the doctor said. "Very perceptive of moods and feelings, very conscious of many things that she can't see." He paused. "And she was always scared of a door on that floor leading from her room to the extra room. She was also very frightened of the dark."

In his seat in a rear pew, Tim Brooks folded his arms before him. Through a veil of haze created by George Osaro's pipe, there was already something unsettling to the doctor's appearance.

Rachel was playing near bedtime one night three years earlier her father said, when she looked up and saw the figure of a man. It came through the wall and stood before her. This he announced as bluntly as if he were diagnosing a common virus.

The girl was terrified. But somehow the vision communicated with her.

" 'I'm keeping track of my place,' the vision said. Then the man disappeared before her eyes. Rachel fled down the stairs and screamed for her parents.

"We didn't believe in such things," Dr. Friedman said. "So we spent a lot of time insisting to our daughter that she must have fallen asleep and dreamed this. But for weeks she wouldn't use the room. And she slept with a light on when we finally coaxed her into moving back in."

Friedman scratched his head. "I suppose we also had another indication that something"—he looked for the right word—"*extraordinary* was happening. We bought Rachel a cat to keep her company. And we told her that the cat would protect her and know if something was wrong. Well, our plan was to reassure her. But the idea backfired. The hair on the cat's back would stand up if you took it to the room. If you put the cat down it would drop its tail between its legs and slink away. And if you tried to carry it through that doorway, it would scratch and claw and fight you till you dropped it. The animal wanted no part of that area of the house."

The apparition didn't appear again to Rachel. And though

she was constantly mindful of the possibility of a reappearance, she did calm down with the passage of time. Gradually, the spookiness became less of a factor of daily life in the house. Then an incident happened two summers later.

"We did some extensive renovations on the upstairs of the house," Dr. Friedman said. "The remodeling called for us to move the master bedroom to the extra room where the ghost had come from. Rachel was moved to the other end of the floor. My son, Jed, was in a room adjoining Rachel's."

He paused for a moment.

"I was there one night," Dr. Friedman continued, "when a feeling of terror came upon me. It surrounded me and held me with fear. It was like a giant hand wrapping itself around me. Honestly, I couldn't talk or move. I wanted to yell and couldn't." He shook his head. "Know what it felt like? It felt like something, some extraordinary presence, was trying to crush me, that's what."

Dr. Friedman knew he couldn't battle this power physically. So he remembered fighting this force intellectually. As a doctor, he tried to figure out what was wrong with him—seizure, heart attack, spastic fit—and do what was necessary to save his life. But equally, he knew that he was locked in combat with something not to be found in any medical journal.

"Eventually, I managed to stamp my foot. Then I got part of my voice back. I managed to let out a muffled grunt. Then a thought came over me. I don't even remember thinking the words. I just blurted them out, surprised to hear my own voice. 'I know,' I said aloud. 'You're just keeping track of your place.'"

The statement, the doctor said, seemed to placate whatever force had gripped him. It gradually released him. There was a point, he remembered, when the feeling was very tactile—something was holding him one second, letting him go the next.

Then he staggered downstairs, terrified. He told his wife what had happened.

"We calmly and methodically made the decision right then," Dr. Friedman said. "We would get out of the house and sell it.

There was no question in our minds that there was some utterly evil presence in that home. We couldn't fight it. Nor did we dare. So the next day we started making preparations to leave."

The preparations continued smoothly for several days. It was the end of August 1991, a quirky, moody time on Nantucket in any case as it directly followed the violent Hurricane Bob. The Friedmans assembled the clothing and belongings they wanted out of the house. They called their real estate broker and cryptically announced that they would list the home for sale but buy another one on the island. The broker didn't understand the logic because the doctor and his wife didn't immediately explain what had happened. But the broker was grateful for the business and accepted it.

"Then my wife and I were in the living room on our final day of packing. We were within minutes of removing our final pieces of luggage. And naturally something happened that both of us will never forget. Something more totally terrifying than I ever thought I would experience in my life."

The meeting hall of the church was very still now. From the back, Tom Brooks surveyed the audience as he held on Dr. Friedman's words along with everyone else.

Dr. and Mrs. Friedman were in the downstairs living area, the doctor recalled. Their children had been sent to stay with grandparents. So they knew themselves to be alone in the house. Then, in midafternoon, they froze. Very distinctly they heard footsteps above them—right in the area upstairs where there had been two incidents.

" 'Richard, let's get out of here. Right now!' my wife Bonnie said to me. And maybe we should have. But I remember thinking and saying, 'No. If we leave it might follow us. Whatever it wants, whatever it is, let's settle everything right here.' "

On the stage near Reverend Osaro, Dr. Friedman sipped from a glass of water.

Bonnie Friedman huddled beside him, Friedman said, and they stood riveted in place as the footsteps above them grew louder. The footfalls neared the central staircase at the front of the house, then slowly descended.

They held their ground as, one by one, the footsteps came down the staircase, which they could not see from where they stood. The sound stopped a few steps from the bottom, held silent for a few seconds, then came the rest of the way, three quick steps in succession. They arrived at the base of the steps with a thud.

Mrs. Friedman gripped her husband. They were looking right at the spot where something should have been standing. But nothing that they could see was there.

"Whatever it was," the doctor said, "it was toying with us. It was invisible."

But it kept walking toward them. The footsteps continued across a bare floor. The sound was like heavy old-fashioned shoes dragging slowly. The pace was deliberate and came straight toward them.

"Bonnie was beside herself now. She was yelling at me, begging to leave. But still I had this fear. I was afraid this thing would follow us wherever we lived, wherever we went, if we didn't settle our business right there."

The footfalls stopped. Still, the Friedmans couldn't see anything. But they *felt*. "It was very palpable," Dr. Friedman said. "Like a change of air pressure in a room. It made us feel low and sickened. Then, somehow a thought was communicated to us. We shuddered and we both felt it at the same instant. We were to turn around. No one said anything. We just both knew at the same time, we were to turn."

There before them, the doctor said, was exactly the same vision their daughter Rachel had described. This was in broad daylight and the figure looked very real. He looked like an old fisherman, the physician remembered, with a straggly beard, an almost misshapen-looking head, clunky boots and a battered mackintosh.

"His eyes were horrible," Dr. Friedman recalled. "Sickly white. Something wrong with the pupils as well as the sockets. *Dead* eyes, that's what they were. They reminded me of a cadaver's."

Dr. Friedman exhaled. "My wife turned away from him and

I could feel her tremble as I held her. No words were spoken. But both Bonnie and I now knew. We were free to go, as long as we left immediately. He had won. This. . . . This ghost, this angry, unsettled spirit, had driven us out. And he was there now to make sure we left."

Dr. and Mrs. Friedman picked up their remaining belongings and turned toward the front door. Richard Friedman was the last to leave.

"I never looked back," he said. "Didn't dare. And I never went back in that house again. It's sitting empty now. The real estate people come by now and then, but we've had no offers. People get a bad feeling just being in there." Dr. Friedman heaved a dismal sigh. "Exactly what will happen eventually, how the next tenants will be treated, I don't know. But there is not enough money in the world to send me into that place again. I don't need it."

He drew out a long breath. With a handkerchief, he dried the palms of his hands. He looked at his audience, which remained very still.

"Sorry I can't be more uplifting," he said. "Sorry I can't relate to you the spirit of a loved one in a contented afterlife, or how a vision from after death came back to save a family homestead. All I know is that our family was run out of our summer home by an evil, malevolent spirit that didn't want us there. That's the bottom line. And that's my story in its entirety."

Reverend Osaro took a half-dozen questions from the audience. Then he glanced at his watch. It was nine thirty-five P.M.

"We have a minute or so left," he said, "and I'd like to claim it, if I may."

No one objected.

"There are those," he said in closing, "who find this whole subject difficult to fathom. And there are those others who want to believe, but can't. I'd like to address that in a word or two."

He weighed what he was about to put forth.

"Nantucket is an aged place," Osaro said. "People have old houses. Generations upon generations have lived on top of each

25

other here. Spirits like to cling to what they have known in their worldly life. So why should it really surprise us when a spirit becomes displaced, when one decides to stay in such close proximity to us that we occasionally catch a glimpse of it?"

There were smiles around the room, Tim Brooks noted. Smiles and nods. Brooks listened to his friend.

"A lot of places have them, of course," Osaro said. "There are probably spirits in every old house, if the truth were known. You know, those displaced things that lurk. That flit by. Those movements or shadows that you see out of the corner of your eye. Then if you quickly look toward them, they're gone and you convince yourself that you didn't see them."

There were a few soft laughs. Brooks folded his arms.

"But we know they exist," Osaro said. "Deep in our human hearts we know. Some of us insist that they don't. But we *know*. Don't we?"

From the corner of his eye, Brooks was aware of a consensus around the room. The ascent of the converted. Yet, he noted further, there was no indication of this being a crackpot crowd. These were sane, rational people. Businessmen and homemakers. Students. Working people.

"And so," Osaro concluded, "with so many spirits about, is it any wonder that eventually a few of us on our side of death interact occasionally with someone from the other side? Should we really be so incredulous if that happens now and then?"

Osaro paused and looked around. He sensed an unspoken answer from the assemblage.

"I think not," the minister concluded. "And I trust that many of you agree with me." He smiled. "That's our time for tonight," he announced cheerily, his fingers playing with the lip of his pipe. "Thank you all for coming and a special thank you to our panelists for participating."

There was applause. Then the symposium concluded.

Afterward, Tim Brooks remained seated. A number of those who had attended pressed forward to ask individual questions of the participants. Brooks moved forward at this time, too, but waited patiently. Finally the group thinned. Mrs. Rovere and

Dr. Friedman were the only panelists left, aside from the pastor.

"You waiting to see me, Timmy?" George Osaro finally asked.

Brooks nodded.

"I've never known you to come to one of my spiritual evenings," Osaro said.

"First one I've been to," Brooks confirmed.

"What did you think?"

Brooks answered as only a friend could.

"I've never heard such crap in my life," Tim Brooks said softly. "I'm amazed *anyone* could believe a word of it."

"Ah, Timmy. . . . Always the doubting Thomas, right? Believe me, your day will arrive, too."

Brooks scoffed again. He was about to give his pal the minister some more heat on the subject when he realized that time wouldn't permit it.

The maintenance staff, volunteers all, was taking over the meeting hall. They were straightening chairs and sweeping the floor.

And more important, one by one, the lights in the church were going off.

Part One
The Discovery

—*Let every soul be subject
unto the higher powers.*
THE EPISTLE OF PAUL
TO THE ROMANS

One

Ever since she had been a little girl, Mary Elizabeth DiMarco had loved to sleep under the stars.

At four-fifteen on Friday afternoon July tenth, Mary Elizabeth looked at the office clock and felt a flutter of excitement. She had almost finished her day of work at the Kramer Insurance Agency in Barnstable, Massachusetts. Mary Elizabeth, Beth to her friends, held a thirty-hour-per-week summer job at Kramer's. But with the labors of the week almost concluded, she could turn her attention to what lay immediately ahead.

She would rendezvous with her boyfriend, whom she knew from the university, for the weekend. On this occasion, for two glorious summer nights, they could both sleep under the stars. She was in love with him. And when she thought about the forty-eight hours ahead of her, the flutter of excitement swelled to a deep tremor.

Portly, fifty-two-year-old Charlie Kramer, who owned the office, was an agreeable family man for whom it was not difficult to work. His agency ran smoothly, almost by itself. The most difficult decision left to Kramer each day was whether to wear his belt above or below his paunch. Thus he allowed his "girls," as he called them, to leave a shade early on summer Fridays if their office work was complete. Insurance claims tended to arrive on Monday mornings. Most afternoons were usually spent invoicing. And few policyholders ever rushed in to pay a bill late on a Friday in mid-July.

So when the office clock marked four-thirty P.M.—official Kramer Insurance Time the staff called it—Beth took her cue. Work finished. Fun begins. She turned her attention to the two travel bags she had stashed in a closet near her desk. One was a blue crushable duffel, packed with leisure clothes, swim wear, tanning lotion and toiletries. The other was a sleeping bag.

Beth disappeared into the washroom and changed from a respectable "businesslike" print blouse and dark skirt and pumps to a pair of red shorts, a blue University of Michigan sweatshirt, and brand new white Nike sneakers with floppy pink socks. She said goodbye to Ramona and Millie, two older coworkers with families whom Mr. Kramer employed full time and year round. As Beth tidied her desk, the two women checked out her change of attire. The persona of the serious young female office worker had been transformed back into fun-seeking college girl. Then they spotted her two traveling bags.

"Off for a weekend?" Millie probed.

"Nantucket Island."

Millie and Ramona made the appropriately envious clucking sounds. "Ever been there before?" Ramona asked.

"No."

"Going alone?"

"With a friend," Beth DiMarco said. "My friend has been there before."

Hesitation. Millie and Ramona looked at each other. "A *boy*friend?" Ramona asked.

Mary Elizabeth grinned sheepishly, rolled her eyes and didn't answer further. "Maybe," she answered. Then, "What do you ladies of the world think?" she added coyly.

The two secretaries laughed conspiratorially.

"I never had the nerve to go away with a guy when I was a kid," the fiftyish Millie complained to her younger peer. "I was raised strict Cat'lic in north Boston. My father would have shot me and my boyfriend, too."

"I would of done it," said the other woman, turning around

32

at her desk. "But I never got asked." They looked back indulgently to the pretty college student.

"What's your guy's name?" Millie asked amiably, taking the lead in the inquiry.

"Eddie."

"Does he have a last name?"

"Just Eddie."

Beth pondered the point for a moment, then reached to her purse. She flipped open a wallet and presented Millie and Ramona with a color snapshot of her with Eddie on the University of Michigan campus. Millie fumbled with a pair of glasses. Ramona needed no such assistance.

The picture showed a nice-looking sandy-haired boy a few inches taller than Beth. He held his arm around her waist. Eddie wore a red football jersey with a huge white 12 on its front. Beth was snuggled close to him, her head resting against his shoulder. They appeared to be at an outdoor party on a bright football afternoon in the early autumn.

The photograph seemed to please Millie and Ramona. It made a strong case that this was a young couple in love. So anything naughty they did, the ladies decided, could be indulged, as long as it was being done responsibly. Modern times, after all. Millie and Ramona made low oooh-ing sounds to each other. Mary Elizabeth blushed.

"Does he treat you okay?" Millie asked, suddenly very serious. She accompanied the question with a slight nod, hoping to evoke the correct response.

"Eddie treats me real well," Beth answered honestly. When the two women continued to look at her, Beth felt compelled to add more.

"I'm twenty-one years old," Beth said patiently. "I know what I'm doing."

"I didn't when I was twenty," Ramona said, more as a general statement than to either other woman. "I didn't know anything about you-know-what until the night I was married." She sighed. "Ah," she half teased, now shaking her head, "you college girls today. . . . With your sexy college novels and your

MTV and your pills . . . God bless you. You know everything I didn't."

"Your parents don't mind?" Millie asked.

"My parents don't know," Beth said. "And it has to stay that way for a while. Okay?"

"Be careful, honey," Millie said, reluctantly extending her approval. She released the photo and allowed Beth to tuck it back into her wallet. "And have a good time."

Beth had every intention of doing both.

After work, Beth took a bus to the ferry depot. There she met Eddie, who had arrived via a different bus from Providence, where he held a summer job doing landscape work. He met her with a kiss and a strong embrace, and swirled her off her feet. Beth and Eddie had known each other for five years, since high school, when his family had moved to Massachusetts from Maryland. It was less than a coincidence that they had applied to the same university. And they still acted as if they were newly in love.

The steamship to Nantucket took two hours and twenty minutes. But the time passed quickly. If Beth and Eddie hadn't seen each other for a day or two, there was always much catching up to do. The boat was crowded. They sat with each other in a corner of the top deck, outdoors. Eddie sipped from a bottle of Heinekin. Beth drank a diet cola. Eddie disappeared to smoke a cigarette on the sly. When he returned, she chided him for what she called his "filthy unhealthful habit." If he had one vice, this was it: sneaking off to have a cancer stick. He half kidded her that he hadn't been smoking at all. Rather, he had been scouting locations on the boat, looking for a little nook where they might make love quickly without being caught.

"Your breath smells like an ashtray," she answered, "and what kind of tart do you think I am, anyway?"

"A terrific tart," he kidded. "If I were a wealthy ugly old Arab I'd buy you for my palace. You'd be my sex slave."

"Who needs a palace?" Beth answered.

The boat arrived at Steamboat Wharf on Nantucket Island at half-past eight. Hungry, they wandered to a busy tavern at the foot of the wharf. Both had been paid that day. They had cashed their checks. To each of them, a few hundred dollars felt like a fortune. Anything was possible. Beth ordered a shrimp salad. Eddie ordered a two-pound lobster. They split a bottle of California Chablis, held hands across the table and wandered out of the restaurant arm in arm shortly after ten.

There was a noisy bar on South Water Street where live music was performed. There was a ten-minute wait at the door, but they stood in line, still carrying their travel bags, and listened to a blues-based rock band for an hour. When they came out, the street was still busy. It was a Friday night and the excitement of a summer weekend was in the air. But it was decision time. Would they find lodging in an inn or guest house? Or would they go do something exciting?

When Eddie brought up the question, Beth looked upward at the brilliantly clear sky. Then she cupped a free hand to his ear and whispered. "Outside," she said. "At least for tonight." Such an arrangement was, after all, her passion.

"Okay," Eddie said. "I know where."

He did. He knew not because he had done this with other girls. He hadn't. He knew because friends who worked on the island had told him where.

They walked up Main Street through the center of town. As the street lamps became more intermittent, they passed a trio of old whaling mansions, then a civil war monument. Then they were on a quiet stretch of upper Main on a narrow, shadowy deserted sidewalk. Eddie held her hand.

"You sure you know where you're going?" she asked.

"Trust me," he said.

She did. He used an old cemetery as a guidepost, and turned right at the corner of the graveyard. Less than five minutes later, he guided her off onto a side street. They tiptoed across someone's lawn, giggled as they climbed across a rear fence, and then were at the edge of an open field. Making their way carefully in the moonlight, they found a protected corner of the field, shielded by a pair of wide old trees, yet beneath a wide starry sky.

Eddie made the announcement. "This is the place," he said.

He was right. It was perfect.

They dropped their bags. They stood for a moment and kissed. Then Eddie laid a plastic sheet across a flat grassy section of ground. They unwound their sleeping bags and spread them one next to each other. They lay in each other's arms kissing for a few minutes.

Even as a child, when she had spent summer nights on the second-floor deck of her parents' summer home in Wellfleet, Beth had preferred stars to a ceiling. It had been so safe and snug back then, out under the sky with blankets and pillows and her two older sisters, her parents sleeping protectively a few rooms away. But a night like this, as a big girl with her boyfriend, cozied into a sleeping bag on an historic island twenty-five miles off the coast of the American mainland, well, this would be magnificent as well.

Then Eddie drew away from her for a moment. In the dimness, Beth could see him put a finger to his lips.

"I thought I heard something," he whispered.

They lay very still and listened. Beth reached to her sweatshirt and pulled it to her in case a flashlight suddenly pierced the darkness. But nothing followed. If Eddie had heard something, they decided, it had been a night bird. Or a cat. Or a raccoon. Or something that need not concern them.

A full minute passed. Whatever had been nearby—if it had been anything at all—had vanished. Beth and Eddie giggled again. Then they playfully undressed each other. They used their hands and their lips to tease each other's body for a few minutes. Then, unleashing the physical passion that had been building since they had last seen each other two weeks earlier, they made love twice on his sleeping bag. Afterward, arms and legs still intertwined, they lay together and spoke softly for many minutes until first she drifted into a pleasant even sleep. Then he followed.

There was nothing, after all, comparable to sleeping under the stars with someone she loved.

Two

The bedroom was dim, long and low and had once been a maid's quarters. Sometime in the early part of the twentieth century, someone had restored the 1730s New England house and put a great deal of love and care into it. The problem was that many years later, witnesses were later to attest, the aging edifice assumed an attitude of its own. The house, partially through the events that surrounded it, would become an ominous, "otherworldly" place. So seen in retrospect, the unnatural horror of what eventually transpired was readily predictable.

But that's not anything that Annette Carlson knew when she bought her home. All she knew, when the troubles began, was that she had been in the midst of a deep satisfying sleep and she was enjoying a very pleasant dream.

In it, she saw herself on a stage somewhere in a distant, timeless place. Music was playing. Annette would remember the music very clearly because it was a type that she had always liked, a catchy syncopated ragtime melody from an upright piano. The vision wasn't so strange because Annette Carlson was already a successful film actress, a name readily recognized both within the trade and—more importantly—by the public.

But she had performed on the legitimate stage in New York and Chicago. When she was a little younger, back in her twenties, before she was fully established in her profession, before fame and an Academy Award had been thrust upon her, she had performed summer stock in the Northeast and she had acted at some playhouses in California as well.

But something started to tug Annette gently away from her dream. Something happening in the present time and place pulled her out of her reverie and socked her back into the present, which was a warm, midsummer night in the 1990s.

Something.

The something was the touch of a woman's fingers gently stroking her forehead and temple—the feeling of a motherly hand running across her hair.

A voice inside her told her to cling to her dream. It was safer there. In her subconscious, in the mind's eye within her dream, Annette gazed upon herself from a medium distance. She was on stage in a great music hall in the 1920s. She was playing New York. There was a man on stage performing with her, but he was to her left, and a step behind her. Annette couldn't discern his face, but she had a comfortable sense about him, as if she were in love with him.

But then the music began to fade. The fingers upon her face became more insistent. The music was all but gone. So was the vision of the music hall. She traveled through a tunnel of darkness—it was a sensation much like plunging in a free fall—and into the present.

Fingers.

Yes, definitely. Fingers and a soft hand were caressing her head. Annette opened her eyes.

For a moment, she thought that her dream had switched gears and that she had been catapulted into a nightmare. They disbelieved, but they definitely focused.

A woman in a white dress was seated at the edge of Annette's bed. She was older than Annette and had a kindly consoling look on her face. There was a beatific cast to her eyes, almost one of concern. Annette would remember this very well.

But the woman was transparent. Annette had the sense of looking through a veil of light, for she could clearly see what was behind the woman.

"Poor dear," the woman said. That's when Annette bolted upright, too stunned and frightened to scream.

"I came to warn you," the vision said next. "Everyone on the island is in danger." It spoke, or in some other way it conveyed that thought. Coming out of her hazy sleepiness, Annette took that message from somewhere, even though the spirit's lips never seemed to move.

Then Annette was awake. Wide-eyed awake. She lunged at the apparition, swiping at it, as if to drive it away. Her hand passed through it.

The woman in white stood. She receded more than she walked, a hurt pouting look across her face. And there was an unnatural flow to her movement, a gliding more than a stepping, an evenness of motion that did not look real.

The specter drifted backward toward the front of the room. It disappeared either out of the door or into a closet. Or maybe it just dissipated. Annette, looking right at it, couldn't tell which. Somehow it was gone, faded into the air.

Annette grasped the lamp at the bedside and turned it on. Harsh yellowish light flooded the room.

The sudden brightness hurt her eyes. She blinked. She looked around. The lamp illuminated all the familiar furnishings, doors and windows. For several minutes she sat very still and studied her surroundings.

Then she picked up a heavy flashlight—one that she kept at her bedside and which she could also use as a club—and rose from bed, clad only in a thin summer nightgown.

She approached the closet door. Gripping the flashlight as a weapon, she stood by the closet and slowly moved her hand to the door. Then abruptly she flung it open.

Nothing.

She pulled a beaded chain that lit a closet light. Still nothing. Only her clothing on hangers. Her many shoes along the floor. A few purses and shoulder bags on shelves. Everything exactly the way she had left it. She turned off the closet light and closed the door.

She walked out the bedroom. To her left on the second-floor

landing were the steps that led down to the ground level of the house. The stairs were old and wooden and creaked noisily upon even the lightest footfall. It was impossible for a human to walk upon them without being heard.

Annette then realized: the woman—or the apparition or whatever it had been if it had been anything at all—hadn't made any noise on the stairs.

Annette listened. Then she walked downstairs, preceded by the beam of her flashlight.

An uneasy feeling crept upon her. She turned a light on in the downstairs landing. She swept the flashlight around. Annette had this terrible feeling—one that she really couldn't shake this time—that something horrible was imminent. She stepped into the living room and turned a light on there, too.

More nothing. A little wave of relief washed over her.

There were thirteen windows on the main floor. They were old fashioned and paned twelve-over-twelve. All thirteen were securely locked, except for two, which bore screens. The screens were undisturbed, bearing nothing more unusual than a moist film from the humidity of the previous day. The windows themselves were set in a position in which they could only open six inches. Too small for an intruder to slip through.

The front door was bolted twice, just as she had left it before retiring. The rear door of the house was just off from the kitchen. It was locked tightly and the screen door beyond it was hooked from the inside. Annette had secured the doors herself shortly after nine P.M.

Outside there was a ground-level bulkhead which led to the basement. But by shining a light from the kitchen window, Annette could see that the padlock upon the hatch was undisturbed. Further, the door that led from the interior of the old house to the basement was locked from the kitchen side.

"See?" she finally said to herself. "There is nothing in this house. Except me."

She sighed. She was starting to feel foolish.

She returned upstairs, but checked that floor, too. Two empty bedrooms, normally set aside for guests. An extra bathroom. A room that Annette hoped to use as a sewing or reading room but which now was empty. At the end, she arrived at a set of back stairs that led to an attic. But the attic remained sealed by padlock. She shined the flashlight up toward it.

The beam from her light was upon the undisturbed lock.

Then she walked back to bed and climbed in. For several minutes, until her tired eyes closed by themselves, she scanned the room. Annette waited for the woman in white to appear again.

But the woman didn't. And Annette slept.

It was something else altogether that made Annette's eyes open a second time that same night. This time it was a feeling, more than an actual appearance. Nor did Annette recall being pulled out of a dream. This time it was a *sense* of something, almost the way a feral animal has a sense of impending danger.

All of a sudden, Annette realized that she was sitting up and awake, looking through the bedroom. There was only a dim light outside from the moon past the drawn shades. She saw only the outlines of tables, two chairs, two dressers and a desk. The familiar furniture took on no evil contours in the darkness. Only comfort and familiarity.

She looked at the clock. It was four-thirty A.M. now. A real hour of darkness. A real hour of . . .

The hour of the wolf. Wasn't that what Ingmar Bergman had called it? Damn her background in films! Why did she have to think of that? Yet in truth, as sleepy, half-formed thoughts danced before her, wasn't this the time of the morning that spirits walked? That weakened patients in hospitals expired before they could welcome the renewal of another dawn? That the dead rose? That—?

Abruptly, she grabbed the flashlight. She needed light. She needed a voice from an all-night radio station. Maybe a drink of something from the refrigerator. Maybe ten minutes of Laurel and Hardy or Murphy Brown or Bob Newhart or Steve Martin or *anyone* on the VCR.

Anything rational. Anything to return her to reality or the light of day.

She took the flashlight in hand and left the room. There was no ghost, no apparition, no woman in white at the top of the stairs. She went down, the steps creaking predictably beneath her bare feet.

She went to the kitchen, which was beneath the bedroom. She threw on the lights. She was reassured by the sink and the Formica kitchen counter and the table where she ate breakfast. The refrigerator hummed. She looked at the bolted door to the basement. It hadn't moved.

Tentatively, she went from room to room again on the ground floor, checking windows. Again, nothing had changed. She went back to the kitchen and sat down at the table.

So why do I have this feeling? she asked herself again. Why this sense of . . . of . . . whatever it is?

She turned on the radio. She tuned in an all-news radio station from New York. The radio played softly and she listened for several minutes.

Then she realized. Whatever it was, whatever was disturbing her, was *outside*. She had an overbearing sense of it, a feeling that her world was somehow encircled. Whatever malevolent force was there was in a small evil orbit around her home.

It made no sense, other than that she felt it in a way that she had never felt anything before. Very cautiously, she went to the kitchen window. She peered out.

Nothing.

Fact was, it was a starry night with almost a full moon. There was a soothing bluish light across the lawn beside her home. Somewhere deep in her subconscious, Bing Crosby was crooning.

"Moonlight becomes you . . ."

She thought of her mother, deceased for three years now. Mom and Dad had romanced to Crosby. Somewhere was she listening to him, too?

Why these weird thoughts? she asked herself. What was happening tonight? Through the kitchen window, she used the

43

flashlight to shine a beam across the lawn. Nothing caught her attention.

She flicked off the flashlight. The moonlight dimmed very suddenly, then slowly brightened. It caused a flash of fear within Annette because she couldn't see what had caused it. She looked at the moon and the sky around it. If there was a cloud scudding around the moon, she couldn't see it. So why had there been a few instants of darkness?

That feeling was back upon her. There was something somewhere. She couldn't escape the idea of being encircled. It was as if the very thought of it held her in its grip.

A foolish urge was upon her. Another one that she couldn't fully explain. She wanted to *know*. She wanted to *confront* whatever it was. She wanted to drive it out of whatever creepy part of her mind it was composing itself.

She went to the rear door of the house and unlocked it. She unlatched the screen door and stepped out. There was a brick landing for a few feet, then grass, which was cold and damp against her bare feet.

She must have been an odd vision herself, she thought, wearing only a nightgown, bearing the heavy flashlight in her right fist. She turned first to her left, then to her right. She threw the yellow beam of the torch in every direction, as if to ward off the intruding presence. The scent of the air was sweet, but under the canopy of stars, the reign of the night was undisputed and unchallenged.

Then, rallying her courage, she actually heard herself speak. "Okay," she said softly but bravely. "Where are you? Let's see you! Out in the open! Let's go!"

Annette did not have long to wait.

She felt something slowly creep over her. Initially, it was like a feeling of nausea, but it quickly turned into a sensation of deep illness.

She turned. She peered through the night. She was looking at something that was very dark and shapeless. It was moving slowly across the lawn in her direction. But she couldn't tell what it was.

If it resembled anything at all, it was like a small, very dense, very dark cloud. It crept slowly along the ground and approached her. She stood silent and riveted, the way one is transfixed in a nightmare—unable to scream, unable to move—until with heart pounding and face sweating, one bolts upright and awake.

She found herself speaking. "What in God's name . . . ?" she began to ask. The Devil risen hot from hell, she would later remember thinking, couldn't have scared her more.

The dark mass approached her. Then it enshrouded her. She knew she wasn't imagining it. She was caught in the icy midst of it. She shivered, despite the warm night. She couldn't see the house behind her, the stars above her or the cast of light upon the lawn before her. Even the length of her arm seemed to disappear in the near darkness.

Then the sensation began to pass. Gradually, the moonlight beyond became more clearly visible until she could see the whole lawn again.

She turned.

The astonishing presence was behind her now. A low, thick, amorphous black mass that was at her doorway. And she stood with mouth agape, watching helplessly, as it dissipated before her eyes, growing smaller and narrower.

Annette realized what it was doing. It was entering her house.

She came into the house after it. There in the kitchen, she thought she saw the tail end of it. It had massed toward the door to the cellar and seemed to be seeping under it, as if drawn by a strong draft. She watched it disappear.

Annette closed her eyes in fright, then buried her face in her hands. She felt her heart pound.

Then she screamed. Her hands moved away from her face and her eyes came wide open.

Sleepwalking! she convinced herself. That's what you're doing again, Annie! Sleepwalking!

She felt her heart race. A film of sweat was upon her neck. She looked around the quiet kitchen.

Yeah. Sleepwalking. Not for the first time in your life. Probably not for the last, either!

She blew out a long breath.

Jesus! What a dream!

Wasn't it?

She looked at the cellar door. "Something went down there," she whispered to no one. "Something not . . ."

Something not human, she wanted to say aloud. Wanted to, but couldn't.

A presence, she wanted to say. Something evil lurks in my cellar.

She stared at the door, trying to decide whether to venture past it. On the one hand, nothing good could happen by going down there. On the other hand, she was determined on another important point: she would never again allow the unbridled thoughts of her own mind to run away with her. To control her life. To push her over the edge, as they once had done so very recently.

No, never again, she thought. It's bad enough that I was sleepwalking.

She paused, "Wasn't I?" she mused.

So she would prove to herself that there was nothing downstairs. That she had dreamed everything. That she, Annette Carlson, was back in control and not yielding to the subconscious wanderings of an overactive imagination.

"And if there *is* anything there," she said aloud to buoy her spirits, "I'll pull it out by its hairy talons."

She shivered at the prospect.

Then she unbolted the cellar door. She opened it. She reached into the cellar stairwell and flipped on the light.

She looked down the steps and saw nothing.

She took one step down, then another. On the fourth step she stopped. She stood perfectly still, waited and listened.

Something? Or nothing?

Nothing. She continued step by step until she stood on the basement floor.

The cellar of the antique house was dark and musty. It was

a warren of old furniture left by the previous owner and packing crates that Annette hadn't opened. It was a domain of spiders and shadows, and, if the truth were known, too many mice.

Then there was the "real scary stuff," as the real estate agents had called it—the oil burner, the hot water tank and the plumbing system. Most of the floor was concrete, except for one stretch adjacent to the furnace, which was undisturbed earth—necessary, the real estate people had further explained, for the control of moisture.

She reached above her and pulled a cloth string on an extra light. A bare bulb illuminated above her head. It threw her shadow in every direction. Annette stood on the cold concrete and looked around.

She half expected something with claws to attack her. But nothing did.

An uneasy moment of thought. Then, "Okay," she finally said. "Enough."

She turned off the extra light. She walked slowly up the stairs. She folded her arms across her breasts.

Abruptly, almost to the top, she froze. With a strange look on her face, she turned. She looked back down the steps. Something had alarmed her.

"But there's nothing here," she spoke softly in reassurance. "Nothing at all."

Her gaze swept vigilantly in every direction, as if she had been *certain* that everything was all right, but . . .

The antique house gave one of its habitual nocturnal creaks.

Annette continued back up the steps and into the kitchen.

She flipped off the light and closed the door. She firmly bolted it.

She sighed. "Come on! No question about it!" she reassured herself. She was very much alone.

Annette moved into her living room and put a light on against the night. She sat up in a Queen Anne chair, a radio softly playing an all-night rock station from Boston. Her eyes wandered across the furnishings of the living room: an antique rocker by the old brick fireplace. A club chair. A second sofa.

Behind her was the massive oak china cabinet that she would have preferred to have moved to the dining room. But the damned thing was bolted to the wall, as had once been the custom to steady oversized cabinets filled with breakables. Annette and three moving men had been unable to budge it an inch. So there the cabinet had remained, out of proportion to every other piece in the room.

On the radio, Paul Simon sang about a girl with diamonds on the soles of her shoes. Annette loved Paul Simon. Her thoughts instinctively settled with the sound of his voice.

Then she looked around on the tables of the room. Somewhere, she recalled, she had left four new scripts that her agent Joe Harris in Los Angeles had sent her to read. There were also two new hardcover novels that her ever-alert agent had shipped her by Federal Express. There were possible film roles in each of the six for her. She could have her choice probably, and could be working again in a few weeks. She could name her dates. All she had to do was decide what interested her, and—

Well, actually, where *were* the scripts and books? She had left them nearby on an end table. She was certain. But they weren't there anymore. Her gaze traveled around the room until she saw them on the lowest shelf of the china cabinet. She must have moved them. She was constantly doing that, misplacing scripts and books that she meant to read.

Annette might have easily risen to go fetch one of the scripts. But in truth, she didn't feel like reading. She was thinking of what she thought had happened. If it had been a dream, she decided in the half light of her wakefulness, it had had a terrible, terrible clarity. So she remained on edge.

She counted the quarter hours. Outside, very gradually, the sky lightened. She sat motionless, thinking and rooting for the sunrise, her eyes trying to close, half expecting something else to happen.

But nothing did. A bright clear morning dawned, instead.

Three

Timothy Brooks shifted his green Mazda Miata into neutral and allowed the car to coast. On his dashboard the local FM station played a fifteen-year-old ballad by James Taylor. Beneath the dashboard, a concealed police radio squawked intermittently. It had been a report on that radio six minutes earlier that had detoured Brooks from his plans: some early morning basketball, one-on-one with his friend, the endlessly quirky Rev. George Andrew Osaro, pastor and spiritualist. On Saturday mornings, the minister made a worthy hoop opponent. Next to Brooks in the front seat of the Miata, a basketball rolled slightly with the movements of the small automobile.

Brooks slowed his car and looked across an otherwise vacant field to an assemblage of vehicles. There were two private cars, a cream-colored ambulance with orange and blue markings, and an armada of dark blue law enforcement vehicles, an equal representation of Nantucket town cops and Massachusetts State Police. Thus Brooks knew he was in the right place.

He shifted the Miata back into first gear and turned off the road and onto the grass. Very slowly, very cautiously, he drove across the field. It was shortly past seven A.M. on Saturday morning, July 11.

This was Brooks' favorite time of the year. It was midsummer on a resort island where no two summer days were alike, but each was usually a gem in its own way. Low humidity, bright sunshine. Clean clear air. Twenty-five miles at sea off the southeastern coast of Cape Cod. Unique beaches, many of them unspoiled. There was an air of leisure combining with one of sophistication, a place where painters, bankers, vacationers, surf bums, yachtsmen and everyone else could hang out in peaceful coexistence.

Typically, the sun was strong and the sky was a brilliant blue on this July morning. Had there not been the scent of premature death in the air, this might have been mistaken for a day created in Heaven.

Brooks continued across the field, stopping a hundred feet short of the other vehicles. A cordon of yellow ribbon had already been set up around a crime scene. The perimeter had been established by two Massachusetts State troopers—one male and one female.

Brooks stopped his car and stepped from it. Heads turned in his direction at the sound of his door closing. Then the heads turned back to the business before them.

This morning, Brooks wore a sailor's yellow windbreaker, a light blue T-shirt, red sweatpants and four-year-old sneakers. He looked fit and strong, like a lifeguard on his way to work, and would have appreciated that suggestion had anyone made it to him. But Tim Brooks was in a different line of work, altogether.

He walked toward the conclave of uniformed and nonuniformed men. They surrounded something bulky and lifeless that lay beneath a gray blanket in a grassy patch of field.

A state cop in uniform, a big hulking bear of a man whose nameplate proclaimed him to be R. Hennessy, stepped in Brooks' direction and put up a large hand.

"Sorry, sir!" the trooper said brusquely, sorry about nothing. "Crime scene. Have to ask you to leave."

Brooks stopped short. "Jesus," he said, reaching into his shirt pocket. "How long have you worked on this island?"

"Eight weeks," the trooper answered.

"I've been here seven years," Brooks said.

The state cop didn't move until Brooks pulled out a small flat black leather case. Brooks flipped it open. A silver shield therein identified him as a detective of the Nantucket town police. The state cop, thoroughly unimpressed, glanced at it, then reacted to it as if it were day-old bread.

"Okay," Hennessy finally said. He allowed Brooks to pass.

Brooks walked through the wet grass to the small cluster of men and women. He was in time to see a paramedic from the ambulance pull the gray blanket away from the victim's head.

Brooks peered downward and looked for the first time—but not the last time—into the face of Mary Elizabeth DiMarco.

"God Almighty," Brooks said.

Several of those assembled—cops and medical people and one reporter from the Nantucket *Inquirer & Mirror*—glanced back. Then they looked away from him again.

Bill Agannis, a paunchy, gruff man with a weathered face and prematurely white hair, was the Lieutenant of Detectives. He was Brooks' ultimate boss, as well as the assistant chief on the island. Agannis stood a few feet from the dead woman. Through some sort of personal radar, Agannis knew Brooks was there.

Bill Agannis wore no expression at all. He just stared at the dead girl, his thoughts alternating between the needlessness of this having to happen, the solemnity of the personal tragedy and the amount of trouble the death would inevitably cause for his department.

Not too far from Agannis was the lieutenant's inevitable shadow: a big, amiable dog named Boomer. Boomer was part German Shepherd and part Labrador retriever with a little heaven-knew-what-else sprinkled in. He was a big friendly mutt who liked everyone except, for some reason, Reverend Osaro, whom he wouldn't go near. Boomer lay in the grass about fifty feet from his master, relaxed and dispassionate, eyes alert, ears attentive. Boomer was always happy to be part of things, as long as Bill Agannis was present.

Then there were two other detectives, Al Rodzienko and Dick Gelman, both in civilian clothes. Gelman held a walkie-talkie. They were militantly blue collar, fortyish men with sullen brown eyes. Facially, they vaguely resembled each other, but

Rodzienko, a Russian-American, was four inches taller. Gelman, the smaller man, had thinning hair, slicked back in vintage Gordon Gekko style. They made no effort to conceal their distaste for Brooks or his arrival. They spoke to each other in low tones and immediately stopped talking when Brooks drew too close.

"We don't need you here, Brooks," Gelman said.

"I thought I'd see if you morons needed help," Brooks answered.

"We don't," answered Rodzienko. "So beat it."

Lieutenant Agannis finally turned. He looked with annoyance at the entire contingent of plainclothes detectives on his small force—all three of them, bickering as usual. They were a triumvirate of men who routinely split two-to-one—Gelman and Rodzienko vs. Brooks—over any issue, from police procedure to whether the sun would rise the next day.

The lieutenant's gaze swept back and forth over Brooks, Gelman and Rodzienko. "Shut the fuck up, will ya?" he snapped. "All three of you!"

They did. For a few moments.

Agannis reached to his pocket and found a red and white pack of cigarettes. He was the last Marlboro Man on the police force, a chain smoker who didn't believe the Surgeon General of the United States any more than he trusted any other representative of the federal government—and he had a persistent, hacking, phlegmy cough to prove it. He lit up with no apologies whatsoever and inhaled deeply.

A female ambulance attendant pulled the blanket from the dead girl's seminude corpse. Brooks angled for a clearer view as the paramedics prepared a body bag.

Brooks could see that the victim had been a very pretty girl. From her face and her body, he guessed that she was around twenty, maybe a shade older. And he could see that her head was at an impossible angle, like an owl whose neck had been wrung. There was blood caked upon her hair and through her mouth.

Brooks grimaced. He was no stranger to death. But he sometimes felt himself shrinking away from his job when confronted by the violence inflicted by some humans upon others. He often wondered whether that aspect of his personality—a weakness in the face of the worst that a policeman's job could offer—was why he'd chosen to be a small town cop instead of a big city one. Yet he had no difficulty accepting even the lowest and most uncivilized forms of social behavior.

Brooks stared downward. There was an expression on the dead girl's face that chilled him, one of torment and terror unlike any he had seen on any other corpse. Ever.

She saw an emissary of the Devil coming to cart her away! said an unwelcome mysterious voice that Brooks was surprised to hear inside him. *Dumb broad! What was she doing out here in the field overnight, anyway?*

He shivered. Where had that thought come from? He felt himself recoiling. Then he suppressed all the other unwelcome, unwarranted notions. Blaming the victim was wrong. This was someone's daughter. Someone's sister. Just a college kid out for a good time, but who had run afoul of the wrong person.

Christ! What a world sometimes, he thought. A flutter of fear went through him, wondering about the perpetrator who could have inflicted this on someone.

And yet, he felt a creeping sense of a larger fear, a foreboding of massive danger. A small, distant, terrified instinct somewhere deep within him told him that this was something far out of the ordinary. And he wondered as he had wondered many times in the past, how would he act, how would he bear up, when facing an adversary that was greater than he.

The policeman drew a deep breath. His courage rallied. He looked again at the death scene.

Karma! That was it, Brooks told himself as he gazed upon the wreckage of a recent human life. Brooks was a cop who believed in a lot of things that he could not directly see. Like karma, for example. Vibrations. Things had auras that humans could sometimes sense. And there was enough of the bad stuff in the air here to bottle and ship out of the country.

That was what was bothering him. Along with that horrible expression on the dead girl's face.

A young doctor whom Brooks didn't recognize knelt beside the body. His name was O'Neill, Brooks overheard, and he was on call from the island's only hospital. Brooks guessed that O'Neill had figured he'd be treating second-degree sunburns, broken bones, poison ivy and cuts from fish hooks. Instead, he had drawn the task of confirming the death of a pretty young girl.

"Where's Doctor Youmans this morning?" Brooks asked the ambulance driver. "He normally does the pronouncements."

"Fishing," said Rodzienko, intentionally overhearing. He answered loudly and pointedly cut off the ambulance driver, who was an older black man. "Youmans is a fisherman. Blues are running off Eel Point."

"Normally we call him, anyway," Brooks said. "Have for years."

"Youmans is in his seventies and the lieutenant thinks he's slipping," Rodzienko said with a soft snarl. "So we start working in a few other sawbones."

"Herbert Youmans? *Slipping?*" Brooks asked.

"If you got a beef, see Lieutenant Agannis."

Brooks sighed and moved nearer the doctor. He could see the jitteriness of the young physician's hand. Brooks squatted beside him.

"Broken neck?" Brooks asked sympathetically. He looked carefully and saw no other trauma to her body.

"Maybe." The doctor was assiduously noncommittal. Dr. O'Neill was dark-haired but dewy cheeked. He looked to be about a year out of medical school.

Brooks pursed his lips. The girl's skin had been very fair and very pretty, as had her hair. Brooks was conscious that he had his own nervous tic at a time like this. The fingers of his left hand were slowly and gently fidgeting with the school ring on his right.

"How long's she been dead?" Brooks asked.

"Tough to tell."

"Give us a guess."

"When I'm ready, all right?"

Brooks waited two seconds. "Ever pronounced a crime victim dead before?"

The doctor glanced at him with mounting irritation.

"What do you make of the facial contortions?" Brooks asked.

"Normal."

"The hell it is," Brooks said.

"The facial contortions stem from neurological trauma to the head, neck and the brain," the doctor answered angrily. "Look. If you went to med school, then *you* can fucking do this!"

"No, thanks."

"Then push off! I know what I'm doing, okay?"

The gauntlet was down. Lieutenant Agannis spat on the ground. He watched without yet interceding.

"How long has she been dead?" Brooks asked.

"Couple of hours, maybe."

"Can you do any better than that? Your pronouncement right here is likely to end up as official."

Furious, the doctor looked up at him. "You in charge here or do you just think you are?"

"Jesus Christ, Brooks. Leave the man alone," Lieutenant Agannis finally growled. "State law: A physician has to pronounce her dead before we can move her. Or is there finally a sticky point of law that you've forgotten?"

"I haven't forgotten. I was just curious what her temperature is," Brooks said, standing.

"They'll do a complete postmortem in Hyannis," the doctor said.

"Yeah," Brooks said. "And it'll take us three days to get it and half the time the PMs from Hyannis are fucked up. Right?"

Lieutenant Agannis considered the point through a long cloud of smoke.

"So what's her temperature right now?" Brooks asked, still standing. "Did anyone take it?" He looked around. "Seems to me that might be useful," he suggested.

"I'm not taking a temperature," Dr. O'Neill said. "Dead is dead. I'll give you a time estimate."

"She doesn't have a cold, you know, Brooks," Dick Gelman said. Gelman grinned, unwrapping two sticks of spearmint chewing gum. He stuffed both into his mouth at once. "Or did you just want to get off on seeing a thermometer stuck in—"

"That's enough, Gelman," Lieutenant Agannis snorted. He gazed on the body.

The doctor hesitantly lifted the dead girl's arm, which was still limp. "I'd say she died sometime shortly before dawn," O'Neill said. "Two to three hours ago."

"So between four and five A.M.? That's your guess?" Brooks asked.

"That's my guess," O'Neill answered without looking up.

"What's your point, Tim?" Agannis asked.

"What do we get here, Lieutenant?" Brooks asked. "Only an occasional homicide, right? Usually it's a gunshot. Sometimes vehicular. Get a stabbing now and then, too, don't we? We even had a poisoning about five years ago."

Brooks looked at his chief and the two other detectives.

"But when's the last time we found a body out in a field from overnight?" No one answered, so Brooks continued. "I don't remember one and I've been here since 1986."

There was an uneasy movement of feet in the wet grass. Brooks stooped down again.

"So what?" Rodzienko asked.

"I used to work in a different part of the country on a different police force," Brooks said to the physician. "And I remember something scientific: A body cools at one and a half degrees per hour."

"What are you? A med school flunk-out?" the doctor asked.

Rodzienko couldn't miss his opportunity. "No," he barked. "Timmy's a law school flunk-out. Became a cop instead."

Rodzienko and Gelman laughed, as did the team from the ambulance.

Brooks continued undeterred. "It's up to you, Lieutenant," he said to Bill Agannis. "But if we get an accurate temperature

56

right now," he said, "rather than later, when the chances of inaccuracy are greater, we'd know exactly when—"

"Detective Brooks has a point," Agannis said quietly. "Take the temperature, Doctor. It won't hurt."

The physician made no secret of his anger. Then he placed a mercury swatch above the dead girl's left breast. A minute later, a reading of 91.8 suggested that the time of death might have been shortly after two A.M.

"This is not the most accurate form of measurement," the doctor said irritably to Brooks.

"This usually works for us."

"Then you're in the dark ages out here."

"What pocket of enlightened civilization do you normally live in?" Brooks asked.

"New York."

"Figures."

"If you hate the place, that's your problem," the doctor answered. He stood and removed a pair of latex gloves. He signaled that the ambulance staff could place the body in the bag.

"Hey, doc?" Rodzienko asked.

The doctor looked to the more receptive member of the Nantucket Police Department. "Don't worry much about Timmy Brooks. He never misses a chance to show someone up. It's just that normally he ends up showing himself up instead."

"Figures again," the doctor said.

"Jesus!" Lieutenant Agannis snarled again. "You got a dead college kid lying here! Would you guys—?"

"I just thought we might want some ball park numbers," Brooks said softly.

"It shouldn't matter much to you," Gelman said. "First, it's not your case. Second, we already got a suspect."

"Yeah," Rodzienko added. "Hate to break your heart, Brooks. But this one just may have been wrapped without you."

Detective Rodzienko motioned toward a police cruiser twenty yards to their right, parked at the edge of the field where it was bordered by the stone wall of the cemetery. There two uniformed officers stood with a distraught young man who looked to be about the same age as the dead female. He had red hair, wore jeans and a University of Michigan sweatshirt and had the build of a college athlete in a fast noncontact sport. Brooks knew he was from off-island. He had never seen him before.

"Who is he?" Brooks asked.

"His name is Eddie Lloyd," Lieutenant Agannis said. "He says he came to the island with the girl last night. Says they did some drinking, heard some music at the Atlantic Cafe, came up here and camped out. He banged her, but he alleges it was consensual. He says he staggered off to take a leak in the middle of the night, fell down drunk and couldn't find his way back to her. Woke up at dawn, came back over here, and found her dead."

"Who called in the initial report?" Brooks asked.

"The kid did," Agannis said, meaning Eddie.

Brooks took a long look at the youth. "What do you think?" he asked his chief.

Agannis shrugged again. "Ah, who knows?" he said with disgust. He drew heavily on his fifth Marlboro of the morning. Then he dropped the smoldering butt. He killed it with his toe. "These days who the hell knows anything?"

"Does his story check?" Brooks pressed.

"Brooksie, baby," Gelman interrupted. "We got the report less than an hour ago. So we treat him like any other smart-assed college kid who comes here during the summer. We read him his Miranda and figure he's lying through his teeth."

Brooks studied the devastated youth braced against the po-lice car. Eddie had a police officer on each side of him. The boy thought the cops were there to console and support him. He didn't even realize that he was tentatively in custody. Brooks looked back at the smirking Gelman and Rodzienko.

"That kid's shattered," Brooks finally said. "Any idiot can see that. You guys don't have any suspect."

"It's not your case," Dick Gelman answered. "So get your ass out of here, would you?"

"Know what else, Brooksie?" Rodzienko said. "You and your college diploma wouldn't know a rape-murder if one French kissed you on your buns."

The young detective was readying his response when his superior's voice interrupted.

"Brooks!" Lieutenant Agannis bellowed. "Get the hell over here!"

Agannis motioned that they were to walk out of everyone's earshot. Reluctantly, Brooks came along. At the same time, Agannis jerked his head toward Detective Gelman, leaving him to proceed.

Brooks walked several feet in silence with his commanding officer. Boomer gathered himself to all four legs, followed and plopped down behind the lieutenant, a jingle of the collar and loud sigh marking his relocation.

"Holy shit, you're obnoxious," the lieutenant finally said. "I got to remind you again what the rules are?"

"Aw, Christ, Lieutenant. . . ."

"Gelman and Rodzienko were on duty. They were here first. It's your day off, for God's sake, and I've asked you ten times already not to antagonize those guys. What do you want? An official reprimand?"

Brooks blew out a long breath. "Look . . ." he began.

"No 'look' about it! First cops on the scene own the case, unless they ask out of it. Clear enough?"

Brooks stared at his shoes and then looked at the remains of the young woman being loaded into the ambulance. Gelman and Rodzienko began to take charge of the scene.

"Yeah. Clear," he said.

"Can't you let one frigging thing come down on this island without wanting to put your own personal paw prints on it?"

"No," Brooks said sullenly. "It's a character flaw. I probably *can't* let anything go down on this island without wanting to put my personal paw prints on it."

"This time you have to."

"You wait," Brooks promised. "What these guys know about

a homicide investigation you could stuff sideways into a thimble."

"This might be open and shut," Agannis said quietly. "I don't think there was anyone around the girl except her boyfriend."

"Chief," Brooks protested, "you can tell just by looking at the kid that—"

"Enough!" Agannis snapped. "Get out of here or I'll assign you to the A & P parking lot to watch for auto break-ins. And I mean it!" The lieutenant's eyes were ablaze.

Brooks backed off. "Yeah," he said. "Fine. Okay." He paused.

Agannis took one step to walk away.

"I don't know why you're not using Herb Youmans anymore," Brooks said.

"He's starting to hear bells, Tim," Agannis said. "I think he's on the edge of senility."

"Never seemed that way to me."

Agannis looked him up and down. "Then maybe you're on the edge of it, too," he growled.

Agannis turned his back and walked away. A wave of resignation swept Brooks. He eyed the paramedics as they closed the ambulance doors behind the young woman's body.

"Just great," Brooks mumbled to himself.

Eunuch! proclaimed the new unwelcome voice within him. *Professionally, consider that your balls were just chopped off!*

Where *was* this voice coming from, he asked himself again. Subconscious thoughts? He couldn't even recognize the sentiments as his own. Brooks frowned. Was he receiving signals from somewhere?

No, that was an idiotic idea, he concluded. The stress of a homicide had merely triggered something deeper in his psyche than he had even known was there. Brooks indulged himself in a long profane oath, completely silent and to himself. He tried to withdraw from the crime scene.

The ambulance put on its lights but not its siren. Slowly, it pulled away from the spot where Beth DiMarco had died.

Brooks' eyes jumped instinctively to the self-confessed boyfriend of the deceased. Eddie was crying now—real loud noisy tears— as the van pulled away. The boyfriend asked if he could accompany the body. The police were not permitting it.

Rodzienko and Gelman had moved over to him by now as well, ready to escort him to the Gray Room, a somber, windowless interrogation chamber in police headquarters on South Water Street. The Gray Room was furnished with a steel table, the tape recorder, the notepads, the three chairs and the single door. There Rodzienko and Gelman would inevitably work their unimaginative "good cop-bad cop" routine on him, hammering away looking for a confession, whether one was there to be had or not.

Unfortunate Eddie, Brooks thought. The poor dumb kid didn't even realize that for him the worst was yet to come.

Angrily, Brooks walked back toward his car, feeling the amused eyes of a couple of state troopers upon him as he passed. He reached his car, got in, and turned the key. The ignition came to life and the Miata's rotary engine purred.

Brooks backed his car slowly across the field. When he had enough space, he made a U-turn. He found the road again.

Murder. Bloody murder, he thought to himself.

Jesus! What were things coming to on this island? It used to be that there would be one homicide every two or three years. Brooks remembered the most recent one. It had involved a couple of blue collar soreheads in pickup trucks who got into a beery territorial brawl over a girl—the ex-wife of one guy was bedding down with the other—until one of them decided to settle it with a shotgun. Now one guy was buried, the other guy was doing twenty-five years to life, and the woman was happy as a clam with yet someone else.

Less than five minutes after leaving the scene of Beth DiMarco's slaying, Tim Brooks pulled into a parking lot behind the island's only high school.

From the basketball court, George Osaro waved. Given the early hour, Osaro was alone. He already had a ball in play and was sinking shot after shot. Brooks stopped his car and stepped out. He pulled off his sweatpants. He wore shorts underneath. He left his own ball in the car.

Brooks walked toward the asphalt basketball court. Osaro waved to his friend, then ignored him.

Above and beyond being a Japanese-American, Osaro was not the typical local pastor. He was given to alternating swings of deep introspection and philanthropy, but could also tell some of the most vulgar jokes on the island. His few close friends knew he had a mouth to match his jokes. And yet he also possessed a keen mind to wrestle with the complexities of his philosophies and his many interests, the latter running from spiritualism and local history to tennis and roundball.

In the latter, in one-on-one against Tim Brooks, Osaro made a surprisingly equitable opponent. He gave away five inches of height but against Brooks, his senior, got back five years in age. Their "even five-against-five exchange," they called it. And normally, in games to fifty points, each would win about half. It was small, crafty, agile, quick and inside against tall, driving, strong and outside. The equation washed perfectly; it was a rare outing when one man would triumph by more than three hoops.

Brooks arrived at the edge of the court. "Have you made a shot yet, you turkey?" he asked.

Osaro readied himself, then used a one-handed set shot from twenty feet out to pop a ball through a hoop. No rim. Swish. The ball obediently rolled back to him and the pastor sank one off the backboard from fifteen feet.

"See that one?" Osaro asked. "Screw you."

"First two of the day, huh?" Brooks asked. "I'd like to see you do that with someone taller than forty-eight inches guarding you."

"Get out here and you will."

Brooks stalked onto the court.

"Where have you been, man?" Osaro asked. "I've been here half an hour."

"You wouldn't believe me if I told you."

"Try me."

Osaro passed the ball to Brooks on one big friendly bounce.

"We had a homicide," said Brooks.

Osaro stopped. "No, really?" He frowned in disbelief and genuine dismay. "Who and where?"

Brooks was silent for a moment. He aimed the ball toward the hoop from the left corner of the court, his favorite game shot from about a dozen feet out. It missed everything—backboard, hoop and net. A genuinely miserable shot. Normally, Osaro might have needled his friend over an airball. At this moment, however, he said nothing.

"Looks like a college girl," Brooks said as Osaro retrieved the errant shot. "From off-island."

"Got a suspect?"

"Not really." Brooks made a sour expression and shrugged as Osaro tossed the ball back to him. "I doubt it. Two of my partners are making a travesty of the justice system as we speak."

"Oh. Gelman and Rodzienko, huh?" Osaro asked.

"That's them," Brooks said disdainfully. He took the same shot as earlier, this time missing off the rim.

"Want to warm up a little?" Osaro asked. He readied a shot of his own.

"Broken neck," Brooks said. "And the poor girl wore an expression right out of a Vincent Price movie."

Osaro didn't shoot. "What?" he asked.

Brooks repeated, word for word. A look that Brooks didn't understand, one of confusion and dismay, one that he didn't remember ever seeing before, crossed his friend's face.

"That mean anything to you?" Brooks asked.

"No," Osaro said. "Should it?"

"You reacted strangely."

Reverend Osaro shrugged and shook his head, innocently and convincingly this time. "No, no," he said softly. "I was just reacting to the horror of it. That's all."

"That's enough," said Brooks, seeking grounds for agreement.

Again, Osaro bounced the ball on one hop to the detective.

Brooks walked to the free throw line. From the foul line, he had reigned as a prince since he was sixteen years old. He shot till he missed.

This time, eleven straight.

"I'm ready," Brooks said when the twelfth rolled around the rim and failed to drop.

"You sure?"

"I'm sure. What's the game? Fifty points?"

"If you think an old guy such as yourself can remain standing that long," Osaro taunted with a straight face.

"Fuck you, parson," Brooks said. With those words, he felt good for the first time all day.

But the feeling didn't last. Some intangible was missing from Tim Brooks' game that day. He had never hit so many rims in his life. That, or Osaro was making him miss.

For whatever the reason, the young clergyman triumphed fifty to thirty-six. The match was chalked up by both as a freak game, seeing how, in the five years that they had played each other, it was the most lopsided match in their frequent competition.

Four

Annette Carlson had been ten years old when she first considered the notion of survival after death.

The occasion had been the death of her cocker spaniel, a personality pooch named Bailey who had come out on the short end of a collision with a milk truck. Annette had asked her father where Bailey would go, where his spirit would rest. She always remembered asking, "Are there dogs in Heaven, Daddy?"

Stephen Carlson had reassured his daughter. "Heaven is as you would want it to be," he said, placing an arm around his little girl. "I'm sure Bailey's there already, chasing cats up trees and rabbits across a field."

The response had been appropriate. It elicited a tear-streaked smile from a little girl. In the years that passed, looking back upon it, Annette, or Annie now to her intimates, could always recall similar tears and smiles from the memory of that conversation.

Survival after death. Tears and smiles. These became the leitmotifs for a young actress's life.

Transplanted from Omaha, Nebraska to Portland, Oregon when she was seven, Annette grew up happy, if not carefree. She was a quiet child, given to somber reflection, and more likely to approach any event more as a spectator than a participant.

But when she was fourteen, she became more self-assured.

Approaching her midteens, she wanted to be part of what was going on, particularly if it involved performing. It was then that she acquired her first professional admirer in the person of Mr. Harvey, the English teacher and drama coach at South Portland High School.

Annette had been into ballet at the time and was walking through the high school gym on her way to private instruction. Meanwhile, chaos was breaking out on the school stage. The school was three days away from presenting its annual production. This year it was *My Fair Lady*. And earlier that morning, the school's Eliza Doolittle had been diagnosed with mononucleosis.

Annette had watched the movie fifty times. She tugged on Mr. Harvey's sleeve after that day's rehearsal.

"I can play Eliza," he said.

"I'm sure you could, Netty," Mr. Harvey said. "But there's only three days."

"I already know the role."

"How could you?"

She lied and said she had watched the movie a hundred times instead of fifty.

He looked at her and blinked. She was a long-legged, gawky American teenager with straight blond hair and a pretty face. Her? Eliza Doolittle? But the other girl had left school with a temperature of 102.8.

"Can you sing?" Mr. Harvey asked in desperation.

She showed him. Then three nights later, she was sensational before a packed auditorium. The only thing embarrassing about her performance was how much better she was than everyone else. Mr. Harvey, who became her first serious acting coach, was stunned. Then he got chills. She was that good. A career was launched.

She stayed in the Northwest to go to college. She took the lead in almost every major production to come out of the University of Oregon during her four years there. Over summers, she traveled to locations around the country that other girls only read about in *Glamour* and *Mademoiselle*. She landed jobs in summer stock and after graduation went to southern California to try to win entry to the Screen Actors' Guild.

The latter took her another year, and she only managed it by carrying a successful role Off-Broadway in New York. From there she was spotted by a film producer who thought she looked just right—he really *did* think so—for an ingenue role in an upcoming film. So Annette landed back in Los Angeles by way of lower Manhattan.

Her first role was as a saucy, witty upstairs neighbor who befriended the female lead in a thriller called *Passport to Fear*. Annette had twenty-six lines and ended up dead twenty-eight minutes into the film. But she gave the public and the film industry the classic who-the-hell-was-*that* performance. How could anyone whom no one had heard of be so good?

Other roles quickly materialized. She played a newspaper reporter in another thriller, made some money on a seventeen-day shoot, did a made-for-TV movie shot in Arkansas, then went back to Los Angeles and prepared for big-time lightning to strike.

She was what directors dreamed about. She was beautiful, sexy and smart. She could give a good character performance and carry a main role, too. She could do it in a film, on television or even on a stage. Plus she was a joy to work with.

No wonder then that she won the lead female role in *Only the Living*, a big-budget studio production based on a best-selling novel by a well-known author. Two dozen other actresses had read for the part. *Only the Living* was a horror thriller set in New England, the type of film with knives coming through doors and name actors lurking in every shadow. But as a piece of slick major league entertainment it worked. The studio campaigned hard for her at Oscar time and Annette came out a winner. Not just the nomination, but she took home the gold statuette as well.

Tears and smiles. Survival after death. The formula visited itself upon her on Academy Award night, too. Watching from the family home in Oregon, Annette's mother suffered a cerebral hemorrhage an hour after the awards. She died two days later at the age of fifty-three.

It was a shock and a loss with which Annette had extreme difficulty coping. She had had friends and lovers over the years since university, but no one had ever been as close as her parents. She found herself with sudden fame and wealth, often unable to appear in public without being bothered for autographs or pestered by would-be screenwriters. Yet part of her life seemed gone, a voice of love from the other end of a telephone was missing. Her father seemed suddenly very old. Annette worried about him as well.

A new boyfriend entered her life. His name was Ty. He was tall, dark haired, twenty-eight, and gorgeous. He was also the worst mistake of her life. He was abusive, untrustworthy and introduced her to sedatives and speedballs. He cheated on her flagrantly and, because it was a weak point in her life, she kept coming back to him. When he finally dumped her, she sank into a long depression, made worse by a drug complication that on two occasions had actually led to hallucinations.

She began to have nightmares: often a dark window would open to her childhood home and she would talk to her departed mother. She sleepwalked: often she would awake to find herself at the edge of a flight of stairs. Once she was near a seventh-story window at the Bel Air Hotel. Another time she awoke to find herself outside in the street when staying at a girlfriend's house in Princeton, New Jersey. On that occasion, a car horn awakened her. Not surprisingly, she obsessed about sudden mortality.

Psychiatric attention helped, the best that money could buy in New York and Los Angeles. She even spent two weeks under a pseudonym as an inpatient at a mental hospital in Fairfield, Connecticut. The doctors were terrific. But—temporarily at least—a man named David McIntyre helped even more.

She had first met David at a party in Brentwood at the sprawling $2,000,000 home of her agent, Joe Harris. This was about ten months after her Academy Award and it was Annette who spoke to him first.

David was a big charmingly unpretentious Texan. He had studied at the University of Texas in Austin and originally had come west to be a stand-up comedian. But he didn't look right for that. Nor did he have the face or delivery or, for that matter, the material. So instead, David had been making money writing good scripts that were optioned but never produced and repairing the structure of lesser scripts based on other people's ideas. At this latter art, that of a script doctor, David was a master.

At Joe Harris' party they had stood in the corner and compared notes about the technique of creating character before a camera—the writer's view as opposed to the actor's view. David fiddled with a toothpick and sipped papaya juice as he spoke. McIntyre, too, was one of Joe Harris' clients.

David, eyeing her carefully, announced after about an hour that he'd said everything he had to say at this particular party. "Let's split," he said.

"What?"

Would she like to leave with him, he repeated. She considered it an affront at first.

"Leave to do *what?*" she asked.

He looked her straight in the eye. "I dunno," he drawled. "There's got to be something more interesting than standing around West Hollywood. Let's go bowling."

A pause. "Are you kidding?"

"No."

"I've never bowled."

"Ah," he said. "A virgin. Come along." He held out an arm to lead her.

Intrigued, she disappeared to find her coat.

David turned out to be a free spirit, indeed. They drove to Culver City and found an art deco alley with pink and blue pastel pins. It was only in the middle of the second game, when she began to attract the attention of several middle-aged men in rayon shirts, that David started to catch on to something he had missed.

"We're getting stared at," he said. "Is one of us famous? I know it's not me."

Annette Carlson said nothing. He looked back at her.

"I never did get your name," he said. "Guess I should have."

She gave it.

He thought for a moment. "Didn't you just win something?"

"An Oscar."

"What'd you do? Something technical?"

"Best Actress."

"Oh. How 'bout that," he said, as if in a revelation. "I never watch that stupid Oscars show. And I didn't recognize you. I don't much go to movies. I can't stand the scripts that get produced."

"But you fix other people's scripts for a living."

"Well, hell, yes! Of course I do!" he boomed as if it were self-evident. "If they stink less after I'm finished with them, I've done a public service, haven't I?"

She smiled and shook her head.

"Hey, how's this?" David continued. "When I get my own scripts produced, I promise to start going to more films, okay?"

"Good idea."

"Thanks." They both started to laugh. "By the way," he said, "congratulations."

"On what? The Oscar?"

"No. You broke a hundred twenty-five on your first game."

"Is that good?"

He blinked. "What else did you do well on your first time?" he asked.

She smiled like the Cheshire cat. "I'll never tell," she teased.

"Good. Don't."

They didn't sleep together that night. She wasn't attuned to casual sexual relationships. But over the next days, she realized that this was not meant to be casual. David, in his unpretentious straightforward manner was a perfect soulmate for her, a pillar of sanity and common sense.

Eventually, after they had known each other for several weeks, they did become lovers. And when Annette confessed to him about her mental condition, her obsession with her mother's passing, her suspicions that all the adulation and money heaped upon her would disappear overnight, it was always David McIntyre who was there to pull her up when she was emotionally down.

She was in love with him. He made her laugh.

He would do stand-up routines just for her. He would skewer mutual acquaintances—usually from New York or Los Angeles—with offbeat, off-color imitations of them. Then he would perform with a ventriloquist dummy. Annette's mother had bequeathed her a prize possession from her childhood, a life-size, four-foot-tall Charlie McCarthy doll, just like the one the famed Edgar Bergen had performed with from the 1930s into the 1950s. The dummy was in perfect condition. He wore top hat and tie, clown's expression and a monocle, just like the original. David's routines, performed for Annette alone, were irreverent and riotous, updated for the 1990s.

Best of all, David wasn't even married. There was no wife somewhere to get bent out of shape and cause trouble. No personal baggage at all. His only real hang-up was his professional obsession: finally getting an original screenplay of his own produced. It would take time, she assured him, but it would eventually happen. She had read his work and knew how good it was.

She had hoped to marry him. And had David not died in the crash of a private airplane in Santa Barbara in March 1991, she probably would have.

Again, tears and smiles. Survival after death. Mourning. The rebuilding of her shattered emotions. Sleepwalking. Back to the psychiatrists. It was as if Annette's life was trapped on a tragic cycle, always doomed to repeat itself. She found herself unable to even approach a relationship with another man.

Worse, she lacked concentration upon her work. The supermarket tabloids and the movie star magazines would not lay off her. Every other week they manufactured an imaginative new spin on the "curse" that was upon Annette Carlson: how astrologers and Gypsy fortune-tellers agreed that she was doomed to always be unlucky in love and—when the hacks at the tabloids finally found out about it—how psychiatrists would always be unable to help her.

Her life teetered on the brink of disaster, both professionally and emotionally. It was agent Joe Harris who finally suggested a partial solution.

"Bury yourself in your work for a while," he said to her one day at his office on Olympic Boulevard. "I'll find you the right projects. Rack up the money. Then buy a place of your own," Harris said. "Buy something far away. Out of the orbit of New York and Los Angeles. Some place where you can go, be alone, take the phone off the hook, be yourself and think. This is your life we're talking about, Annie. Don't squander a moment of it."

Annette was listening.

"Joe knows best," Joe Harris said as a coda to his speech. "Trust Joe."

She did.

Annette completed another television movie and another feature. In terms of financial ledgers, she found herself to be a lucky woman. After taxes, she had more than four hundred thousand dollars in cash. Thus, she was able to go house shopping.

It took her a year to find what she wanted, looking in various quiet corners of the United States. But when an antique house on Cort Street in Nantucket came on the market, and when a realtor whom she trusted couriered her the information on the property, Annette took the plunge.

The house had been owned by Daniel and Martha Shipley, whom Annette met only at the lawyer's office for the closing. The Shipleys were a couple in their seventies from western Massachusetts. They had habitually summered in Nantucket, but their two sons had now grown. They were anxious to sell 17 Cort Street, buy a smaller place and divide their retirement years between New England and Palm Beach.

The house even came partially furnished. Everything was in move-in condition. The only blemish was a horrible old china cabinet in the living room, the dark hulking oak monstrosity that had been bolted to the wall by a previous owner—long before the Shipleys—many decades ago.

But the cabinet wasn't important. What was significant was that Annette Carlson was again taking the first steps of putting her life back together. She had wealth and fame in her youth. She had an apartment in Los Angeles and a home to retreat to in the Northeast. She had even stopped seeing her head doctors and had mercifully fallen off the pages of the tabloids.

There was no particular man in her life now, but she did not yet consider that a priority. The possibility of a new relationship was, in fact, something she still retreated from. The pain of the previous tragedy remained too great. So Annette's biggest challenge now was not slipping back into the depressions and tormented mental states that had gripped her after her mother's passing and after David's sudden death. That, and selecting just the right script to do next—just the right offer out of the many that Joe Harris was sending her way.

There were a few smiles now, even if a few tears appeared at low moments. And as for survival of death, well, she seemed to have finally survived David's.

Everything was finally moving forward, she would later recall. It was moving very smoothly. And it remained so right up until the specter in white first stroked her forehead. If the specter had been there at all.

Five

Midway through Saturday afternoon, less than twelve hours after the death of Beth DiMarco, Detectives Dick Gelman and Al Rodzienko proceeded with all the subtlety of a pair of jack-hammers. But they were making progress. Or at least they thought they were.

They had Eddie seated at the long steel table in the Gray Room. And they were working on him. Eddie's father, Arthur Lloyd, was an executive with a medical supply company in Brockton. Lloyd Senior was flying to the island that afternoon from Boston to be with his son. A local attorney named Ned Schwinn had met with Eddie to make the interrogation legal. Now Schwinn sat outside the Gray Room at a cost of a hundred dollars an hour, kibbitzing with the cops, all of whom he knew personally. This was great work for a small-town mouthpiece who made most of his living by overcharging his longtime friends for title searches. But Schwinn was there until an off-island counsel could be retained, if such proved necessary.

Increasingly, it looked as if it would.

"You and Beth must have had a fight," Rodzienko suggested over and over as the walls of the Gray Room reverberated with his voice. "Was she seeing another guy? Did you think she'd been unfaithful to you?" Rodzienko was playing the tough guy, pacing the room, snarling, accusing. Sweat poured off him as he circled his young suspect.

Gelman sat dispassionately, almost sympathetically. "What

happened, Eddie?" he would say softly at the prearranged moments when his partner would be "called" from the room. "Come on. Tell me. Get this over with."

"*Nothing* happened," Eddie explained more times than he could count, often choking with tears, fatigue, or both. Then he would run through his version of the evening again, recounting detail after detail. Unobtrusively, a tape recorder ran. Any small inconsistencies or tiny misstatements would loom larger when the two detectives eventually reviewed the cassettes.

"We made love twice," Eddie said. "We both fell asleep. In the middle of the night I got up to take a leak. I don't know what time it was. I wandered off and—"

"Where'd you go, Eddie?"

"I don't know. It was dark. There was this bunch of trees."

"Which bunch? How far did you walk?"

"I don't know."

"You were there. Why don't you know?"

"I don't remember."

"What else don't you remember, Eddie?"

"Why didn't you come right back?" Gelman soothed.

"What time was it?" Rodzienko pressed.

"I told you. I don't know."

"Why don't you know? Were you wearing a watch?"

"I didn't look at my watch."

"Sounds strange to me," Rodzienko said. "Most people, when they wake up in the middle of the night, it's the first thing they do, look at a watch. Huh?"

"I didn't," Eddie Lloyd said.

"Maybe 'cause you were too busy with something else. Like you'd just had a big fight with your girl."

"I passed out, I tell you."

"Eddie, there was no one else *there*," Rodzienko said.

Young Lloyd shook his head.

"Eddie, listen to this," Rodzienko said, swinging his leg across a chair and seating himself directly in front of the young man. "You and the girl had a disagreement. You hit her. You hit her hard. You didn't mean to hit her hard but she'd done something to hurt you, didn't she?"

"No!" The boy was crying, shaking his head.

"Slept with someone else, didn't she?" Rodzienko pressed. "I bet that was it. Fucking around behind your back. Turned out to be a little Italian slut, didn't she?"

"No!"

"Maybe she *said* something to you," Rodzienko tried next, his voice rising. "Something that pissed you off, huh?" He thought about it. "Did she tell you that you weren't making her come? Was that it? Did she call you a lousy fucker?"

"No!" the boy insisted.

Feigning sudden rage, Rodzienko sprung up from his chair so violently and abruptly that his movement made Lloyd recoil. "Ah, fuck, Eddie!" Rodzienko snapped. "What'm I gonna do with you, huh?"

The detective paced off to a corner of the room. There he opened a pack of Juicy Fruit gum and immediately went to work on three sticks at once.

It was his partner's turn. "It's no shame, Eddie," Gelman said softly. "Girls do things sometimes. They start seeing another guy. They say something mean. It's like, they *give* you reasons to lash out sometimes, right?" Gelman paused. "I understand why you were so angry. You didn't mean to do it, right? Tell us you didn't mean to do it. You're young and you have a clean record."

Eddie glanced up at the mention of no previous arrests. Yes, he realized to his horror, the detectives had already checked.

"Courts take that into account," Gelman said. "You're a good kid. I know that. It was an accident that she died, right?"

Eddie looked from Rodzienko to Gelman.

"Tell us that you didn't mean to hurt her," Gelman said. "But you hit her, right? And she accidentally died."

"That's not what happened!"

"Then what *did* happen?"

"I've told you!"

"Eddie, we know you're not telling the truth," Rodzienko

said calmly. "See, you were the only one there besides Beth. So it had to be you who hurt her."

"No," he said, shaking his head. "Not me. I didn't." His face sank into his hands and he began to cry again. "Where's my father?" he finally asked. He sobbed. "He should have been here by now."

There was a long silence in the room.

Rodzienko came back. He sat down in Eddie's face again.

"Your old man's going to be pretty disappointed," the detective said. "Lying like this. Gonna put the whole family through a trial. Not facing up to what you done."

Rodzienko paused. "Maybe you were real drunk, Eddie. So drunk that you barely remember doing it? Is that okay? I can accept that. Tell me that's what happened and we can go with that." He paused. "Yes?" he said hopefully. "Can we make that deal, Eddie? Will you tell me that?"

Eddie looked up and saw both detectives staring at him, waiting for their moment of triumph. Their eyes were fixed and intense like a pair of stubborn but dutiful terriers.

"I didn't hurt her!" Eddie moaned. "I loved her. I would never have hurt her."

Rodzienko stood and leaned on the table, bracing himself with clenched fists against the metal tabletop. "We *know* you hurt her, Eddie!" he roared eye to eye. "So don't give us bullshit! There was no one else there! Understand me? *No one else there!*"

Muffled desperate sobs sounded from the boy. In the adjoining room, attorney Ned Schwinn affably split a warm Diet Pepsi with one of the female police dispatchers.

"Know what I think?" Rodzienko said to his partner. "I think Eddie here lured her out there with malice. He was planning to kill her. That's why he won't admit it was an accident. It wasn't an accident. That's why he won't talk."

Rodzienko gathered some papers.

"Well, Eddie's making a big mistake. This was his time to tell us he didn't mean to do it. Now we're gonna prove that he did mean it. That's only gonna make it worse, huh?"

Silence, not a confession, from Eddie Lloyd. Rodzienko left the room. For several seconds Eddie and Gelman sat without speaking. Finally Gelman looked at his suspect.

"Come on, Eddie," Gelman said softly. "Ignore my partner. He's a prick. Talk to me, instead. Tell me what happened and I'll keep Detective Rodzienko off your ass."

Eddie shook his head. His eyes were crimson. Dark circles were emerging beneath them.

"I don't know anymore," Eddie cried. "I want my father."

Arthur Lloyd, Eddie's father, arrived late on Saturday afternoon. The questioning of his son continued into the evening. Beth DiMarco's shattered parents arrived on an earlier flight. The two families did not know each other. Gelman and Rodzienko kept them apart.

Eddie would be released that evening in his father's custody on the condition that neither of them leave the island and that Eddie return for further questioning on Sunday morning. Rodzienko and Gelman then returned to the field where the girl was slain, accompanied by two State Troopers and a canine. They searched for anything that might reflect further on Beth DiMarco's death.

The dog didn't care much for the site of the murder. And the search team found nothing.

Elsewhere on the island, late on that same afternoon, Tim Brooks rolled his Miata to a halt at the end of a dirt driveway leading to the old farm house. A big female collie named Clara barked wildly at the arrival of the car, circling it and alerting her master. Brooks cut his ignition and stepped out.

Clara recognized him and stopped barking, coming over closer to where Brooks could pet her and where she could bang her rapidly wagging tail against his car.

"Hello, Timmy," Peter McCloy said, coming out of the building to greet the detective. The farmer was a somber-looking man, thin with untrimmed gray hair that circled a head that was bald on top. He was about fifty but appeared older.

"Sorry to have to call you," he said. He frowned. "Ain't it your day off?"

"It's no problem, Pete," Brooks answered, stepping out of his car. "Not your fault. The department got real busy today. What happened?"

"Aahh . . ." McCloy grimaced and shook his head, too disgusted to even begin a description. He waved with an arm, indicating that the young detective should follow. "You'll see."

McCloy's farm was located down a dirt lane off Cliff Road, the route that led along the shoreline leaving town toward Dionis Beach. The farm was a throwback to a previous age, one of the last working livestock farms on Nantucket. Nestled between expensive housing and a wildlife preserve, it was small, modest, and marginally profitable. It had been worked by four generations of McCloys since 1892.

"I just don't understand stuff like this," Peter McCloy said. "Never did. Never will. Why would someone do something like this?"

There was something hot and oppressive about the farm, particularly late on a midsummer Saturday when the sun had been pounding it for twelve hours. McCloy, in a wrinkled white shirt, overalls and heavy shoes, led Brooks through a dirt patch where grass never grew. He guided him toward his livestock pens where mostly he kept chickens and a few rabbits. In the middle was the largest individual pen, about fifty feet in width and slightly oval in shape, enclosed by tightly meshed wire. There was a small man-made pond in the center and a little hutch that provided shade and a nesting area. This was where the McCloys had always kept their ducks. For Brooks, the day that had begun with a homicide and continued with a basketball game was about to take an even more macabre turn.

"I ain't touched nothing," McCloy said as he led Brooks closer. "I wanted you to see. You're my witness. I already took some pictures. Then I can get on with burying my birds and filing a claim. Criminal loss. I'm insured, but I just don't know how people can do something like this. How do people sleep at night, Timmy? Answer me that."

Brooks didn't have an answer. Led to the scene of the atrocity, Brooks stopped short in revulsion. He could feel his own senses, particularly that of decency, recoil. He uttered a low profanity and felt himself grimace.

"Pretty fucking disgusting, ain't it?" Peter McCloy said in a low angry voice. "Murdering good birds. And it don't make no sense, either."

Brooks stared.

Someone, in plain daylight under an open sky, had massacred McCloy's ducks. The whole pen of them. Eighteen birds lay in little pathetic feathered heaps around the pen where for years they had led a safe, protected existence. Their necks had been wrung, each and every one, for no apparent reason. Then their bodies had been left in six clumps of three, arranged neatly with almost a pathologically intense touch.

"I don't understand why people do stuff like this," McCloy repeated. "A dozen and a half perfectly good birds. What's it accomplish? Does this make someone feel good?"

"I don't know, Pete," Brooks said, consoling and continuing to stare.

"Normally, we're pretty lucky with livestock on this island. You know that. There ain't no foxes. Some hawks. A couple of dogs get carried away sometimes . . ."

McCloy shook his head.

"Can I go in?" Brooks asked, indicating the pen.

"Sure."

Brooks entered through a gate in the fence, walking carefully so as not to obliterate any clues to the source of the carnage. He pulled out a notebook to record the incident in the police register. McCloy watched him and waited on the outside.

"When did it happen?" Brooks asked.

"That's the funny thing."

Brooks looked at the farmer.

"I came out here to feed the birds at about five P.M. They were fine then. Took their feed. I came back half an hour later and they were all dead. Exactly like you see. I was around back with my hens. That's the funny part, Timmy. I didn't hear no car. Clara never barked. The ducks never kicked up a ruckus. There's no footprints. And my wife," McCloy said, turning to indicate a window in the house that overlooked the pen and the pond, "was right there in the kitchen baking some berry pies. She didn't see nothing, either. So how can this have happened?"

Brooks thought about it for a moment and had no answer.

"May I?" Brooks asked. He looked down to one of the birds and wanted to move it with the toe of his shoe.

"Sure," said the farmer. He watched. "You can see no animal was capable of doing this. A human done it. Or a couple of humans." He paused. "Eighteen birds in a couple of minutes, all neat and stacked up. Someone's a walking slaughterhouse, I'll tell you that."

Brooks nudged a white feathered carcass. Farmer McCloy was right. The crime, the massacre, made no earthly sense. One bird after another had been killed with eerie precision. Someone very strong, very fast and very silent had been bent upon some very vile mischief. Then the killer had left the corpses in their all-too-cute mocking arrangement.

"Know what I think?" Peter McCloy said.

"What's that?"

"I think you got a real sick-o who done something like this," he said. "Can't be an islander. Got to be someone from off-island."

Brooks only nodded, trying to factor all the details, the sum of which made no apparent sense.

"Ever seen anything like this before?" McCloy finally asked.

"No," Brooks answered. He looked at the six piles of dead birds, moving slowly from one to the next. Each bird had been killed exactly the same way, with no other marks on its body. An image of the DiMarco girl lying dead at his feet returned to him, then vanished.

Brooks' gaze eventually returned to the farmer.

"I guess I have to ask you this, Pete," Brooks said. "You don't have a clue as to who might have done this? Made any new enemies lately? Got any old ones?"

"Me? Ha!" McCloy spit angrily on the bare ground. "Wish I had. Then this would make more sense."

"Yeah," Brooks said. "It would. Anyone you know want to drive you out of business?"

"Who'd want this business? I'm in debt up to my ass."

"Anyone after the land?"

"There's better land than this that you could buy tomorrow."

The farmer's logic seemed impeccable. Brooks nodded. He walked out of the gate and closed it.

"I'm sorry, Pete," he said. "I'll file the report. Come by and sign it when you get a chance. We'll ask around, see if anyone's heard anything. Okay?"

McCloy nodded.

"You should see my wife," McCloy said. "She's real upset. These birds were kind of hers. Used to come down and feed them out of her hand. Know what I mean?"

"I know what you mean." For a moment in passing, Brooks put a hand on the older man's shoulder. McCloy drew a deep breath and was steady again.

Brooks stopped by the house and said a few words of sympathy to the farmer's wife. She nodded and said little. Brooks promised that he'd investigate as best he could. She thanked him.

Wally Crossman, one of the town insurance agents, turned up with the claims forms just as Brooks was leaving. Crossman inspected the damage and also nodded sympathetically. As Brooks pulled out of the driveway, the farmer started to gather the little corpses onto a wheelbarrow. Nearby, he already had a shovel leaning against his barn.

Six

Timothy Brooks was the second son of a workaholic journalist named Joshua Brooks, a man who was successively the bureau chief in Baltimore, St. Louis, Dallas and Los Angeles for a national news weekly and who spent an average of ten non-sleeping hours a week at home. Timothy's mother taught school, played the piano and died of cancer when Tim, the youngest of her three children was fifteen. Such were the guide-posts of his parents' lives.

An older sister took a degree in French and became a university instructor in Rhode Island. An older brother became a dentist. Timothy was sent away to an academically competitive private school in Pennsylvania a year after his mother died, his father having little idea what else to do with him. There he came close to excelling—doing poorly in nothing and very well in almost everything, socially, academically and athletically. And as a secondary school student, a pattern emerged that would follow in later life: he was well liked and respected, but showed an unerring propensity for poking his nose into the business of others. Yet at this juncture, such traits were considered quaint.

University followed—a big-name place in the Northeast where he was a starting guard on the basketball team for his final two years. He was good enough to star in the intercollegiate ranks, but not big enough to pursue professional hoops. It was a tough lesson in life right there.

So he earned a bachelor's degree in American Civilization, which upon graduation qualified him to do just about nothing other than drive a cab and bear testament to the reality of what he had studied. Many of his friends were going to law school, so he took a plunge at it, himself, much to the immense pleasure of his father who—for reasons known only to himself—insisted that his offspring have discernibly white-collar professions.

Tim Brooks astonished even himself with his LSAT scores and gained admission to a law school that was within everyone's Top Fifteen list. After the first round of midterm exams, he held a first quintile position in his class. He was also bored silly. And he could never picture himself as an adult putting on a suit each day and poring over contracts, torts and stipulations. So at Christmas vacation, he walked.

"The problem with lawyers," he remarked to his father as he announced his decision, "is that they have no natural predators."

"So what the hell are you going to do?" Joshua Brooks angrily asked his son. "Be a cop or a fireman?"

Timothy thought about it. "Not a bad idea," he answered. But it didn't happen quite that quickly.

Tim Brooks was hanging around Chicago at the time, following the Bulls, Blackhawks and Cubs while he pursued an environmentally concerned art student from New York. Her name was Heather Gold. He had first met her in New York the previous winter where a gallery in SoHo was showing some of her tamer canvases.

Heather was in her late twenties, a woman with slow-burning eyes and very fair skin. She was so wan and plain that she was strikingly pretty. She played the piccolo and had a streak of gray in her long black hair. And as her lovers knew, a small red tulip had been tattooed just below her bikini line. The tulip, she freely told Tim Brooks, had been administered in honor of her English professor during her freshman year at Vassar.

"He was my first sex partner," Heather explained. *Sex partner.* In reference to most of her previous relationships, Heather assiduously avoided the word "lover."

For a fee from Cook County, she painted shockingly technicolored multiracial murals on public building exteriors. She also liked to suggest that she was a witch, and Brooks witnessed nothing within her footloose unconventional life-style to indicate that she wasn't. She was the strangest woman for whom he had ever fallen. And at this point in his life, with school finished and nothing but uncertainty ahead of him, he was truly smitten.

For several weeks at age twenty-three, Brooks considered marrying her. He finally took a long chance and broached the subject one night in bed while he watched the orange glow of her marijuana cigarette after making love. She considered the proposition very gravely for about ten days, a space of time during which she answered his request with a deafening silence. Then she suggested they each start, as she put it, "screwing some other people." She went on to explain her philosophy. "Permanent relationships suck," Heather pronounced.

A week thereafter, Brooks arrived on the West Coast with three hundred fifty dollars and a '76 Colony Park station wagon filled with clothes and books. But he was older and wiser. He saw an ad that said that the Police Department of San Jose, California, was hiring recent college graduates. So he registered for the recruitment exam.

He passed the test with the highest grades in the history of the department. He spent a year on patrol and distinguished himself again by sauntering in and out of other cops' cases, invited or not. Then he gravitated to the troublesome beats that the veterans liked to avoid. His good manners and easy bearing were often confused for softness. But by the end of the year he had as many commendations as men who had been in the department for more than five years. He didn't *look* like a supercop. He didn't *act* like a supercop. Yet his results indicated that he might have been on that path.

"So that's it? A cop?" his father asked him over the long distance telephone one day. "With that good head on your shoulders, with all that education, all you've become is a cop?"

"It was that or a fireman," Tim Brooks answered facetiously. "You made the suggestion, yourself."

Joshua Brooks hung up on his younger son and the two men stopped speaking for several months.

Within another year Tim studied for a detective's shield in San Jose, tested well and won it. As usual, he went for the most challenging work, going into undercover narcotics in the dicey sections of the city. It was nerve-shattering stuff, without a gun, without a shield, but sometimes wearing a wire.

Once, an insane dealer put a pistol to the front of Brooks' head and made fun noises about airing out his brain with a hole from a thirty-eight. The dealer wanted to see if a backup squad would break down the doors. As it happened, due to a mix-up in timing the backups were on a pizza run and never knew that Brooks was looking into the open end of a Smith & Wesson. And when no one broke down the doors, the dealer put his weapon away. But this was one of two defining moments of Brooks' police career on the West Coast.

The other moment came under the command of one Captain Harold G. Barcus, the controversial commander of the San Jose Homicide Division. Barcus was known as "Blood and Thunder" in the press, an appellation which suggested the contempt he held for such irksome concepts as due process and civil rights.

Barcus eventually drew a bead on a lowlife named Jerome Tweedy who seemed to have a hand in every dirty bit of non-Mafia business in the city. Barcus asked for Brooks' help on an undercover squad that would make Tweedy, a longtime nemesis, a priority target.

The San Jose Police Department and the local underworld exchanged threats. One thing led to another. Then a member of the detective squad named Ted Hamlin was shot to death opening his mailbox one night. Two months later, primarily on some strongly circumstantial evidence channeled from Blood and Thunder to Brooks—to which Brooks diligently testified in court—a jury decided that Tweedy had been the gunman. Eventually, Tweedy gasped for his final breath in a California gas chamber.

At the execution, Barcus joyfully served as an official state witness.

"Well, I watched the exterminators do him in," the captain confessed to Brooks and a few other of his narcs over a beer a few days later. "I watched them spray in the Raid. I watched Tweedy gag and kick and choke and barf and fart until it was over." Barcus grinned and mused further. "Gosh," he concluded sweetly as he drummed his fingers on the bar. "I wonder what Jerome was really doing the night Ted Hamlin got whacked."

A month later, Brooks resigned from the San Jose Police Department. He turned in his shield and his weapon, withdrew every nickel from his pension fund, and, to use his words, "went on the bum" for a couple of years.

He worked as a store detective in San Francisco, then took a post in industrial security in an aerospace plant in Seattle. Again, he was bored silly. One day on a lark, he pushed off from the Pacific Coast and went to Hawaii, planning to stay for as long as his money lasted.

It lasted two years. And so did a string of knockout girlfriends who were more than generous with their favors. But by then it was 1984 and even perfect waves in paradise could get boring. He assembled his old credentials and tried to latch on as a cop in Honolulu. He had no luck. Wanderlust beset him again. One May, he set out for the Lower Forty-eight again and found himself on the East Coast by August.

There, on another whim, he attended a convention of law enforcement placement officers at the New York Coliseum. Impressed by Brooks' university degree, clean record and straightforward respectability, several recruiters pressed business cards in his hands. He soon found himself sifting through job opportunities, trying to decide which he considered attractive.

If any.

As it happened, it was now the mid-1980s. The island of Nantucket, thirty miles at sea off the southeastern shoreline of Massachusetts, had found itself with a ticklish problem. There was not just quick big-city Wall Street money coming to the island, but there was a trickle of dirty money as well. The town was looking to add a detective or two with some big-city street smarts—exactly what Brooks had developed in San Jose.

The island made him an offer.

Brooks accepted. He began in January 1986 and had been a detective on the Nantucket Police Department ever since. It wasn't Nirvana and sometimes it still bothered him that his father's condemning prophesy had proven correct:

"With that good head on your shoulders, with all that education, all you've become is a cop?"

Well, yes. That's what he *had* become. It wasn't perfect and more and more he nurtured the hope of finding a steady woman someday—not a strong likelihood on an island where he already knew almost all of the seven thousand year-round residents. But life itself wasn't perfect and this wasn't hell, either. So, as he closed out his thirties, it would have to do.

Still unresolved, of course, was the question that only he could ask himself and only he could ultimately answer? Had he walked away from San Jose in disgust? Or had he left the department because he wasn't up to the challenges of being a policeman in a big city?

Did he really have the inner courage to carry a badge and protect the public? Or had he now settled into a comfortable small-town department where few cases which required true street-style courage would ever come his way?

He didn't have answers yet. And he didn't know if he ever would.

But that, resolutely, was how Tim Brooks might have told the story of his own life. Or at least that's how he would have told it up until a July morning in the early 1990s when a college girl from Cape Cod was found dead in an open field.

From a deep, dead sleep in the middle of the night, Annette came alert. Her eyes opened as if in response to some unseen cue. She lay in bed for several seconds, thinking. She wondered why she was awake in the darkness in the first hours of Sunday.

Then Annette knew, though she didn't see her. The visitor was back. The specter. The woman in white. Two nights in a row.

Hell. Call it what it was. *The ghost.*

Annette felt her flesh creep. She looked around the room.

There was no movement. There were no shadows, no enigmatic configurations of light and darkness. Just quiet. Just stillness.

And yet, Annette knew. She knew the ghost—or *a* ghost—was somewhere.

Annette rose from bed. She went to the top of the stairs. Then slowly, she descended. The house was cool, chilly for a summer night. Almost abnormally so.

Annette arrived at the landing at the base of the steps. She moved into the living room and saw her. The woman in white—the ghost—was standing near the fireplace. She turned, the spirit did, when Annette entered the room. The ghost acknowledged the living owner's presence, but she went about her tasks. She stood by the hearth for many minutes, staring, as if she were considering a matter of great sorrow.

It was a whitish transparent presence that Annette saw again, clearly visible through the darkness, as if illuminated by some soft low hidden spotlight. And it was definitely a woman. This time, however, Annette had a sense that the woman was much younger. This was perhaps a woman of less than Annette's own age.

Then, with a flash, Annette made a realization. This was a different woman, altogether. Younger. Prettier. A second woman in white. Annette then had another sense, much like an idea coming to her from somewhere unknown: the sorrow this woman felt was very fresh and very painful.

And, strangely enough, Annette's fear was now gone. She watched this new specter with fascination. She backed away from the room and slowly seated herself on the bottom step of the staircase and gazed into the living room. It was as if she were too riveted to flee, yet too fascinated not to watch.

The ghost turned and sat down in a rocker near the hearth. Annette would later remember feeling that the woman was finally content about something—maybe just pleased to have been seen—and smiled, though later Annette wouldn't remember seeing her smile. Again, it was just a *sense*.

Then Annette felt another sensation that was new. She felt an idea forming inside her, a thought that she couldn't immediately unravel. Nor could she give words to it. It was just a feeling. It was not a pleasant one. It was one of caution, almost one of foreboding or dread. It was much like the feeling one has when one knows something is bothering one but cannot quite place it.

Or maybe it was that there was another presence somewhere nearby, but Annette couldn't quite place it.

Annette looked downward for a moment, then back up. She stared at the ghost. The woman seemed to still be in her chair, gently rocking. Annette felt the woman was facing her, but she couldn't see clearly enough to determine the woman's expression.

Then the feelings within Annette started to fade. And with them faded the vision in the living room. Seconds later, the ghost was gone.

Annette stared at the place for what seemed like many minutes but which was probably a much shorter time. She had the urge to step forward and turn the room lights on but, in a funny sort of reaction, hesitated. She didn't know whether light would antagonize the specter.

So she waited for several more minutes. Then she stood. Her hand found the old light switch near the door of the living room. Annette turned on the room lights. The room was suddenly bright.

Annette squinted. The room was empty. Not a soul there. The only thing moving was the rocking chair, which, right before Annette's eyes, was moving very slightly, as if someone had left it a minute or two earlier. Then it eased to a gentle halt, as if guided by an unseen hand.

Annette felt a deep shiver. She held one of her hands in the

90

other. The room was very still now, very empty and very comfortable. Then she suddenly knew that the presence was gone. It was a very palpable feeling, as if she had felt the woman brush invisibly past her and leave the room.

"Gone," Annette thought to herself. "Sure. Gone. Gone to where?"

The unsettling thought—the ominous one she had sensed a few minutes earlier—started to form again within her. And then that vanished as well. Yet for some reason she wasn't frightened. And she congratulated herself on her courage.

"You should be scared," she mumbled to herself. "You saw a ghost again! You should be scared, but you're not. Brave girl. Very good!"

She blew out a long breath to reassure herself.

She recalled that it was not unlike her conquest of professional fear several years ago. Fear of audiences while upon a stage. Fear of auditions. Fear of a live television camera. Fear of—

Tired, she looked for a place to sit. She avoided the rocker and chose the sofa. It was half-past three in the morning. She studied the furniture that surrounded her. The rocker. The side tables. Some antique chairs. The huge old china cabinet that no one could budge.

A few moments later, remaining in the living room, Annette closed her eyes. Just for a minute, she told herself. She would just close her fatigued eyes for a minute. Then she would climb the stairs again and go back to bed.

Her mind worked overtime.

"Ghosts," she whispered in the quiet room. "Oh, yeah. Sure. All the time. We believe that, don't we?"

Her eyes opened a crack. The room was quiet and cozy.

There really has to be a rational explanation for this, she thought. I mean, what's going on here? Have to find the rational explanation tomorrow.

In her sleepiness, she considered it further.

Right. First thing tomorrow morning. That's what I'll do.

Instead of going back upstairs to bed, she fell asleep on the sofa. There she remained. She dozed for several hours till her eyes opened at half-past eight the next morning, when the light from a gray cloudy morning seeped into Annette's living room.

She made herself coffee and breakfast. Then, her resolution firm now, she reached for the telephone.

"Ghosts," she reassured herself as she pressed a number into a modern pushbutton telephone. "What utter rubbish."

Elsewhere on the island that Sunday morning, the interrogation continued. Tim Brooks was nominally off duty at the time, but was in the police building catching up on paperwork. His office bordered the office used by Rodzienko and Gelman, and was within twenty feet of the Gray Room as well.

Brooks studied the interrogation, or as much of it as he could see and hear. He watched the greatly shaken Arthur Lloyd bring his son to the precinct. He watched the boy submit to another torturous morning of questioning. From his desk, Brooks could hear much of the conversation in the Gray Room.

Then, toward noon, as Brooks worked at his desk, a familiar figure with white hair lurched into Brooks' doorway. Brooks looked up. Captain Agannis' eyes were fixed upon him.

"What are you doing here, today, Tim? Working? Jerking off? Or just eavesdropping on your peers?" Lieutenant Agannis asked.

"All of the above."

"Figures," Agannis growled. The lieutenant always sounded as if his head ached.

"Got time for a nuisance run today?" Agannis asked. Whenever the lieutenant asked, it was strongly suggested that the officer in question make the time.

"Sure," Brooks said after a pause.

"Come down to my office, Timmy, will ya?"

Brooks followed his superior through a corridor. The walls here were green, just as they were in Brooks' office. And, like Brooks' walls, the paint was starting to peel. Agannis led him to the higher rent district of the building, right next to the chief's office. The paint was flaking there, too. Under the rules of the new nineties austerity, all decorating costs had been whacked from the town budget.

Agannis led Brooks into the assistant chief's office. Agannis trudged behind his own desk and landed heavily in a leather swivel chair. Boomer, seated on a mat beneath a window, raised his head expectantly and recognized the younger policeman. Boomer gave a halfhearted wag of his tail and then settled back into his afternoon snooze.

"What have you got?" Brooks finally inquired.

"The old Ritter woman. The one who walks around at night," Agannis said, leaping into the subject at hand. "Helen Ritter. You remember her?"

"Of course," Brooks said. He seated himself on a wooden chair across from the lieutenant.

"Seen her recently?"

Brooks shrugged. "Maybe a week or ten days ago."

"How'd she seem?"

"About the same as ever."

Agannis foraged through the top drawer of his desk as he spoke. He found a battered soft pack of Marlboros that contained a few final smokes. His thick fingers intruded into the pack.

"Harmless old hen. Sweet old woman, actually," Agannis said, shaking his head slightly and rambling off on a brief tangent. "You know, she was a schoolteacher on this island forever. I had her myself when I was in eleventh grade."

"Is that right?"

"It is."

"Must have been a hundred years ago," Brooks suggested.

Agannis grinned and lit a Marlboro. He inhaled deeply and savored the smoke.

The cigarette in his mouth was slightly bent. For a moment, through a strange cast of light that filtered through the fresh cloud of smoke, Brooks' commanding officer looked horribly ancient and his skin seemed to take on the hue of granite. From somewhere there was a fragment of sunlight from outside.

Through the haze, it illuminated one side of Agannis' face and made a hollow out of his eye on the opposite side.

Brooks blinked as if his vision hadn't focused properly. Then, just as abruptly, the light from outside shifted and Agannis looked normal again.

Lieutenant Agannis sighed.

"We got a complaint from an address on Cort Street this morning," Agannis said. "Some single woman lives there. New to the island. I don't know who the hell she is. Summer resident probably. Wealthy if she's at that address. I think the house was sold recently. Anyway, she thinks there was a woman wandering about her property the last two nights. Or something."

"On her lawn or driveway or what?" Brooks asked.

"Inside the house," Agannis said.

"She saw someone?"

Agannis inhaled a new rush of smoke and nodded. "She says she did."

"And she filed an actual complaint?" Brooks inquired.

"Nah. She just asked us to look into it." Agannis glanced down at a paper on his blotter. "She phoned an hour ago." Lieutenant Agannis paused. "Check with the dispatcher, will ya? I don't even know the name. We got a call this morning around ten thirty."

Brooks nodded.

"The woman said that she would like the visits to stop. Of course, if she'd lock her fucking doors at night it would help, too, wouldn't it?"

Brooks acknowledged that it might.

The lieutenant wrote down the address. Seventeen Cort Street.

Brooks took the slip of paper from him as Agannis further enveloped himself in a cloud of his own making. He raised his eyes and locked into those of the younger man.

"Looks like our Mrs. Ritter is on the prowl again," he said. "Or at least that's my guess. See if you can settle things down, will ya, Timmy?"

"I'll handle it," Brooks assured his commander. He nodded

and took the address. Then he departed from the lieutenant's office.

As the detective reentered the corridor with the peeling green paint and approached his own office again, the interrogation of Eddie Lloyd was still in progress. Brooks knew because he heard Rodzienko bellowing in his best "bad cop" voice, followed by the irate voice of Arthur Lloyd rising to his son's defense. It was enough to send Ned Schwinn hurrying back into the Gray Room from the spot where he had nearly taken root outside.

Seven

The gray overcast darkened on Sunday morning until it became heavily humid and was accompanied by intermittent showers. Kept away from the beaches, tennis courts and golf courses by the weather, vacationers and weekenders clustered in the center of Nantucket town, prowling through stores, lining up for breakfast at the inns and guest houses, and waiting near The Hub for the deliveries from the mainland of the New York and Boston newspapers. From Brant Point, the foghorn sounded mournfully every seven seconds.

Annette spent most of the morning quietly tidying her house. There were a few small pieces of extra furniture that had cluttered rooms. These she moved to the spacious attic. She swept and vacuumed the top two floors of the house as well. Then she made a final series of trips to the attic, neatly storing suitcases and packing cartons in an area separate from the furniture.

Even the Charlie McCarthy dummy, after some deliberation, made a trip to the topmost floor. There the dummy was carefully laid on a table and, to protect him from dust, beneath a heavy white sheet. Annette loved the dummy, but the poignant reminder of her late mother remained painful. Better to keep it out of sight for a while, she decided. It was the future she wished to live for. Not the past.

Her housekeeping complete, Annette was filled with a sense of accomplishment.

* * *

Early on Sunday afternoon, the rain let up and there was a sharp knock on the front door of 17 Cort Street. Annette raised her eyes from the script that she was reading. She was in the living room of her house. She waited several seconds and made no effort to respond.

Silence followed.

Then came a series of knocks. Annette's eyes left the story before her. In dismay, through her reading glasses, they settled upon the eighteenth-century hearth across the room.

She waited.

Annette was deeply annoyed to have a visitor. Enough of her time belonged to other people. Those hours which were hers, she tried to guard religiously. So she didn't even move to the window of the room to peek out.

"Go away," she said softly. She meant it. After a few moments, a longer silence returned. She saw it as a victory and returned to her work.

Annette had two ways of reading a movie script.

Method One: She would read the first fifteen pages and make a decision whether or not to continue. If the story just plain didn't interest her, she would stop. Or, if the screenwriter hadn't set out his or her themes, characters, plots and subplots within the initial quarter hour of screen time, she could conclude that the structure of the story was already faulty. How could anyone hope that all of those vital elements would come together later when bad craftsmanship was already apparent? So after fifteen minutes, bingo. If it didn't work by then, it would land with a vengeful thud in the waste basket. It didn't merit return postage.

In truth, of course, Annette rarely received any scripts in this category. It was Joe Harris' job to screen out the clearly unprofessional efforts.

Then, Method Two: If Annette liked the story as well as the character being offered to her *and* if the script passed the fifteen-minute litmus test, she would continue. Thereupon, she needed to read the complete work in one sitting—exactly the way the story would be presented on screen.

One sitting. About an hour of reading time. Not one sitting with three interruptions, but *one* uninterrupted read. An intrusion, even after seventy pages, meant losing the feel of the story and the characters. She would have to go back to the beginning.

Blessedly, there was no more knocking. A small wave of relaxation came over her. Annette sipped from a glass of diet Coke on the table by the sofa. Her eyes returned to the script on her lap.

This one was titled *Rumor of Guilt*. It was a murder mystery set in Philadelphia, but which would be filmed in Vancouver. The author was an Englishman named Horace Westerly. Westerly was a successful television writer and a Joe Harris client. He had also had two previous scripts produced as feature films. When restraining from all substance abuse, Joe Harris had said, Westerly wrote well. *Rumor of Guilt* presented Annette with the role of a young woman who is suspected of poisoning a former lover so that her current husband won't learn of her affair. In trying to prove her innocence, the woman gradually reveals the affair, creates the impression that she *is* culpable and frames herself of murder.

Joe Harris thought the script was very cleverly written and had great possibilities, though it also reflected the author's cynical view of the world. So far, Annette agreed on all counts. Her gaze drifted back to page thirty-one.

Then there was a harder rapping at the front door. Annette's eyes left the script again and her anger built rapidly. She had bought a house clear across the country to be left alone. She had closed her doors this afternoon. She had taken her phone off the hook.

Why couldn't the world take a hint? She didn't want to be bothered.

Fact was, had the weather not been dreary when the day began, she probably would have hauled the scripts off to an isolated beach on the south shore of the island. There the sea gulls, terns and greenhead flies didn't give a damn who was a movie star.

There she could have sat in blissful isolation, listening to the surf pound and reading the material Joe Harris had sent her.

Again, the knocking.

Furious, she stayed where she sat. Surely, whoever it was would inevitably go away. She would outlast this intruder. She waited for peace and quiet to return. When a silence of two minutes had followed, she allowed her eyes to settle back into the story.

But already, her attention had been sabotaged. Well, she thought, she hadn't *moved* yet. Maybe she could retain the atmosphere of Horace Westerly's story and—

The final time, the knocking was so loud and insistent that it almost caused her to jump. And it came from a different source now. It was on the door at the rear of the house, the one next to the kitchen. It was loud and sharp. Seconds later, it was accompanied by an unfamiliar male voice calling out.

"Hello . . . ? Anyone home?"

Annette muttered a long, low, single-syllable profanity. She laid aside her reading glasses on the table by her chair, putting them next to the glass of soda. She slammed the script down and stalked to the rear door. She peeked through the kitchen window.

Her visitor—her nuisance—was a sandy-haired man in a blue short-sleeved shirt and tan slacks.

Someone local, obviously. A workman, no doubt. Or a salesman. Or someone from the town. Or—much, much worse—some complete dip! An autograph seeker or a hopelessly untalented buffoon with a half-written half-baked hopelessly unprofessional script home somewhere in his sock drawer. She would give him, she decided, living hell. She flung open the wooden interior door but kept the screen in place.

"Yes?" she snapped. "What is it?"

"Hello," the man said. He smiled engagingly. The blue of his shirt matched his eyes. "Sorry to bother you."

"You are bothering me!" Her tone ranged between icy and

hostile. "I'm in the middle of something important," she said, folding her arms. "You've come at a terrible time. What do you want?"

He gazed at her for a second and Annette wondered whether or not he had recognized her. "Yes, I'm *the* Annette Carlson," she was prepared to say. "Yes, I'm the actress and would you please go away!"

But the man gave no indication at all that he recognized her or knew who she was. "Am I at seventeen Cort Street?" he asked.

"The number's on the mailbox. Who the hell are you?" she demanded impatiently.

He reached into the breast pocket of his shirt. Her eyes followed his hand. He withdrew a small black leather case, rectangular and smaller than a billfold. Then he opened it to reveal an ornate silver shield and an embossed identification card sealed in plastic.

"I'm Detective Timothy Brooks," he said pleasantly. "Nantucket Police Department. I apologize if I'm here at a bad time. But earlier today I believe you made a nonemergency call to our department."

She looked at his badge and experienced a sinking feeling. Of course! Earlier that morning she had made the call to the police.

Reluctantly, her tone softened. Something within her—something buried deeply in her middle-class American upbringing—still perceived a policeman as a figure of authority and respect.

"Yes. Of course," she said after a final moment of hesitation. "I'm sorry. I'd forgotten."

He returned his badge and ID to his pocket.

He offered his hand. She accepted it. She gave her own name as Ann Carlson. "How did you know I was home?" she asked.

"I have a hunch about those things," he said. He looked past her and saw that no one else appeared to be there. "You told our dispatcher that you've had a prowler the last couple of nights. A 'woman in white'?" he asked. "About two to two-thirty A.M. one night. Last night maybe about three A.M."

"Yes," she said tentatively. "That's correct." She hesitated. Somehow in daylight, the rambling of a nocturnal imagination seemed petty. Silly. Unreal. But, "I suppose you'd better come in," she said.

"Thank you."

Annette stepped away from the door and allowed him to enter. She walked him to the living room and invited him to sit down. He chose the rocker. She picked the sofa.

Then Annette explained why she had called. She tried to be very rational and straightforward. She wasn't crazy, after all, she kept reminding herself. And she was sure that she had seen *something*.

She described it the way she had remembered it, but cut out any supernatural implications. There had been a woman in her room, she said, then maybe another one—she couldn't be sure—puttering around downstairs the next night. Both times, the intruder was gone before the lights went on.

"Scary, huh?" he asked.

"Yes," she admitted. "It was."

"Some prowlers can move very quickly when they've been spotted," he said.

"I guess so." She drew a breath. "The house was properly locked. I don't know how anyone could have gotten in. Or out."

He nodded.

"Why didn't you call us when it was happening?" Tim Brooks asked.

Her eyes lowered. "I don't know. Middle of the night. Single woman with a crazy story." Her eyes rose. "Besides, it was over by the time I would have called. So I didn't know what kind of response I'd get."

"We would have sent a patrol car," Brooks said. "If there's a problem, it's our job to investigate. Will you remember that for the future?"

She felt somehow reassured.

"Okay," she said.

"And you don't think you were dreaming?"

She hesitated. "No."

"Have you changed your locks recently?" he asked. "How do you know someone doesn't have a key?"

"I don't," she admitted.

"Look," he said steadily, "if you actually saw something, chances are you had a prowler. And I'll make you a bet that there's at least one access to this house that doesn't lock properly. Friendly bet, okay? May I take a look?"

"Be my guest," Annette said.

Brooks stood. He walked to the front door of the house and examined it. It was securely locked. Then he walked through the living room, looking carefully at the lower panes of each window. Once, he stopped to feel something, making sure a pane was firm. When he was satisfied that it was, he went to the next window.

From there he walked into the dining room. Annette did not follow. She knew what he was doing. He was examining all of the entry points to the house. She heard him in the kitchen next.

Finally, Brooks fiddled with the back door and its locks. There was a moment of silence, followed by more jiggling with the latches. Then she heard his voice.

"Ms. Carlson?" he called.

"Yes?"

"Would you mind coming here for a moment?"

When she arrived, the detective was standing by the back door, which he held open.

"Look at this," he said. He motioned to the doorknob.

She looked where he indicated. "What about it?" she asked.

"Does it feel like it's locked?"

She held her hand on it and tested it. It did.

"Same as the other night?"

"The same."

"Lock me out," he requested as he stepped through the doorway. "Lock both doors, then stand inside and wait."

She closed both the screen door and the heavier rear door, dropping a hook into a small eye on the screen door, and turning a lock on the wooden one.

She stepped back.

"Ready?" he called from outside.

"Ready!" she answered.

Annette stood within the interior vestibule and watched. Behind her, some newspapers rustled, distracting her. A breeze must have rippled through the kitchen window, she thought. But she hadn't felt one.

"Watch carefully!" the policeman called.

She couldn't see through the door, but she could hear. Tim Brooks fussed with the screen. He did something abrupt to it. She heard the hook and eye come unlatched with a small rattle.

Annette felt a surge of anxiety. She felt her palms begin to sweat, transposing the sounds of the policeman breaking in to those of an imagined intruder.

She stared at the doorknob before her. It started to turn, gently at first, then more forcibly. It moved rapidly from one side to the other as Brooks twisted it.

Annette felt a tremor of something. But she couldn't tell what.

Fear? But, why? It was only the detective's hand on the other side of the door.

Wasn't it?

Or were the two of them starting to investigate something they shouldn't—trying to assess answers to questions best left unasked?

Silly! she told herself. Get this notion out of your head, girl!

She watched carefully. The doorknob turned firmly from one side to the other, Timothy's hand continuing to work from the outside. Then the knob turned more sharply. Annette took her eyes off it because a soft creak in the room behind her startled her. But the footfall, if it had been one, or the heat, or the wind again, was invisible.

She sensed the ghost anew, or one of the ghosts. And then, just as fast, her sense of it was gone. She looked all through the room and there was nothing.

No presence. Nothing. An empty welcoming room.

She turned her attention back to the doorknob. Brooks

twisted it a final time all the way to the left. Then he jerked it hard in the opposite direction.

It made a muffled snapping noise, and for some reason the only corresponding sound Annette could think of was that of the neck being snapped on a small animal. She had no idea where such an image might have come from. Nor did she have time to consider it. For slowly, the door opened.

Unnerved, Annette stepped backward.

"Boo," the cop said. He grinned amiably. "So much for on-site building security, right?"

She looked at him, then at the doorknob again, then back to the policeman. She tried to sort out the implications. But as he opened the door and stepped into the house, Annette suffered one of those tremors again. She almost felt as if something had slipped icily past her and departed the house.

She glanced around, anxious and distracted. Oh, hell. Oh, hell, she cursed at herself. Get a grip on yourself. Stop imagining all this crap. Keep control of your mind. It's daytime, anyway!

"How did you do that?" she asked Brooks.

He produced a credit card.

"There's enough slack in the screen door so that someone can jimmy the hook upward from the outside," he said. "All you need is a piece of hard plastic. Like a credit card. As for the doorknob . . ." He shrugged. "Try it yourself," he offered.

She moved to the spot where he stood. Then he talked her into standing outside the closed door and trying the knob from the rear doorstep. At first, when the door was locked, the knob seemed steady. But when Annette moved it rapidly back and forth, and then applied some force, the knob gave way. There was no surprise. It had done the same for Tim Brooks.

She raised her eyes and looked at him.

"Look," he said. "I might be able to clear up this whole intrigue very quickly. It might connect with something else I know about." He paused. "But I'd need to drive you around a few corners from here to meet someone. It would take maybe another half an hour of your time. Half an hour, maximum," he promised. "Even though I know you just told me that you're in the middle of something important."

She hesitated.

He nudged her toward a decision. "It might give you some peace of mind if this works out the way I think it might," he promised.

"When would you need this 'thirty minutes, maximum'?"

"How about right now?" He smiled hopefully and waited. "I have a car," he said.

So much for the script, she thought. So much for getting it read in one sitting. Well, better now than later. Let's get rid of this, God damn it all. Next time I don't go near the door unless it's on fire.

"All right," she said. "Thirty minutes, maximum. Like you promised."

She locked her house. Then Tim Brooks led her to his car which was parked around front. Despite the rain of an earlier hour, the Miata had its top down.

Annette's eyes rose to look at her house as she stepped into Brooks' car. She would later remember thinking, as the old building sat in the mist of a gray afternoon, with the foghorn still moaning in the distance, that it looked like the coziest, most tranquil place in the world.

She would always remember that vision and that thought, and, of course, years later from a darker perspective, the irony contained therein.

Eight

The Mid Island Convalescent Home was located on a narrow side road which was one left turn beyond upper Main Street. It was a rambling white wooden house in transmogrified Victorian. Its gables rose above the surrounding foliage. There were three steps upward to the front porch, over which hung a small sign which proclaimed the name of the establishment.

There were numerous chairs on the front porch, scattered in whatever arrangement the elderly residents had last left them.

Mid Island had been established in the 1950s as a care center for older island residents, men and women in their seventies and eighties who remained mostly self-sufficient but who also needed a guiding hand. There were never more than seventeen residents, as that was the number of rooms, and half were in the category of Mrs. Helen Ritter, the longtime Nantucket resident and former schoolteacher. That is, while a guardian eye was kept upon her, she was free to come and go as she wished. Within reason.

Tim Brooks parked his car in a semicircular driveway before the front porch. An old man sat near the front door, rocking in a cane chair and quietly listening to the Boston Red Sox on a transistor radio. It was a timeless scene from a New England summer. Brooks nodded to him. The old man nodded back. The Sox had the bases filled with one out, bottom of the first. But Mo Vaughn lined into a double play—first baseman, unassisted—as Brooks led Annette through the front door.

"What *are* we doing here?" she asked softly and with some irritation.

"Looking for your prowler," Brooks answered.

There was a nurse at the front desk, a matronly woman with gray hair, a porcine face and a name tag. Her name was Amanda. She knew Timothy Brooks and greeted him with a smile. The detective asked if Mrs. Ritter could receive two visitors.

"I think she'd be pleased," Amanda said kindly. "She's upstairs."

"Third floor?" Brooks asked.

"Try the lounge," Amanda said. The third-floor porter could knock on the door to her room if Mrs. Ritter wasn't out in the common area.

Annette Carlson followed, saying nothing.

There was a modern elevator by the central stairwell. The policeman and the actress took it to the third floor, which was also the top floor at Mid Island. They stepped out into a quiet corridor.

The porter's name was Mike Silva. He was a moody man in his late twenties who was washing the tiled floor. Silva knew Brooks, and initially glanced at him with disinterest. Then he looked at the policeman more attentively.

"Hey, Brooks," Silva called. "Anything new on the college girl?"

"It's still being investigated, Mike," Brooks answered.

"They still talking to a suspect?"

"That's about all I can tell you, Mike," Brooks continued. "Today I'm looking for Mrs. Ritter."

Silva nodded in the general direction of the lounge. Again, Annette followed closely. She asked what the porter had meant about a college girl and Brooks told her that there had been a murder on the island the previous Saturday morning.

"A *murder? Here?*" Annette answered.

"And if the truth were known," Brooks grumbled, "the real killer is probably long gone. Could be halfway across the United States by now."

"Still . . ." Annette said softly. "A *murder* . . ."

It was the first time she had heard of the slaying. It shocked her.

"The *Inquirer & Mirror* comes out on Thursdays," he added. "So does the *Beacon*. But the story will be all over the place long before then."

Brooks stopped short as they passed a residential doorway. The woman he sought, a white-haired lady who looked to be at least in her late seventies, was stepping out of a friend's room. She carried an aluminum cane but wasn't using it. She did, however, appear intent on where she was going.

Brooks stopped, smiled and greeted her.

"Hello, Mrs. Ritter," he said, speaking gently so as not to surprise her. "May I give you a hand with anything?"

She was an aged, frail woman with white hair. At the sound of his voice, she hesitated into a stop. Then her eyes stolidly raised themselves. There was a moment's hesitation before they found the speaker and locked onto Brooks. There was another painful moment still before a labored flash of recognition.

Then, "Why, Timmy," she said. "How nice to see you again." Her eyes went quickly to Annette and back again. "Is this your new wife?"

"No, just a friend," said Brooks.

"Where *is* your wife?" she pressed.

"You know where, Mrs. Ritter. I'm not married."

"A nice boy like you should be," she said very properly. "Maybe this will be the girl," she suggested next, nodding toward Annette, approving her at the same time. "Oh, shush," the old woman said next, more to herself than to her guests. "Why do I say things like that? Rushing things a bit, aren't I?"

"Just a trifle," Brooks answered. "Do you have a moment to chat?"

Mrs. Ritter said yes. In fact, she had all afternoon.

Brooks offered her an arm. Mrs. Ritter took it and the policeman guided her. He felt close to her full weight on his wrist.

"I just came by to say hello and see how you were doing," Brooks said.

"Doing?" she answered. "How am I ever doing? One day at a time," she said. "With God's will. That's all."

Mrs. Ritter's room was nearby. Brooks pushed the door open to allow her passage. With his head he motioned that Annette was to follow.

The three of them entered a small, densely furnished room. Brooks helped her to a chair. She edged her way off his arm and seated herself. Brooks sat down on the edge of a chaise longue across from her. Annette sat on the edge of a bed.

From a lifetime, from what she had once had in her own home, the old woman had packed her favorite pieces into a single room. There was a lady's writing desk, neatly arranged with pens and writing paper and a small dresser that she had frequently told Brooks had once been her mother's. There was a pink barrel chair and beside it, bearing nothing, was her prized possession, a small square antique tea table with four legs.

This was her "checkerboard table," as she called it. It had been made from walnut wood in the early nineteenth century by a cabinet maker in Salem and still bore his initials underneath. A painted checkerboard, in sixty-four distinct but faded red and black squares, was clearly delineated on the tabletop. But two of the table's legs, Brooks noted sadly, were cracked.

"Have they been feeding you all right here?" Tim Brooks asked.

She complained about the food.

"How 'bout your old students?" he asked. "You must have a million of them. Anyone come see you?"

She admitted that several people dropped by each week to say hello. Tim Brooks knew this but listened anyway.

"Billy came by last week," she said. "You know Billy, don't you? He's a policeman, too."

By 'Billy' she meant Lt. William Agannis, fifty-nine years old, chief of detectives and still a boy to her. Brooks nodded.

"That snotty little Japanese man comes by, too," she added almost indignantly.

"Who's that?"

"The minister."

"Reverend Osaro," Brooks said, helping her with the name of his basketball opponent. "He's the pastor of Mrs. Ritter's church," Brooks announced for Annette's edification.

"That's nice that he comes by," Annette said.

Mrs. Ritter gave a dismal sigh.

"The weather's been nice recently," Brooks tried next. "How much have you been getting out?"

"Out?" she said. "Oh, maybe once a week I take a walk. That's all."

"With one of the other residents here?" Brooks asked.

"Usually."

"During the day?"

"During the day."

Detective Brooks moved toward the subject matter of his visit. "I was wondering, Mrs. Ritter," he asked gently. "You haven't been up to any of your tricks, have you?" he asked.

"Me?"

"You."

"What tricks?"

"The ones that scare people. Going out for walks late at night?"

"Good Heavens," she said. "No! Wouldn't dare. All these hippies and drug addicts coming to the island in the summer. Not safe at night anymore."

"So you haven't been out at night at all?" he pressed. "Not even when you might have been feeling a little lonely sometimes? Maybe—"

"I haven't gone anywhere, Timmy," she said. "I haven't been out of"—she lowered her voice so that any nursing personnel wouldn't overhear and take offense—"this damned place for three weeks." She leaned back. "And I haven't been out at night since, you know—"

"The last time I gave you a ride back?"

"Yes," she said. Her aged eyes looked directly into his. "You know I'd tell you the truth, Timmy," she said.

"Yes," he said. "I know that." He made a mental note to ask

the night nurse if it were at all possible that she may have slipped out.

"Then why are you asking me?" Mrs. Ritter demanded. "You have a funny look on your face."

"Do I?" He smiled. He turned to Annette. "Here I am a professional detective and Mrs. Ritter can still see right through me."

"I certainly *can!*" she said succinctly.

"What am I going to do? My career will be ruined."

Mrs. Ritter's eyes twinkled. "I won't tell anyone, Timmy," she said, consciously continuing the joke. She eased back in her chair and folded her hands. Her gaze wandered the room for a moment, then settled on Annette.

"I taught school on this island for fifty years," she boasted, emphasizing the fifty. "I know when a young man is being less than candid." Now she focused even more intently on Annette. "You're a very pretty young girl," she said. "You'd do well to learn some of the danger signs as well."

"Yes, I should, Mrs. Ritter," Annette said. The old woman took a very deep look at Annette.

"Men can't be trusted," Mrs. Ritter continued, citing the wisdom of the ages. "Never at all with a pretty girl."

"Shame on all of us," Tim Brooks said.

"Well, maybe Timmy here you can trust. I trust Timmy." She took his hand and gave it a squeeze. Then Mrs. Ritter considered the presence of Annette Carlson very carefully. "I know you," she finally said. "You're a movie star."

Annette smiled graciously. "I've been in a few films," she answered.

"More than a few," Mrs. Ritter said. "And you won an award. I saw you in that movie. Oh, I forget the name. With that handsome Italian man. The man with the real black hair and the wonderful voice."

Annette knew exactly who she meant. Tim Brooks rolled his eyes.

"The film was *Passport To Fear,*" Annette answered.

"That's the one," Mrs. Ritter said, as if they would never

have thought of it without her. She was much more animated now. "You were terrific in that."

"Thank you," Annette said again. "You're very kind."

"You got killed off early," Mrs. Ritter said, recalling with remarkable clarity. "Such a shame. I liked you better than the other girl who was in the film. I don't know her name."

Annette supplied it.

"You were much better than she was. Should have kept you around to the end." She paused. "I don't know who writes those silly things." She shook her head. "But who am I to judge? I'm just an old schoolteacher waiting out the time that's left to me. God willing, Heaven could only be a few hours away for any of us." She shrugged then smiled ruefully. "You in any more movies?" she asked.

"I'm in a television movie that will be broadcast this fall," Annette said patiently. "I think it will be shown in October. And I'm choosing another script for after that."

"For a television show?"

"For a movie. In a movie theater."

"Well, you choose very carefully, dearie," she said boldly. "And don't you trust anyone but yourself. A girl has to be careful of her career. When I was a teacher, I looked out for mine. No one else looks out for you."

Brooks came slowly to his feet. "We have to be going, Mrs. Ritter," Brooks said next. "I just stopped in to say hello and make sure you were all right."

"That's kind of you, Timmy. But, 'all right'? Ha!" She snorted and motioned contemptuously to her confines. Then she made a complacent face. "I suppose," she said with a sigh, "all I can do is make the best of it."

Brooks leaned forward and gave her a kiss on the forehead.

"You take care of yourself, Mrs. Ritter," he said. "And stay out of trouble."

"Hmph," she said. "Not much trouble a woman of my age can get into, is there?"

"I'll stop by and see you again next week," he said.

She sighed again. "Bless you, Timmy."

A few minutes later, Tim Brooks accompanied Annette down the entrance lobby of Mid Island Convalescent. He excused himself for a moment and spoke privately with the facility's daytime manager. Then he and Annette walked out to his car.

"So what was that all about?" she asked.

"Ever seen her before?"

"That old woman?"

"Who else?"

"Of course not." Annette said. "Why?"

He followed her to the passenger side and opened the car door.

"You're sure?"

"I'm sure. Tell me why."

"I'll explain in the car," he said.

Annette settled into the car. Brooks joined her a moment later, started the ignition and buckled into his seat belt.

"This goes back maybe two years," Brooks said. "Mrs. Ritter had her own home. Not far from here, not far from Cort Street. She used to go out for walks after dark. Just waltz out of her home, go up and down the street, looking for doors that were unlocked. Then she'd walk into people's homes." He paused. "I'm talking about two, three, four in the morning." He paused again. "Same time as your visitor."

Annette folded her arms and listened.

"There's still a small-town feel among a lot of people here," Brooks said, guiding the car out of the driveway and pulling onto a quiet road. "Doors don't get locked very carefully in a lot of houses."

"So what did Mrs. Ritter do?" Annette asked. "Once she was in these houses."

"She'd make herself at home," Brooks said. "Look for people who hadn't lived there for thirty years." He paused as he turned onto Main Street. "That, and scare the hell out of the current residents who heard voices in the house."

Annette nodded. A sad smile crossed her face as she watched the town float by her window. There was still a bustle in the main shopping district: daytrippers from off-island.

"I get it," she said. "A solitary old lady late at night. Wandering around at loose ends."

"Poor old dear," Tim Brooks said. He glanced at his passenger as he drove. "Want to hear more?"

"Sure."

"More than once, people have reported that she would come upstairs into their bedrooms. She'd sit in a room. She'd sit on the edge of a bed."

Annette looked away.

Brooks continued. "She'd check on children. Mrs. Ritter's nighttime prowlings scared the hell out of dozens of people on this island. You wake up, see someone wandering through your room, sitting on your bed. Well, you can imagine."

"I don't have to," Annette said, looking back to him.

"Of course not. Sounds kind of familiar, doesn't it?"

She admitted that it did.

"She never hurt anyone, of course," Brooks said. "Problem was, she was out in the streets late at night. In the summer, we get these drunk kids speeding home after the bars close. Then we also get city people. New York and Boston. They think they're vulnerable in their houses so they bring guns. Everyone got kind of worried that she was going to get herself hurt. Know what I mean?"

Annette knew.

"She doesn't have family. No children. Husband died a quarter century ago. Arrangements were made to move her into Mid Island for her own good. She's not happy, but deep down, she knows she's a whole lot safer." He paused. "See, I used to work nights a lot on the island, so it was me who brought her home a lot. That's how I personally landed in the case."

"And you're still keeping an eye on her?" Annette asked.

Brooks seemed almost embarrassed by the question.

"People forget: being a policeman is protecting the public," he said. "Sometimes you protect people from harm they might bring upon themselves."

He took his eyes off the road long enough to watch a girl in red shorts bicycle past them from the opposite direction. The girl was half Annette's age.

"Mrs. Ritter is a sweet old lady. Yeah, I know her faculties are slipping. Whose aren't? But she gave her whole life to teaching school on this island. I think she's earned a little something from the rest of us. So I help keep an eye on her. A lot of us do."

The girl on the bike was gone from his rearview mirror.

Annette was quiet as the car eased to a stop in front of her house on Cort Street.

"The night staff was supposed to be watchful, make sure she didn't wander off again," Brooks said. "My guess is. . . . Well, you see what I'm saying?" he said.

"I see."

"They're not always so alert, the night staff," Brooks said.

Annette nodded. They sat together in the parked car.

Brooks waited. "So what do you think?" he asked. "Is our mystery solved or not?"

"What I saw in my house didn't look like her at all."

He thought about it for a moment and sighed. "Ms. Carlson?" he asked.

"What?" She waited.

"Tell me again what you think you saw. I have a hunch that you left something out."

She was silent for a moment. Then she spoke.

"Neither woman had any contrasting color. They were all white. Like beams from stage lights. Yet they had form. And faces. And they conveyed thoughts to me. Two different times."

She fell silent again. Then, with an arch to her eyebrow, as if to discount even her own version of the events, "They looked like ghosts," she added. "Or what I imagine ghosts would look like."

Her words elicited half a smile from him. Polite but noncommittal. Indulgent and supportive, but skeptical.

"But that's silly, isn't it?" she asked. "Ghosts, I mean."

"I've never been much of a believer," he allowed.

She nodded.

"The first night, when I reached out to chase it away," she continued, "my arm flowed right through it, just like reaching through a beam of light."

His right forefinger was gently massaging the steering wheel of the Miata.

"No low moaning?" he asked. "No dragging chains? No skeletal hands or red beady eyes glaring out of the darkness?"

"No," she said. "And I wasn't drunk and I don't do drugs."

Expecting a curt dismissal, Annette was surprised when Brooks began to nod gently. Then he surprised her again. "You were there," he said. "You know what you remember. And that's the real reason you didn't phone the police at the time it happened," he concluded.

She nodded.

"Well, it makes more sense now," Brooks said. "In one way, at least."

"So what do you make of it?" Annette asked. "You think I'm a crazy lady from the West Coast, don't you? Movie actress, right? Must have a few screws loose?"

"Well, not yet, anyway," he assured her. "But there's still time."

"What you're saying is you *do* think I'm crazy. And you don't believe in ghosts. Let me tell you something. That's how I felt up until two nights ago, too."

"I have a friend on this island," Brooks answered thoughtfully. "Mrs. Ritter mentioned him. George Osaro. He's the pastor of one of the local churches as well as one of my best friends. We play basketball. He's always been into this stuff. Spirits. Spooks. Ghosts. Whatever he calls them."

There was a brightness as the sun almost broke through the clouds. Then from somewhere a shadow crossed Brooks' face.

"Every summer George has a symposium on this island about encounters with the supernatural," Brooks said. "He holds it in the church hall and always brings out a crowd."

"Are you suggesting that I go?" she asked, accusation in her tone. She had no intention of attending such an event.

"Nope," he said quickly. "Fact is, you just missed it. It was held about three weeks ago."

"I'm sure it was interesting."

Brooks shrugged. "What did your ghost say to you?" he asked.

Annette had almost forgotten. But the words came back. "She said, 'I came to warn you. Everyone on the island is in danger.' "

For some reason that he couldn't readily understand, her response gave him pause. It hung in the air and disturbed him.

"George never seems to lack for new material or new 'sightings' on this island," he continued. "But then again, we're overlooking something else rather obvious."

"What's that?"

"Just because Mrs. Ritter wasn't in your house doesn't mean you didn't have a different prowler. A real flesh-and-blood one, I mean."

"I know what I saw," she repeated.

"I'm sure you do."

Detective Brooks fished through his shirt pocket until he found one of his business cards. He found a pencil almost as easily. On the back of the card, he began to write.

"In case your visitor drops by again," he said, "I'm giving you my home phone number. Call me at the police station or call me at home. Any time, day or night."

He handed her the card. She accepted it.

"You mean it?" she asked.

"I'd like to meet her, too," he said. "Or one of them."

She thanked him and she stepped out of the car.

"I promise," Annette said. "If it comes back, I'll phone you."

"Do something else for me, too," he said.

"What's that?"

"Get that lock replaced. I'll give you the name of a repairman."

Annette nodded and gave him a grudging smile. "Right away," she agreed.

Then she turned and walked back to her house, feeling the

detective's eyes—or some pair of eyes—upon her every step she took.

On Monday morning, Annette hired the home repair contractor to change all the exterior locks on her doors. The man's name was Emmet Hughes. He was a cheerful, chubby, ruddy-faced man who specialized at any sort of household repair job. To him, changing a series of locks was a simple assignment. By eleven A.M. on a clear sunny morning, the new locks were in place and Hughes had been paid in cash by 17 Cort Street's owner.

Then on Tuesday afternoon, the nursing staff of Mid Island Convalescent moved Mrs. Ritter to a more secure room on the second floor. There she resided across from the duty nurse's desk. In the ensuing days, she frequently complained about the new accommodations. The elevator never came to the second floor when she needed it, she grumbled. Her new room was drafty and she was too far from the steps. Even worse, her residency status had been downgraded and she was not permitted to set foot outside the home without a chaperon.

Timothy Brooks stopped by 17 Cort Street that same afternoon to advise Annette of the change in Mrs. Ritter's tenancy. Annette received the detective cordially. She thanked him but still professed doubt that the events at Mid Island Convalescent could in any way reflect upon what happened at the Carlson residence.

"I know what I saw," she told him again.

He nodded indulgently.

And yet, and yet . . .

Simultaneous to the tighter leash held on the old woman, the spectral manifestations had ceased at 17 Cort Street. There were no unwelcome visitors to Annette's bedroom at any hour of the day or night. Or at least none that Annette saw.

Thus the mystery, the petty nocturnal dramas of July eleven and twelve, did indeed appear solved through normal phenomenon. Secretly, however, Annette kept her own counsel. If there were supernatural presences in her home, she decided, they hadn't harmed her. They had only frightened her. So on one hand, she was prepared to live with things she couldn't readily explain. And on the other hand, she took comfort in the fact that the overt problems had ceased.

She gave a careful reading to *Rumor of Guilt* by Horace Westerly. While she found much to commend in the script, the role being offered to her wasn't entirely to her liking. It was good. It was quite good, in fact. But it remained too similar to roles she had already played. With some careful consideration, she returned the script to Joe Harris with a note praising its quality, but declining the role. Thereupon she started in on another dozen scripts Joe Harris had procured for her.

What film she would do next was not the only question that remained unanswered. Nor, with Mrs. Ritter under a form of Senior Citizen House arrest, were all of the smaller mysteries at 17 Cort Street resolved.

There was the matter of Annette's reading glasses, for example.

When she returned from Mid Island Convalescent on the previous Sunday afternoon, she had gone immediately back to the script in an attempt to finish it.

But her eyeglasses had not been where she had remembered leaving them. She was certain she had placed them on the end table by the sofa, right next to her soft drink. Instead, she eventually found them on the bottom shelf of the china cabinet. They were right in the open. But again, they were not where she recalled leaving them.

The sight of them in a different place gave her pause for a moment, accompanied by a tingle of goose bumps. Yes, this was a room in which she felt she had seen a restless spirit. And yes, the glasses seemed to have moved.

But she also knew that she was frequently unmindful of where she had left things. Where was her driver's license, for example, which she had apparently misplaced four days earlier? Where had she mislaid a French eyeliner that had vanished since the previous Tuesday? Why had a gold hoop earring, one of a pair, turned up on the kitchen floor when she was certain she had left the pair on a dresser upstairs? And so on.

So what if she thought she had put the glasses on the end table? When Detective Brooks was distracting her with his bothersome knocking, she might easily have put them down somewhere else.

It was that simple, wasn't it? Things didn't fly across the room by themselves.

But then there was the mahogany chest upstairs, a big old one that dominated the bedroom and which she used to store clothes.

Getting ready for sleep on Thursday night, Annette banged her bare right foot against the leg of the dresser. She whacked the smallest two toes on her foot very hard, raising a dreadful bruise and even drawing a few drops of blood.

In examining the dresser and trying to figure out why she had tripped where she had never had trouble passing before, Annette made a strange discovery. The impression that the dresser's legs had made upon the carpet beneath it showed that the chest had been moved at least three inches to the left. That was what had caused her to miscalculate her step and bang her foot.

Annette stared at the impressions on the carpet. She knew she hadn't moved the dresser. Nor could she have. It was a big, heavy hunk of furniture, much too heavy for her, something of a companion piece to the china cabinet in the living room. Like the china cabinet downstairs, Annette disliked its bulky gracelessness. But the dresser had come with the house. It was too big and difficult to remove. And it did serve a purpose.

Yet when it was filled with clothing, as it was now, the dresser probably weighed four hundred pounds. She wondered how it could possibly have shifted even that short distance. Or was she just plain wrong about where the legs of the bureau had once stood? Had the other impressions on the carpet been there since she moved in and she had never noticed?

Or—and this she found to be absolutely unbelievable—had

someone been in the house while she was out? And had that person moved the dresser?

If so, *who?*

If so, *why?*

She went to bed wondering about this on Thursday night, though her wonder didn't last long. She left the room light on and slept soundly. The night passed peaceably and without interruption. The next morning was sunny and bright.

Annette awoke refreshed, feeling terrific. Only later in the day did she happen to run into Emmet Hughes, the lock repairman, in town. She asked him if he had for any reason been upstairs in her house. Might *he* have moved the dresser?

"Never went above the first floor, Miss Carlson," Hughes answered with a bashful but respectful smile. "Didn't need to go upstairs to change locks."

"Of course not," she agreed.

He shrugged. "You were there the whole time I was," he reminded her. "You remember? I just done the outside doors."

"Of course, Emmet," she said, recalling. "Silly of me to ask."

Hughes concluded the conversation by inquiring if Annette would sign an autograph. "For my niece," he explained. Annette smiled graciously and obliged by signing Hughes' grocery bag, obtained a few minutes earlier from the A & P adjacent to the boat basin.

Yet Annette's spirits were in better shape than those of several other people. There was the emotional agony suffered by Eddie Lloyd and his family, for example.

Detectives Gelman and Rodzienko had done a thorough job on the young man and, in their opinion, had built a sound criminal case.

It was their thesis that Eddie had killed his girlfriend. Stuff like that happened all the time, they felt, and finally it had happened here. They didn't have a confession yet, but figured they soon would. Accordingly, the Lloyd family had been advised that a grand jury in Hyannis would soon bring an indictment for the murder of Mary Elizabeth DiMarco.

Nor was it a time of tranquility for Detective Timothy

Brooks. Much troubled him. First, the case being built against Eddie Lloyd seemed grossly circumstantial at best. Gelman and Rodzienko seemed to have tailored their investigation to suit the preemptive conclusions they had reached minutes after arriving on the murder scene. People either had homicide in their soul or they didn't, Brooks had long felt. One look at the Lloyd kid told him—very unscientifically—that Eddie didn't.

And there had been the expression on the dead girl's face. That stricken look of pure unearthly horror. What on Nantucket Island could have caused that? What, in particular, out there in the darkness in an open field fifty yards from the old cemetery?

Brooks craved an explanation.

And then the 17 Cort Street situation bothered Brooks, too. Two reported intrusions. Annette Carlson's flaky account of it, suggesting the supernatural. There was a disturbing aura about this episode, as well, though Brooks was at a loss to pinpoint it. Maybe it was the sense of the unsettled, even though with the changes to the locks and to Mrs. Ritter's accommodations, no new occurrences had reached Brooks' ears.

But it bothered Tim Brooks enough so that the following Saturday he stopped by the house. Just to say hello. Just to inquire if everything remained all right. But Annette happened to be out at the time and Brooks pursued the matter no further, other than to slowly walk around the house. He was looking for karma again, he supposed.

Well, he found none. He left his business card on the rear doorstep and went on his way. And that concluded a full week in which some matters had ostensibly settled and others had progressed to their next stage.

And that also guided Brooks to the following Sunday morning, July nineteenth, and a rare visit to church. The latter would present him with the opportunity to pose several more questions that had perplexed him recently—questions which, had all of the previous events not transpired upon the heels of each other, he would never have thought to ask.

Nine

In more ways than not, Rev. George Osaro did not fit in at the rambling white church where he was pastor. His name sounded like Boston Italian, but he was the offspring of a Japanese mother, who was a librarian, and a Canadian father, who had been a seaman.

According to the stories he told about himself, but which no one ever was able to verify, he had been raised in Montana, read his way through the local library by the time he was twelve and took the better part of his bachelor's degree in life experience, working alternately as a logger, a supermarket clerk, and a cab driver in Billings. He finally picked up a real sheepskin at a small liberal arts college in northern California. Then, in his midtwenties found his Calling. Or, more accurately, his Calling found him.

Someway, he traveled east and landed at Harvard Divinity. It was as if he had just appeared one day full grown and with little background. At first he simply took courses from the extension division of the God School. Then, impressing a few professors, he was admitted for formal study.

He married a local girl from Sommerville who was an OR nurse at Massachusetts General Hospital. Her name was Carol Ann and they set up shop during his second summer in Cambridge. A son named Paul—Osaro was an expert in the Pauline Epistles—was born during his second winter.

Then George Osaro amazed everyone by writing the most

brilliant thesis the school had seen in fifteen years—something nearly incomprehensible having to do with Shinto influence upon the Christian interpretation of the afterlife among the missions in China in the eleventh century—and was ordained. Mainstream New England Protestantism hadn't been the same since. He became the assistant pastor at Christ and Holy Trinity in 1989 and assumed the full pastor's duties upon the sudden retirement of his predecessor—a starchy old Lutheran cleric named Clarence Hapgood—in 1991.

It was at approximately this same time that Carol Ann, for whatever reason, decided she had had enough. She packed three suitcases and headed back to the Boston area with her son. Brother Osaro had been dividing his time between the church and the basketball court ever since.

Osaro had lively intense eyes, windows to a matching soul. He was equally adept arguing Wittgenstein with graduate students or bickering about a summons with the local traffic enforcement ladies on Nantucket Island or spending hours in deep reflection upon the transcendental qualities of the human consciousness. He also liked NBA basketball, pickup trucks and the novels of James Ellroy. He had probably read everything ever printed surrounding the mysteries of any human afterlife—and, as his annual "Spiritual Nantucket" nights indicated—was always seeking to define new theories of the afterlife in mainstream Protestant terms. This was no easy matter and did not always rest comfortably upon the church hierarchy. But George Osaro was, all who knew him agreed, a singular piece of work.

"Golfers," said Osaro to Tim Brooks. "Golfers. Republicans and the aged. That's my congregation. The latter would be a lot bigger if so many members of our parish didn't belong to all three groups."

The two men stood on a grassy patch of earth outside Christ and Holy Trinity. It was eleven-thirty on Sunday morning. Osaro had concluded his two services. He talked to his friend and greeted an occasional parishioner as the three to four dozen worshippers walked home or to their cars.

"It's not a bad parish and the location is terrific," Osaro allowed. "As far as challenge goes, however." He raised his eyebrows and his narrow shoulders. "What's challenge?" he asked in response to his own question.

Brooks smiled. On down days, he might have asked the same of his own job. But within police work the demands of faith were of a different sort.

Osaro greeted two teenagers. Then an older couple. He carried a bookbag on one arm with several eight-by-ten manila envelopes clutched against it. He smiled broadly. His personal skills were not insubstantial, though, encumbered by books and papers, even in a clerical collar he looked more like a graduate student than an ordained pastor.

"So what's going on?" Osaro finally asked. "You show up for my infamous spirit night, now you show your face on Sunday morning. By my calendar, it's neither Christmas nor Easter. Why are you here, Timmy? Are you trying to give Protestantism a bad name?"

"Oh, I had nothing else to do," Brooks said in jest. "So I thought I'd see what you'd be bantering about."

Osaro chuckled softly. "I don't believe you," he said. "First, you *look* like you've got something on your mind. Second, you left a message on my answering machine. Said you wanted to talk to me."

"I did indeed leave that message," said Brooks. "And I *do* want to talk."

"Your message was bracketed by two from the bishop in Boston," Osaro said somberly. "Allow me to say that whatever the nature is of your conversation, it will be more pleasant than the one with the bishop."

"Oh? Is there a problem?"

"I don't know for sure because I'm not planning to return the call till Monday morning. But I suspect the word of our spiritual evening last month has reached his lofty otherwise-deaf ears."

"Ah. I see."

"He doesn't care for such activities," Osaro said. "Call our bishop 'old time,' rather than 'New Age.' " There was a fervency in his voice as he quietly mocked his superior. But everyone else was out of earshot now. The sidewalk was quiet as was the stretch of grass by the side of the church.

They walked a few paces and were on the asphalt of the parking lot. The cars present were brightly gleaming with sunlight, though they were crisscrossed here and there by the shadows from the branches of several trees.

"Well," Osaro said at length. "Here I am. Talk to me."

"It's funny that the bishop should phone you," Brooks began. "I wanted to ask you something about 'Spiritual Nantucket' as well."

Osaro moaned slightly. "Oh, Lord." He sighed. "Well, out with it. What's on your mind?"

"Tell me a little more about Doctor Friedman," Brooks asked.

"Who?"

"He was the final speaker that evening," Brooks reminded him. "He had some God-awful nasty spirit in his house."

Osaro smiled. "Oh. Yes. *That* Doctor Friedman," he said, as if there were two of them. "What about him?"

"Doctor Friedman's story," Brooks asked. "How much of it can we believe?"

Osaro thought for a moment. He drew a breath, and when he finally answered, his eyes were shadowed from overhead by a low branch of an elm tree. *"You* probably don't believe any of it. As it happens, *I* believe every word of it."

Brooks looked his friend in the eye.

"Tim, the man's a *doctor,"* Osaro said. "A professional person, same as yourself. Think he gets off on making up hobgoblin stories? Think that brings extra tonsilectomies into his office?"

"It takes a leap of faith to accept a story like that," said Brooks, thinking as much about Cort Street as the Friedmans' residence on Milk. "Evil spirits and all. I don't know if I can make that leap just yet."

Osaro arrived at his van, an old Plymouth Voyager that was

white and rusting. The vehicle's most distinguishing feature was a large dent on the right front end where it had once lost a right-of-way challenge with a driver from New Jersey.

Osaro had left the van unlocked. He opened a rear door and tossed in his bookbag and manila envelopes.

"Well, I'm able to take him at his word," Osaro said. "And, if it helps you sleep tonight, Timmy, I've also talked to the rest of the Friedman family. They all saw the same things. His poor kids were scared shitless."

Osaro looked disapprovingly at the interior of his van. "Why the hell does someone move out of a three-hundred-thousand-dollar house, Tim?" he asked without looking back. "Why, if there's not a problem? The Friedmans felt that they had a malevolently haunted house. So they got out."

Osaro folded down a rear seat in his van. The floor of the vehicle was littered with stray papers, maps, empty bags, windshield cleaning solvent and, that most essential of summer equipment, a spray can of de-icer, left over from the previous February. Osaro leaned into the Voyager and made an effort to lend some order to it.

"Tell me something else," Brooks finally said, leaning against the right front door of the van. "I've never asked you, so tell me honestly. How did you get started with this spiritualism stuff?"

"What do you mean?"

"Did you get into this in college? Were your parents into it? Read some book that changed your life? See a light flash one day?" He paused for emphasis. "I've always wanted to know where your interest came from."

"It was either something I read or something I ate. I really don't remember."

"It was a serious question," Brooks pressed.

"Tim," Osaro said, pulling his head out of the car and grimacing slightly, "you didn't 'always wonder' about this. What are you fishing for?"

"Nothing in particular," Brooks said.

"Liar," Osaro said gently as he pushed some old food wrappers into a small trash bag. "You've always belittled this whole subject. Now you're suddenly interested. Before I recite for you my autobiography, you have to tell me: what gives?"

Osaro looked at his friend and waited for an answer. A speckled shadow crossed his face. Branches of a long-diseased elm tree above them rustled in a breeze.

"Let's say it's work related."

"Police business?"

"Maybe."

A pause. Then, "Oh, I see," Osaro said thoughtfully.

The minister put the van's rear seat back up and closed the door.

Brooks expected another airily contentious response from his friend, one tinged with flippancy and the inevitable needle. Thus Brooks was surprised when he drew something more serious.

"Let me tell you something, Tim," George Osaro said. "And it's just *entre nous*, okay? I already have enough funny stories circulating about me without every cop on this island looking at me as if I'm extra whack-o."

"This is strictly between us," Brooks promised.

"For a long time, maybe since I was about ten years old," Osaro began, "I've had this funny *gift*. I didn't set out to become interested in spiritualism and the afterlife. They landed upon me."

Osaro stopped speaking as a well-dressed young couple strolled to a nearby car. Osaro nodded to them. Then he lowered his voice and continued.

"I can walk into a disturbed place and pick up the vibrations," he said. "I can tell you immediately if something's there."

Brooks stared at his friend for several seconds.

"What do you mean by 'disturbed place'?" Brooks finally asked. "And what do you mean by 'something'?"

"A disturbed place is a location such as Doctor Friedman's house. A place where events that might be viewed as paranormal have been reported. And by 'something,' I'm talking about a spiritual presence. A migratory soul, maybe. Or something else, making itself known."

Tim Brooks waited for Reverend Osaro to break into a wide There!-I-had-you-fooled grin, but quickly realized no such sign would be forthcoming.

"Oh, come on," Brooks finally said.

"Okay. *Don't* believe me!" the minister snapped petulantly. "I'd make up something like that, right? You ask me to confide in you, I say I will, and then you accuse me of bullshitting you. Thanks a lot, pal."

Osaro's left hand plunged into his pocket for car keys. The keys came out with a jingle. Brooks was startled by the vehemence of Osaro's response.

"I'm just surprised, that's all," Brooks said apologetically. "We've known each other for nearly five years and you've never uttered a word about this."

"Why *would* I? You never expressed interest in the subject."

Osaro turned to unlock his car, but Brooks placed a hand on his friend's shoulder, stopping him. "I didn't say I didn't believe you."

"You implied as much."

"I didn't mean to. Okay? I'm sorry."

"Okay," Osaro said, accepting the apology. He winked good-naturedly. "Hey, I know how it is. If you haven't experienced it, if you haven't seen it firsthand, it's tough to believe."

Osaro paused and motioned back toward the church.

"The people you heard that evening, Tim," he continued. "My panelists. All of them were skeptics, too. Same as yourself. Every one of them. Then each of them arrived at a point. They could no longer deny the reality of what they had seen or what they had experienced."

Osaro sighed. "And I didn't mean to bite your head off for asking a few questions. This particular subject matter gets me on edge sometimes, too."

"What's this 'gift' of yours got to do with Doctor Friedman's house?" Brooks pressed.

Brooks stepped aside and allowed Osaro to open the driver's door to the van. Osaro climbed into the vehicle.

"Well, that's kind of the point," Reverend Osaro said. "You asked me if I believed the doctor's story." He closed the door and rolled down the window. "Well, hell, man. I went over to Milk Street, myself. And I do *not* care to go back. Whew! That place is . . . is . . ." He searched for an accurate word.

"Is *what?*"

"It's to be avoided, my man. There's something nasty there. Exactly the way Doctor Friedman represented it. I could feel it."

"Then why don't you go back and find out what the 'something' is? Might be damned interesting."

Osaro looked at his friend and hunched his shoulders.

"I simply said I could *feel* these presences," Osaro answered. "I said nothing about wishing to strike up lasting relationships, particularly with the malevolent ones."

Brooks thought about it. "Think I'd be able to feel this malevolent 'something' if I went over?"

The Plymouth's front window was fully open. Osaro started the ignition and looked quizzically at his friend from the shade of the car's interior.

"*Why* on earth would you *want* to?"

"Let's say I'm curious."

"That's a lousy reason."

"What's the address?"

Osaro looked at his friend with disappointment. "I'm going to do you a favor," Osaro said. "I'm not going to tell you."

Osaro put the Voyager in gear. The vehicle lurched forward, but Brooks kept his hand on the side mirror.

"I just have one final question," Brooks said.

"Shoot," Osaro said.

"These people such as your panelists," Brooks said. "The skeptics turned believers. What happens? They get transformed overnight by what they've seen?"

Osaro smiled and shook his head.

"Not at all," the minister said.

"Well, then?"

"There's an earlier point," Osaro said. "It's when they begin to reexamine their earlier posture of doubt. It's like a religious conversion, actually. One set of beliefs gives way to doubts. Then a new set of beliefs sets in. See, that's the key to spiritualism. You have to let the idea meander into your head. Then it makes itself at home. Once it's comfortably ensconced in there, it usually never leaves. And only then can you understand or accept the paranormal."

Osaro paused. "Once you've accepted the idea that the paranormal exists," Osaro said, "then you can accept anything that follows."

"And how do you know when you're at that point?" Brooks asked. "The reexamination point, I mean?"

Osaro laughed. "It's funny. The individual never realizes it himself or herself. But to me it's very clear."

"How?"

"The party in question usually comes around unexpectedly and starts sniffing around the subject. Asks a lot of questions and makes a lot of vague disclaimers and pronouncements. That means the period has set in during which the individual is ready to believe." Osaro paused and grinned. "Such as yourself this Sabbath morning, Tim. Obviously. You're ready to develop the senses that I already have. *You just have to open your mind to it.*"

Brooks considered it, then retreated. "Oh, that's a lot of nonsense," he said. "I'm not ready to believe any of this."

Osaro laughed and shook his head.

"That's what *you* think," the minister said, grinning to emphasize his point. "Tim! You wouldn't be here asking questions if you weren't in the reexamination stage."

Brooks let the remark pass unanswered, as if it hadn't found its mark, which it had.

"What did you see?" Osaro asked. "What did you experience?"

"I neither saw nor experienced anything," Brooks said. He was aware that his response sounded defensive.

"Well, whatever," Osaro said airily. "Have it your way. See you on the basketball court, huh?"

"On the court," Brooks agreed.

Brooks stepped back from the van. Osaro gave him a wink and the vehicle moved forward, leaving Tim Brooks standing alone. Another branch rustled above his head.

Brooks watched the van pull away. Until now, Brooks had thought his friend to be a man of reason and good sense. Yet there had been something within Osaro's manner this morning that was deeply disturbing. As the battered Voyager disappeared, Brooks felt a sense of foreboding creep upon him. He tried hard to dispel it, but failed.

It was as if in discussing these very subjects—of ghosts, of spirits, of the afterlife, of the supernatural—Brooks had conferred credibility upon them. And with credibility, he knew, they acquired a reality of their own.

Osaro's words echoed. "Once you've accepted the idea that the paranormal exists, then you can accept anything that follows." And, "You just have to open your mind to it."

This, from a clergyman of reason and good sense.

Late that same afternoon transpired one of those unavoidable summer tragedies. Or at least, that's what it appeared to be.

A seventeen-year-old boy named Bruce Markley and two friends were swimming in the deep choppy water between Surfside and Cisco beach. This was an isolated stretch of shoreline at an off-hour. There were never any lifeguards in the area. Markley was visiting from Ontario. His two friends were native Nantucketers.

Without any warning, as is usually the case, a wall of sand collapsed beneath the tide about a hundred yards offshore. The underwater shift caused a riptide, sweeping westward. Rips occurred in this area about a dozen times per summer. Regular swimmers were aware of them and knew that when they combined with an erratic undertow, they could be dangerous.

The local boys knew how to survive the rip. They stayed with it, let it carry them under for a moment, then bobbed to the surface and rode it for several hundred feet. Neither had ever been caught in a rip before and the experience was harrowing, but they were experienced swimmers who had always held in their mind how to react if the time came. When the time did come, they didn't panic. Minutes later, with the tide normal again, they made their way to shore.

It was only then, when they were safe, that a sense of dread was upon them. Bruce was missing. They looked back along the surface of the water and couldn't find him. Still, they didn't panic.

The stronger of the two swimmers swam out to look for the Canadian. The other youth ran for help. At the nearest house, the latter boy called the police. Tim Brooks was one of the officers who responded. When Markley was still not located, a Coast Guard helicopter flew in from the rescue station at Brant Point, cruised low over the water, and joined the hunt.

The search took two and a half hours. And by the time Markley's body was located downcurrent at Cisco, bobbing beneath the surface about fifty feet offshore, he had long since drowned. He had made, lifesaving crews speculated, the classic mistake of an inexperienced ocean swimmer caught in a riptide. He had used all his energy in a futile effort to fight the current and swim to shore. In doing so, he had expended his strength. He had then drowned in the undertow.

Brooks was one of the officers who helped pull the body to shore. Medical technicians attempted immediate CPR as well as electric shock to try to revive Bruce Markley. Both efforts failed. Dr. Herbert Youmans, the regular medical examiner, would pronounce Markley dead an hour later at Nantucket Cottage Hospital.

Tragic and regrettable as the death was, it gave greater pause to Tim Brooks than anyone else. Markley's corpse was pulled from the water toward dusk. The rescue teams were working by floodlight, and the latter can sometimes cast strange, horrific shadows. So Brooks wasn't entirely sure of what he had seen.

But he did know that he had caught one quick glimpse of the

boy's white, waterlogged lifeless face before the CPR was attempted and before his body was whisked to an ambulance.

And Brooks read something in the boy's expression that he didn't like. It was a trace of extra terror. Not just the I'm-drowning-oh-my-God-please-save-me! type of terror. Something extra. Something which had an echo from the twisted, contorted death mask worn by Beth DiMarco.

"Crazy! You're imagining this!" Brooks told himself.

No, you're not! came an answering thought a moment later.

Brooks froze. A deep chill gripped him so fiercely that he physically shuddered. He didn't think he had subconsciously responded to his own question. No! God Almighty! He had distinctly heard that other intrusive voice again, communicating with him from God-knew-where, just as it had at the scene of Beth's death.

More thoughts rolled upon him. This time, his own: Bruce Markley had seen something horrendous out in the water in the moments before he died. Yes! Even out in the water! God damn. No one on this island *is* safe!

The voice answered again. *Right!* it croaked.

Brooks waited for more. But nothing more came. He watched the ambulance take the boy away. At the same time, he tried to convince himself how foolish his instincts had become.

Here he was, in all rationality, trying to make a link between the murder of a girl in town and an accidental drowning of a boy at one of the beaches.

Was there a link? If so, where?

Brooks waited for the bizarre internal voice to tell him more. He asked specific questions. He wanted specific answers. But the inner voice—mischievous, elusive and taunting—had fallen silent.

Ten

Through Wednesday afternoon, the humidity built on Nantucket Island. Then toward four P.M. the sky darkened and the trees shook with a wicked wind. The most violent July weather conditions in anyone's memory followed within minutes.

It was a knockout punch of a storm, walloping the island with thunder and lightning much like a hurricane. Then, as quickly as it had hit, it was gone again—the wind subsiding, the rain abating and the sky lightening to a beautifully clear evening.

Annette loved a walk after a storm. Her only regret after this one was that she didn't have anyone with whom to share it. Had there been a man in her life, she would have propped him up onto his feet, pushed him out the door and placed her hand in his. And off they would have gone, listening to wet leaves click and whisper above their heads as they walked.

She thought about this feeling as she left her house. She wondered. What were these stirrings within her? Was she finally ready to find someone new to become part of her life? Was she ready to fall in love again?

Or was she merely experiencing a tinge of loneliness on a moody rainy afternoon?

As she walked from Cort Street, she took no specific path. Yet something directed her toward Vestal Street.

It hadn't been her intention to walk anywhere near the Mid Island Convalescent Home. It just happened. Annette realized that she was near the retirement facility when she recognized the building. It was only a few blocks from Cort Street so it was no surprise when she rounded a corner and recognized the old structure.

She approached it and was struck with a second happenstance. The only person she knew at Mid Island, Mrs. Helen Ritter, formerly of the Nantucket Department of Education, was seated on the front porch, gently rocking.

Annette walked past and looked up.

The old woman nodded and raised a frail hand in recognition. A tangle of white hair framed her face.

"Hello," Annette said.

"How do?" said Mrs. Ritter.

Annette stopped and tried to be friendly. "You weren't out during the storm, were you?" Annette asked.

The old woman cupped a hand near her ear and asked for Annette to repeat. Annette came closer and did.

"Oh, no, no, no," Mrs. Ritter said emphatically. "Sakes alive, no!" She laughed. "I was inside. More sensible there, isn't it? Storms can be beautiful. But I don't truly care for them." Her voice had an occasional creak, like an old house.

Graciously, Annette said she felt much the same way. Then Mrs. Ritter asked if Annette would care to sit for a moment, indicating a ladderback chair beside her. Having no excuse, and not ready yet to return to Cort Street, Annette accepted the invitation.

The old woman rocked gently. A slight breeze, one of the last from the storm, swept across the porch.

"Where do I know you from?" Mrs. Ritter asked after several moments of thought.

Annette reminded her. Timothy Brooks had brought her by a few days earlier. Annette said nothing about movies.

"Ah," the old woman said, still gently rocking in her chair. "Yes." A Pause. "Of course. Timmy." She pondered it for several more seconds. "You didn't do this to me, did you, dearie?" Mrs. Ritter finally asked. With shrewd pinkish eyes, she watched the younger woman.

"Do what to you?"

Mrs. Ritter raised her brows and grimaced. "Have me locked up, of course," she said. "Have me imprisoned." Her gaze traveled across the porch and found an inquisitive sparrow on a railing opposite her. Then the bird flew off. "I'm not allowed to leave this property anymore. Not unless I have my own escort. A chaperon, it would be. And at *my* age!" She shook her head, and made a tisking sound, as if to suggest shame on someone, if not everyone.

Annette felt a pang of guilt. If she had never said anything about a nighttime disturbance, suspicion would never have landed on Mrs. Ritter.

"I'm sorry. But I didn't say anything to the staff here," Annette said. "But I'm sure everyone is concerned with your safety. I'm sure—"

"I'm locked up! I'm a prisoner here," she said again. "All alone. No real family. My students were my family. My little dunderheads," she said with a trailing laugh. "Well, they're all grown now. Still my family, but I'm not theirs."

Helen Ritter thought about it some more. "Not much more left for me now. Except to wait for my final time and place." Another pause, then. "A funny thing, isn't it? You lead a good life. Then they put you away in a jail like this. You have all the time in the world and yet not very much time at all. Isn't that strange?"

She said this so routinely that Annette had no idea how to respond.

So Mrs. Ritter assessed the younger woman in an awkward silence, one that she eventually broke, herself.

"Well, it's done, anyway. So why did you come to see me to start with?" Mrs. Ritter inquired politely.

"Someone was coming into my house at night," Annette confessed. "The first time, it appeared to be an older woman. She scared me."

"Ahhh," Mrs. Ritter said. Her tone bordered between exasperation and understanding. "And Timmy Brooks thought it was me?"

"No, he never said that. He wanted me to meet you just in case it was."

"Did the woman look like me?"

Annette looked at her. "Only remotely."

"So what do you think, dearie?" Mrs. Ritter asked softly, turning and looking her full in the face. "Was it me?"

"I know it wasn't you," Annette said. "I saw the woman who was in my room. And then I saw another woman, a younger woman, downstairs. Neither one was you."

As she glanced away, a new expression took hold of Mrs. Ritter, one of vindication. "Then why can't I go for a walk by myself?" she asked.

"I don't know. That's not something I have any influence upon."

"Where do you live, dearie?" Mrs. Ritter asked.

"Seventeen Cort Street."

"Oh." There was recognition. *"That* house."

"You know it?"

"Very well."

"Ever been in it?"

"Long, long ago. I used to know the occupants." A smile played at the corner of the old woman's lips. "But I used to know everyone."

"Who owned it?"

Mrs. Ritter gazed off. She befuddled Annette. From moment to moment, she was either sharp as a tack or she hazily drifted into her own sphere, not even hearing questions that were posed to her. It was as if Mrs. Ritter inhabited two worlds: one outside her and one deeply within her. She looked back to Annette.

"Who *owned* Seventeen Cort Street?" Annette repeated.

"Yes. I know you do," Mrs. Ritter said, misunderstanding, either intentionally or otherwise. "It's a lovely house." She paused. "Do you have some time today? Will you come upstairs with me?"

"Oh, I don't know if—"

The old woman's hand settled on Annette's. It was very cold.

The iciness of the touch came as such a surprise that Annette was startled. She recoiled slightly. But Mrs. Ritter now seemed very sharp again, her gaze settling very firmly into Annette's eyes.

"Of course you can," she insisted. "The question is only whether you're willing to or not. Now, say yes, young lady. I've something to show you that's very important."

Still, Annette hesitated. In truth, she was searching for an excuse.

But Mrs. Ritter's voice was kindly, patient and convincing. "How much time do I have left before I die?" she asked. "How many opportunities will I have when you come by? *Please,*" she urged. "It's very important. Please come upstairs for five minutes. Then you can leave."

Annette gave it a final second's thought. "All right," she eventually agreed.

With difficulty, Helen Ritter rose from her chair. Annette offered her a hand of support. The old woman accepted it. Mrs. Ritter moved slowly and Annette was patient with her. They walked into the home and past the receptionist who gave Annette a friendly smile after an initial hesitation. Then the two women walked to the elevator.

On the second floor, where Mrs. Ritter lived, they passed the porter, Mike Silva. Annette remembered him from the previous Sunday. Silva barely raised an eye to Mrs. Ritter, but gave Annette a full double take. He stared at her the way certain men often stare at women whom they know are unattainable.

Annette felt his eyes upon her, following her down the hall toward Mrs. Ritter's chamber. For no real reason, Mike Silva made her uncomfortable. He gave her the creeps.

The door to Mrs. Ritter's room was open. They went into the room and both sat down, Mrs. Ritter in her usual chair.

She fumbled for a pair of glasses. It took many painful seconds for her to find them, put them on and allow her eyes to adjust. Then she turned her back to Annette for a moment and reached to a small brown radio that was on her writing desk.

She flicked it on. The dial was already set to a "Beautiful Music" station from Cape Cod.

"Much more cheerful like this, isn't it?" the retired schoolteacher said.

"Much," Annette agreed.

On the radio, a chorus of homogenized American voices mutilated a selection of Franz Lehar. When Mrs. Ritter wasn't looking, Annette turned the volume down.

Mrs. Ritter's attention then landed with a thud upon the checkerboard table a few yards beyond her reach.

"See that little table over there?" she asked.

Annette said that she saw it.

"Slide it over to me."

At first Annette couldn't figure out what the old woman had on her agenda. But the request seemed harmless. Annette went to the table. There was a small pink vase bearing a red plastic rose on top of it. Annette removed it and placed it on the old woman's writing desk. Then Annette slid the antique table to Mrs. Ritter.

"Know what we used to do with this table?" the retired teacher asked in her most matter-of-fact tone. She didn't wait for an answer. "Communicate with the spirits."

"What?"

"Communicate with the spirits," Mrs. Ritter repeated. "Conjure up the dead."

For a moment, Annette thought she had misunderstood. Then an ominous feeling was upon her when she realized that she hadn't.

"I don't know what you mean," Annette finally lied.

"Sounds very clear to me," Mrs. Ritter said gently. Her aged arthritic fingers were working around the edges of the table now. There was something very authoritative about the way she was touching the piece. A lifetime of familiarity, perhaps. A sense of mastery. The old woman's eyes rose quickly, found Annette's, then returned to where her fingers seemed to take the inanimate object's pulse.

"I used to talk to my grandmother with this table," she said as routinely as if she were revealing the time of day. "Grand-mum Lizzie. Born in Inverness. You should have heard her brogue." Mrs. Ritter paused and laughed. "Grandmum Lizzie died in nineteen hundred and four."

"Uh huh."

Annette disbelieved. But she felt a chill anyway.

Mrs. Ritter raised her eyes again. "Don't believe me, do you?"

"I—"

"You will. Eventually." Mrs. Ritter pursed her lips, hummed for two seconds, then continued. "Wouldn't matter right now, anyway, whether you believed in it or not. We're one person short."

Annette felt a second chill that was even deeper. "One person short for what?" she asked.

But Mrs. Ritter didn't hear. Or didn't choose to hear.

"I used to do this when I was a little girl," she said. "My mother owned this table. You need *three* people who believe. That's what I meant when I said we'd still be one person short, even if you believed. This part is very important, you see. Six hands. Three people. The right amount of heartbeats. The correct number of palms. Or maybe it's fingertips. Or maybe it's just the number three. A trinity. I think that's what makes it work. The right equation." There was a longer pause and she concluded. "The right amount of blood."

The old woman seemed convinced of what she was saying.

"My sister, Mother and I," she said. "We used to do it together on Saturday evenings." She paused. "Then my mother died in nineteen forty-seven and another lady joined us. My sister and I and this other lady. A Mrs. Prouty. Lived over on Orange Street. Lovely woman. But she died. Then my sister died. No one's done it since."

" 'Done it'?"

"Turned the table," Mrs. Ritter said. "Not for twenty-five, thirty years."

Then the old woman explained. She spoke like a school-teacher embarking upon a lesson. And her memory was as compendious as her body was spare. But surely she loved her memory more, for she had apparently packed into it the treasures of a lifetime. Now she put everything aside to unburden it.

She brought it all back in minute detail. It was her mother who taught her about "turning tables," she said.

The latter had been a vogue in New England a few generations back, sort of like the great wave of revivalism in the 1920s or the public fixation upon reincarnation in the 1950s. And it all had begun when Helen Ritter was about fifteen years old. Or, as she might have alternatively phrased it, Year One of her lifelong involvement with her checkerboard table.

"Oh, I was a pretty little thing then, I was," Helen said, tilting her head slightly. "Just becoming aware of myself." Unconsciously, she dangled one stiff wrist coquettishly, perhaps recalling a series of adolescent indiscretions that she did not regret. "I married when I was seventeen," she said with a laugh. But that, Annette could tell, was another story.

Helen Ritter had grown up in Fall River, Massachusetts, before moving to Nantucket in the 1920s. As a girl, she, her sister and her mother would seat themselves in a darkened room in the Fall River homestead. They would sit around the checkerboard table, eyes closed, thoughts in unison, gently resting their eager devout fingers on its surface.

" 'Come forth, any spirit in our home!' my mother would demand," Helen Ritter proclaimed. "Very loud and clear, in a voice like that. Have to let the spirits know you mean business. If a spirit was present, the table would start to move."

"Uh huh," said Annette.

"Sometimes it would rise. Other times it would move from side to side. But always the table would *turn* or *tip*. Then it would move one leg. It would tap out a message."

Most tables didn't work, Mrs. Ritter explained. Waste of time trying to levitate a normal table. The schoolmarm's smile appeared here again. But the checkerboard table would move. It *always* did—as long as there were three believers around it. A spirit would come forth. A message would be sounded out.

Tap, tap. Tap. Tap, tap, tap.

They would have the alphabet written out on a piece of paper, Mrs. Ritter recalled, and they would point to letters. One tap meant they were pointing to the wrong letter. Two taps meant they were right. It was always proper to have a pencil and a second sheet of paper handy. Spirits didn't send telegrams. They beat out their thoughts with table legs.

"My blood ran cold the first time it happened," the old woman recalled. "Then I realized it was the ordinary course of things. Never bothered me again."

Annette Carlson sat very still and listened.

"A message could take fifteen minutes to an hour," Mrs. Ritter sang, enjoying this tale as she weaved it. "Then we'd reply with words spoken aloud. Always made a big evening of it, us three ladies. My poor father, he wanted no part. Said we were foolish. Didn't believe. Or he was afraid to believe. Could never tell which."

She spoke now either from memory or from something that closely resembled it. And she spent several minutes—recollecting with remarkable clarity—conversations between her mother and her then-deceased grandmother, trivial tipping table chitchats that must have occurred seventy years into the unlovely past. To Annette's creative mind, the old woman's ramblings were many times wilder than she ever might have imagined.

Aside from Grandmum Lizzie, Helen Ritter forged onward by way of explanation, a legion of other spirits had exchanged greetings from time to time as well.

There had been a Union soldier from the Civil War, she remembered, unable to rest because his fiancé had married another man while he starved to death at Andersonville. There had been a merchant seaman, looking for a family that had been wiped out by influenza while he had voyaged two years around Cape Horn. There was a young woman who had hanged herself and was sorry ever after. And once, Helen Ritter said chillingly but with no further elaboration, they had conjured up an aggressive spirit which identified itself only as Tib.

143

Helen Ritter had believed at the time that Tib was a demon. Something from a nether world. So had her mother. So they shoved the table into a downstairs pantry and stored canned goods upon it. They stayed away from its mystical qualities for several months. Tib never returned.

"Come forth any spirit in our home," Helen Ritter repeated aloud, as she sat in her chamber at Mid Island Convalescent. Then she laughed. She threw her head back and blood rushed to her face.

"Know what I believe?" Mrs. Ritter asked Annette. She didn't wait for an answer. "I think that God's universe is a much stranger, more complicated place than science is willing to recognize. And I think that spirits are around us all the time. Good ones and evil ones. Right now, for example. Watching us. Laughing at us. Close enough to brush against our cheeks, if they wished. But only occasionally, only under the right circumstances can we make contact."

Annette felt that uneasy tingle again. Mrs. Ritter glanced toward the table. Lovingly, she ran her stiff fingers across the top of it. She traced a pair of parallel lines in a light covering of dust. She was breathing more heavily now, perhaps not from any one emotion but from a whole slew of them, washing around within her like mixed drinks.

On the radio came a fifteen-second spot ad for a variety store in Hyannis that boasted Cape Cod's largest selection of postcards and souvenir items. They also sold "overstuffed" sandwiches.

"This table, combined with the right believers, dearie," Mrs. Ritter concluded. "*Those* are the proper circumstances." She smiled sweetly, her eyes open again and alert. "That's all I wanted to say," she said. "I'm tired. I'm going to rest now." There was only a second's pause before she concluded. "I've said all I need to for this lifetime. Don't you agree?"

Annette didn't specifically answer. Mrs. Ritter's eyes glazed and narrowed. She hummed again, her fingers still on the tabletop, as if she were caressing the hand of a beloved but long lost child.

Annette did not want to leave her just like that in her room. On the radio, the announcer was now covering news headlines and sports. But Mrs. Ritter was swaying ever so imperceptibly to the measures of a symphony that only she could hear. So Annette gently removed Mrs. Ritter's hand from the table. Her eyes flickered slightly as Annette eased her arm back into her lap. She smiled with gratitude but suddenly seemed exhausted.

Then Annette moved the checkerboard table back to its position against the wall. She replaced the pink bud vase on top of it.

Annette glanced again at her host. Mrs. Ritter's face was content now and she seemed to drift into a peaceful sleep. Her breathing was even and peaceable. Very quietly, Annette left the room.

A few moments later, Annette stepped into the elevator which would take her from the second floor to the lobby. The door closed. Mike Silva, the porter, was in the elevator with her. Mike shook his head as he punched the button for the lobby.

"Daffy old hen, huh?" Mike said.

"Who?"

"Mrs. Ritter," Silva said. "I seen you in her room."

Annette said nothing, trying to determine whether Silva would eventually move the subject to films.

"More trouble than they're worth, keepin' them alive," the porter muttered.

"You're in a rotten mood today, aren't you?" Annette shot back, her tolerance badly eroded.

"Nah. I'm just talkin' the truth. Stuff most people are 'fraid to say. Lot of people today live too long, know what I mean?"

"And who decides what 'too long' is?" Annette asked.

Silva gave her a pained expression. The elevator rose an extra floor. The door opened on Three. No one got in or out.

"You work here, don't you?" Annette asked.

"Yeah." Silva brushed a renegade lock of hair away from his forehead.

"So having these old people here pays your salary, doesn't it?"

The door closed slowly.

"Yeah," Mike Silva said, quickly grasping the direction of Annette's remarks. "Hey, look. I don't mean nothin' by it. I'm jus' the type of guy that says what's on my mind."

"So I see." Annette was willing to let the conversation drop right there. Silva wasn't.

"She show you that table of hers?" Mike asked. "The 'checkerboard table.' I bet she showed you that."

"She might have. Why?"

The elevator moved slowly downward, past the second floor. It approached the first. There was a mean-spirited glee in Silva's eye. "That means, yes, she did," Silva concluded petulantly. "Did she say how it used to rise into the air?" he asked. "She tell you how she and her sister used to fly the damned thing?"

"She told me a story about it."

"She claims she flew it."

"She didn't *fly* it," Annette answered with a sinking feeling and more than a touch of annoyance. "According to what she said, the table rose gently off the ground."

And she conversed with the departed, Annette might have added. But she didn't.

"Yeah. Sure," Mike Silva chortled. "She flew it."

The door to the lobby opened. The porter stepped out of the elevator first, directly in front of Annette.

"Well, don't that tell you how daffy she is?" Silva insisted impatiently. "I been workin' here for five years and I never seen that table do no lift-off from the ground yet." He laughed. "And probably won't, either, unless someone's got one on strings."

"You never know," Annette said.

A funny thought passed through Annette's mind. *Of course* the checkerboard table wouldn't levitate for Mike Silva. Never in the world.

Mrs. Ritter's concise instructions echoed: To tip an enchanted table, to contact the dead, you needed at least three believers. On most days it was challenge enough to locate two.

So Annette continued toward the front door, giving no voice

to her thoughts. And Mike Silva seemed smitten with the intellectual tidiness of his argument.

"Crazy old dame," Annette heard him repeating as she walked down the front steps and away from Mid Island Convalescent. "Crazy, crazy, crazy."

On the other side of the island, Tim Brooks sat in the bedroom of the small cottage he had purchased three years earlier. He stared at the screen of a television set. The Red Sox were playing Baltimore that evening at Fenway. The game was in the third inning and, if asked, Brooks could not have told the score.

A deep aching pain had been growing within his head over the last several days. Since the last time he went by 17 Cort Street, in fact. Now it was turning serious. A throbbing, pounding right up front across the bridge of his nose.

He began to ask: *What the hell is wrong with me?*

Walks didn't help. Extra sleep didn't help. Some recreational tennis hadn't done the job, either. He called friends. Other cops and civilians. How do you get rid of a titanic headache, he asked.

They offered suggestions.

Go for a long swim in very cold water.

Four aspirin and a nondiet Pepsi Cola.

Apply an ice pack.

Empirin with codeine, by prescription.

Lie in a very dark room for an hour.

Go see a favorite movie.

Go see a lousy movie.

Get your girlfriend to do something new and perverse.

But he didn't have a girlfriend and none of the earlier methods worked, either.

He tried to psyche the problem out of his head. Then on the third night of suffering, Brooks attempted to manufacture his own remedy.

He iced two bottles of imported beer and grilled himself a steak. He planned to rise early the next morning and run five miles before six A.M. Then he would *will* the headache away. The sheer force of positive thinking, exercise and clean air would put him back on track.

He ate dinner and watched a movie on cable television.

Later, toward ten P.M., he found his most comfortable pair of pajamas. They were clean and fresh, neatly folded in a drawer. He showered and dressed for bed. He took a mild nonprescription sleeping pill and pulled his phone off the hook. He was sending himself off early in the direction of dreamland.

It turned into a night of terror.

At first he was unable to fall asleep, despite the alcohol and despite the drug. Then, toward eleven o'clock, he felt himself drifting. But this wasn't any ordinary sleep.

He entered this strange realm by being conscious that he was falling asleep. Then he experienced a sense of tumbling—a feeling of having passed over the edge of some precipice. He had a sense of floating downward through a passageway that grew dimmer by the second.

He was in a half world—half awake, half asleep.

At first, this sensation was accompanied by one of deep tranquility. But then the passageway grew dark. The feeling of tranquility was gone and the place he was in frightened him. He moved his arms to stop his descent.

Simultaneously, he was aware that he was in bed and falling through a dream. He felt his arms flap against his sheets. But then he entered the dream world completely and felt himself plunging.

It was a free-fall through time and consciousness. He saw much of his life in flashback.

Nothing could stop the fall. It only accelerated. The next thing he knew, he had hit bottom with a tremendous impact. Now he was dizzy and staring upward, as if in a stupor.

His body was paralyzed! He could not move and he was transfixed with pain. But the pain had a center point. He saw himself spread-eagled and naked on a wide black slab in a desolate hellish stretch of some phantasmogoric underground.

His arms were spread wide. He tried again to move, but couldn't.

Oh, Holy Jesus! he thought.

There was a beast before him. A small, vicious, fanged, winged demon! Like a harpy. Or a griffin. It was straight out of some horrific fifteenth-century woodcut. And the demon was inclined between his legs.

The monster leaned forward and took Timothy's genitals in its fangs. It tore his flesh and chewed on it. Blood spurted from him as the imp ripped off his penis. The demon's teeth were like a thousand little razors. Its mad eyes were crimson, gleaming and taunting.

In his bedroom, Tim Brooks heard himself scream.

The pain between his legs was excruciating. He heard himself scream again. The beast devoured his groin, braced itself with tiny sharp claws, and was merrily proceeding to eviscerate him.

His heart kicked within his ribs. Sweet fucking Jesus! he thought. This is really happening!

Detective Brooks flailed insanely at his sheets. He thrashed wildly against his bed covers. His arms swung wide, as did his legs. He bolted upright in his bed in the dark room, his heart thundering, his pulse racing, and sweat pouring from his body.

His eyes opened. He knew the dream was over, but his heart still pounded. Then his eyes went wide, the scream still echoing in his throat as well as his ears.

Oh, dear God! Oh, dear God!

There was a flash of terror unlike any that he had ever known before. And he felt his heart kick so hard that he thought it would stop.

In the darkness, he saw a towering black figure before the foot of his bed!

Tall and black and evil and ghostly and—!

He lunged desperately for the light switch on the lamp at bedside. He whacked it. It failed. He whacked it again. Blackness that seemed to last for hours. Then the light came on. At the same moment, he picked up a porcelain pitcher that rested beside the lamp on a night table. He raised it above his head to throw at whatever was standing before him—*seven feet tall!*—in the darkness.

But the room was deserted.

He looked all around. The room remained empty, quiet and still.

Brooks didn't move. He heard his heart, which was thundering. He could hear himself breathing. Distantly, he could hear the water drip in his bathroom.

He turned. He stared at the time on his clock radio. Incredibly, only twenty minutes had passed since he had last checked the time before falling to sleep. Considering the many minutes that he had lain awake, this horrible vision must have been compressed into a tiny sliver of time.

Maybe no more than a few seconds, he guessed.

His pajamas were soaked with sweat, as if he had awakened from a fever. He moved his hand to his genitals. The pain had been so horrible, the image of the demon chewing at him had been so lurid—so *real*—that he needed to reassure himself.

Nothing was missing. He sighed in relief. Relief from pain. Relief from terror.

"Oh, man . . ." he muttered to himself.

He lay back down and tried to allow the pace of his breathing to subside. He had never had such a terrifying dream in his life. Never one as realistic, either. It was almost as if something had come unhinged in reality and Brooks had poked his head into some horrible new universe—one to which he did not care to ever return.

And that immense black figure at the foot of his bed?

Preposterous! There had been nothing there! he kept telling himself. It was a nightmare. Nothing more than a terrible nightmare.

But the realness of that black vision had tingled his spine as well. God Almighty, he thought to himself. He would have sworn on a stack of Bibles that he had actually seen something, that something had actually been there.

No! Be rational! You don't believe in such things!

He worked hard to convince himself.

He felt his nerves settle. His heart returned to a normal pace. Never again, he told himself. Never again, beer and a nonprescription sleeping pill. Diphenhydramine hydrochloride. Jesus! He supposed this was how people went to bed and never woke up.

"Oh, man," he again muttered aloud to himself. He ran his hand through his hair. His scalp was damp like his bedclothes. "Oh, man alive," he said boldly. The sound of his own voice reassured him.

This type of dementia he did not need. Or want. Was he suddenly coming mentally undone? So many cops ended up as drunks or suicides or drug addicts. Or some combination of all three. But never once had he ever thought he would.

He rose from bed. He removed his sweaty bedclothes. He went to the kitchen. He would have liked another beer, but was afraid to consume any more alcohol this evening. He found a ginger ale, instead.

He sat down at his kitchen table and thought back on the horror of his dream. Involuntarily, he replayed little details of it to a chilling and shuddering effect.

It wasn't real! I don't believe in such things! I don't want to believe in such things!

Against this, Reverend Osaro's voice again. "Once you've accepted that the paranormal exists, you can accept anything that follows."

He stayed awake. The clock said two forty-five A.M.

No, George. I'm fighting it off. I won't accept it. Not yet. I do not care to have a seven-foot black ghost standing at the foot of my bed.

He gave in. He drank another beer. His head continued to hammer. Did someone say, "migraine?"

Annette's ghosts were white and shimmery, he reminded himself. They came to warn her. Mine was black. What was he here for?

He didn't turn the light off. But he finally went back to sleep.

The next morning he overslept and then was badly tired

when he finally arose. He never ran the six miles. He dragged himself through his shift.

During the late afternoon, however, his headache magically lifted. He wasn't aware of it diminishing. He only knew that suddenly it was gone. He might have been pleased, but a sense of foreboding was upon him—an instinct, developed after many years as a cop. A sense of impending trouble. Deep down, he suspected that though the headache was gone, it would soon be replaced by something far worse.

Eleven

Annette turned on the television in the living room at 17 Cort Street. It was Friday evening. The CBS Evening News came on via the Boston affiliate. Connie Chung substituted for Dan Rather.

Annette paused for a moment and listened to the headlines. Then she set a place for herself at an antique table on one side of her living room.

One salad fork, one knife and a blue cloth napkin. A flat straw coaster and a matching place mat. She arranged everything very precisely, even though she would be eating alone. She turned up the sound on the television so that she could hear as she walked back and forth between the living room and the kitchen.

In the kitchen she uncorked a Tuscan white wine. She poured herself a glass. She tasted it. She loved the taste of a dry Italian white on a summer evening. She walked the glass back to the living room and carefully set it down on the coaster, keeping an ear on the news.

It was a slow news day. Nothing much had happened. Six minutes into the program the network was into a feature story on declining educational standards in America.

She walked back into the kitchen. With lettuce, tomatoes and some avocado slices, she prepared for herself a crabmeat salad. She added a few slices of apple and pear. She walked back to the living room. Connie Chung broke for a commercial. Annette set down her plate on the place mat and stopped cold.

The wineglass had silently turned over and was on its side. The wine was running over the woodwork of the table.

"Damn!" she said to herself. She hurried to the kitchen, then froze.

If it had fallen over, *why* had it fallen? And why hadn't she heard it?

Annette walked cautiously back to the living room and stared at the wine lying on the table. There was no breeze. The table was level. She had replaced the glass carefully. And unless it had been turned over gently, she wondered again, why wouldn't the glass have broken?

She picked up the wineglass and put it down on the coaster again. It didn't move. Annette stared at it and waited. Still, it wouldn't turn over. There was something about this episode that didn't feel right.

In the back of her mind she suppressed the thought: What's in the room with me?

She checked the rest of her table setting. Everything else was perfectly in place.

Annette put the glass on the edge of the coaster to see whether it would tip. It wouldn't. She stood, folded her arm and watched it. Still it wouldn't move.

Then she leaned forward. She blew at it first from a distance of one foot, then one inch.

It wouldn't tip.

Annette picked up the glass and walked back to the kitchen. She filled up the glass with the same amount of water as it had held of wine. She walked back to the living room. She set the glass on the coaster again.

She stood near it and watched it. It didn't budge. Not a millimeter. Annette leaned over so that her eye was level with the glass. The liquid within it was perfectly still.

"All right," she said aloud. She reached to the glass and placed a finger upon it. "Let's just see," she said.

Very gently, she started to tip the glass. She tipped it for several seconds until its center of balance and gravity took over. The glass inclined farther in the direction that Annette had nudged it.

Then it fell.

It shattered against the wooden tabletop. The water mixed with the wine. It formed a puddle that ran far beyond the shards of broken glass.

Annette stepped back, more frightened than angry. She raised her eyes and looked around the room.

"All right," she said aloud. "Where are you?"

She waited. She now had that sense, that feeling, that she was not alone.

But the room was still, other than the homogenized electronic voice from the television. Nothing moved. Not even a breeze through the screens of an open window.

"Come on," Annette said bravely. "Make yourself known."

No sound. No response from a quiet house. Not a creak on a floorboard. Not a footfall. Not a touch. Not a whisper.

Annette walked to the sitting room off from the living area. No one was there. No one was in the front foyer or the back hallway. She knew no one had gone upstairs. The old staircase was too noisy. It sang out whenever anyone walked upon it. And no one had gone to the basement. The door was locked and closed from the kitchen.

"Please," she said next. "Reveal yourself. Who are you?"

Still, nothing. Yet there remained that *feeling* in the room, something almost palpable.

Annette Carlson stared at the mixture of wine, broken glass and water on the table, seeping into the old pine surface. She looked at the fork, knife, napkin and coaster, otherwise perfectly in place.

Sure, she thought. I'm imagining it, right? The glass turned over by itself. It turned once and didn't break and I knocked it over a second time and it did. This is nuts. I'm nuts. I'll be spending another two weeks under a doctor's care at the Fairfield, Connecticut, funny farm before I know it.

She drew a breath to steady herself.

"This is nuts. The world is nuts. I'm nuts," she repeated aloud.

She walked back to the kitchen, her thoughts askew. She picked up a cloth dish towel, came back to the living room and began to mop the table.

Then her hand froze. When it registered upon her what she was seeing, she recoiled and dropped the towel.

The knife and fork were now inverted. They were facing the wrong way, points downward instead of upward toward the open table.

They had been perfectly in place seconds earlier when she walked back into the kitchen. She knew it! Twice she had looked directly at them. But they had moved within a matter of seconds. She knew that either she was right or she was losing her mind.

Annette stepped backward all the way to the door to the room. Then she unleashed the scream that had been bottled within her for the last several seconds. It was long and shrill and piercing. It could be heard all the way to the street, had anyone been happening by.

And with her scream, she felt the tone of the room change. Annette had temporarily driven something from the chamber.

She leaned back against the wall and screamed again. Then, with the cry of fear out of her system, she bolted to the kitchen, grabbed her purse and fled the house.

Less than thirty minutes later, the small green Miata of Timothy Brooks pulled to a halt in front of 17 Cort Street. Annette, in what remained of the daylight, sat on a lawn chair to the side of the house.

As Tim Brooks stepped out of the car, he could see how shaken she was. He was wearing sweatpants and a wet T-shirt. He walked toward her, carrying a copy of the local weekly newspaper folded under his arm. The edition had just been published an hour earlier. Brooks didn't want his copy blowing out of his open car.

Annette's face was ashen. Her hands were folded across her lap.

"Sorry to take so long," he said. "I had to be paged."

She looked at him and his unlikely attire. "You're a real piece of work for a cop, aren't you?" she said.

He smiled. "How's that?"

"Where were you? At a gym?"

He smiled again. "No such luck." He'd been on his own time when his beeper rang, he said, in a pickup basketball game.

"I called in," he said. "When I recognized your address, I came over."

"Oh," she said. There was something dismal about her tone. "Well, thanks." She looked at him critically. "Do you even own a uniform?" she asked.

"Sure," he said. "Look, I only *appear* to be casual. I'm ready for any occasion."

He indicated the spot around his ankle where he wore the ankle hems of his sweat togs all the way down at his sneaker top. Beneath the gray cloth was the bulge of his service revolver. And from a pocket, he pulled his badge.

"I believe you," she said. "I just came back, myself. I called you from a phone booth."

"Oh?" he asked. He glanced at the house. It looked warm and inviting in the twilight. "Another problem, huh?"

She looked at him for several seconds. "Yeah," she said finally. "Another problem. Like I'll be *damned* if I'm willing to spend another night in my own home."

She opened her mouth to explain and suddenly found herself choking back tears.

"Jesus Christ! Won't somebody help me?" she pleaded. "Won't somebody *do something?*" For several seconds, she buried her face in her hand. He knelt down next to her, surprised at her emotion, and put a comforting hand on her shoulder. He might have done more right there. He might have placed an arm fully around her as he had done with other distraught individuals in various moments of emotion or disaster, but he was struck by the awkwardness of it. Here he was a town cop.

She was a nationally prominent film star. And she was at the brink of emotional collapse, reduced to pleading for his help.

"Now," he said as she quickly gathered herself, "I'm here to listen. Want to tell me what happened?"

She gradually recovered. He sat patiently for several minutes and listened to what she had seen and what she had felt. That latter aspect—what she felt, what she sometimes sensed in the house—was gaining in significance. It was as if she knew when something invisible was present. She had a growing sense of something she couldn't see, and that was almost as upsetting as the things that *were* visible.

He never interrupted her. He let her talk. And as he listened, his own nightmare came back to him.

When she was finished, he offered her a hand. She accepted it. He stood and helped her up to her feet. They would walk through the house together, he suggested. Whatever was there, they would face it down, together.

"I'm sure you screamed pretty well," he said, attempting to cheer her. "Whatever it was is probably safely in Maine by now."

"I wish," she answered without a smile. And he wished that inside, he was as confident as he appeared outside.

She led him first into the living room. The television was still on and when Brooks first entered the house he didn't realize the voices were electronic. Then Annette flicked off the TV with a remote.

The kitchen towel remained where she had dropped it. The puddle and the shards of glass were still on the dining table, making a lovely white stain on the antique wood.

Brooks set down his newspaper on a dry end of the table. He put his hand to the puddle, then raised his fingers to his nose. "Wine," he said slowly, "mixed with water. Exactly as you said."

"Did you doubt me?"

"In my line of work," he answered, "I confirm for myself as much as I can."

She stood with arms folded, watching him. He raised his

eyebrows as if to indicate that first, he had believed her all along and second, there was nothing to fear. The gesture even elicited a small smile from her.

He picked up the towel. "May I?" he asked.

She nodded. He mopped the puddle and dried the table. He set aside the broken glass. His gaze rose and settled into her eyes.

"Tell me candidly. Do you sense anything in the room right now? Any presence other than ours?"

She took the measure of the room. "No," she finally said, to her own relief. Brooks realized that it was to his relief as well.

"If the situation changes," he warned, "tell me right away. If we go into another room and you feel something different, tell me straight out."

She nodded.

"Promise?" he asked.

"Promise," she said.

They walked through all the downstairs rooms, entering the kitchen last. He put his hand on the door to the cellar.

"Does this unlock?" he asked.

"It's been locked," she said. "No point to go down there."

He paused. He eyed the door. He rapped on it to see how secure it was. He had a funny instinct that he should have a look. A bad vibration, he would have termed it.

"You're sure?"

She shook her head again. "I'm sure. Don't bother."

He released the knob. "All right," he said. "Some other time, huh?"

"Some other time."

He retraced his path through the downstairs rooms. She asked him what he was looking for.

"Some of the very old houses on this island have hidden passageways," Tim Brooks said. "Secret rooms. Trapdoors to basements. Fake walls. Trick doors at the side of fireplaces. These are all little architectural quirks that are left over from the time settlers thought they might have to hide from the Indians and other hostiles," he said. "In many cases, these things have

159

remained in the structures of the houses, sometimes out in the open, sometimes hidden. Some have remained hidden for two hundred years."

Here was an interesting theory, one which would eliminate the supernatural aspect from some of the events at 17 Cort Street. She was almost relieved to hear it, though it then implied that something human was skulking around her home and that thought was just as chilling.

He continued, moving his hand across walls, rapping gently here and there, looking for a hollow or a previously unknown hinge.

"If someone's playing a now-you-see-me-now-you-don't game," he said as he searched, "nothing would be more useful than a passageway you don't know about."

Beside the hearth in the living room, where Annette had seen the young woman one night, a few loose bricks caught the detective's attention. For several seconds he stared at them. They were about head high. He removed them. For a moment, he thought they would reveal a lever that would crank open a small passageway between the wall and the brickwork, just narrow enough for a thin adult to squeeze through.

But he was wrong. Throughout the first floor, he found nothing. There was nothing on the second floor, either.

She considered it pointless to search in the attic, but Brooks insisted. They climbed the stairs together. He went first.

The floor groaned beneath his footfall. It was a spooky stretch of space, this attic, complete with cobwebs, dusty windows and a pair of bare sixty-watt bulbs that hung from the ceiling. It was also very hot and oppressively stuffy.

Brooks walked around the space. He examined the locations where Annette had stashed her suitcases and the pieces of furniture that she had not wanted downstairs. She had left everything covered with sheets.

Annette stayed at the top of the steps. For some reason, this room was starting to make her nervous. For an instant she sensed something. She opened her mouth to warn him. Then what she sensed was gone. So she held silent. Annette didn't want to appear any more foolish than she already felt.

Brooks stopped. His gaze settled upon one of the sheets. He turned to Annette.

"May I?" he asked.

She nodded.

To the policeman's trained eye, the small reclining form under the sheet was clearly human, perhaps the size of a child. He slowly pulled back the sheet, and as he did something flashed within him and he jumped slightly. He found himself looking at a small human head attached to small immobile shoulders. The eyes were closed. The small face bearing a single eyepiece was lifeless and wooden.

He started to blurt something out just as recognition came upon him.

"What's this?" he asked with a bemused smile.

"I meant to tell you he was there," she explained. "That's Charlie McCarthy," she said. "A copy of the ventriloquist's dummy Edgar Bergen used to use." She paused. "It was my mother's."

"I haven't seen one of these in years," Brooks said. Charlie looked like he'd been pleasantly embalmed, pickled maybe, then sealed in acrylic, monocle and all. He remained in perfect condition—for a dummy.

Intrigued, Brooks reached to the back of the dummy's jacket where he found the controls. He opened Charlie's eyes, moved the dummy's head from side to side and rolled his eyes as if he were possessed. Tim Brooks made Charlie open his silent mouth, but he thought better of putting any words therein.

"Edgar Bergen. Father of 'Murphy Brown'," Brooks said with a thoughtful smile. "You're in entertainment, Miss Carlson. I might have known."

Brooks set the dummy's head back down. The eyes closed. The policeman pulled the sheet back over the lifeless body. A tiny painless funeral.

"You know they put Edgar Bergen on a postage stamp a few

years ago," she offered. "It shows you there's always hope for an actor."

"Always. Look at Ronald Reagan," he said.

Now they both laughed.

"Or John Wilkes Booth," he added.

He straightened the sheet back across the dummy's head and scanned the rest of the attic, enduring a tiny descent into boredom. There was nothing wrong with this room. He was convinced. "Let's go back downstairs," Brooks said. They both turned. On the way down, he advised her to keep at least one of the windows in the attic open at least an inch—maybe several inches if she put in a screen.

"It will keep the rest of the house cooler in the summer," he said. "And it will keep the musty smell from building up there."

"Thanks," she said. "I've never owned a house in this area before."

"Being a town cop," he said, "is a full-service job."

They walked back down two flights of steps. Annette drew a deep breath and began to relax. No, there didn't seem to be anything strange in the house right now. She felt more assured just having the detective there. When they arrived on the first floor, she found that she did not like the idea that he would soon leave.

"Well?" she asked. "What do you think?"

"Honestly?"

"Yes."

"Based on the evidence that's been placed in front of me," he said, "it looks like someone spilled a glass of wine, then mixed it with some water. Then you called me."

Annette stared at him with disappointment. "Damn," she said. "Is that all you can say?"

"I'm sorry," Tim Brooks said. "That sounded flip. Let me rephrase."

"You don't have to."

"No, I should," he said. He glanced around the living room. "Mind if I sit down?"

"I wish you would," she said. "And while you're sitting, I hope a dish flies in the air directly at you."

He sat in the rocker across the room from her and considered her remark. "Now, that would be interesting," he said. "Trouble is, no one would believe me."

"Then you know how I feel," she said.

He looked at her with growing approval. "A point well taken," he said.

She sat on the sofa, where she normally might read scripts or a book. Or watch the television.

"Look," he said. "If you're having a problem in this house, I'm willing to do whatever I can. What's your gut feeling? Be as frank as you want because that's how I'm going to be with you." He paused, then asked, "What do you think is going on?"

"I think there's some sort of"—she searched for the right term—"*force* at work in this house. It's the absolute truth."

"I'm just curious," he said. "Who else might have had access to the house?"

"No one," she said. *No one human,* she meant to say, but didn't.

"What about the locks?" Brooks asked. "Were they changed?"

Annette said Emmet Hughes had done the job. Brooks nodded.

"What about this afternoon?" Brooks asked next. "Were your doors locked when the wineglass fell over?"

Annette thought back. She conceded that she had never been in the habit of locking doors outside of a city. So two doors to the house had been open. For a moment, a knowing look crossed Brooks' face. Then he politely reminded her that someone could have quietly walked in and out. It sounded unlikely, he admitted, but she had to admit that it was not impossible.

She nodded again. As he spoke she wished again that an object would fly off the table but nothing did. There was an awkward pause and then he shifted the conversation once again.

"Look," he said, "I'll try to be as up-front about this as

163

possible. You're in films. The public—and this does not mean *me*—holds a certain bias about film people. Film people and publicity."

She looked at him.

"Are you following what I'm saying?" he asked.

She thought about it. "That we get too much of it?"

"In a way, yes," Brooks answered. "But that wasn't exactly what I meant." He exhaled. "Counting tonight when you came out to the street to telephone me, we've had three reported 'incidents' out of this house. Three circumstances under which you might strongly be suggesting a 'supernatural' occurrence. That's if I'm using the right word."

"So?"

"Miss Carlson," he said. "None of this has gone beyond the police force yet. In fact, nothing has gone beyond me. But when it does, *if* it does—"

Annette folded her arms and Brooks knew that she finally had figured his point.

"—if it does," she said, "people are going to say we're engineering a publicity stunt."

"That could happen," Tim Brooks said.

"And what do you think?"

"In all candor?"

"Yes."

"I've never in my life believed in ghost stories," he said. "But the other night in my own home, I had a terrifying dream. I turned the light on and the room was empty. But I could have sworn . . ." He shrugged.

"Why are you telling me this?" Annette asked.

"To let you know that I'm more sympathetic than you might suspect. That I might be more willing to believe than I was a week ago."

Her eyes found his and embraced them.

"I'll tell you something else," he said. "I have an instinct for witnesses: which ones are lying, which ones are holding back, which ones are telling the truth."

"And?"

He chose his words with a precision that would have done justice to a trial lawyer.

"You look to me like you're awfully upset about what might be transpiring in this building," Brooks said. "I don't know what's going on. But I have the sense that you don't know, either."

She leaned back in the rocker. It creaked on the wooden floorboards, much as it had the night she had watched the apparition of a young woman in that same spot.

"What I'm saying is," he concluded, "that I take you at your word."

"Thank you," she said.

"But now if you don't mind, I'll tell you a story," he offered. "You can take from it what you want. This is something I know about firsthand. It's also a reason why I sometimes have trouble believing what I've seen with my own eyes. May I?" he asked.

"Be my guest," she said.

"A few years ago there was a ghost reported at the U.S. Military Academy at West Point. A friend of mine was a tennis instructor there and he told me about it. Seemed like there was a phantom in a blue-and-white uniform that had been seen in one of the buildings. It was early in the month of November when it first appeared."

It was Annette's turn to listen and wait.

"First one cadet saw it. Then another. Then a few more. Then some officers. The phantom was spectral. It had color, but it appeared like a beam of light. Made no noise. No sound. Didn't say anything. Those who saw it told their friends. Others saw it. There you had it. A full-fledged verified haunting before the levelheaded future leaders of the United States Army."

Brooks let the moment hang in the air. "And so?" Annette finally asked.

"There must have been twelve to sixteen witnesses eventually," Brooks said. "Cadets, officers and civilian employees of the academy. They all knew what they had seen. And what they had seen was a ghost." He paused. "Well, not really, as it turned out. The solution was much more prosaic."

Somewhere upstairs in the old house a warm floorboard creaked with discontent in the cooling air of evening.

"The hoax was revealed the day of the Army-Navy football game in Philadelphia," Brooks explained. "A few Midshipmen from the Naval Academy had stationed themselves within the West Point compound. They had a slide projector. What had looked like a beam of light *was* a beam of light. They were showing a slide of a soldier from the War of eighteen twelve. They shot the beam through a dormitory window. Those who saw it believed it to be a ghost."

Annette considered it.

"Great story," she finally said. "But I haven't seen anyone around here yet with a projector."

"I'm sure you haven't," he said. "And you probably won't. But my point is a larger one. I think someone's doing something to you here. I don't know who or how. But I still think there's a natural explanation somewhere."

Any disagreement that might have followed was averted by the shrill ring of the telephone. Annette excused herself and went to the kitchen to answer. Then she returned to explain that the caller was Joe Harris, her agent, phoning from California. She would be a few minutes, she apologized.

As Annette carried on a conversation in the kitchen, Tim Brooks sat in the living room without moving. He looked around, assessing a comfortable room. It struck him that there was a smattering of pieces in the room that must have been left by the previous inhabitants, not the least of which was the massive china cabinet. The rest must have been shipped in by Annette.

Well, at least she hadn't turned the place into Beverly Hills east, he thought to himself. An Academy Award actress. A real beauty in person. And here he was sitting, having a normal talk with her. How many tens of thousands of men would have paid good money to trade places with him at this moment?

And yet she seemed so normal. So collected. So together. And yet again, she told these bizarre stories.

He heard her talking with her agent and wondered how these

166

people lived, these celebrities who flew coast to coast the way another person might go to the shore for a day. Thinking about it triggered a touch of restlessness that remained in Brooks' spirit, the instincts that had taken him all over the country in his earlier years. A touch of discontent was suddenly upon him as he realized that she could jet out of there tomorrow morning. And he was stuck with a shoe-leather-style job.

She was talking in subdued tones now and Brooks did his best not to eavesdrop. Police business was one thing. Personal phone calls were another. The call reminded him, in fact, that—attractive as she was—she was socially out of his reach and would always remain so. He wondered if she had a regular lover—or a half dozen of them, all wealthy, handsome and famous—back in California.

He picked up the edition of the *Inquirer & Mirror* that he had carried in from outside. There it was, all over the front page.

Murder.

Beth DiMarco. A picture of her in life. A story of what had happened. A mention of the suspect being questioned. Plenty of self-serving quotes from Detectives Gelman and Rodzienko. And a plea from the police for anyone who knew anything further to come forward.

For the sake of young Eddie, someone better, Brooks found himself thinking. Here was a problem he hadn't even approached yet. He was convinced—no, he *knew*—that Gelman and Rodzienko were barking up the wrong tree. What would he, Brooks, do when the indictment was handed down?

He sighed. Forget about seeing a knife or a fork or a plate fly across the room. What he wanted was for Mary Beth DiMarco's killer to magically appear. That would solve years of problems for lots of people. He sighed again and placed down the newspaper as Annette returned to the room.

He spoke to her as she sat down. He waited for a response. But he knew that he had suddenly lost her attention. Instead of listening, instead of excusing herself for the time spent on the phone, she was staring at the front page of the newspaper that he had set beside the sofa.

"What's wrong?" he finally asked.

She was staring with wide mystified eyes. Eyes that told more than surprise. Eyes tinged with anxiety.

"Who's *that?*" Annette said urgently.

"Who's what?"

"That girl?" she asked. He followed her gaze to the lead story of the local newspaper. "That picture?"

He picked up the paper and looked again at Beth DiMarco. To make sure that he understood what Annette was asking, he turned the paper toward her and gave her a good look.

Then he saw something terrible in Annette's eyes. Somehow he knew what she was going to say.

Brooks felt a long low tingle, something which ran along the skin from the base of his backbone, up his spine and to the nape of his neck.

"That's *her,*" Annette said, looking past the headline to the photo. "That's the young woman I saw the second night. Who is she? And why was she in my house?"

Twelve

On Saturday morning, Annette sought a temporary retreat from her Nantucket home. She found an isolated strip of beach beyond Dionis on the south shore. She brought with her a pair of novels purchased from Mitchell's Book Corner that morning, a stack of scripts, a blanket, a beach chair and an umbrella. She also had some fruit and some bottled mineral water for lunch. She spent a peaceful day, reading, swimming, and sunning herself. She enjoyed the solitude. She enjoyed being left alone.

She also enjoyed being away from 17 Cort Street.

But she returned to her house just past six P.M. She showered and washed her hair. Then she went downstairs, found some classical music on the radio and tuned three radios to it throughout the ground floor of the house. Then she busied herself in the kitchen as she prepared a light dinner.

She would eat in the dining room, she decided. She put out a blue linen place mat, a matching napkin, and one setting of tableware, though she did not yet set the place. She returned to the kitchen and was still thinking about the various scripts she had read. Then she suddenly went very still.

She heard something. Then, clearly, she heard the rattle of the tableware that she had left on her dining-room table.

"Oh, God," she muttered to herself. "Not again."

Annette slowly turned the corner from the kitchen to her dining room and stopped short when she saw a frail human figure before her.

Annette's heart leaped, then settled as she recognized the intruder. Suddenly, everything was familiar and safe. Suddenly, an awful lot made sense.

"Mrs. Ritter," Annette said to the old woman inspecting Annette's dining table. "What are you doing here?"

Mrs. Ritter looked up and smiled.

"Just visiting. Just looking," Mrs. Ritter said. Her face was healthier and happier than the last time Annette had seen her.

Annette sighed. "You have to stop scaring me," Annette said gently. Annette paused to think. "Do your friends at Mid Island know where you are?"

Mrs. Ritter laughed. "No," she admitted. "They know I went out. But they don't know exactly where to."

"And you've been here before, haven't you?"

The old woman gave Annette a mischievous expression. Then she nodded. "I've always loved this house," she admitted.

The old lady's eyes gleamed merrily. The escape from the nursing home had served her spirit well.

Annette sighed again, this time with relief. So the mystery of the silverware had come to this. It had been Mrs. Ritter all along. Could a rational solution concerning the strange intrusions at night be far behind?

The visitations were now readily explainable in terms of a lonely old woman going for a walk—seeking attention, some sort of human companionship—yet not wanting to admit what she'd done, as she knew she'd be kept under tighter rein.

Annette's whole world made sense again. "Mrs. Ritter?" Annette said.

"Yes, dear?"

"You startled me. I wish I had known you were coming."

"Oh, I had no way of telling you," Mrs. Ritter said. "Believe me. I would have called. Dear Lord," she said. "I didn't know I'd be able to come by."

"How did you get here?"

"A lovely peaceful walk."

"From Mid Island?"

"That's right, dearie."

"You must be feeling particularly chipper today," Annette said. She came a few paces beyond the kitchen and neared the other woman. "You're feeling well?"

"Oh, today? Today I'm fine," Mrs. Ritter insisted. "You?"

"I'm fine, too."

Annette was at a loss what to do with her guest. Mrs. Ritter in turn seemed preoccupied with the table setting. She kept looking back to it.

"Eating alone, I see," Helen Ritter said. She inspected the table very critically. "I don't think that's good," she said. "You eat alone, you stay alone. You should get married," the old lady suggested tactlessly. "Make some nice babies."

"Maybe someday," Annette answered indulgently. "I'm sure someday."

Mrs. Ritter reached to the table settings. Her fingers were more nimble today. Perhaps the arthritis had abated, Annette thought. Maybe that was an explanation. On the days that her flesh and bones would allow, she made her exits from the home. Maybe it was that simple.

"You'll marry the policeman," Mrs. Ritter said out of the blue.

"What?"

"Timmy. The policeman."

Annette smiled indulgently. "The policeman is a very nice man. But we're not romantic."

Mrs. Ritter's eyes were alive. "Oh, but you will be, dear. You'll marry the policeman. Your Hollywood friends won't understand, but you'll be happy because he loves you."

There was an undertone to this that Annette didn't like. Goose bumps rose on her arms. For a moment, Annette didn't respond, as she considered Mrs. Ritter's words.

"Daffy old hen, huh?" Mike Silva, the porter at Mid Island Convalescent, had said. "Crazy, crazy, crazy."

Annette had resented Mike's words at the time. But now, there seemed to be a bitter verity to Silva's mean-spirited assessment. What right or logic did she have to blithely predict a marital involvement with someone Annette barely knew? And why did she need to wander around other people's houses?

The guest fingered the tableware. She moved a fork.

"So it's you who has been playing games with me?" Annette asked.

"Excuse me?"

"Reversing my forks and knives? You've been here to do that before."

"No, no, dearie," Mrs. Ritter said. "As you can see, I just *corrected* them. They were piled together in the wrong place."

"I hadn't set the table yet."

"Oh." Mrs. Ritter sounded hurt. "I'm sorry. I didn't realize. I'm making a pest of myself, aren't I?"

"Not at all," Annette relented. "You may set the place for me." She felt sorry for the lonely old woman. She wondered if she should ask her to stay for dinner. Yes, she decided, that's what she would do. Then Annette would accompany her back to Mid Island. Annette would walk over herself to make sure Mrs. Ritter arrived safely.

Then another thought was upon Annette. The staff at Mid Island had probably called the police. If Mrs. Ritter was missing, they were probably combing the island.

"I'm afraid the young girl keeps reversing them on you," Mrs. Ritter said, neatly setting a serving place for a single diner.

"What young girl?"

"The young girl whom you said was sitting in your rocking chair that night," Mrs. Ritter said. "Mary Elizabeth."

"Who?"

"The college girl who was murdered. She's a very nice young lady and her soul lives in this house with you now. She will be here until it is her time to pass onward."

Now a full and horrible shiver overtook Annette. "Mrs. Ritter, please . . . !"

"Why are you alarmed?" Mrs. Ritter asked calmly. "Did you think you were alone?" She laughed. "Don't worry. Mary Elizabeth is very much your friend. She won't harm you."

"Come on now, Mrs. Ritter," Annette answered.

"No, no. For real." Helen Ritter was very animated and sure of herself, her intonation rising. "Mary Elizabeth is here with you now." She glanced around as if to locate something. Then her eyes seemed to find something just behind Annette. She nodded toward the wall by the doorway where Annette stood. "There she is," Mrs. Ritter said happily. "Dear girl! She's standing right there. Close enough to put a hand on your shoulder."

"Please stop that!" Annette snapped. "I don't like it! And I know it's you who moved my place settings."

Something swept against Annette's cheek. It felt like a cobweb. Feathery light. Glancing. Brushing. Annette felt a flash of alarm and struck at it with her own hand. Nothing was there. Already it was gone. Fingers?

"That was Mary Elizabeth," the old woman said. "She caressed you. Can't you see her?"

"No! There's nothing there!"

"Of course there is," Mrs. Ritter said calmly, patiently.

The feathery glancing touch was at Annette's cheek again. Annette struck at it furiously and again whatever it was eluded her.

Annette quickly stepped away from where she stood. She looked in each direction. She saw only Mrs. Ritter.

"Pity you can't see her," the old woman said. Helen Ritter shrugged. All eighty-six years of her. She raised her eyebrows and made a pained Well-I-tried-to-tell-you smile.

What should I do? Annette wondered. I want this woman out of my house. Call Mid Island? Call the police? Call Tim Brooks? She considered the options.

"And I know what you are thinking," Mrs. Ritter said. "So I don't wish to stay for dinner. Thank you very much, anyway."

Annette decided she would call Mid Island first. She could very nicely ask the nurses if Mrs. Ritter was really allowed to be at liberty like this. Then she would phone Tim. The old lady looked at Annette.

"Could you get me a glass of water?" she asked. "Before you make those phone calls."

"How did you know I was going to make a phone call."

"Oh, you're going to call and check up on me!" she scolded. "Think I don't know how you think? You go ahead and call the nurses and the policeman if it pleases you. But could you get me my drink first?"

"I'll get you some water."

Annette returned to the kitchen, mildly shaken. She found a small glass and drew some water from the tap. She heard Mrs. Ritter walk to the living room. Creaking floorboards again. Annette followed and found the old woman sitting on the rocker near the hearth.

Annette handed her the water.

"Just set it on the table beside me," she requested.

Annette did exactly that. Mrs. Ritter studied the glass. "Have you ever given much thought to your own death?" Mrs. Ritter asked, looking up to meet Annette's gaze.

"No. I really haven't," Annette lied. The old woman was starting to scare her.

"I have," Mrs. Ritter said brightly. "I'm not sure anymore what the big fuss is about. I don't know what everyone's so afraid of. Death should be seen as a liberation." She shrugged. "Well, that's just my thinking today, anyway."

"Well, that's very brave of you."

"It's not brave, dearie. It's just realistic."

The old woman laughed. She reached to the water and sipped. "Now you make your calls if it makes you feel better."

"Then maybe I can walk you home," Annette suggested.

Mrs. Ritter shrugged. She looked at the younger woman and her eyes tingled with mischief. "I made it here by myself," she said, sounding a note of independence, "and I can be on my way by myself, too, thank you very much."

The old woman stared contemplatively off into the middle distance for several seconds.

"Did I ever tell you this?" Mrs. Ritter asked. "My sister used to live in this house. That's why I came by. Just to see how it looks once again. My dear sister. She was a music hall star. Did you know that?"

"Was she?"

"Died many years ago. Life's very unfair and unequal," she continued gently. "She had so few years, I've had so many."

Again, Mrs. Ritter shrugged. And again, Annette felt another surge of fear. A music hall star: she remembered that haunting music she heard in her dream the first night a woman in white appeared, the syncopated ragtime beat plunked out on a piano, the sense of being on a stage long ago in New York City.

"A lot of stage people used to come to this island in the twenties and thirties," Mrs. Ritter said. "Stayed down in Siasconset where it was cheap. The theaters in New York and Boston closed down in the summer. Cities were unbearable." She paused. "Heat. Summer heat."

"Of course," said Annette. "Why did your sister die so young?" Annette asked. Instantly, she knew she had touched upon the wrong subject. Mrs. Ritter's face twisted into a fearsome expression.

"Oh!" the old woman snapped, fervently shaking her head. "The less said the better. It's many years. Doesn't matter anymore to anyone living, does it?"

"I'd like to know," Annette said.

Mrs. Ritter smiled cryptically and finished her glass of water. "I think you'd better make that call now. I'm very tired."

Annette nodded warily.

"And remember, I just came to warn you, dearie," Mrs. Ritter concluded plaintively. "Heaven knows, the whole island is in danger."

These words echoed ominously in Annette's ear. She stared disbelievingly at Mrs. Ritter. Then, thoroughly frightened, she returned to the kitchen. For a moment she couldn't find the telephone book.

"You don't know the number at Mid Island, do you, Mrs. Ritter?" Annette called out.

No answer.

Deaf as a haddock, Annette thought, but only when she wanted to be. Annette located the directory wedged against the wall behind the kitchen table. It had apparently fallen down but

175

looked as if a strong arm had stuffed it there. Why, she wondered, wasn't anything where she had put it anymore?

Mid Island's line was busy. Annette hung up and waited a moment. Yes, she would return Mrs. Ritter personally to Mid Island. And she would have to do it soon. Who knew how long she'd been out?

Annette dialed the numbers for Detective Brooks, office and home. He was at neither location. She left a message for him on his beeper.

Annette walked back to the living room and stopped short. The room was empty.

"Mrs. Ritter?" she called. "Mrs. Ritter, where are you?"

There was no answer. Not a soul present. Annette stared at the empty room.

"Come on, Mrs. Ritter," she said softly. "Don't do this to me." Then she said louder, "Don't scare me like this, okay?" Louder still. "It's not funny. Not a game."

There was a slight creak in a floorboard toward the front entrance hall, just beyond Annette's view. Always, it seemed in this house, there was something just beyond Annette's view.

Annette walked through her living room. She rounded the corner. The front hall was empty, too. So was the dining room. No one had gone upstairs. Annette looked back into the living room. She turned on the light.

The little rocking chair, the one near the fireplace, was rocking very gently. Wind? An unbalanced floor? Sure. Of course. The rocker looked like someone had just got up and left it.

It settled to a halt. And when it did, another thought come up behind Annette, surrounded her and took hold. The thought was so firm, so real, so convincing that immediately Annette realized its truth.

Mrs. Ritter. Just passing through. Just stopping to say goodbye. And to "warn" me. About who? About what?

Then, with a shock, Annette sensed that she knew exactly what had happened.

"Come on, Mrs. Ritter," she called. "Please! Stop this!"

She took a final look in two closets. She knew no one had

gone upstairs. Or downstairs to the cellar. The steps creaked remorselessly. Not a chance.

Annette went to the front door. It was locked from within. She went to the back door. The same.

"Oh, dear God," she said. Then she was struck with a thought. The drinking glass in the living room! She ran back to it. It was still where the old woman had left it. Annette didn't touch it. But it was empty and dry.

"I'm not going crazy," she said. *"I'm not."*

Not going crazy. But she *knew.*

Annette went back to the kitchen and grabbed the telephone. Again the nursing home's line was busy. Fine thing, she told herself, slamming the phone down. Great if there were an emergency! Then she ran out the back door without trying to lock it.

At the end of her short driveway, she scanned the street in both directions. For a moment, she thought she saw Mrs. Ritter a block away, a thin figure moving steadily in the shadows beneath an elm tree. Annette jogged toward the spot. But as Annette approached, the figure receded like a mirage until it wasn't there. A little girl was nearby instead, a little girl in a dress from the 1950s. She looked at Annette sweetly and curiously, but said nothing.

Annette searched in every direction. But when she turned back to the child to ask if an old lady had passed, the child had vanished, too. There was nothing near Annette except pleasant evening shadows and the moving leaves from a bush.

She even wondered if she had really seen the little girl.

Annette began to run again. She arrived at Mid Island within three minutes. Mrs. Ritter hadn't been on the street and hadn't been on any path to the convalescent home.

Annette burst into the building. There was a new employee on the evening reception desk, and there was no one on the telephone.

"Hello?" the woman said, looking up. "May I—?"

"Helen Ritter," Annette demanded. "Room Twenty. I need to see her."

Mike Silva appeared at a downstairs doorway. He grinned as if he received a sexual thrill every time he saw her. There was something particularly devious in his expression today. "Hello, Miss Carlson," he said.

Annette ignored him.

"Who?" the woman at the desk asked. "I'm sorry. I just started to work here. I don't know the name." She fumbled with a computerized directory.

"Mrs. Helen Rit—! Never mind!"

"Hey! Miss Carlson?" Silva demanded.

Annette turned and rushed past both of them. She didn't bother with the elevator. Instead, she ran up the front steps. The building was quiet. It was mealtime in the refectory. There was a dull distant murmur of aged voices in the dining area.

Annette went to room Twenty. The door was closed. Annette, her pulse pounding, put a hand to the doorknob and threw the door open. What she had known was confirmed.

"Oh, God," she said softly, her voice almost breaking.

Mrs. Ritter's bed had been stripped, the mattress removed. It awaited a new tenant. The dresser drawers had been left open and were empty. There were two large suitcases near the door, presumably packed with the old woman's clothing. The window was half open, as if to air out the room. All furniture had been pushed against one wall. The chamber smelled of an antiseptic cleaning solution: pine-scented mortality.

Annette felt tears in her own eyes. Then she felt a sudden hand on her shoulder. A strong hand. A man's.

Annette whirled. Silently, Mike Silva had arrived beside her. His eyes were trained into hers. She pushed his hand away.

"Mrs. Ritter?" Silva said. "That's what I try to tell you."

Annette shuddered.

"They try to call you downstairs," he said. "Since this morning. I guess you not been home."

"I was out most of the day," she answered. Annette formed the next sentence several seconds before she asked it.

"Is that when she died?" Annette asked. "This morning?"

"Never woke up this morning," Mike Silva said. "No come

to breakfast, then the nurses find her. Very peaceful. Never knew what happened." Annette let the reality of it sink in as Mike continued to talk. "Sometime these real old people go like that." Silva snapped his fingers. A loud jarring pop. Death could be that simple.

"Sure," said Annette.

In Annette's mind, the old schoolteacher was speaking. "I'm not sure anymore what the big fuss is all about. I don't know what everyone's so afraid of. Death should be seen as a liberation."

Mike Silva's tone of voice changed. He sounded more sympathetic. "You liked the old girl, huh?" he said.

Annette nodded.

"She liked you. You were very kind," he said. "You gave her some happiness in her last days." He paused. "You need help with the table?"

Annette turned toward Silva and stared at him. "With what?" she asked.

"The checkerboard table. That's why they try to call you. That's why you here now, no?"

"I have no idea what you're talking about."

"I show you."

Silva led Annette into the room. "Hey, you know I used to make jokes about her flying that silly checkerboard table," he said. "I don't mean no harm, lady." Mike walked to where the furniture was lined against the wall. "I ain't a bad guy," he said.

Maybe not, Annette decided, but he still gave her the creeps.

"She leave you her favorite possession," the porter continued. "See?" He pointed to the checkerboard table.

And somewhere in a corner of Annette's mind, Mrs. Ritter was chattering about tipping the table: "Communicate with the spirits! Conjure up the dead!" Sure. And you needed three people who believed. Now the original believer was gone.

Mike continued to talk, sometimes aimlessly. Annette had a way of tuning him in and out. But as it happened, Mike, who worked seventy hours a week at Mid Island, always had his ears open. He knew too much about everyone's business.

179

The checkerboard table had been set aside within Mrs. Ritter's room. From the bottom of it hung a small white tag, much like one that would display a price in a Goodwill store.

"I got to tell you somethin'," Mike said. "I got to show you somethin', too."

Mrs. Ritter had left a will, the porter explained. That was held downstairs, waiting the arrival of Ned Schwinn, the mouthpiece of inevitability for estates in Nantucket which had no one to closely monitor them. But subsequent to the will, which had last been updated in 1990, Mrs. Ritter had also left some specific instructions. *Very recent* instructions. The table had been left to Annette, the only person who had ever admired it.

"How do you know?" Annette asked.

"She tell me last week," Mike said, as if it were obvious. "She tell me that she want that lawyer to come over to change her will. Mister Schwinn. You pardon me, Miss Carlson, but Mister Ned Schwinn's a real dickhead jackoff. He never come by unless he smell cash. You ask for weeks, he never come. So Mrs. Ritter tells me. She always talked to Mike. You hear what I saying?"

"Uh huh," Annette said steadily.

"Your friend Mike be rough sometimes. I no mean to be. But I see a lot here. I see old people, they give me specific instructions. Do this if I die. Do that. 'Never mind the will, don't let my no-good daughter-in-law get my rings.' And so on." Mike paused. "So don't wait around for no will to be read, pretty lady. Things disappear. Sons. Nephews. Cousins. They don't care nothing for these people when they're alive, then grab what they can get when these old people are dead. Vultures. I show you."

Silva led Annette to the table. There was a tag upon it, unmistakably in Helen Ritter's dottering handwriting, bequeathing the table to Annette Carlson.

"You take it now?" Mike asked. "That's what she say she wanted. Get it out of here before somebody steal it."

Silva looked around. "There was this little pink glass that

180

used to sit on it," he said. "That's already gone. See what I mean?"

"All right," Annette said. "I'll take the table now."

She placed her hands on it. The walnut wood had a warm, mellow texture, rich and solid and welcoming to its new owner. Yet it was light enough for a woman to carry.

"You got a car?" Silva asked.

"I can walk."

"Now's a good time."

Now was. Mike took the table under his arm. He led Annette to the back stairs, the fire exit of the home, and down one flight. No use having extra eyes upon them while walking through the lobby. They came to the rear door of the building, a fire exit. Mike braced it open with the morning's Boston *Globe*, keeping the lock from catching. Then he carefully handed the checkerboard table to Annette Carlson.

"I glad you come over," he said. "She felt strong that you should have it." He looked at the table, then at Annette.

"Hey? Why you come by if you don't know she's dead?"

Annette opened her mouth to speak. Then she realized. Mrs. Ritter passed my way a final time. Oh, Christ! She sent me to pick up the table.

"I just felt like dropping in," Annette said.

"Yeah. Well, good you did, huh?" Silva said. "Funny little table. Somebody'd of stolen it." He shrugged. "Must mean something."

"It must," Annette agreed. "Thank you."

He looked at her strangely. Another question formed on his lips. He hesitated, then grinned. "You gonna try to fly it?"

"You never know, Mike," she said. She found herself smiling. "If I ever found the right number of people, maybe I would."

He shrugged again and grinned. "Yeah," he said. "Got to follow her instructions, don't you? Well," he said, "so long."

"So long."

The checkerboard table was even lighter than Annette had first thought. She had no trouble walking it home as a calm evening settled upon the island.

Tim Brooks' car was parked in the semicircular driveway before Annette's house. He was leaning against the front of his car when he saw her. For a moment he watched her walk up Cort Street, carrying the checkerboard table. Then he walked toward her, taking the table when he reached her side.

"Hello," he said.

"I've had more problems," she said. "In the house."

They both stopped. "Uh huh," he said.

"Want to hear?" she asked.

"I came when you called, didn't I?"

"Mrs. Ritter . . ." she began.

"I know. She died." He looked at the table and recognized it.

"She left me this," Annette said.

Brooks nodded. They started walking back toward her house.

"I saw Mrs. Ritter earlier today," Annette said calmly.

He frowned. "Just before she died?"

"No," she said. "Just after. In my house. She visited."

His head turned toward her. As they walked, she related the whole day to him—the tinkering with the place setting, the visit by Mrs. Ritter toward six in the evening, her disappearance, the glass of water, and then her run to Mid Island.

They stopped on her front lawn, not far from his car. She continued to talk. He listened attentively as he always did, saying very little. A question here. A nod there.

She finished her story.

"What do you think?" she finally asked.

"Come on," he said, trying to cheer her. "I'll walk inside with you. If there's a problem, I won't leave."

"Thank you."

He carried the checkerboard table indoors. She took it from him in the living room and placed it against the far wall opposite the fireplace. The table fit perfectly into the previously empty spot. That it should fit so well was, to Annette, bizarre in and of itself.

She stepped back from it. The top of the table looked empty. It cried out for something. She placed a pewter candlestick upon it. The stick held a pink candle. The pinkness reminded her of the stolen vase. And the vase reminded her of Mrs. Ritter.

Impulsively, without saying anything, Annette lit the candle. In memory. And to cheer the room.

Brooks watched her silently.

"Follow me," Annette asked.

The policeman did. From the living room to the dining room, he trailed her.

"There's the place setting," she said. "Exactly as I left it. Or I should say, as Mrs. Ritter left it."

"Uh huh," he said.

She turned upon him with irritation. "You don't believe me, do you?" she snapped. "When it comes right down to it, you don't believe me!"

"I'm trying hard to," he said. "I believe something's going on here and—"

"Oh, thanks!" she snapped, her anger rising. "I'm terrified, no one will help me, and you think 'something's going on'! What's the matter with everyone around here?" she cried. "Why can't—?"

He placed a hand on hers. "I'm on your side," he said calmly. "I'm trying to help. I'm trying to find answers."

Annette moaned in desperation. The urge was upon her to run upstairs, pack her bags and take the next flight out of this place. At least the lunacy in Los Angeles was predictable.

Brooks, thinking that his gesture might be misread, released her hand.

"I've had a brutal day, myself," he said. "I had a forcible arrest in the morning. We had to close Orange Street due to a moped accident at the lunch hour. Then in the late afternoon I learned our department succeeded in getting an indictment in the Mary Elizabeth DiMarco case."

"What?" Annette asked, looking up.

"The boyfriend," he said. "Eddie. Indicted for murder. He's being arrested."

Annette opened her mouth to respond.

But another force answered, instead.

As Annette Carlson and Timothy Brooks stood in the dining room, they heard first the distinctive crash of a piece of china. Then another. It came from the living room. It was followed by an avalanche of matching, tingling, crashing sounds, followed closely by the sound of more plates and cups tumbling rapidly from shelves onto the floor.

Then, in a continuation, there were more heavy sounds. Destruction. Shattering. The tormented ripping away of ancient wood and antique bolts, culminating in a tremendous, hideous thundering crash.

They both thought: What in God's name . . . ! ?

They turned. They moved quickly into the front entrance foyer. They stood in the door that led to the living room. They watched with mutual fear and a total lack of comprehension.

The huge china cabinet, the one that no four men together could budge, the one that had been solidly bolted to the east wall of the house, had been ripped from its sturdy moorings and propelled inexplicably and violently forward.

Ripped and propelled by a power that neither Annette nor Tim could see.

There had been no earthquake and there had been no sonic boom. No quirk in the atmosphere. Nor had the huge cabinet, in excess of eight hundred pounds, simply tipped. *It had been thrown several feet!*

From where Annette and the policeman stood, trying to comprehend the incomprehensible, it was quite clear what had happened. The cabinet had flown forward away from the wall, heaved by some hideously powerful force. It had been launched with great strength, because its bottom had moved seven or eight feet from the wall. And it had flown through the air and torn up whatever lamps and chairs and rugs and electrical cords had been in its path. It was as if it had existed in a doll's house and had been walloped by some tremendous invisible fist.

For several seconds Annette stared at the wreckage. The actuality of this, like seeing Mrs. Ritter, like the visit from the young woman in white, like the stories about the checkerboard table, was so estranged to reality that it was difficult to absorb. But there it was before both of them. No one could tell her she had imagined this. She even had a witness.

The contents of the cabinet, Annette's china, most of it cracked or crushed, were buried beneath a mountain of splintered wood. It lay in all corners of the room, as well as beneath the wreckage of the old cabinet itself. White dust rose. Powder from aged plaster, pouring forth from the deep wounds in the wall, rose and misted.

Annette stood in the doorway and stared, trying to make some sense out of it. Across the room, in the direction that the cabinet had flown, Mrs. Ritter's table stood in the safe corner where Annette had placed it only moments earlier. It was unscathed. The little pewter candlestick upon it hadn't moved, either. Upon it, the pink candle gently burned.

But as if that was not enough, both Annette and Timothy then saw what they would forever perceive to be the culprit. Nothing within their life experience could have readied them for the terror they then felt.

From under the crashed cabinet, from the corners of the room, there gathered dark pieces of a cloud. At first it looked like the low masses of condensation that sit upon a field at dawn, or steam from dry ice. But gradually it came together and began to take shape. It formed and came apart and tried to form again. Annette, in her wide-eyed terror, stepped away from the doorway. The cloud rose and Annette recognized it.

She recalled it from the night of the first woman in white, the dark mass that she had witnessed across her lawn, cutting her off from the stars. It formed and reformed. It almost tried to take a human form, but then it became amorphous again.

Suddenly there was a foul smell in the room. It was an unspeakably putrid and repulsive odor, reminding Brooks of a month-old decaying body he had once found in the trunk of a stolen car in San Jose.

The smell of rotting flesh, of death itself.

And the air temperature dropped. It tumbled through reality. It plunged into freezing and beyond.

Slowly, as if rising from the very lowest thresholds of their own hearing, both human witnesses became aware of the low horrible sound of a man moaning in great agony. The sound was unmistakable. It didn't come from anywhere, but they both heard it. It was inside their heads and it accompanied the sudden assemblage of the cloudy mass into a single black presence in her home.

Annette's back was against the wall near the front door. She pressed herself against Tim Brooks. Instinctively, he wrapped an arm around her and held her tightly. She shielded her eyes from the horror.

He didn't. He watched.

Transfixed, he gazed upon the black form as if he were studying Death itself. He thought to reach for his pistol but realized how pointless and pathetic that gesture would be.

The mass took something close to a human form. Arms. Shoulders. A torso. Then it came apart again, dismembered. And he knew it was the same figure—the same presence—that had lurked by the foot of his bed during his nightmare.

This isn't happening, he thought. This isn't real.

But it was.

The only sound now was Annette screaming. Frantic. Hysterical. Hellish. Bloodcurdling. A scream into Brooks' ear unlike one that she had ever uttered before or could ever launch again.

A scream that could raise demons.

The mass approached. It was like a huge cloud. Darkness moved toward them.

Annette screamed again. And again it did not a damned bit of good. The stench and the coldness grew more intense.

On Mrs. Ritter's walnut wood table, the pink candle burned peacefully. Then the flame flickered and wanted to expire. It wavered and was almost out. But it stayed and grew strong again.

186

The black cloud recoiled from the humans. It eased away. It struggled to find a shape again but could retain none.

It withdrew in the direction of the rear of the house. It withdrew toward the kitchen.

Tim Brooks watched it recede. Then, taking a chance, he left Annette behind and followed.

The black presence turned a corner—or seemed to—and drifted into her kitchen. It traveled with the ease and waywardness of a thin trail of smoke.

Tim Brooks watched it go. He pursued. Then the dark vision dissipated into the air. Brooks stared at the space into which it had vanished. He stared, doubting the credibility of his own eyes for the first time in his life.

It was a cloud of dust, he tried to tell himself. Dust and particles stirred up from the collapse of the bookcase. That's all. Our eyes are playing tricks on us.

He knew he was lying to himself.

Silence. Total silence within 17 Cort Street.

Sobs followed. Muffled crying. Brooks turned back to the woman he had left. He rushed to her.

Annette was cowering against the front door, her arms trembling, her eyes wide, red and wretched. She sobbed uncontrollably. And he felt the question shoot through him: why wasn't he every bit as shattered?

He held her. He held her tightly and her body convulsed against his. He reached beyond her and opened the front door of the house. He led her out into the evening.

"It's all right," he assured her. "You're all right. You're not hurt."

But in the back of his mind, many thoughts were in open revolt with each other. He struggled to make sense of what he had witnessed.

"I believe you," he said next. "I believe you. All right? I believe everything you've told me, okay? Now we'll do something about it. I promise."

And as she fought to control herself, each of his promises posed a larger question.

187

Yes, he believed her.

But he had no idea what they would do.

And deep in his own soul, he knew that things were not all right. And they would probably never be all right again in either of their lives.

Part Two
The Haunting

*—You have seen, but you
do not yet believe . . .*
JOHN 6:36–37

Thirteen

The sun had set into a pinkish orange sky, so it was already dusk of the following Monday when Tim Brooks stopped by the rector's house of Christ and Holy Trinity Church. Brooks stood at the door and knocked twice. He found a home that was silent. The battered old Voyager was missing from the driveway, as well.

Brooks prowled further, walking to the rear of the house, hoping to find Osaro at work on his lawn. Instead, he came upon a back door which remained as unyielding as the front. And, in the lessening light of evening, scattered across the property was some of the flotsam from Osaro's broken marriage.

There was a small tricycle that Osaro's son Paul had outgrown. There was a screened gazebo that had once been Carol Ann's joy on summer evenings. There was also a four-foot-high cardboard and plastic basketball standard, hoop and net, meant for a child who was no longer there. Little mundane tombstones to failed relationships as a husband and father, Brooks thought to himself. He wondered if he, Brooks, could have done any better. The question also entered his head about Osaro's spiritual interests, and whether they had someway compromised the man's marriage. But it was only an idle musing.

So instead of reaching conclusions, Brooks stood behind the silent rectory and took it all in. He filed all the details and in the end, he came away with a strange sense of condemnation and abandonment from Reverend Osaro's domain, one he had never felt before.

Why, Brooks wondered, should the small details of a man's life give a greater impression than the man himself? As he climbed back into his car, he realized that this was often the case. In considering the whole, one must always consider even the smallest part.

Brooks guessed that the minister might be working late. He drove the next two blocks and saw George Osaro's dented white van in the church parking lot. The funny thing was, it had always made Brooks slightly uneasy to visit his friend here. There was always something awkward about it. That same sense of disquietude was upon Brooks again now, stronger than ever.

Nonetheless, Detective Brooks parked his car in the parish lot. Then he walked to the church and entered.

Despite the hour, there was activity at Christ and Holy Trinity. The pleasant gray-haired ladies who volunteer were busy with something in the vestry as well as downstairs. They directed the policeman to Reverend Osaro's office.

Brooks found George Osaro in his small tidy study downstairs from the pews and around the corner from his much discussed basement meeting hall. The pastor's study was across the corridor from a kitchen. The door was open when Brooks arrived.

Osaro was hunched over a letter, writing it in longhand, a green desk lamp throwing a bright beam across his desk, his dark eyes fixed and intense behind the round lenses of his glasses. The windows were high upon the basement walls and afforded insufficient light as the evening closed in on the daylight.

Tim Brooks knocked.

George Osaro never looked up.

"Hello, Tim," Osaro said ruminatively. "Something on your mind?" He didn't wait for an answer. "Come in. Sit down," he said. "Give me a moment, then talk to me."

"Thanks," Brooks said.

Brooks entered the office and seated himself. Osaro still hadn't looked up. He was concluding a letter in his small spidery handwriting. He wished to complete his thoughts.

Brooks looked past him and saw that the high window to Osaro's study overlooked the east lawn of the church, not the parking area. So Brooks, always alive with suspicion, wondered how the minister knew he was coming. Brooks also knew that his friend loved to play such mind games.

Finally, with an eyebrow raised, one eye peered from above his round eyeglasses. Osaro gazed at him with mock reproach.

"What are you doing here, you filthy heathen?" Osaro asked in an excessively somber voice. "Seeking confidential absolution for carnal sins past, present and—inevitably—future? Come as a supplicant, have you? Down on your hands and knees to beg for a merciful God's forgiveness?"

"Nope," said Brooks. "Not a chance."

"Well, then," Osaro said softly. "The pastor of this fucking parish sees no spirit of contrition at all. Congratulations! You're excommunicated immediately and damned to hell in the bargain!"

"You can't excommunicate me, you fraud," Brooks replied with unfailing logic. "I'm not a member of your church."

"Details, details," said Osaro airily. "I'll excommunicate anyone I damned well wish. The other day I was catching up on some back business and excommunicated Spiro Agnew. I'm thinking about Stalin next, but I do have to have priorities."

They both grinned with the joke.

"We're breaking away from the mother church here, Timmy," Reverend Osaro continued. "Setting up our own outrageous little sect. Want to play John to my Jesus? Or, more tastelessly, Goebels to my Hitler?"

"Nope," said Brooks steadily, not continuing the banter. "Neither. But I wonder if I might talk to you about something."

"Oh, Lord." Osaro sighed. "Sounds serious again."

"It's a serious question on an arcane subject."

"Police or personal?"

"A bit of both."

"Ah. I see. One of those." Osaro smiled. "We have to behave like adults for a few minutes, huh?"

Tim Brooks nodded. Reverend Osaro sighed a second time. He held up a hand, asking his friend to wait.

Then the pastor put his signature upon the letter he had completed. He glanced at it for thirty seconds and set down his pen. Then he looked up again.

"Sure," said Osaro, removing his glasses. He reached for a cup of steaming tea. "Sorry to keep you waiting and forgive the flippancy."

"No problem."

Osaro smiled amiably, the grin crinkling his face. For some reason, Brooks noted, today the minister looked as if he had just passed from youth to middle age.

"What's on your mind, Tim?" Osaro asked. He steadied his glasses along the bridge of his nose. Then he pulled a tea bag out of the cup and threw it into a plastic waste basket where it landed sloppily, with a small soggy thud. "Hope it's better than what's on mine."

"What's on yours?" Brooks asked.

Brooks reached to a lamp next to him and turned it on, lifting himself from the shadows of the room.

" 'Spiritual Nantucket'," Osaro said. "Or 'Ghost Night,' as it seemed to be known in the local vernacular. Ready for this? I have received not one, not two, but *three* complaints to date from the archdiocese about it. Actually, 'complaint' is too mild a word. *'Reprimands'* would be more accurate."

Osaro thumbed a trio of letters on the side of his desk.

"Remember those phone messages which I told you were waiting for me? Well, if I value my position in this parish," the pastor said, looking angrily at the correspondences, "I'm told by those who hold a terrible swift sword above me, I'm not to engage in any such quote malarkey and pop hocus-pocus unquote again on church property. And if I know what's good for me, I'm further informed, I won't dirty my proboscis with it anywhere else on the face of this planet, either."

Osaro shook his head in extreme annoyance.

"That's what I'm responding to right now," Osaro continued, indicating the letter he had just finished. "God." He sighed. "You'd think I'd appeared on 'The Oprah Winfrey Show' with the Swedish Bikini Team and performed an exorcism in the nude." He grimaced and gazed contemptuously at the letters.

Sometimes when Osaro spoke, an extraordinary stillness came over him, as if he were listening to his own voice being played back to him. This was one of those moments.

The minister continued.

"I'm still assigned to this parish, but just barely. Stuffy old farts in Boston," he said. "Got a letter from Bishop Albrecht, himself, I did. An intemperate letter, at that. God, the man's a bore, Tim! Why doesn't someone just send him to bed with a glass of milk? But established hierarchies tend to breed that sort of anally retentive white-bread reactionary, I suppose. Aren't police departments much the same?"

"Frequently they are," Brooks concurred and smiled sympathetically.

"Anyway," Osaro continued, "if you also wish to take me to task about 'Spiritual Nantucket' at this late date, feel free. But you've been deprived of the honor of being the first."

His pipe was unlit in an ashtray at his elbow. The ashtray bore the logo of the Copley Plaza Hotel in Boston, from where the minister had borrowed it three years earlier.

"I haven't budged from this study in two hours," Osaro said. "I'm sitting here scribbling inane letters of apology to the clerical halfwits who are my titular superiors. I have to get the words just right, you know. Just the right blend of sincere humiliation and fake contrition or I'll be in the unenviable position of having to repeat the task."

"Jesus, you're in a great mood," Brooks said.

"You would be, too, if you were I."

Once more, Brooks went on to agree and say that he understood.

Osaro again peered over his glasses at his visitor. Then he

opened a desk drawer and ferreted out some postage stamps. He set three aside on the desktop.

"I really don't know what you or anyone else thinks or expects of me, Tim," Osaro said softly. He spoke with exasperation. "I know that Bill Agannis' dog doesn't like me, but everyone else remains a bit of a mystery. Then again, maybe my ancestry is against me," he suggested easily. "Maybe half-Japanese equals full Japanese and that doesn't settle too well in these parts."

Osaro brooded for a moment.

"I don't think that has anything to do with anything else," Brooks said.

"Maybe. But I'll tell you something," Osaro began. "Seven days a week on this island I serve up religion to a comfortable well-fed congregation that really isn't very interested. Then one or two times a year, I'm not averse to giving a little spiritualism to anyone who's got five bucks to spare. It kicks in a little extra to the church budget." He thought about it. "But some people think that's inconsistent. So I won't be doing it again."

Osaro leaned back in his chair. He folded his arms behind his head. Two rings of sweat stained the underarms of his pale green shirt.

" 'Some people,' " Tim Brooks answered, "must include the bishop."

Osaro grimaced. Some of the volunteers were busy in the corridor. One of the gray-haired ladies went by humming an Andrew Lloyd Webber tune. Osaro rose and shut his door.

"Christ, the bishop's a fucking bore!" Osaro said quietly. In his soft, vaguely Asian accent he had a faculty for lifting even obscenities to eloquence. "He accuses me of being into witchcraft. Or voodoo, not that he would know what either is. Or atheism, or— Ah, who knows what the idiotic old man thinks? On one hand he accuses me of some vague practice of mysticism, then the same day he turns around and ordains a bull dyke as pastor of a rural parish in Vermont."

Osaro clenched his teeth in disgust. Then he sat down again.

"Anyway," he concluded in a tone of injured virtue, "nothing could be further from the truth."

"A couple of Sundays ago," Brooks said, guiding the conversation back to where he desired, "we had a talk in the church parking lot. You told me you could go into a 'disturbed' place— usually a building—and, you know, 'pick up the vibrations.' You said you could tell if there was 'anything there.' "

Osaro raised his eyes again. Brooks now had Osaro's full attention.

"Yes," Osaro answered, speaking slowly. From somewhere his interest in the conversation had been raised to a keener level. "Yes, that's not bullshit. Very often I can do that."

"You called it a 'gift,' " Brooks reminded him.

Osaro gave him a hopeless smile. Brooks knew the minister to be a man of moods. Today's was definitely down.

"Is that what I called it?" Osaro asked. " 'A gift'? How dreadfully fulsome of me. It's not really a gift. It's not even a talent. For me, it's just a sense that's there. Like touch. Or smell. Or sight. It's an ability nature gave me. I didn't ask for it." He paused thoughtfully. "And I'm not sure I want it."

"But most people don't have that ability," Brooks offered. "Nor do they even think they do."

"I wouldn't say that most people don't have it," Reverend Osaro countered, disagreeing immediately. "I think many people probably do, but they don't channel it." He gave it a second's thought. "Know what percentage of Americans believed they've communicated with someone dead, Timmy? According to a nineteen-ninety-two survey in *USA Today?*"

"I would have no idea."

"Sixty-seven percent. Two-thirds of the great unwashed proletariat. Two out of every three adults you see on the street. That's either a lot of crackpots or most people have sensed something at one time."

"Or else a lot of people *think* they have," Brooks offered for the sake of argument.

"My sense is just developed, that's all," Osaro said. "I'm

aware of mine. If you hang around me long enough, you'll develop the same sense."

"No way."

"Oh, yes, you will! You'll see! And all of this, as I keep trying to tell people, is not even inconsistent with Christianity. Not entirely, at least. Why *shouldn't* we receive signals from another world from time to time? Isn't that the much-maligned bill of goods all of us guys with the reversed collars have been trying to sell for twenty centuries? So why should everyone be so distrustful when it actually happens? The Bible even attempts to prepare us: 'What sign can You give us to see, so that we may believe You?' John 6:30-31. Explain it to me, Timmy," Osaro said, fiddling with his pipe. "Why does everyone assume either evil or lunacy whenever we try to rationally discuss life after death? Why does everyone want to see horns and a pointed tail when one could just as easily assume wings and a halo?"

Brooks shrugged and opened his hands to suggest that he remained sympathetic. "I wish I knew," he said simply.

"The Resurrection is supernatural," Osaro continued without a trace of apology or irony. "Holy Ghost, Saint Esprit and all that? How about Easter? The day of greatest joy in our faith, is it not? What is Easter other than a promise of eternal life?" Osaro looked at his visitor impassively. "You've been to church enough to know about Easter, haven't you?" he teased.

"As I've told you before, I'm a good Protestant. Christmas and Easter. Those are the two days I drop by."

"Greater faith I have never seen," Osaro said in a mock-Old Lace Irish accent, his sense of wit and irony putting in a brief appearance. For a first-generation American, Osaro could also do a great Jimmy Cagney imitation whenever he was so inclined.

"The problem we have," Osaro said, "is that if the Archangel Gabriel appeared to trumpet the Last Judgment the only coverage he'd get would be in the supermarket tabloids—right along with the Elvis sightings—plus six minutes on 'Geraldo.' "

Again, Brooks smiled.

"Sorry," Osaro then said. "I'm giving you a diatribe. That's not what you came for. What did you want to talk about?"

"I want to know something straight-on," Brooks said. "I want a candid answer. As honest and accurate as you can make it. No crap, all right? Promise?"

Osaro opened his hands again. "Ask me anything."

"All this 'spirit' stuff," Brooks began. "I know it's a fascination of yours. But where does it fit in? Is this something that amuses you? Something you're trying to learn more about? Or have you become your own convert?"

As a trained investigator, Brooks had a method with questions: he would launch an armada of them at once, then lie back in wait and see what he had hit.

"When you say 'something's there,' " Brooks continued, "are we talking about a matter of faith? Or do you think there's really something tangibly present?"

Brooks was surprised to see George Osaro's face go quite dark. The minister folded his arms.

"Congratulations, Timmy," he answered. "I've been waiting for years for someone to ask me that question."

Osaro stared downward, apparently weighing his response. He held this posture for several seconds until he looked up again and found the policeman's gaze still fixed upon him.

"Okay," Osaro said, speaking quietly again. "Brutally honest, right? And it goes no farther than this room?"

Brooks promised.

"Yes, when I sense something I think that something is very clearly there," Osaro said. "It's there, and I think it's physically ready to come forth. All it needs is the invitation or maybe the specific occasion. And know what? Most of this scares the living bejesus out of me."

"Why?"

Again, Osaro measured his words with caution.

"Well, first off," he answered, "I think what we're talking about exists on at least two discernible levels. First there's the spirit world. Human souls. The psyche of men and women which still seem to drift across our level of living." He paused.

"Nantucket seems to be a unique little patch of the world. Difficult to leave. Perhaps that's why we might have a population of worldly spirits—benign, wandering, migratory souls—who simply *don't* leave."

Osaro shrugged and looked his friend in the eye.

" 'Ghosts,' some people would call these," Osaro explained, "though I don't care for the term, as you know."

"Uh huh," said Brooks. For some reason, he felt a strange tingle as the subject misted out into the open.

"Then there's the rest of the nether world," Osaro said respectfully. "The stuff that the fucking bishop is always trying to hang on me. The stuff I wouldn't dare go near. The occult. Black masses. The cabala. Demonology."

"Why wouldn't you go near it?"

"First off, the lunatic asylums of this country are filled with people who have messed around with it too much. I struggle to keep it balanced, myself."

Brooks fidgeted with his fingers on the arm of his chair. "Fine so far," he said. "Keep talking."

"Second," George Osaro said, "it seems to me that there's an awful lot we don't know about the human spirit. Where it comes from. More importantly: *where it goes.* Perhaps every earthly death gives birth to a thousand new lives." He continued to weigh his thoughts. "It also seems as though we know very little about reality. What it really is. How many dimensions it has. Are there three? Four? Ten? Six million? The same number as there are angels dancing on the head of a pin? And what are the full reaches of each of these realities, Tim? Got a guess?"

Osaro drew a breath and sipped his tea, about which he had almost forgotten. "I'm used to being pulled in two different spiritual directions, Tim. See, I'm Japanese, but I'm American. I'm a Christian, but I've studied Shinto. I'm a true believer, but I harbor grave doubts." He looked at his friend. "Are you following me?" he asked.

"No. I asked what scares you," Brooks answered.

"I'm trying to draw an analogy. Try to stay on my wave-length with this, all right?"

"All right."

"I sometimes think that we have a foot on at least two different planes: the reality we know and at least one other reality that we sometimes sense, but may not be entirely capable of understanding. That's what I meant about being Japanese but also being an American. Or being a believer and a doubter. Both of those forces are within all of us. Now, sometimes we are very firmly planted in the reality we expect to be in. Regular, normal, everyday life, right?"

"Right."

"But then there's the other region. Sometimes that other door opens up. That other reality is staring us right in the face. We try to dismiss it, but it's there and we're looking right at it. Then we make all these excuses about why we didn't really see it or can't really believe it. But, oh brother, it's there, isn't it? We know because we've gotten a glimpse of it. The realm of those no longer living with us. 'The dead,' if you wish. 'Spirits,' as I prefer. We know it's there. But most of us just can't fathom it. See, the difference between Mary Rovere, Leon Kane, Doctor Friedman and the rest of the world is that those people stopped rejecting what they had experienced. Instead, they embraced it. Now they believe."

"Why does it scare you?" Brooks asked.

"Only part of it does. But doesn't it scare you?"

Brooks shrugged.

"Come on. Answer me," Osaro insisted good-naturedly. "I answered you."

"If I decided that I believed in it," Brooks said, "then, yes. It would scare me."

"Why?"

"Well, it's . . . it's an unknown. It's—"

"Exactly! Suddenly a dark window is drawn up. The mysteri-ous door opens. You might see some familiar faces. Spirits of those you know, maybe. A wonderful grandparent you loved long ago as a child. A young friend who died of illness seven years ago. But travel beyond that, Tim. Take the next logical step, and bang! You may be looking into a horrible chasm. A big black inexplicable void. No maps, no points of reference, and not much literature which is of any use. Boy, oh boy!" The minister shook his head. "That's not *intimidating?*"

"But, for the sake of argument," Brooks continued, "if you believe in God and Christ—"

"That's the upside," Osaro said, taking up the argument. "The reassuring part. But then you have to believe in Hell and the Devil as well, don't you? If there's an afterlife for Good, then why wouldn't there be one for Evil, too? And when you contact that alternative parallel universe, what are we dealing with? Benevolent familiar spirits? Or the satanic ones? If we don't know immediately, might we be better off just leaving it alone? How do we know *it* or *they* will leave us alone once we've made contact?"

Osaro posed his questions quickly, as if he had spent many hours on the various points. Then he tried to answer them.

"You heard what Doctor Friedman had to say," Osaro said, almost angrily. "You and I can't explain what was going on in that house. Nor can anyone else. So let's face it. There was some malevolent presence there. And its will was in opposition to the human presence."

Two weeks earlier, Brooks might have suggested that Dr. Friedman had been having an elaborate joke at everyone's expense. But Brooks had seen the wreckage of Annette Carlson's china cabinet. He had seen—or thought he had seen—the misty black cloud that had seemed to try to take on the configuration of a large man. So the thought didn't occur to him.

Instead, very slowly, very ominously, at the back of his neck he felt something like hands. Icy hands. Cold as mortality, lightly touching. He brushed at the base of his neck and the touch was gone. He supposed it had been some quirky draft. Yet he noticed that his palms were moistening, too.

". . . and, of course, being a Christian *is* a matter of faith," Osaro continued, as Brooks tuned back in. "So there's always another darker possibility. Something even more horrible."

"What's that?"

"As a Christian, one could always be wrong. Perhaps none of *our* theology works at all. Maybe Buddha was right and Jesus was wrong. Maybe I should forget the Ten Commandments and embrace the 'eightfold noble path.' "

Brooks felt distinctly uncomfortable. Osaro studied his friend carefully. He must have sensed Brooks' reactions because he made an abrupt attempt to change the conversation.

"Oh, for heaven sakes," the minister said. "What in God's name are we talking about? I can't believe you came here to dick around with this. Why *are* you here, Tim? Have the collection plates been audited? Am I being arrested?"

"There's a house on this island," Brooks said steadily. "I need you to visit it with me. Soon. Then tell me what you think."

"About what?"

A momentary pause, then Brooks answered. "It's a disturbed place. There's something in it."

"Pretty damned sure of yourself, aren't you? For someone who was a doubter less than a week ago."

"I have my reasons."

"I guess so." Then, pondering the request, Osaro backtracked. "What sort of 'something?' "

"Same as Doctor Friedman's," Brooks answered.

The clergyman thought about it for a few more seconds. "Which house?" he finally asked.

"Seventeen Cort Street."

Osaro frowned and tried to place the address. "That's not one that I've ever heard about," he said pensively. "Must be something new." Then he frowned painfully and asked, "Isn't that over near where some movie actress just moved in?"

"Not *near*, George. That's the house. An older couple owned the place for years. A Mr. and Mrs. Shipley."

"Of course," Osaro said. "They're parishioners here. They're still on the island."

"They sold Seventeen Court Street and bought a smaller place farther out of town," said Brooks, who had that morning researched the property's ownership as well as any history of disturbances. "The transaction was in May of this year."

There was another moment's hesitation from the pastor. Then Osaro's mood changed. "Oh, these damned Hollywood people!" he growled. "They're worse than the rude fucking New Yorkers. What's this girl want? Publicity?"

"No. I don't think so," Brooks answered.

"What's her name again?" Osaro asked.

"Annette Carlson. She's well known."

Reverend Osaro thought he'd heard the name. But he didn't go to many movies, he confessed, and wouldn't have recognized her. So he considered the request for several additional seconds.

"Well, I've never heard of any problem at that address before," he concluded skeptically. "Let me tell you. There are old houses around Nantucket, plenty of them, with spiritual inhabitants. There's no doubt in my mind. But it's always the same houses. And the same spirits, even though they might take a decade or two off between appearances. We don't just hatch out new ones. See what I mean? That's what makes it credible. Generation after generation, people see the same things. They get the same feelings."

Brooks told him about the two sightings of a woman in white. Or two different women in white, if one took the view that it was an older woman the first time and someone bearing a resemblance to the late Mary Elizabeth DiMarco the second. And then there had been the appearance of Mrs. Ritter a few hours after she had died. And finally, ominously, Brooks told about the china cabinet.

"I saw the damage myself," Brooks said. "I don't think five strong men could have thrown that cabinet and smashed it like that." He stopped short of mentioning the black presence.

Osaro listened intently and without interrupting.

"So maybe she just gave the fucking china cabinet one big yank from the top," Osaro suggested. "I've seen some clever frauds from time to time. You'd be surprised—"

"The cabinet was bolted to the wall, George. Two antique iron bolts, torn completely out of the woodwork. Ripped loose right at that moment by something very, very strong. We were in the next room, George, and no one else was in the house."

Osaro's skepticism softened. "Is she living there now? This actress?" he asked.

"She's checked into a guest house," Brooks said. "Doesn't want to stay in the house again alone. Not just yet. I don't know that she'll even go back to it. She's talking about selling and going back to California."

Osaro pursed his lips. "That scared, huh?"

"Legitimately."

Osaro sighed. He glanced again at his desk.

"You heard what I told you, right? How the frigging archdiocese is on my ass about this stuff already?"

Brooks nodded. "This is not church property we're going to," the policeman said. "You're on your own time and it's private. No one has to know. We're not going to take pictures and we don't have to send the bishop an invitation."

Osaro wavered. He smiled wanly, unconvinced. He sighed with displeasure and ran his hand through his hair.

"I can't do it," he said softly.

"Come on, George," Brooks continued. "Just come over and get a feel of the place. You said you had this gift. Well, I want to know what you think is there. That's all. I promise. Sniff around the address once, then you're out of it."

"This isn't crackpot stuff, is it?" Osaro asked, wavering slightly. "You're absolutely sure?"

Brooks sighed and revealed what he had held back until that moment. He told about the black vision in the house, as well as the figure that he sensed, or saw, or thought he had seen, at the time of his nightmare.

Osaro's eyes locked, stunned, upon his friend. When Brooks finished his explanation, Osaro waited several seconds to let everything sink in before he answered.

"Then the answer is 'no' more than ever," Osaro finally said.

"Why?"

"First, I'm not in a position right now to flagrantly disobey

Bishop Albrecht. But second, and much more importantly, I have no desire to help raise a malevolent spirit."

"How would you help raise it?"

"By doing battle with it! Fight with one of these and you'll lose every time! Plus, you strengthen it through conflict."

"Please?"

"Tim, I told you. This is the occult! This is demonology! This is the stuff I don't touch!" Osaro was impassioned. "Whatever this spirit wants, let it run its course. Let it have its way and go back to whatever sphere of reality it came from. Trust me. That's the only path."

"All right," Brooks finally said with a sigh. He rose to leave. "I can't make you help."

"I'm sorry," Osaro said. "Right now, I feel like my hands have been tied."

Brooks nodded in disappointment. "There's one other thing," he said. "It's been bothering me since I sat down here fifteen minutes ago."

"Yes?"

"You were at your desk writing when I arrived. Never looked up, greeted me by name, but claimed you hadn't been out of your study for an hour. You can't see the parking lot from where you're sitting, but you knew I was coming. How?"

"Telepathic powers," Osaro said. His tone was carefully measured so that Brooks had to guess whether he was teasing or not. "I developed them at seminary."

"Bullshit," Brooks said. "The only thing you developed in three years at seminary was a two-handed jump shot. And not even a very good one."

Osaro grinned. "You're the detective. What do you think?"

"You were lying when you said you hadn't left the room. You saw me coming from the window in the kitchen. That's where you made your tea, which was hot when I sat down. You heard the footsteps of a man approaching your office. All of your volunteers are women. So you guessed the footsteps were mine."

Osaro leaned back in his chair. He raised his eyebrows and

nodded appreciatively. *"Very* good!" said Osaro. "You're absolutely right."

Brooks smiled.

"But you know what, Tim?" Osaro said quickly and soberly. "Everything else I said? You know. About those levels of reality? The different planes? The afterlife? The malevolent spirits?"

"Yeah?"

"Take it in dead earnest, my man. I meant every word of it. Particularly," he concluded, "the part about a door opening to the unknown. And the part about being scared."

"I think you're being a bit dire," Brooks said.

"Think so?"

"Yes."

"Do you know how this particular door to the unknown got opened?" Osaro asked.

Brooks thought about it, then shook his head.

"Then you won't know how to close it, either," Osaro said. "Timmy, do everyone on this island a favor. Drop this. Burn the house down if you have to. Just don't mess around with what you can't control or understand."

"George, we're not living in the Middle Ages."

"Thank God for that! But I do have a bit of knowledge about what we're talking about. Okay? So see if you can take someone else's advice for a change."

"You're reacting as if I'm bringing demons up from Hell, itself, Parson. And that if I don't watch what I do, they'll come up one by one in all their evil and blackness and take over our island."

Osaro saw nothing amusing about Brooks' remark. He pursed his lips. His gaze settled deeply into Brooks' eyes.

"Let's put it this way," Osaro answered. "First there was one at Doctor Friedman's house on Milk Street. Now there's one at the Carlson home on Cort Street. So as a matter of fact, Tim, you're right. What you described—a whole legion of them invading this wealthy, beautiful isolated island we call Nantucket, provoked by something bent out of shape in their universe— Well, yes. That is *exactly* what I fear."

When Brooks returned to police headquarters, a surprise waited for him. Dr. Herbert Youmans, the island's regular medical examiner, had stopped by. When Youmans had learned that Brooks was out, he left no message. Only a business card on Brooks' desk.

"Did he say what he wanted?" Brooks asked the receptionist.

"He said it was nothing really urgent," she said with a shrug.

Tim Brooks gazed at Youmans' card. The medical examiner rarely came by the police station. Of late, he had been particularly scarce, since Lieutenant Agannis seemed bent upon phasing him out in favor of a brigade of younger and, in Brooks' opinion, less reliable physicians. So the doctor had probably cruised through very quickly.

Dr. Youmans was semiretired and barely worked twenty hours a week. Brooks picked up a telephone and called the doctor's office number. His nurse said he was out. When Brooks called Youmans' home, his wife revealed that the doctor had gone fishing.

"Blue fish off Smith's Point this time," she ranted. "And guess who gets to clean 'em. Not Herb! I feel like I work in a seafood store I've cleaned so many darned fish this last week."

"Please tell him I called," was the detective's only message.

Brooks gazed at the pathologist's card again, as if it might tell him something by itself. It didn't. Seconds later his phone rang. A woman in Siasconset had reported some malicious vandalism in the library of her house and wanted the police to take a look. By the luck of the draw, Timothy Brooks was the detective assigned to the case.

He drove out to the woman's home and parked in her driveway. She was waiting outside for him.

Her name was Mrs. Thelma Lewis. She was a widow in her sixties and was deeply frightened. Brooks did what he could to settle her. Then she showed him what had happened. And, like the day when Timothy Brooks had been led to the massacred ducks, his initial reaction was one of revulsion.

Someone had entered Mrs. Lewis' house overnight or in the early morning when Mrs. Lewis went out for a walk. The someone had come with a large antique knife, a macabre old carving utensil that was rusted all along the length of the blade. The intruder had taken nothing and apparently touched very little. In fact, little in the house had been touched—with one glaring exception.

In Mrs. Lewis' library there was a large print reproduction of DaVinci's *Last Supper*. The print had been savagely vandalized.

The intruder had used the blade of the rusted knife to carve the large letters F U C K in the print. Then he had thrust the knife directly into the figure of Christ standing among his apostles.

The knife remained stuck where the intruder had left it, the blade horizontal, jutting into the figure of Jesus below the chin and above the shoulders.

Straight through the throat, probably not by coincidence.

Brooks suddenly felt a deep anxiety, an anxiety that built to a shudder and then to fear. He repressed it and didn't let Mrs. Lewis sense it.

"How horrible," he heard himself saying as he attempted to comfort the woman. She refused to even look at the destruction and desecration any further. But Brooks' eyes were riveted, examining the subtext of this act, the underlying horror, depravity and sacrilege.

Mrs. Lewis said that her doors had been locked at all times. And the knife was not hers. And who, she said, in another eerie echo of the McCloy farm incident, would do something like this? What sort of madman?

What sort, indeed? Brooks asked himself.

Brooks used a paper towel from the woman's kitchen to remove the carving knife from the print. He was careful to preserve any fingerprints that may have been upon it.

But even pulling the knife from the wall was a struggle. It had been plunged deep into the woodwork beneath the print.

Brooks needed both hands and all of his strength to dislodge it.

He decided to take both the print and the knife to the police station to be examined as evidence and chauffeured Mrs. Lewis there also to file a complaint. As he drove, however, his thoughts began to focus.

More and more, he sensed that a confrontation was coming with an enemy that George Osaro deeply feared and that he, Brooks, had not yet even begun to understand.

Fourteen

Annette telephoned Tim Brooks the next morning. She asked him to meet her on one of the uncrowded beaches at Madaket. She wanted to talk and walk. He agreed.

She was waiting when he pulled his Miata to a halt at the side of a sandswept road. She wore a pale blue T-shirt and a short yellow skirt. She watched him through dark glasses, big round owlish ones. He greeted her with a smile and a wave. He walked to where she stood.

On the beach, away from Cort Street, the source of her torment, he was conscious of her in a different way. How attractive she was. How delicate her face was. How beautiful her tan arms and legs were in the sunlight. The entire way she stood there and held herself was—

"Hello," he said, cutting off any impropriety within his own thoughts.

"Hi," she answered. She smiled slightly. "I wanted to talk somewhere away from the house. Is this okay?"

"It happens to be one of my favorite places on the island. You can see why."

She agreed that the shoreline was beautiful. Then, "Look," she said. "Again we're speaking in confidence. Can we?"

"Of course."

"Good." She drew a breath. "Let's walk," she said. They turned away from the sun. She held a pair of sandals in her right hand, dangling them by the ankle laces. The beach was beauti-

211

ful, but remote, populated with only a few bathers, a few families, and one diehard fisherman.

"I wanted to have this conversation away from the house," she said. "You'll understand why. Never know who or what is listening within those walls." She glanced to him from behind her dark glasses. "Know what I mean?" she asked.

"I know what you mean," he answered.

"Do you think we're crazy, you and I?" she asked next. "Mentally unbalanced? A few screws loose here and there? And that's why we think we see things?"

"No," he said.

"That's your honest impression?" she pressed.

"That's my professional response," he said. "But, remember. I'm a detective not a doctor."

She kept walking.

"So maybe we *are* both crazy," she said. "Or delusional."

"Doubt it, Miss Carlson," he assured her again. "But why are you trying to make that point?"

She smiled secretively. To the casual observer, they might have been any young couple on a vacation.

"You can call me Annette," she said. "And I'll drop the 'Detective Brooks' stuff and call you Tim. Or Timothy," she said. "Whichever you prefer."

"Either," he said.

She was silent for a few steps. "I'm not trying to make the point that one or both of us is crazy or delusional," she said. "I'm trying to rule it out."

He was confused and admitted it.

She drew a breath. "I want to tell you something so that you don't get the wrong idea. A few years ago, after my mother's death, I was under a doctor's care for depression," she said, a breeze gently tossing her hair. "I was even hospitalized for a short time in Connecticut. I've recovered. Completely. Or at least I think I have."

He walked by her side and listened.

"I don't want to slip back," she said. "I don't want these

212

'occurrences,' at Seventeen Cort Street to push me backward. Do you know what I'm saying?"

He thought he did, and said so.

"So I've made arrangements to see a doctor in Boston. Tomorrow. He's a psychiatrist. I want to know I'm sane and not slipping."

"Have you ever seen him before?" Brooks asked. A bright red Frisbee, thrown by a handsome blond boy of about ten, eluded a second boy and landed in the sand near Annette. Brooks picked it up and threw it back, a fine smooth throw with a dash of backspin. The Frisbee caught a current and sailed upward as if it were ascending in an elevator shaft. It delighted the boys who laughed at the funny trajectory and gave chase.

"The doctor's name is Gary Rossling," Annette said. "He's the former associate of a doctor I was seeing in California. Studied at Berkeley with him, or maybe it was UCLA. I don't know." She sighed. "I called this morning and had copies of my records sent to his office in Boston."

"I'm still not sure why you're sharing this with me," Brooks said. "You certainly don't have to."

"I'm telling you because I'm going to see this new psychiatrist in Boston tomorrow," she explained. "I don't want you to think that I'm not coming back. And I also didn't want you to think that I was crazy all along."

"You have no danger of either," he said.

"Good," she said. "Thank you."

She walked several more steps in silence and Brooks knew that she was summoning up the nerve to move the conversation to its next level.

"I've been doing a lot of thinking," she said. "About the house. About this thing that's in it." Her gaze settled into his again, then she looked to the distance. "A haunted house. That's what I have, don't I? That's what these things are called."

"I suppose they are."

They continued to walk. She formed her thoughts. "When I was a little girl," she said, "my father fell ill. I was about

213

thirteen. He couldn't work. The bank foreclosed on him. Took our home. We rented and lived in apartments for a few years. Finally, my father got some money together and we bought a new home."

Brooks listened.

"He always told me, and I always told myself, that if I had any financial success as an actress, I should buy my own place. Buy it with cash and then hang on to it forever. Then it's mine. It's my home and no one can take it from me." She smiled sweetly. "I always wanted a quirky antique house in the Northeast. Something with charm and a lot of character. That's what I have now on Cort Street," she said.

"With maybe a bit more character than you bargained for," he suggested.

"Quite a bit more," she said. "But the fact is, this is my house. This spirit that's in it. This ghost. Or these many ghosts. I don't care what world these things came from. This is my home now. I'm not letting them run me out."

"You're very brave," he said.

"No. Just a stubborn bitch from Hollywood."

He laughed. "I don't think that at all."

She stopped walking.

"You mentioned something about a friend of yours," she said. "A priest? A man who knows about similar hauntings on the island?"

Brooks nodded.

"He's not a priest. He's a Lutheran pastor," Brooks said. "I wanted to bring him over to the house, in fact. Talked to him just yesterday. He says he has . . . this gift. He can tell if something's present."

She seemed to accept that such talents existed.

"We know something is there," she said. "I want to know how to lose it."

"Sometimes he can tell exactly what's there," Brooks said. "To my mind, that would be the first step in understanding how to get rid of it."

She nodded. "How to exorcise it?" she asked.

"So to speak."

She considered this for a moment. "What's his name?"

"Reverend George Osaro."

"Will he come over?" she asked hopefully.

Brooks told her about the minister's current antagonisms with the archdiocese over exactly this type of thing.

"Damn," she said.

"It doesn't mean he won't change his mind eventually," Brooks said. "I'm hopeful that he will."

Annette nodded, mildly despondent.

He tried to pick up the mood.

"I wonder if *I* could take another tour of your house," he asked. "I'd like to have a serious walk-through. See if I can sense anything. Or see anything new."

"We could do it right now," she suggested.

"I have to go back to my office and I have some other pieces of business," he said. "Tomorrow?"

"I fly to Boston tomorrow. Remember?"

"Ah. Yes. Of course."

"So it would have to wait till Thursday," she said. "Unless you want to do it tomorrow by yourself."

"Alone?"

"Yes," she said. "There's a big grayish-brown rock in the flower garden just beneath the kitchen window. I can leave a key there."

"That doesn't bother you?" he asked. "If I go in by myself."

"I might prefer it that way." She laughed.

He smiled.

"Do you need a lift to the airport then?" he asked. "I can drop you and pick you up. Tomorrow's my day off, to the extent that I ever take one."

"That would be great," she said. "I accept."

Then, impulsively, she surprised him as well as herself. She leaned forward and kissed him lightly on the cheek. She gave him a smile and thanked him again. Then she turned. He walked with her, back to where they had left their cars.

He watched her drive away, still feeling the spot on his cheek that her lips had touched.

Returning to Cort Street, Annette parked her car in front of the house. She walked to the back door and found a courier pack that had arrived during the afternoon. She hefted it in her hand. It felt like three more scripts to read. The package bore the return address of Joe Harris in Los Angeles.

Annette walked into the house and opened it. It was in fact three scripts, just as she had guessed. But the scripts were related. They were Part One through Part Three of a planned big-budget TV production, a miniseries based on a best-selling World War II-era novel titled *Message From Berlin*.

She groaned when she realized what they were.

"Oh, Joe," Annette muttered hopelessly, setting the scripts aside. "You know I hate working in TV." There was a covering letter clipped to the top script. She decided it could wait, as she had no desire to involve herself in a network movie.

Somewhere upstairs in the house, the floorboards gave a distant creak. Not once, but twice, and in different spots. Annette glanced at the ceiling above her, and felt her heart skip for a moment.

"Go away," she said aloud. There was no further noise from above.

In the evening, she called Emmet Hughes, the island handyman, and hired him to fix the plaster in the living room where the old cabinet had fallen—or been thrown—forward.

Half an hour later, Annette was more relaxed. She was comfortably at work in the kitchen of her house. A foul mood seemed to have partially lifted. Her world shone as a brighter place.

Annette considered the steps she had taken that day—the hiring of Emmet Hughes, the handyman, and the immediate appointment with Dr. Gary Rossling, the psychiatrist. Annette came to view them as positives. In putting anything in order, she concluded, first steps had to be taken in every direction.

216

Additionally, of course, she had fixed her resolve to battle for her house. How dare these spirits—if they were spirits—think they could drive her out—if indeed that was what they thought.

She smiled. Overall, she managed to convince herself that she was pleased.

That same evening at seven, Tim Brooks stood at the foul line on the basketball court behind the high school. He was alone. He drew a breath and lofted the ball in a perfect arc toward the hoop.

Swish. Not even a rim.

He repeated. Swish again. A third shot matched the uncanny accuracy of the first two.

If there was one thing in life Tim Brooks could always do successfully, it was sink foul shots. Particularly when he was angry. Foul shots focused his attention and worked off his anxieties. Therapy. That's what it was.

He should write a book some day, he told himself as he retrieved a shot that had rolled off the court. He envisioned the title: *The Foul Shot Method of Stress Management.*

Yeah, sure, he thought to himself. Make a million bucks and quit my job. Make a million bucks and marry an actress.

"Yeah, sure!" he muttered aloud.

In his quiet, methodical way, Timothy Brooks was in a rage.

He walked back to the free throw line. He tossed two more shots up in quick succession, hardly aiming. One skinned the rim and settled through the net. Another swept around the rim and fell in. So did the next one. He dropped nine more in succession, missed one, then methodically sank eight more in a row before missing two.

"Come on, God damn you!" he cursed at himself. "Concentrate!"

He went back to the foul line, shooting, retrieving, shooting, retrieving. Eighteen hits in a row. Finally! Much more like it.

If only, he reckoned, he could channel the other forces and

events in his life as neatly as he could direct a twelve-inch round ball through a sixteen-inch hoop.

His thoughts weren't even on basketball. He finally admitted to himself that they were upon Annette Carlson.

Out of your league, he told himself. Untouchable. Unapproachable. Probably has some hunk back in California who sends her into ecstasy, you halfwit! That or she sleeps with every weasel-faced producer in town to land those top roles!

All of this came to Tim Brooks as he shot baskets. He felt a deep wave of discontent sweep over him.

This was not how he had envisioned things when he was growing up. In his fantasies then, all desirable things were attainable. When he finally met the woman who sent his heart spinning, he had imagined, he would woo her, court her, romance her and enjoy success with her. Later he would marry her. And spend a long happy life raising two adorable children with her.

Life, he had long since learned, was not like that. Annette Carlson was successful in her field, young, pretty, single, and all she would ever be to him was a facet of a strange breaking-and-entering case and a chapter in another Nantucket ghost story.

He took a shot from the top of the key. Swish.

Annette has her career, he thought. Elsewhere.

Another shot from the foul line. Swish.

Annette has a lover. Elsewhere.

A jump shot from the corner. Swish.

Annette has a life of her own. Elsewhere.

He walked over to a plastic bottle of chilled water that he had brought with him. He drank.

There was no room in Annette Carlson's life to ever include him. He was a town cop. Nothing more. Nothing less. The reality of his situation settled upon him. For the first time in his life, when he suddenly wanted to be more, he realized that he couldn't.

Some of his father's choicer words haunted him from years gone by.

"Is that all you aspire to, son? Is that all you want to be? With your potential? With the education you have?"

"Come on, Dad," he grumbled aloud. "Leave me alone. Good cops are hard to come by."

No one answered. A touch of incipient madness. Talking to himself on a public basketball court in the dying light of a summer evening.

Sullenly, he set down the water bottle and walked back to the foul line. Where the hell was George Osaro?

God damned little Jap!

The thought came to him involuntarily, as so many seemed to over the last few days. Immediately, he was ashamed of himself. George was his friend. And Tim Brooks hated few aspects of human misbehavior quite as much as he hated bigotry.

God damned little Jap!

The sentence was within his mind again like an acid flash. This time he practically had to physically reject it.

Then he realized. It was that involuntary inner voice that seemed to spring from nowhere yapping at him again.

"Go away," he said aloud. It did. It was as if a little imp, whispering in his ear, had been dispatched. But Brooks could almost hear a little patter of demonic laughter as the imp departed.

Back to the foul line. There Timothy Brooks reigned. He authored another string of consecutive foul shots. This time he hit fifteen consecutively before one kissed the rim, skipped to the backboard, rebounded onto the rim again and then fell away. Fifteen straight. His personal record on this court was forty-one. In game competition in high school he once had twenty-two. In college, he'd sunk nineteen. In the second round of the National Invitational Tournament one year, he had been twelve for twelve.

He started again. This time he was at nine when he heard the readily recognizable sound of Osaro's white Voyager and its cranky, grumbling engine.

The van rolled to a halt in the parking lot. Aiming for his

eleventh in a row, Brooks heard the Voyager's door slam shut. Retrieving the ball, Brooks saw his friend step out from the van and start toward the court.

Osaro held up a hand. Brooks smiled and waved back. Then he took another shot and missed.

"Ah. You're in terrific form," Osaro said, reaching the court. Osaro knew better than anyone how well Brooks could shoot fouls. It was a hallmark of their friendship that Osaro would never acknowledge a successful skein of shots. But he would be all over his friend when the detective missed.

"Shut up," said Brooks. "I was fine till you arrived."

"Likely story."

"You put any new dents in that piece of junk you're driving since I saw you last?"

"Fuck you, cop. You shoot any unarmed children since *I* saw *you* last."

"Yeah, two. But they deserved it."

Underhanded, Brooks tossed the ball to Osaro as hard as he could. Osaro made a clean catch of the ball—two arms cradled against his chest—and would not acknowledge that the force of Brooks' throw might have knocked the wind out of him had he not been looking.

Brooks grinned. So did Osaro. Osaro took a shot from twenty feet out on the left side. It rebounded off the backboard and went through the hoop.

"Lucky," said Brooks.

"I'm ready," said Osaro.

"You sure?"

"You saw that hoop. I'm ready, man."

"You got first ball in-bounds," Brooks said, settling in and taking his mind off Annette Carlson and 17 Cort Street for the first time that day. "Play," he said.

They played until dark. For a while, some teenagers played another game on the adjoining court.

Playing with unusual intensity, the policeman demolished the pastor 50–32, then 50–38.

220

"Jesus Christ," muttered George Osaro as they walked back to their cars in the lot. "What's eating you today?"

Brooks shrugged. "I just needed some exercise," he lied. "Nothing's bothering me at all."

Osaro let Brooks' response hang in the air for almost a full minute. He said nothing further until the two of them were almost to their cars.

"Liar," Osaro finally said. "You're involved with either a woman or a case. Or both. Think I'm an idiot?"

"George . . ."

Osaro laughed. "I told you, Timmy," he said. "I got this gift. I see things that you don't. I *feel* things that you don't. I've got an altogether superior intellect."

He laughed again.

"Don't ever doubt that for a second," Osaro continued. "Nostradamus predicted that Asian people would eventually triumph in the world. Are you forgetting that?"

"Nostradamus said 'Chinese.' "

"Don't get picky!"

They reached their cars.

"Think I don't know you're falling in love, Timmy?" Osaro murmured to close the evening. "Think I can't read your thoughts? Think I can't tell?"

Fifteen

Early the next morning, Wednesday, the twenty-ninth of July, Tim Brooks picked up Annette at her house and drove her to the airport. She would take a forty-minute flight to Boston. She would take the ferry across Boston Bay, then a taxi to the doctor's office. There she would keep her appointment with Gary Rossling, M.D.

Brooks returned to 17 Cort Street. He parked his car on the street before the quiet house. He used the extra house key that she kept under a rock in the garden.

The rear door opened and Brooks entered the house.

In the midmorning, 17 Cort Street was very quiet. Very still. Peaceful as a tomb.

Somewhere in the distance, Brooks heard the sound of two children talking. He glanced at the window that overlooked the front lawn. A boy and a girl were passing the house on bicycles.

Several minutes went by. He looked through the downstairs. Then he heard a distant thump somewhere upstairs.

He thought nothing about it. Frequently crows or sea gulls landed on the roof and clawed at the shingles. Then he heard the same sound again. A second time he dismissed it. Then when it happened a third time, he went to investigate.

He walked to the base of the stairs. The sound came from on high in the house. Timothy's first instinct was to walk upstairs, all the way to the attic if necessary. Then he entertained a better idea.

He walked to the back door. He would throw something at whatever bird was on the roof. More direct. And secretly, more fun. The Audubon Society be damned!

He walked outside. Squinting in the sunlight, he looked up to the roof.

Oh, really? he thought.

There was nothing there. For a moment, he was puzzled.

So they flew away when they heard the back door open! The little feathered buggers!

He grinned. Well, too bad. He would have enjoyed heaving a stone at something today. Not that he could hit the ocean from the end of a pier in his current mood. He went back into the house.

Another thump. A heavier one this time.

What the hell? he wondered.

He was irritated now. Something made him think of his boyhood back in Ohio. His mean-spirited uncle Marty used to prowl a barn with a twenty-two-caliber rifle, blowing away field mice. Not a bad idea. Timothy Brooks was a lifelong hawk on the subject of household pests. What use did they serve, anyway?

Two more thumps.

Ah, screw it! he thought.

He walked up the front stairs. The noises, intermittent as they were, grew louder as he drew closer. But they weren't on the second floor. He passed the bedroom door and continued to search. For that matter, he decided as he heard the sound again, they were too close to be on the roof. And they weren't the sounds of branches brushing against the outer walls of the house. He could tell that, too.

The noises were . . . *within* the house.

In the attic.

Brooks moved through the second floor. He stepped carefully to the landing below the back staircase that rose to the attic. A tiny wave of anxiety overtook him.

Squirrels? he wondered. A raccoon? A bird that somehow had crept under the eaves?

Sure, cop! Come and get me!

He recalled that there was only one window to the attic and Annette had carefully placed a screen upon it. The screen, he knew, was still in place. He had just seen it when he was outside.

"So what the hell is up there?" he said aloud.

I am, you ass. Wreacking havoc!

Then he realized. That second voice within him, the involuntary one, was addressing him again. Why? Maybe he should listen this time. Maybe it would tell him something.

The voice came back. *I'll tell you something when I'm damned ready, scum!*

Brooks' anxiety turned to something heavier. His instincts told him not to fool with whatever was on the other side of the attic door. Then he collected his thoughts rationally. He gave himself a good mental lecture.

Scared? The alien voice asked him. Mocked him. Then it vanished, as if something were lifted from him.

Tim Brooks stood at the base of the stairs, gazing upward. But as he stared at the door at the top of the steps, he felt his heart start to flutter. Above him, stark and mysterious, firm and unyielding, the attic door remained tightly shut. Ominously.

Oh, hell! Where does Annette keep the key, anyway? he wondered. Probably on her key chain which is probably with her in Boston. A lot of good it's doing me there! he concluded. Damn! Better tell her to leave it here in the future.

More thumps. Then a few taps. Then there was a loud bang. With the flashlight in his hand, Timothy took a step up the final stairs in the house. Just one step. Then another. Then a third.

He stopped short. Then he recoiled. There was movement on the other side of the door. It sounded like a human. Or maybe a large animal. Claws or talons against the wood of the attic floor.

Impossible! I'm not ready to believe this! he thought.

The attic was locked from the outside. What could possibly be in there?

But then there was another loud bang in the attic, so sharp that it jolted him. And this bang was as if something hard and

224

wooden had been hurled against the wall, then fallen to the floorboards and rolled.

Yes. Definitely, it had rolled! It sounded like a croquet ball rolling on a wooden floor.

He whispered, What in God's name . . . ?

Brooks felt himself turning against this confrontation. But he summoned up his nerve.

"Hey!" he yelled. "Get out of there!"

A human voice—his own voice—echoed through the silence of the upper floor and the attic. It resounded. It echoed almost as if it belonged to someone else.

Timothy held still. Whatever was in the attic, a squirrel, a raccoon, a cat, or a . . . Whatever it was, it had been silenced. Scared off by a human voice! Or at least stilled by one!

He drew a breath and summoned up more nerve.

There were six more steps to the top landing and to the attic door. Brooks reckoned that he would climb them, knock hard on the door, shake the doorknob as if he were coming in and scare off whatever was in there for good!

That's what he reckoned. But he never took another step forward.

He was lifting his foot to climb further when he encountered a blast of cold air. Not just cold. Frigid. Icy. As if someone had opened a freezer door. The air enveloped him and seemed to enclose him.

He looked all around. There was nowhere for a draft to come from. And anyway, the blast seemed to have come from the attic and the attic door remained closed.

Physically, at least, it was closed. He would later remember thinking. But spiritually, it's wide open, isn't it? As open and beckoning as a freshly dug grave!

Gaping open. Beckoning.

Brooks suppressed a deeply sickened feeling as the cold air held him. Then—

Oh, God! What's this? I do not believe this!

—it almost felt as if a force were pushing hard against him.

Oh, dear God! Something horrible is here!

Brooks was at a loss to describe or understand it. But he felt it. He knew he felt it. He suffered a fresh perception: Something evil! Yes, something deeply evil hovers just out of sight.

He was suddenly deeply afraid it was going to attack and kill him.

Then another idea seemed to slip inside him from somewhere. It was something like the nightmare he had had at his home, the dark deathly one with the little demon chewing at his gonads. Instinctively, he put a hand to his testicles to protect himself.

He expected to feel the pain. He expected the nightmare to be fulfilled.

Then he suddenly had a very different feeling. Almost as if he knew he were being watched.

But from where? By whom?

Brooks heard a voice. It was his own. Self-defensive. Almost involuntary.

"All right!" he shouted. "I'm going! I'm leaving!"

He stepped back, off balance. Almost as if he were being shoved. And he retreated quickly down the attic steps. He was almost screaming. He had the overwhelming sense that something was there beside him. Something invisible! Chasing him, physically repelling him down those steps.

Something driving him away from the attic door.

He arrived at the base of the stairs and he kept going for several feet. The iciness was gone. He stood stock-still, his heart pounding. Nothing pursued him anymore, but he kept backing away.

"Okay," he said aloud. "I'm going. Okay? I'm going. See?"

He felt like a fool. But he kept his promise. He went back downstairs.

He found a few bottles of beer in Annette's refrigerator and opened one. Then he sat in the kitchen for several minutes, thinking and listening.

Eventually, he retreated outdoors into the bright sunlight. He felt safer out there. He looked at his watch. Only three hours until it would be time to head to Nantucket airport and fetch Annette.

Three hours.

His heart was still fluttering. He kept looking up toward the attic, but from the outdoors he saw nothing.

Had this really happened? Had he imagined it?

And why had he backed off? Why hadn't he stood up to whatever enemy was there?

Cowardice? Was that the word for it?

There was no way, he realized, that he could ever describe what had just happened to him. To someone who hadn't experienced it, it was indescribable.

It was difficult enough, he realized, to play it back in detail to himself.

Three hours.

Brooks started to mark the minutes. He figured he would live that long. But had anyone asked him at that particular moment, he would not have been so sure of his answer.

Sixteen

The offices of Gary Rossling, M.D., were on a tree-lined city street in Cambridge. Dr. Rossling, the psychiatrist, had a pair of graduate degrees from Harvard, tacked on top of an undergraduate sheepskin from the University of California at Berkeley. Now he was in a lucrative private practice, wrote influential articles for half of the best professional publications, and was affiliated with the Department of Psychiatry at Massachusetts General Hospital. There he was already a full professor.

This much Annette knew after arriving at the address of his private practice and spending five minutes in the waiting room. Yet when the door to his inner office finally opened, Dr. Rossling was not what Annette had expected.

Annette had anticipated a small intense man with a pinched, shrewd face. He'd be bearded perhaps, dark but graying, and inevitably with glasses. An aging Robin Williams from *Awakenings*. Or any of a hundred faded cliché-ridden portraits of Sigmund Freud.

Instead, Rossling was a young man, probably no more than thirty-five. He was handsome and tall, his hair reddish blond. His name may have been Austrian but his face was Irish. There were no eyeglasses and his stature and bearing were more those of a college baseball coach than a university lecturer.

Annette's most recent therapist in Los Angeles had faxed Dr. Rossling a copy of her medical history, including three pages pertaining to her hospitalization for depression in Connecticut.

Rossling had apparently read everything thoroughly before their meeting.

"Hello, hello," he said when he met her, coming to his office door. He offered his hand.

"I'm Gary Rossling," he said. "Come in. Sit down. Make yourself comfortable. We should talk a little before any of the professional mumbo jumbo."

From that opening, Annette had a feeling she was going to like him. For a moment her gaze settled upon his hands. They were large and strong. Like those of a boxer she had once met on a film set in Los Angeles. Powerful. Positive. Affirmative. At the fringe of her consciousness flashed a warning about disturbed women who become sexually involved with their psychotherapists.

Disturbed women? Her? Annette? Well, she had come to Dr. Rossling's office on her own volition, hadn't she?

She tuned out the thought.

He eased into an hour session, asking casual, nonpersonal questions at the outset. Then he posed a lengthy series of questions relating to her background. The questions tended to be clinical in nature and also addressed the time when Annette had been taking drugs.

When that line of discussion ended, Dr. Rossling invited Annette into the next room. He termed it his "conference" room. It was actually his examining area.

It was a comfortably furnished chamber, primarily in a gentle shade of green. The light was subdued. There was a couch. But more than anything else, the couch seemed to exist more to observe the conventions of a doctor's office and confirm patients' expectation.

Annette didn't use it and was not invited to. She sat in a leather armchair across a short coffee table from Dr. Rossling. He sat in an identical chair across from her. A pad of yellow legal paper lay across his lap and in his left hand—she noticed immediately that he was left-handed—a sharp Ticonderoga pencil stood sentry.

"Tell me why you feel the need to talk to someone again," Dr. Rossling asked.

Annette thought about it and asked a question in return. "With all honesty?"

"Any other way is a waste of time for both of us," he said.

"I think I'm seeing ghosts," she said, raising her eyes to meet the doctor's as she hit the key word.

For an instant Dr. Rossling looked surprised, almost amused. This changed quickly to a look of puzzlement.

Then, "Ghosts, huh?" he asked softly.

"Ghosts," Annette Carlson said. "I think. . . . Oh, I don't know what I think. . . . Maybe it's tied up with tension. You know, work pressures, combined with"—she hesitated here for a moment and Dr. Rossling caught it—"my mother's death two years ago. On Academy Awards' night she had a stroke." She looked up. "I'm sure it's all in my records."

Dr. Rossling nodded without looking at the records. He had read carefully. He recalled.

"What do they look like?" the psychiatrist finally asked. "These things you see."

She told him.

He received her account very pensively. Mostly, he listened in silence, making occasional notes to himself on his yellow pad. He asked a question from time to time also, usually pertaining to a small detail of what she said she had observed.

Annette's account took more than half an hour. Toward the end of it, Dr. Rossling flipped the first page of his notepad and began a second sheet of observations. He had written down, Annette realized, more than she had thought. Those large, strong hands obviously wrote quickly.

Finally she concluded. There was a pause in the room for several seconds before Gary Rossling looked up from what he was writing.

"This is not to take issue with you," he said with understanding. "But I don't know much about ghosts. I don't think I've ever met one. Never knowingly had the experience. I don't dismiss anything, though." He approached it rationally. "I suppose I'd find it very interesting if it happened. Do you find it interesting?"

"I don't find it interesting or uninteresting," Annette said, almost with irritation. "I live with it. More than anything, I find it frightening."

"Upsetting? Unsettling?"

"Very."

"And you'd like it to stop?"

"Yes."

"That's good. That's a start." Dr. Rossling folded his arms. His gaze settled into Annette's. "Why do you think you're still seeing them if you don't want to see them?" he asked.

Annette thought about it. She shrugged.

"Because I don't think there's anything wrong with me," she said. "I think what I'm seeing is actually there."

Dr. Rossling smiled. He wrote something down. "Who knows?" he added philosophically and without looking up. "Maybe it is. Or maybe *something* is. 'Actually there,' I mean."

He then guided her through a final sequence of questions. Some of them backtracked over territory covered in the transcripts. Others addressed her mental state at the time she had received her Academy Award. Her mental state, and how it wrapped itself around her mother's sudden passing.

"Were there things that you and your mother had planned to do that you never got to do?" he asked. "How much do you think your grief intermingled with guilt?"

And so on.

Annette answered as best as she could. Fifty minutes of the hour session had soon been filled.

"All right," Dr. Rossling said when Annette appeared to be talked out. "I think that's enough for today. At least on your part. Maybe *I* should gab a little."

He was still making notes. She smiled hopefully as he looked up and put down his pencil. Yet the doctor appeared disturbed.

"Oh, come on," Annette finally demanded. "At least tell me something."

Dr. Rossling sighed, gently tapping a finger on his writing

tablet. "Well," he said, "it's somewhat perplexing. Quite clearly, you're an intelligent woman. Educated. Well balanced. Stable. In control of your faculties of reason." He paused. "Yet you entertain these disturbing visions."

"And I want to be rid of them."

"And you want to be rid of them," he affirmed. He scratched his temple for a moment and exhaled thoughtfully. "It would be completely irresponsible and unprofessional for me to attempt any sort of diagnosis or conclusion after one meeting."

"But you must have something to send me out the door with," she pressed again.

Dr. Rossling pursed his lips. "I'll sell you a few thoughts. Check that. I'll toss them in free for the admission price you've already paid." He smiled. He gave her a wink. He motioned to the adjoining room, the one they had come from.

"Come back into my office," he said. "That's the place to talk."

Annette followed him. Her eyes had accustomed themselves to the diminished light of Dr. Rossling's examination room. The bright Cambridge daylight outside filtered through a venetian blind. The return was so jarring that Annette realized immediately how different the moods of the two rooms were, just as the psychiatrist had intended.

"Look," he said, sitting down, "you're an adult patient. You're not manic depressive. I doubt that you're schizoid or a closet psychotic. Very obviously, you lead as normal a life as anyone in your profession—no offense—could hope to. You're well suited to functioning among sane people in a normal society."

He watched her closely as she settled into a chair.

"Overall, and I stress that these are just preliminary impressions," he continued, "your mental health would seem fine. Your previous bout with depression seems to have enjoyed a full recovery. And I take you at your word that you're not abusing any substance."

He waited for reassurance.

"I'm not," she promised him.

232

"Good." He switched gears. "I suppose we could do an electroencephalogram to see if we turn up any brain-wave abnormality," he said. "But I'd rather reject doing one at this time. I see that one was done three years ago when you underwent depression and the EEG back then didn't show much of interest at all. I see no reason to do one diagnostically now when your overall mental state would appear to be much better than it was three years ago. Unless you *wanted* one now," the psychiatrist said warily. "And even if you did, I'd argue against it."

"I don't want one," Annette said.

"Quite frankly," Dr. Rossling continued, speaking slowly and looking at her carefully, "judging by our conversation, I'm strongly tempted to suggest that there's some external physical force at work here. Something completely divorced from your mental health or your faculties of psychological perception."

Annette frowned. "In plain English, what do you mean by 'an external force?'"

"Sorry," he said. "I'm not accusing anyone. But might someone be instigating these 'ghost' appearances?"

"I still don't get you. What do you mean?"

"Could someone be having a mean joke with you? A complex prank, perhaps? Oh, maybe there might not even be any malice to it, Ms. Carlson. I've heard about some really convincing performances. And I'm sure you *do* know people who'd be adept at 'special effects' of a fairly sophisticated sort. I've seen stranger things from—"

"No," she said, cutting him off. "I don't think that's a possibility." She hesitated for a moment. "And even if it were, how would you explain the appearance of Mrs. Ritter several hours after she died?"

"Well," he said somberly, playing detective for a moment, "there are certainly possibilities of fraud there. Don't you think? Did you ever check the official coroner's report of exactly when she died?"

"No," Annette allowed.

"Okay," Dr. Rossling continued. "Now, I might be putting

233

myself out of business on this tack, but have you reported what you've seen to the police?"

"Yes."

"And?"

She thought of Tim Brooks. "The investigating detective didn't believe what I was seeing, either," she said without expression. "Then he witnessed one of these incidents, himself."

Dr. Rossling was surprised by the response. He weighed it. "He did, huh?"

"That's right."

"And he took what he saw to be a ghost, too?" His eyes narrowed. "I'm understanding this correctly?"

"You are."

Dr. Rossling was clearly puzzled. Annette half expected a comment about dumb cops. But the psychiatrist only fingered his notepad.

"I see," he finally said at the end of several seconds. "That's right. You told me you had a witness to the most recent incident. That gentleman was a policeman?"

She nodded.

For several seconds Dr. Rossling pondered the point. Then he wrote something down.

"Okay, then," Rossling finally said. "I'd like to exclude the actual existence of ghosts to start with. Not because I necessarily disbelieve. Rather, because we should look first at the more *likely* explanation of what's going on. Barring the existence of some merry pranksters, again, that leads us invariably to stress and trauma, as well as opthalmic misperception and disorientation. Even, in a very broad sense, hallucination. Are you following me?"

Annette answered that yes, she was.

"Again, these are just initial impressions," the doctor said. "But I think you're very much in control of yourself and capable of understanding what I'm going to discuss."

Annette sat very still and listened. They had already run past their scheduled sixty minutes.

"Hallucination takes many forms," Dr. Rossling explained.

"Normally, when not chemically induced, it stems from hysteria. Hysteria, too, can take a variety of forms. It can be very broad or—possibly in your case—very, very narrow and focused upon one line of thought. Accepting mortality, for example. Your own. That of your mother. Potentially that of your father. Or maybe of a friend."

Dr. Rossling smiled reassuringly.

"Somewhere in the dark recesses of the sprawling psychiatric industry," he said, "they even have a word for this: 'thanatophobia.' Great term, isn't it? Comes from 'thanatology,' which is the scientific study of the phenomena surrounding death. It's a deep fear of people dying, often very well obscured within the psyche. It tends to afflict children more than adults, or at least people who have never survived a close death before." He paused. "Obviously, that aspect of it doesn't apply to your case, though in a larger sense I suppose it could *if* enough remained unsettled in your own unconsciousness." He thought for a moment. "I should have asked earlier: are there any other deaths in the last few years that deeply affected you? Not just in your personal and private life. But maybe something public? A famous person? Someone in your industry whom you had always respected or hoped to work with?"

Annette searched for a name. Then she shook her head. "No," she answered. "No one."

Again he paused. "It might be significant that the specters you've seen are women. But right now, I couldn't say. I'd only be guessing."

Annette nodded.

The doctor continued. "So obviously, we're looking for something more elusive. Something deeper, perhaps. And obviously again, I'd like to discuss these problems with you further, as long as you continue to feel the need to talk."

He tapped gently on his desk. Thinking. Searching. Maybe pondering.

"I suspect deep down there probably *is* something," he said. "And we should try to get at it."

"Uh huh."

" 'Ghosts,' " he said again. "This really isn't exactly my line. But I will tell you a story that I believe to be germane to what we're discussing." For a moment he focused on some inner thought. "And I have to tell you: This is what's really troubling me today," he said. He glanced at his watch. A Rolex. "Do you have a few extra minutes? We're running over our time, but I won't charge you."

Annette had the extra minutes and didn't care about the charges.

"My theories would tend toward believing that such apparitions originate in the mind," he said. "Even if the experiences are shared with another individual, as you say one was. My feelings lead me to recall a paper I read a few years ago in the psychiatric journals. It was very striking. The content stayed with me. It concerned a local group, I think it was the Boston Society for Psychic Research. Something like that. I'm sure I could find the material if I looked for it."

Somewhere outside there was the sound of a car horn, followed by skidding tires, metal crunching metal and then angry voices. Yes, this is metropolitan Boston, Annette thought. The doctor read her mind and smiled.

"The Society attempted an experiment one summer," Dr. Rossling continued. "They wanted to determine whether ghosts were actually the spirits of the dead, some sort of disembodied entity, or figments of the unconscious mind. So they set about to manufacture a 'ghost.' "

Dr. Rossling leaned back in his chair.

"There were three male doctors who were involved. Two psychologists and a psychiatrist. They invented a case history of a man named Charles," he continued, "a contemporary and friend of Abraham Lincoln. Charles had an affair with a black woman named Althea. When Charles' wife found out about it, she had Althea accused of murder. Althea was convicted and hanged. Ultimately, Charles committed suicide on the same day Lincoln was shot."

Annette listened.

"The researchers created a suitable background for their

ghost—an old plantation house in South Carolina—and spent summer weekends there trying to conjure up the spirit that they had invented."

"Conjure up how?"

"So-called seances. No medium. Just the three of them and an ordinary table in this old mansion."

A table. Annette felt something morbid come over her, a sense of foreboding that lay coiled within her like a length of rope, ready to unravel and tighten at anytime.

"A table," she repeated aloud.

"Something small. Card table size," he said, sensing no significance to the act of contacting spirits through a table.

"Please continue," Annette said.

"They worked on it for six or seven months," Dr. Rossling said, recalling. "Finally, they were just about to give up when they felt a sharp rap on their table one night. They used a code to communicate with their 'spirit.' One rap for yes. Two raps for no. The spirit, or whatever was rapping, claimed to be Charles. It repeated the story they had created. At later sentences, before a television camera, the spirit—or something—actually was seen to levitate the table. It could also move small objects around the room through what the Society termed 'psychokinesis.' That's moving objects through mental force rather than physical. 'Charles' even threw the table once."

Dr. Rossling drew a breath. Annette was very still, conscious of her heartbeat. The psychiatrist continued.

"The three men involved considered the experiment a triumph," Rossling said. "They contended that the 'Charles' persona was wholly a product of their creativity. And the appearance of his spirit was a product of their unconscious minds."

"So?" Annette asked.

Dr. Rossling had now run far past his allotted hour with her. There was the sound of some discussion in the waiting room.

"The truth is," the psychiatrist said, "that what the three researchers did was very unscientific. They held a number of seances until their original prophesy was fulfilled. They kept their 'research' going, in other words, until they arrived at the results they wanted. The most likely explanation for what happened is that the three researchers induced a mutual self-hypnosis on each other. Thus they shared the same hallucination because they had decided in advance what the hallucination would be."

Annette smiled slightly, following the doctor's logic. Temporarily, something about the story mildly relieved her.

"Even people who ardently believe in such things as poltergeists and feral spirits totally discredit the Boston Society's conclusions. They maintain that the spirit that descended upon them—if indeed one did, as you know I'm a skeptic—could have been *any* bored spirit, wandering through eternity, looking for something to do."

The doctor shrugged playfully. He rolled his eyes. Then he turned serious again.

"But that's not the point of my telling you this story," he said. He stood as their time together came to an end.

"No? What is?" She stood, too.

"For some reason, the whole episode evolved under an ill star," Dr. Rossling said. "I don't know any of the circumstances surrounding the private lives of any of the three men. But about a year after the final seance, one of the researchers murdered one of the other two. Came into the laboratory one day with a kitchen carving knife from home. Day after Easter, if I recall. He slashed his psychiatrist friend along the jugular vein. Ear to ear. A week or so later, the third member of the team suffered what has to be called a psychotic break with reality. Mental breakdown. Never came out of it. So that's my point. Within two years after seeing their ghost—or their hallucination—one man was dead, one was serving a twenty-five-year prison sentence for homicide and the other was in an insane asylum."

He let this sink in.

"So what I'm saying, Miss Carlson," he said softly, "is that *I* take your story and your problem very seriously. These things—the alleged manifestation of spirits—can translate very easily into a very bad case of stress-related hysteria. I want you to come back. And I want to help you dispose of what you're seeing while we can still keep things under control."

The doctor paused.

"Is anyone staying with you at the present time?"

"No."

"Is there anyone on Nantucket you could call if you needed to be with someone urgently?"

Timothy Brooks, she thought. So, "Yes," Annette answered.

"I think that's constructive," Dr. Rossling said. "A rational voice nearby is a healthy counterpoint. Can you come back some time next week?"

Annette nodded. On her way out, she made a follow-up appointment.

On the evening of the same day, just past six, Brooks was waiting with the car at the airport in Nantucket. As soon as Annette saw him, she knew something was wrong. Moments after that, she had an inkling as to what it might be.

"You saw something, didn't you?" she asked. "You were in the house alone and something happened."

He exhaled long and hard as he pulled his car out of the airport parking lot. "Maybe worse than saw," he admitted. "I heard. I felt."

"Uh oh," she said. "Let's hear about it."

He explained as they drove back to Cort Street. The knocks and the thumps. The rattling of something hard rolling across the attic floorboards. The icy blast at the top of the stairs. The sense that something was chasing him away from the door.

Then they rode part of the way in silence, each alone with individual thoughts. He asked a few questions about Dr. Rossling, but the questions were intended only to break the tension. There was no question about what was on either of their minds. And perhaps they shared the same visions telepathically, for the discussion quickly drifted from Dr. Rossling back to the house and what had transpired there.

To her own amazement, it was Annette's turn to be the skeptic, or at least play the role of the Devil's advocate.

"Icy air," she said, pondering the point. "There's always the possibility that it wasn't as cold as you thought. A strong draft could have emanated from a sudden wind outside. You know how leaky the roofs of some of these old houses can be. Well," she added, "maybe you don't."

He drove and listened to this in brooding, unsettled silence.

"And as for thinking that something was there pushing you back down," she suggested, "you are probably a man of strong imagination. So it's always possible that you—"

At first he wasn't sure whether she was serious or not, whether she was trying to tweak him for his previous reluctance to believe.

Then, "That's bull," he said softly and sullenly. "I heard it. I felt it."

"But you didn't actually *see* anything," she answered.

"If I'd had the key to that damned door, I would have seen it," he muttered, anger and tension coming together in his tone. "It was scratching around on the other side. Where *is* the key?"

"Right here," she answered.

Her keys were already clenched in her hand. With a jingle, she held up a silver chain bearing at least a dozen keys. Keys for Massachusetts. Keys for California. Keys for a mailbox. Keys for her father's home in Oregon, the one she grew up in and hadn't lived in for eleven years.

He looked at the keys, then looked away. He turned the car onto Main Street. They were minutes from Cort Street. He looked at the road ahead and so did she.

For a moment Annette thought she had spotted the little blond girl in the 1950s style dress, the one who had appeared and disappeared so quickly the evening she had followed Mrs. Ritter's ghost back to Mid Island Convalescent. Then Annette realized with a start that all she was looking at was the light from the setting sun playing illusory tricks through a white picket fence. There was no little girl at all.

Minutes later, they were in the driveway at Number Seventeen. For a moment, they sat.

"Are we going up?" she asked. "To the attic?"

Brooks looked toward the uppermost points of the house, the section of slanting roof just above the attic and the one attic window, which was still neatly screened.

"I am if you are," he said.

"If it's an hallucination," she said, echoing Dr. Rossling's thoughts, "I want to stop seeing it. If it's real, we might as well find out what it wants, and try to get rid of it. I want my house back. Right?" She looked to him for confidence.

"Let's do it now," he said. "Before it's dark."

They entered the house through the rear door. The structure was quiet. Annette turned on a light and held still. She saw nothing and heard nothing.

She didn't sense anything, either. She motioned with her head and they walked upstairs together. A minute and a half later, they were standing at the base of the attic stairs, shining a flashlight upward.

She took the first step. But Timothy placed a hand on her shoulder, stopping her and motioned that he would go first. She nodded.

She held the light and walked up the steps, one by one. He waited for the icy blast to materialize again. Halfway up the steps it still hadn't. The attic door and its lock grew larger in front of him.

He reached behind him and took the key from her. Three steps from the top he stopped. Then he went the final distance, stair by stair.

He was at the top. Still no resistance.

"Still with me?" he asked.

"Still with you." Gently, she touched his arm with her hand. Gratitude. Moral support. He appreciated both.

He placed the key in the lock. At first the mechanism resisted. Then it gave way stubbornly. A loud click announced that the lock had opened.

Brooks could feel sweat streaming down his brow. With a wet

palm he put his hand against the doorknob. He turned it slowly. The latch opened. He gave the door a push. It went wide open in complete silence.

Brooks stepped into the attic. Annette was right behind him. The room was stuffy but quiet. It was dim and shadowy, but there was enough light to enable them to see. The sheets still appeared to be over the furnishings where Annette had left them. David swept the room with the flashlight.

Annette's hand went to the light switch. She turned on the three bare bulbs that hung at various points.

At first nothing struck them as being askew. Her gaze ran around the room. Then suddenly it settled.

"Oh, Christ!" she said aloud.

"What?" he blurted.

"That!" She raised a hand, finger extended, and pointing toward the sheet that had rested upon the ventriloquist's doll. The Charlie McCarthy dummy. That was the one sheet in the room that had been disturbed. It was wrinkled and badly disheveled. As she looked closer, the doll's hand was visible from beneath the sheet, hanging limp like a dead man's.

Not how she had left it at all. Not the way he had seen it last, either.

"Now what?" she said softly. It was either a rhetorical question or a statement.

Annette walked cautiously to where the dummy had lain neatly beneath a sheet. Her hand had a quiver to it as she reached to the small wooden body.

"Annette, careful," Tim warned, his voice barely above a whisper. "Want me to do that?"

But by this time, she was undeterred. At least for the moment. "No," she said.

She held the sheet in her hand, then yanked it back. She dropped it with a shriek, raised her hand to her mouth in horror and looked away.

She recoiled into Timothy's arms. He held her tightly as he looked, too.

He muttered a low, mild oath. But he did not avert his eyes. He stared, transfixed. Stupefied. Astonished.

Someone—or something—had smashed and mutilated the doll. Its clothing had been removed and its limbs had been spread out in all four directions, as if it had been tied to stakes.

Then, as if with some blunt instrument, all four limbs had been smashed. They had each been broken in single crucial points, the arms above the bare elbows, the legs above the knees.

Thump. Thump. Thump. In his memory, Brooks could still hear it.

But the mutilation of the limbs wasn't even the worst part. Charlie McCarthy's head was gone. Whatever force had broken the arms had finished the project—or maybe had started it—with a decapitation.

Annette started to cry. Brooks tried to pull her from the room.

"Who the hell is doing this?" she cried. "Why won't it stop?"

Timothy tried to get her out of the attic again, but she would not leave. Not until she had located the dummy's head.

It was lying clear across the attic. It looked to have been pitched across the room and against the attic wall.

Then it had rolled—Brooks had heard it roll—until it lodged in a corner.

The clothes? The doll's black top hat? A small pile was found under the table upon which the dummy rested. Compactly arranged. Neatly folded. Almost in a mocking fashion.

Annette took the mangled doll in her arms. She held the head and retrieved the clothes. She found a small canvas duffel bag and put the doll, its many broken parts and its attire, all together in the bag.

"I know a puppet man in West Hollywood," she said between sobs. "Brilliant man. Works in films. He can fix anything."

"Of course, he can," Brooks assured her.

"We're fighting back, Tim," she said to him, recovering, her will growing stronger. "This was my mother's. We'll ship him out to be repaired tomorrow. Right? Tomorrow!"

"Tomorrow," Brooks agreed.

Shaken, they left the attic. They relocked the door. No force followed them. No icy air. No sense of being pushed or pursued.

They walked downstairs. Annette laid the duffel bag nearby on a sofa in the living room. She collapsed onto the sofa and looked at Timothy.

"Where do you live on this island?" she asked.

He described his lodgings on the opposite shore.

"Do you have a guest room?"

"I have a sofa," he said.

"Can I use it? Tonight? To sleep?"

For an instant, he didn't realize she was serious. Then it hit him.

"Well, yes. Of course. But—"

"Thanks. I'll only be a minute."

She disappeared upstairs to collect a few things for overnight. Stunned once again, he might have been euphoric. But that voice was back. The one inside him. The one he didn't like.

You can put the dummy's head back on, you pious scumbag! it croaked. *Won't be so easy with two human heads. Yours and hers! Yours and hers! Ah, what a lovely day for some more decapitations!*

Something feeling like ice crystals flowed through his veins.

"Go away," he whispered.

The voice dissolved in laughter.

Moments later, Brooks was more than relieved when Annette returned again downstairs and gave him a brave smile.

"All right," she said. "Let's go."

Seventeen

Brooks drove to his cottage. He parked in his driveway and led Annette to the front door.

"It's humble," he warned her, "but it's home."

His cottage was cozier in the evening than during the day. Night had a way of hiding many of its shortcomings. He turned on a pair of Cape Cod-style lamps in the living room. The softness of their light gave the room a homey touch.

She looked around and smiled. "I like it," she said. "You decorated this by yourself?"

"Me and the local thrift shop," he said with a smile.

"You did well." She meant it.

"For a policeman's salary . . ." he said with a shrug. "I could do worse. I'll say this much, there's probably nothing like it in Beverly Hills."

"I wouldn't know," she said, "I spend as little time there as possible."

He laughed. He carried her overnight bag into the bedroom and dropped it just inside the door. Then he offered her a seat in the living room. She relaxed into a club chair that he had once bought for fifteen dollars.

"I'm giving you my bedroom for the night," he said. "It will just take a moment to get it ready for you."

She protested, saying that she would sleep on the sofa. He said that he wouldn't hear of such an arrangement and told her not to argue. She was, after all, a guest.

"But I invited myself," he said.

"And I accepted your invitation," he reminded her. "So sit tight, okay?"

She waited as he quickly straightened his bedroom and remade the bed with fresh sheets.

"Can I get you something to drink?" he asked, returning to the living room. "Try to pick something I have."

"White wine?"

"Good guess. You win. It was that or beer."

"Beer was my second choice."

He went to his kitchen and retrieved a bottle of Chablis from his refrigerator. He opened it and poured two glasses of wine. He walked back to the living room and handed one to Annette. He set the other down on a coffee table in front of a sofa.

He leaned over his CD player, turned it on, and reached for a box of disks that lay beside the player. His hand came up with Joan Sutherland singing arias from an Italian opera. He went with it and set the disk into place.

She watched him the entire time, sipping liberally from the Chablis. She didn't speak until Dame Joan began to sing.

"What kind of cop are you?" she finally asked when he sat down on the sofa across from her.

"I'm a town cop."

"That's not what I mean," she said. "You're a detective and you seem to spend most of your off hours playing pickup basketball. You live on an island in the Northeast but you're from the Midwest. You should be solidly blue collar, but you pop Verdi onto your CD player."

"That's Puccini," he said.

She looked him in the eye.

"I know. It's *Tosca*. I was testing you."

"And I passed?"

"You're just becoming more and more unusual as a cop."

"I'll bet that you don't personally know very many cops," he said.

She sipped more wine. "Point," she said. "I don't. I played

246

a policewoman on television once but we didn't have a technical advisor on the set."

"What movie was that?" he asked. "Or what TV show?"

"Neither. It was a commercial for radial tires. An actor and I would swagger out of a police car and do a twenty-second speil about driving safety, all predicated on the brand of tires we were pitching. I think it was Goodyear. Or maybe it was Goodrich. Which one of them has the blimp?"

"Fuji," he said.

They both laughed. In a funny way, it sounded glamorous. *Acting* at being a cop.

"I missed that commercial," he finally said. "And here I thought I'd seen all of your work."

"Have you?" She was surprised, almost to the point of embarrassment.

"All the movies," he said. "None of the commercials."

"You never told me you'd seen my films."

"You didn't ask," he said. "Does it surprise you?"

"No, no," she said, setting down the wineglass. "It's just that. . . . Sometimes it's the first thing people say when I meet them." She imitated such a greeting: " 'Oh, Miss Carlson. I've seen *all* of your films . . .' And so on."

"Does it get tiresome?"

"It's well meaning, but yes. It gets tiresome."

"I figured as much. That's why I didn't mention it," he said. He looked at her glass, which was almost empty.

"More wine?" he asked. She accepted.

He guided the line of conversation farther afield. He moved through a half hour's worth of topics. Anything but ghosts, spirits, 17 Cort Street or his friend, George Andrew Osaro.

"Tell me something else," he finally asked.

"What's that?"

"Are you hungry?"

She allowed that she hadn't eaten since morning.

"Then we're in the wrong place," he said. "Let's go out, okay?"

"Only if you let me pay," she said.

"We'll do it dutch," he suggested. "How's that?"

"Okay."

They drove back into town and went for a late supper at one of the less formal restaurants near the ferry terminal on Straight Wharf. The place was crowded and noisy which allowed them just the reassuring atmosphere they needed to discuss the events of the day, from Dr. Rossling to the decapitated dummy in her attic to the collapse of the china cabinet in her home several days earlier.

They didn't leave until after eleven, at which time they drove past 17 Cort Street. The house was dark and quiet, almost ominous. They didn't speak as they passed it. Annette wished that she had left some lights on, but didn't feel like going back.

They arrived at Brooks' cottage at about eleven thirty. Annette excused herself a few minutes later. She disappeared into the bedroom and closed the door.

Tim Brooks settled in to spend the night in his living room. He drew the two large shades that covered the pair of windows that overlooked his front yard. He threw an extra pillow on the sofa. He kept his service revolver near him. He placed it under the sofa. It was out of view but within his reach.

Then he eased himself onto the sofa and lay back. He read a novel for almost half an hour, then felt drowsy. He turned the room lights off just past midnight.

Drifting toward sleep, his body gave one of those involuntary jumps that one suffers sometimes on the threshold of a dream. In any case, Brooks thought he felt something touch his shoulder in the darkness. At first he sensed it was Annette, but then—as his eyes opened a crack—he realized that her door was still shut.

So he whirled.

There was nothing there. He remained wakeful for several minutes, then settled back to sleep. He feared that he would have a second manifestation of his black nightmare. The dream with the black ghost. But nothing bothered him when he tried to sleep a second time.

Something, however lifted him from a peaceful rest toward

three A.M. From where he slept, all light in the living room had been sealed off from the outside. But the door leading down the hall to his kitchen was now open, even though he was certain he had closed it.

Light from outside, moonlight and one street lamp, flowed through a window over his dining alcove in the kitchen.

That light flowed down the hallway toward the living room. And as Brooks looked at it with sleepy eyes, he did not like the way it appeared. The light cast a long shadow that had a bizarre configuration. It was as if a man were standing in the doorway of Brooks' kitchen. The arms, legs and torso were defined quite clearly. But the rest was bizarre and in defiance of nature.

The figure was headless.

Brooks stared at this and gradually came to a greater wakefulness. It is impossible that anyone has come in here, he thought to himself.

He further wondered if the figure was that of Annette, and that he wasn't seeing clearly. And that her head was lowered.

Or is it an intruder? he wondered.

Gradually his hand moved from his bed. It went to the base of the sofa and pushed underneath. His wet palm settled upon the handle of his pistol.

He drew the weapon. In the darkness, he could hear the steel of the gun withdrawing from the leather of the holster.

Brooks rolled slowly off the sofa and onto the floor. He inched his way across the carpet.

What *was* casting that shadow? He moved on the floor for several feet, commando style, until he was almost in a position to see around the corner.

Then he was around the corner. He was at a terrible angle from which to see. Similarly, it was a terrible vision that was before him. Whatever was there *did* seem to be the figure of an intruder.

But it made no sense. He had been right the first time. It had no head!

Tall and black and—

It had no head!

No, this was not another dream. Using both hands he cradled the pistol before him. Sweat poured from his brow. He gave considerable thought to firing a bullet to see what would happen. But his instincts of safety with a firearm were too professional. Shooting first was against everything he had ever learned.

Shooting first was how innocent people got killed.

He held the figure in his sight. Then he spoke.

"Who's there?" he asked.

No answer.

"Talk to me. Don't move! Talk to me."

The figure seemed to shift slightly, almost as if it were floating not walking.

"Jesus!" he said. "Last chance! Talk or I'll shoot."

The arms of the figure seemed to move. But the feet didn't.

For some reason, a thought about George Osaro crossed his consciousness, then flew away again.

His finger tightened on the trigger.

Go ahead! Pull it! something inside him said.

Still, some other impulse urged restraint.

Brooks wanted to see—wanted to know—before he pulled a trigger.

He quietly rolled to the wall near his front door. He kept his eyes on the figure in the darkness. Brooks rose to a knee. His sweaty left palm groped upward along the wall until it found a light switch.

He threw it on.

Light—bright lights from three hundred watts of track lighting—flooded the room. Brooks squinted and blinked. He stared at the spot at the end of the hallway that led to the kitchen.

Empty! Empty as a desert canyon.

There was no figure present. Just thin air and a vacant space.

Still, he wasn't reassured. He let his eyes adjust. He kept his gun trained before him. Then slowly he walked down the hallway to the kitchen.

The door was ajar. Not the way he remembered leaving it. But he could have been mistaken.

He also could have been right.

An old enemy from my days in San Jose, he thought idly. Come to do business. Come to settle accounts.

He took several steps.

Bullshit! he thought to himself. I know I saw something!

He reached the kitchen door. He pushed it all the way open. It clattered.

Nothing.

An empty kitchen. The door to the outside was locked from within.

Abruptly, Tim Brooks sensed something—a malevolent, scheming presence—behind him. He turned suddenly, the pistol out.

Nothing again.

He drew a long breath and let it out slowly. What was going on? Some mind-game of hide-and-seek. *Cache-cache* with a poltergeist?

He searched every corner of the kitchen, the hallway and the living room. There is nothing here! he told himself over and over. Nothing!

He went back to the light switch in the living room. He crouched down and turned off the track lighting. He allowed his eyes to adjust and looked to the same spot at the end of the hall, wondering if he would see the same figure in the darkness.

He didn't. It was gone.

Then again, several minutes had passed. The moon had shifted in the sky outside. Different shadows would be cast into the house by now.

He waited several minutes in the darkness. When nothing happened, when nothing moved, when no other shadow accosted him, he went back to the sofa.

Wearily, he settled down to sleep again. He put the pistol back in his holster.

A wonderful way to live, he thought to himself, sleeping with a gun under your body.

Then suddenly he was jolted. *And a wonderful way to die,* cackled that irrepressibly petulant voice came to him at will now.

Brooks' heart raced. He recognized the voice. He knew it wasn't part of his subconscious. It was coming from God-knew-where and he was hearing it God-knew-how.

After many seconds, Brooks answered it.

"Why don't you just make yourself known?" Timothy whispered aloud to the darkness.

Silence followed. Brooks concentrated.

Then, *In time. In time,* came the silent response. *When YOU choose to contact me.*

"And how will I do that?" Brooks whispered again.

Elusive and coy. Taunting and mischievous. In a half-completed arc of sleep, Brooks listened again for an answer. None was forthcoming for several seconds.

Then, *How would you like a deep dark sleep?* the voice asked, not really in response. *A long sleep in a closed rosewood box, with your arms folded across your chest.*

"Shut up! You can't kill me," Brooks said aloud.

You and the girl in the next room. I'll kill both of you when the time is right. The voice almost had a texture now, rasping and shrill as it addressed the detective. Merry, devious and impishly clever. *Maybe you'd like to be buried together. Maybe in the same box. Arms and legs intertwined. Fetid genitals interlocking as your earthly flesh rots . . .*

"Where in God's name are you?" Brooks whispered. His voice was loud. His eyes searched the darkness. Sweat rolled from his forehead.

Waiting, the voice answered.

"Waiting where?"

Nearby.

"Waiting for what?"

The right time.

"The right time for what?"

To kill, the voice chirped. *To drag someone unwillingly into the afterlife. To put someone else in a box in a cold earthen hole.*

"So you've killed before?"

Oh, yes.

Brooks' next question was instinctive. "Did you kill the college girl?"

Of course I did.

"Why?"

The voice laughed.

"And you decapitated the dummy?"

My work, too.

"Why?"

Why not?

"Have there been others?"

Of course.

"Who?"

You'll know soon enough.

"Will you kill again?"

Yes.

"When?"

When I am ready.

"Who will you kill?"

You'll see, my dear ass! I'll arrange for you to make the discovery.

"A man or a woman?"

Anyone I want on this damned island.

"If you already know, prove it. Tell me who."

A man.

Brooks thought about it.

"God! Not George!"

The voice laughed inside Brooks' head.

Osaro is already a dead man! the voice proclaimed.

"No. I won't believe you."

But the voice was mocking him savagely now. *If you love Georgie Jap so much, why don't you fuck him?*

"Go to hell!"

I've been there! I'm back! There was a pause. *There's a beautiful woman in your bedroom, Timmy. Why don't you go in there and sodomize her?*

Brooks didn't answer. He wondered what world he was traveling through.

Might as well screw a famous actress, Timmy Boy! You've accomplished nothing else of note in your underachieving life.

Again, Brooks resisted the bait.

Go in there and offer her your cock, boy. Don't you think she's enjoyed hundreds of others?

"Will you be watching?"

Of course.

"Then you *are* nearby."

I said I was.

"Prove it."

My pleasure, my dear Detective Swine!

Two sharp noises like a pair of shots exploded in the room a few feet away from where Brooks lay.

Dull bluish light flooded in.

Brooks bolted upward, as if electrified. Instinctively, one hand was under the sofa and came out again with his service revolver. He was on his feet and his other hand groped for the nearest lamp.

He threw on the light. The room was empty. He felt something like a pair of strong wings flapping in his chest and he knew it was fear.

Fear of the unknown.

Fear of another world parallel to this one, reaching out to take him in.

Fear of everything he had never dared to even imagine.

Fear of things that were usually only murmured on the lips of nightmares.

Fear unlike anything he had ever known.

Pure cold fear.

The voice in his head was still, having established its point.

The room, too, was still, with the exception of the dangling eye-cords of the two window shades which had suddenly shot skyward in the darkness, causing the noise in the room, causing Brooks to bolt upright, causing sweat to flood over his body.

The two cords swung very slightly, settling again. The detective stared at them. The only sound was that of his heart, which was thundering.

"You did that, didn't you?" Brooks finally said aloud. "How? With a physical touch? With telepathy? Tell me how."

But there was no answer.

Insane distant laughter.

Brooks watched the two shades. And it occurred to him that the spirit—or the demon, or the ghost, or whatever it was—had shot two shades skyward to prove his own existence. If one shade just had suddenly snapped and bolted upward, Brooks might have chalked it up to coincidence.

Two was beyond coincidence. *Two* proved that the spirit who owned the voice existed. It was as real as any other adversary he had ever known.

Somewhere distantly, Brooks was aware of the insane laughter.

Slowly, he went to the bedroom door. He quietly pushed it open. He saw Annette sleeping. He stood very still and could hear her breathing.

He closed the room again but left the door open a crack.

Then he settled back onto the sofa, laying the gun beneath the pillow again. His stomach still churned. His eyes were so tired they stung.

Each time his eyelids closed, he battled to lift them. As time began to pass, he saw four A.M. come. Then four thirty.

Timothy?

The voice had waited until Brooks was barely conscious, until sleep had all but wrapped its warm tentacles around him.

Timothy?

"What?" Brooks said aloud to the lit room. He jerked his head up with a start.

That was me before. That was me who touched your shoulder in the darkness. Remember . . . ? When you were just approaching sleep . . . ?

Brooks trembled this time. He thought of checking on Annette again, but he was too exhausted to lift his feet. He wondered if he had dreamed this final exchange or actually partaken in it.

He scanned the room. Empty. Silent. Creepy.

His enemy was nowhere, meaning it was everywhere.

Tim Brooks now knew what it was like to be haunted. To be reached by something on the other side of one of those dark windows.

He thought of George Osaro and understood why the minister wanted no contact with an unknown of this sort. Yet he also knew, Brooks did, that he was locked in combat with this undefinable force. How could there be any escape from it?

Sweat dreams, my impotent friend! And don't forget. Your dear George Osaro is a dead man!

Brooks left the lamp on. Eventually he slept, albeit in a sitting position. When he awakened next, it was a gentler hand that nudged his shoulder.

This one was visible.

The hand was Annette's. The clear light of another morning had blessedly arrived.

She sat down on the edge of the sofa. She looked relieved, rested and very beautiful.

"Stayed up most of the night, didn't you?" she asked.

He nodded. Eyes bleary. Head pounding.

She shook her head in sympathy. "I knew you wouldn't be comfortable out here," she said. "I'm sorry. I can't put you out again in your own home."

"Annette, no. That's not it. I—"

"I owe you breakfast. Anything in your refrigerator?" she asked.

He nodded. "You'd be surprised," he croaked. "I'm strong on breakfast."

She was amazed.

"Then I'll make some," she said.

She kissed him on the forehead, then stood. She turned her attention to the preparation of toast, juice and coffee.

As she worked, Brooks moved to a living-room window and moodily stared out at the new day. A typical midsummer morning on the island, he thought to himself. The promise of sun and some humidity. In terms of police work, it would probably be as uneventful as any other. The occasional shoplifter. A car break-in. A stolen bicycle. Most people would be at their jobs, at the beaches, on their boats or playing tennis or golf.

A typical day on a resort island. But for him, he brooded, a day unlike any previous one.

He now knew that whatever was haunting 17 Cort Street had the ability to follow both Annette and him. It could get into his head. Communicate its vile thoughts. Threaten. Cajole. Shoot window shades skyward. Butcher a dummy.

It was vicious. Malevolent. And it could kill. It already had. Was there anything it couldn't do?

And what in God's name was Brooks going to do about it?

"We're ready," Annette said from the kitchen.

They ate breakfast together.

When he left for work, he gave her a lift back into town.

Eighteen

A crowd of reporters jammed the front entrance of the Nantucket police headquarters when Tim Brooks arrived for work that morning. He immediately recognized the tools of their profession. The print journalists held small tape recorders against their notepads. The television people were equipped with minicams and microphones.

Brooks knew the reason for the commotion. That day there was to be an indictment in the murder of Mary Elizabeth DiMarco: Eddie Lloyd on a charge of second-degree murder. The two detectives who had worked on the case would be making full statements.

Brooks passed the reporters and recognized several from off-island. He passed the civilian receptionist and walked the corridor to his office.

He had not even seated himself at his desk when he saw that he had had a visitor. Another business card from Dr. Herbert Youmans, the island's medical examiner emeritus. This time, in Youmans' neat penmanship, a note had been written upon it:

"Timmy," it said. "I'm fishing at Sankaty today, but we should talk, you and I. Important." It was signed simply, "Herb."

A moment passed. In the distance, Brooks could hear the gaggle of reporters being called to order. A slow stampede of anxious footsteps in a distant corridor indicated that the knights of the keyboards were being ushered to a conference room.

There, Detectives Rodzienko and Gelman would make a statement and answer questions.

Brooks stared at the note and then an impulse was upon him. He walked to the police parking lot and signed out a vehicle with four-wheel drive. Seven minutes later, Brooks was on the Milestone Road driving in the direction of Siasconset on the southeastern end of the island. Twenty-five minutes later, he was winding his way along a lonely strip of beach directly below the crumbling lighthouse at Sankaty. Thereupon, he found exactly what he was looking for, a solitary fisherman casting a line into the ocean in bold sunlight. The man was standing not far from his own four-by-four Jeep Cherokee.

The figure, which had been very still, came to life when Brooks walked to him.

"Well, hullo, Timmy," the fisherman said affably.

"Hello, doc," Brooks answered. He found himself staring into the ruddy pink face and doleful brown eyes of Herbert Youmans, M.D., seventy-one years old, local mystic and angler extraordinaire.

"Hell of a crowd back there at the police station this morning," the doctor said, now adding an edge of irritation to his voice.

"Hell of a crowd," Brooks agreed.

"Horrible thing, that girl getting killed like that," Youmans said, shaking his head. The doctor was a burly stooped man with a shaggy mustache and thinning white hair. "The island's not like it used to be, is it, Timmy? Something like that would never have happened a few years ago."

"It's a nasty world," Brooks agreed, not addressing Dr. Youmans' point. He watched as Youmans wound his reel, dragging a lure through very still ocean water. He remained silent until the lure came up out of the water and Youmans cast it forty yards back out into the ocean.

"I took the liberty of wandering down to your office," the doctor explained. "I felt I needed to have a word with you. And I didn't feel like waiting with all those two-bit scribblers. So I left again. Hope you don't mind."

"No problem," Brooks said. "You're always welcome in my office, doc."

"Thanks, Timmy." Youmans' eyes searched the younger man. "You probably know that your commander's trying to phase me out. Thinks I'm soft in the head."

"I haven't heard much about it," Brooks said.

"Well, I'm not so soft in the head that I don't know that Bill Agannis can be a stubborn asshole sometimes," the doctor said. "You can bank on that."

Brooks grinned in response. Even a vulgarity from Dr. Youmans rang with authority.

Youmans let his lure play in the water for several seconds. Normally in this location, one of Youmans' favorite for blues or bass, there was a gentle surf. Today the water was smooth, resembling polished marble as the sun played upon it.

"I tried to reach you by phone a few times," Brooks said. "Missed you each time. How are the bluefish?"

"One evening at Surfside they were so thick you could walk across them," Youmans said. "Caught fourteen, threw back twelve. The next day it was spottier. Ah, hell. Fish are like women. You never know, do you?"

Brooks shook his head.

" 'Course, I didn't bring you here to talk to you about fish, Timmy. Or women. You know that."

"I do. So what's up?"

"There's an oversized manila envelope on the seat of my Jeep, Timmy," the doctor said. "It bears my name, plus a return address to the local hospital. Go get it."

Brooks walked back up the beach to Youmans' Jeep and found the envelope. The fisherman was casting again when Brooks returned. Youmans had the stodgy slow movements of an older man whose body didn't always obey his command. But somehow his beech pole followed his wishes.

"Open it," said Youmans of the envelope, slowly winding his lure toward shore again. "I came across something a little quirky. The DiMarco case. It's worthy of note by someone. I mentioned it to your friends back there in town. Gelman and Rodzienko." He made a dispirited expression.

"Uh huh," said Brooks. The doctor was a bookish learned man at heart. Yale '42. He was no Bolshevik himself, but he didn't care much for the other cops' latter-day "Miami Vice" mentality, either.

"Your colleagues—those two other detectives—didn't seem to appreciate my thoughts," he explained, understating the obvious and wrapping an extra layer of disdain around the word *detectives*. "Then I mentioned it to Lieutenant Agannis and he didn't seem to want to know about it, either."

The doctor paused.

"*I* don't even know what to make of it," the doctor continued. "But you like to worry about everything, Timmy. And you like to poke your nose into everyone's business, too. So I thought I'd drop it on you, as well."

"I'm honored," Brooks said, gently facetious. He grinned reluctantly to indicate that Youmans could ramble onward.

"Do as I say. Open the envelope," said the doctor.

Brooks did. The water rippled slightly into surf.

The detective pulled out a pair of X rays, each ten by fifteen inches and centered upon two different skeletal images of human torsos, viewed from the shoulders upward. Brooks held one X ray in his right hand and the other in his left. His brows knitted as he glanced back and forth.

"So what are these?" the policeman finally asked.

"Part of two official PMs," Dr. Youmans said. "Postmortems on both DiMarco and the Canadian boy who died at the beach. Markley? Was that his name?"

Brooks said it was as he continued to look at the black and white transparencies. He held them against the sky. There was plenty of light. After a moment, he lowered them and looked at the doctor.

Youmans held his fishing rod in one hand and moved unsteadily to a spot at Brooks' side. He pointed with a forefinger as he spoke.

"Heaven knows, each taken individually, there's nothing

unusual about either of these," the doctor explained. "Taken together . . . ? What is it S.J. Perlman used to say? They put 'a Charlie Horse in the long arm of coincidence.'"

Brooks still didn't understand. Dr. Youmans forged ahead.

"The DiMarco girl died of a massive trauma to the head and neck," the doctor affirmed. "You know all that, so bear with me."

Brooks raised the X rays again and Youmans pointed to shaded areas as he spoke, shadows and fracture marks on the X rays.

"Her neck was broken," Youmans said. "Spinal cord severed. But you know, that's not enough to kill a human. It's enough to leave a human paralyzed and it *can* kill you without medical intervention. But it doesn't kill you by itself. You following this? If I remember, your forensic instincts were always pretty sharp, Timmy."

Brooks said he was following. So far.

"It's the way she landed," Youmans said. "It's just my theory and I'm just a white-haired old island doctor, Timmy. Which is to say that no one wants to listen to me. But I think she was maybe lifted to a great height. Ten, fifteen feet. Maybe twenty. Then smashed downward. That accounts for the trauma to the parietal portion of the cranium you see here"—he continued to point as he spoke—"as well as the fracture marks to the left clavicle."

He paused and let Brooks lower the X rays. But both men still viewed them.

"I think the head was smashed downward into the ground," the doctor said. "Then the deceased's neck was twisted around in such a way that she couldn't draw breath. Similarly, Timmy, look at this. See this spot here?"

Youmans' blunt finger moved authoritatively to the top of the deceased girl's neck.

"That's where the occipital bone meets the 'atlas,' the first vertebrae," the doctor said. "The 'atlas' is the part of the neck that supports the head. The joints here were torn as if they'd been caught in a machine. Ripped the spinal cord right where it should pass through the occipital bone. Again, that's enough to cause paralysis. But it was the fact that her trachea was crushed—you can see that here—that caused her to expire."

Brooks blinked twice and pondered the point. "Died instantly?" he asked.

"Let's say, 'very quickly.' By suffocation. A human being can't draw breath following a trauma of that sort. No access to oxygen."

Brooks thought about it for a moment more.

"Well, how is that inconsistent with what Gelman and Rodzienko allege?" the detective asked. "They claim Eddie Lloyd beat her and strangled her."

A disturbing look crossed the doctor's face. He worked his lure back to shore and put down his pole for a moment.

"I suppose what your peers are saying isn't totally inconsistent with the injuries," Youmans said. "They claim that the Lloyd boy assaulted her ferociously. Beat her around the head, causing the trauma marks, then strangled her. When she resisted, the struggle caused the injuries to her vertebrae and subsequently to the trachea."

"But you don't think that?" Brooks probed.

"Timmy, I don't know what to think. It's an arguable point. And they'll parade another physician into court—some young hotshot with a fresh med school diploma. They'll get the testimony they want no matter what I say." He paused. "There's only one thing I can maintain for sure. No one can refute me. And this is what bothers me. This is why I'm here."

"I'm waiting," Brooks said. "What is it?"

"The body of the Canadian boy shows parallel injuries. And that's being marked death by drowning."

It took a moment to sink in. Then, "What?" Brooks said loudly and incredulously.

"The same God damned injuries," the physician repeated. "Look at this," Youmans said, moving to the second X ray and taking it in his hand. "It's frightening how similar the trauma is."

It was. Similar and frightening.

There were almost identical injuries to the head and the

neck, Dr. Youmans explained. He pointed to the parallel markings from one X ray to the other. Once again, it was as if the neck area had been battered by some great force or dropped against something hard from a great height.

"What could be out there in a riptide that could cause similar injuries?" Brooks asked.

Youmans shook his head. "And what's out there in a vacant field at night that could pick up a girl and smash her down to the ground from an elevation of fifteen feet?" the medical examiner asked.

Brooks stared at the doctor. At the back of his neck he felt the icy hands of fear again. Touching him. Taunting him. Caressing him. Goose bumps rose.

Fear of what? Brooks asked himself.

Fear of something tall, black and supernatural. Something homicidal that moves in the darkness. Something that talked to him through his subconscious. Some power that he did not yet understand.

"I suppose Markley could have been pulled into the undertow and battered against some underground rocks," the doctor mused. "I suppose it's possible that his neck was wrenched violently by the force of the riptide." He paused. "I suppose a lot of things for the sake of argument." He raised his eyes to meet Brooks' gaze. "But I don't really believe any damned bit of it."

"What's the official medical cause of death?" Brooks asked.

"Death by drowning," Youmans affirmed with a nod. "That's as accurate as it is misleading. Sure, drowning: just as everyone knew all along. But what happened first, Timmy? The trauma to the neck? Or the drowning? If the deceased drowned in the riptide, then the injuries about the cranium and vertebrae could then have followed as the tide carried his inert body."

"But if the trauma to the neck came first?" Brooks asked, reasoning along with the doctor. "If something . . . some force . . . wrenched his neck in the water . . . ?"

"Then Markley's spinal cord would have been severed, resulting in paralysis," Dr. Youmans said, taking up his pole again. "Paralyzed, he would have been unable to swim. And he would have drowned."

Brooks considered it. "I don't suppose there's any way to tell which happened first," he asked.

Youmans shook his head. "Fate is mocking us on this one," he said.

Fate, huh? Brooks wondered.

"It's very strange, Timmy," Dr. Youmans concluded. "In fifty years as a practicing MD I've never seen this exact injury. Now I've seen it twice in four weeks, both times resulting in a fatality. One on land, one in the water, but both in the same community." He drew a breath. "If this were epidemiology, we'd be on to something."

Brooks caught the strong pulse of suspicion in Dr. Youmans' tone. He could also tell that the doctor wasn't quite finished. Youmans threw another long cast into the ocean and let his lure settle.

"Timmy, you're pretty well read. An educated sort of young swine for a policeman," Youmans announced easily. "May I ask you something unusual in this context? A literary question?"

"Sure."

"Did you ever read Poe's short story, *Murder in the Rue Morgue?* Or maybe you saw the old film with the wonderful Bela Lugosi?"

"Can't slip a classic past me, doc. That's the story with the trained ape that goes around Paris killing people," Brooks said. "Right?"

"Right," Dr. Youmans said, nodding. "Well, I can't help but being reminded of that story here. You see why? In the Poe story, the killer was so strong that it seemed superhuman. Which in fact, it was. The strength. The ferocity of the injuries to the victims. The apparent senselessness and inhumanity of the attacks."

Brooks measured the physician very carefully and made a last-ditch plea for a rational worldly argument.

"Doc," Brooks said. "Markley drowned, right? We're not

talking about an attack in the water. He was swimming with friends and there was a riptide. There's half a dozen witnesses to that."

With a free hand, the doctor worked a butterscotch Life Saver out of a roll. Brooks returned the X rays to their envelope.

"Uh huh," the medical examiner said. "That's the conventional wisdom around here, isn't it? Accident. The boy drowned. And did anyone bother to think about the fact that he was the best swimmer of the three?"

"I checked that angle, doc. He was also used to lake swimming in Ontario. He was inexperienced with ocean and heavy surf."

"Uh huh," Dr. Youmans said again. "Yeah. Maybe."

The Life Saver made a clicking sound against the older man's teeth. Then Dr. Youmans' gaze settled directly upon the detective. Brooks was aware of an extra tension, an extra sense of interrogation within the doctor's eyes.

"What are you suggesting?" Brooks finally asked.

"Tell me honestly, Timmy," the medical examiner said after a heavy pause. "Is there something strange happening on this island? Something the police aren't talking about? Something that's being kept from the public?"

"What makes you ask me that?"

"Two reasons. First, it's a hunch I have. And second"— Youmans nodded toward the X rays—"on account of everything I just said."

Brooks thought about his response for several moments. He was surprised when Dr. Youmans kept speaking.

"I've been coming out on this water for more than half a century, Tim," Youmans said. "I've seen a lot of sunlight. A lot of very bright days. But what's always struck me," he said as he worked his line again, "is the hard face of the ocean's surface. Yet right through that impenetrable surface there's another world. One we can't even begin to comprehend." The old man's brow furrowed and he glanced at his younger friend. "Imagine that. We're inches away from another world, we touch it, we see it, we dip into it now and then. But we don't understand it at all."

Brooks thought about it. "So?" he asked.

Youmans shrugged. "Something very strange happened to the DiMarco girl and the Canadian boy. I could almost prove it if anyone would listen to me. So I'm asking you again. What's this all about, Timmy?"

But, to his abiding shame, Brooks was now able to lie easily.

"There's absolutely nothing, doc," Brooks said. "Nothing unusual is going on at all."

But Brooks also asked if he could hang onto the X rays. "Just for the record," he repeated with a forced smile. "And just in case."

When his shift ended late that afternoon, Tim Brooks drove to George Osaro's church. The pastor was not in his office. Nor had any of the church's daily volunteers seen the minister that day. And Reverend Osaro's appointment book, the church secretary revealed when Brooks inquired, was blank for that date.

Unusual.

Normally, there was *something* each day.

Brooks continued to the minister's house. There was a strange stillness there, too. No battered van in the driveway. No Reverend Osaro. Brooks stood for several minutes on the pastor's front step, trying to pick up vibrations.

Brooks had an extra sense sometimes, a faculty that any good detective develops over the years. It was an ability to add all the odd parts of a mystery and still come out with a higher total than one should. Something told him—something hollered out at him—that there was something unnatural about his friend's disappearance.

Brooks held this thought for several seconds. Then another unwelcome idea was upon him and battled with his calmer more rational instincts. Something told him that George was lying dead somewhere, his spirit gone from his body.

Brooks suppressed a nasty tremor and rejected the notion.

No, he thought. Not so. George Osaro is alive. But where? And what is he doing? And why did he leave no word at the church as to where he could be reached?

Brooks played with the idea of breaking into Osaro's house. Had Brooks been a private citizen, he might have. But as a policeman, there were proper procedures to be followed. Unofficial break-ins were not part of any regulations or orthodoxy.

Brooks walked back to his car, pursued anew by aggressive questions from an unquiet place in his mind.

There are perfectly logical answers for each of those questions, he told himself. Aren't there?

Reverend Osaro did not schedule a particular day off each week. Osaro worked as his parish needed him, Monday through Sunday, fifty-two weeks a year. He grabbed a day of leisure when his appointment book happened to come up empty. No weddings to plan . . . no funerals . . . no meetings with the trustees of the church. . . . And so on.

Brooks started his car and pulled away from the parish house, still deep in thought.

George had taken some time for himself, right? A long walk on one of the remote beaches, perhaps, followed by a day trip to Hyannis via ferry. Whatever it was, the man had a right to his own business. Maybe he had a dentist's appointment off-island.

No, Brooks reminded himself next. Something like that would have appeared on the pastor's calendar.

Brooks sighed, pulling onto Orange Street. This unbanishable feeling was upon him. He needed to locate the pastor.

He took a perfunctory drive past the basketball courts. A father played with a young boy, shirts off, one-on-one in the diminishing sunshine of late afternoon. Brooks next drove out past the beaches which he knew the minister to like, eyes sharpened for the white Voyager. Still nothing. He also came up cold in the airport parking lot and the ferry parking spaces.

Still no Voyager. No George Osaro.

Brooks returned home, his sense of troubles mounting, and with no hint where to look next for his missing friend.

He drove back to his office and sat at his desk. He pulled out the X rays that Dr. Youmans had given earlier. He studied them again. In the injuries to the necks of Mary Beth DiMarco and Bruce Markley, Brooks heard troubling echoes.

Echoes of the head torn off the dummy.

Echoes of the eighteen murdered ducks, their necks wrenched.

An echo even of the malicious vandalism at the home of Thelma Lewis, the knife in the painting lodged at the throat of Jesus Christ.

Brooks picked up his telephone and punched in Annette Carlson's number. She answered on the third ring. He was relieved.

No, she said, she had had no problems at 17 Cort Street that day. And yes, she said she felt secure enough to pass the night there.

"But leave your phone on the hook, Tim," she said, "in case I change my mind at two A.M."

He said he would. He set down the phone. Only a few seconds passed between the moment the receiver landed on the hook and the moment when Brooks heard a knock at his open door.

His eyes rose. A woman.

His second visitor of the day was Andrea Ward, best known as a regional busybody, which was another way of saying that she was a reporter for the *Hyannis Eagle*. Actually, not just *a* reporter. She was probably the best in the region. She had big-city skills and big-time perseverance. And when she was on to something, she knew just how to knock the wind out of an official version of a story.

"Hello, Detective Tim Brooks," she said with mock formality. "You're working late."

"Not really," he said. "Just making a few phone calls." Whenever someone called him by his full name, an inner alarm went off. It always forewarned trouble.

"Mind if I sit down?" she asked theatrically.

"I can't stop you," Brooks said. Momentarily, she hesitated, trying to find subtext to his answer. "And wouldn't if I could," he said. "Sit," he offered.

She did.

Andrea was an attractive woman in her midforties, slim and smooth with dark hair and sexy gray eyes that made many people—usually men—talk to her much too much for their own good. Tim Brooks had known her for a few years. She frequently surfaced on Nantucket, chasing down stories of regional interest, some significant, some not, some pertaining to police activity, some merely human interest.

She had been a print reporter in New York for many years, working police beats and City Hall for first the *New York Post* and then the *Times*. But neither paper had elevated her to the larger, national stories that she craved. At the same time, she despaired of the normal cheek-to-jowl daily living that marked her stay in the Big Apple. So she moved to San Francisco and then Boston. She finally got the beats that she wanted and realized that big-time stories were filled with the same petty liars and con artists as the small ones. It was only the scope of what they had done that made them any different.

Better, she had decided in the mid-1980s when she had had enough of this, to turn inward.

Thereupon, she married a doctor, changed her last name, had a child, chucked her career, moved to Falmouth with her husband, divorced her husband the first time he committed adultery, wrote a trashy novel that never got published, reclaimed her maiden name, gained custody of her child, and picked up her reporting career again with the Hyannis paper. All this and more within the years 1986 through 1991. When Andrea Ward moved, she moved quickly. Some would say equally that she knocked over everything in her path. And she also brought a great wild card to her current vocation: she was a stringer for one of the national wire services. So one never knew whether something Andrea Ward was working on would turn up buried on page eight of the *Hyannis Eagle* or prominently displayed in one hundred seventy-five daily papers around the country.

"What do you think about all this excitement?" she asked, motioning with her head toward the chambers beyond Brooks' office.

"All what?"

"The murder indictment. Against that boy."

"What are you doing, Andrea? Nosing around for an extra quote?"

"Maybe," she answered. "Maybe not."

She rolled her eyes as if to suggest that even she didn't know what she was nosing around for: Curiosity, she frequently maintained, was its own reward—sort of an intellectual promiscuity.

Brooks answered with a shrug. "I can't tell you much that you don't already know. It's not my case," he said.

"I know it's not your case," Andrea Ward answered. "I asked you what you thought."

"I know what you asked me," he parried. "And you also know what I answered."

"In other words, you have your doubts, as well."

"Andrea, don't try to put words in my mouth," he said. "The officers investigating the case have their reasons for asking for an indictment. Talk to them."

"I did."

"Then why are you talking to me?"

Conversations with Andrea tended to resemble a beam of light in the universe, constantly bending back to where they had begun.

Andrea lounged in her chair. "I didn't like their answers." She set aside her leather shoulder bag.

"They probably didn't like your questions."

"They never do," She smiled. "For that matter, why the fuck should they?"

Andrea crossed her legs, which, by anyone's standards, were still the stuff that turned men's heads on the street. Once, a few years earlier, Tim Brooks had learned that Andrea was interested in having an affair with him. He learned this because she told him. Straight out. "What are you doing tonight, Tim? How about this: Let's get in bed together at my hotel room," she had suggested with a casualness that had surprised even him. He had gracefully declined, though he wasn't even sure why. Perhaps some little internal mechanism had warned him that this was a relationship best left unfulfilled.

All of this flashed back into his mind as she sat before him and as he answered her subtly venomous questions.

"Well, those are the only official answers you get," he said. "Whatever I might think has no bearing on the case."

"Sure," she said thoughtfully. "But, I think of you as one of the more intelligent members of this police force, Tim. I have some doubts about this case. I was wondering if you shared them. Care to talk? Off the record?"

He leaned back in his own chair. "I'll listen," he answered. "Off the record."

"Well, when the DiMarco girl was murdered," she said, "it was a pretty big story on the Cape. I spent some time on it. Talked to the girl's family. It wasn't any secret that the Lloyd boy was a suspect. So I spent some time talking to him, too."

Brooks said nothing and indicated nothing. All the time, Andrea Ward's eyes searched him.

"He's not a killer, Tim," she concluded. "Eddie Lloyd said he wandered away from where they were sleeping in the middle of the night. Fell down drunk. Never hurt her. Know what? I got a pretty good bullshit detector from working in New York, Boston and Frisco all those years. My needle doesn't move when I talk to Eddie. I believe him. I think your department's trying to string him up 'cause they don't know what else to do with the murder."

It was remarkable, in Brooks' opinion, how quickly Andrea Ward could jab to the heart of the matter.

"Then why don't you help him prove his case?" Brooks replied.

"I'm doing what I can."

"Good for you," he said flatly.

"Are you on my side?"

"I'm not on anyone's side. I'm an employee here."

She paused. "I know you don't like those other two detectives," she said. "I also know that you wouldn't let an innocent boy get hammered for no reason."

"You're right about that much," he said.

"Trouble is," she mused, "a jury is going to want to convict *someone*. A heavy circumstantial case can be made against him." She paused and mused further. "Of course, a *good* defense lawyer, an Alan Dershowitz, would make hamburger out of the state's case. But that's not what Eddie Lloyd is going to have. He's going to have some local yokel from Cape Cod, a hundred-dollar-an-hour mouthpiece who'll make more mistakes than there are peanuts in a bag. The type of lawyer who'll want to plead him guilty to second-degree manslaughter even if the kid's innocent."

"Andrea, I sympathize. But what do you want from me?"

Inadvertently, he realized he was fingering the manila folder that Dr. Youmans had left with him. When he realized he was doing it, he stopped.

"Who do you think killed the girl?" Andrea asked.

Brooks blew out a long breath. "I have no idea," he said.

She held him in her gaze for a full ten seconds. He knew the game. She was waiting for him to speak further. He kept silent. He gave her a forced smile.

"I can't offer you another suspect, Andrea," he said. "Honestly I can't. And neither can anyone else in this department."

"You can't offer me one or you don't have one to offer?" she inquired. "There's a slight difference."

"I don't have one to offer," he said.

Another ten seconds of searching his eyes. Then she reached for her handbag and rose. "Okay," she said. "I just thought I'd drop by and chat."

"It's always appreciated," he said in a tone that suggested that sometimes it wasn't.

"I also wanted someone in this department to know that I was still investigating the case. And you never know when I might find something juicy to embarrass the department."

273

He shrugged again.

"You do what you feel you have to do, Andrea," he said "can't control that."

"Thanks," she said. She moved to his door and stopped.

"What else?" he asked before she turned.

She had a big conspiratorial smile now.

"Timmy? Could that be termed a 'date' that you were on last night?" she asked.

"What?"

"I've been on the island for two days. You know, I may wear glasses, but I could have sworn I saw Detective Timothy Brooks of the Nantucket Police Department—that's you I believe—out to dinner with Annette Carlson. The aforesaid is of Academy Award fame."

"Must have been some highly attractive couple who looked like us."

"Nope," she said. "Try again."

Brooks sighed. "Come on, Andrea. Don't print crap like that."

"Why not? Oscar-winning actress dates local cop. You could turn into the luckiest working guy since Larry the Truck Driver married the *National Velvet* girl."

"I'm asking you as a friend not to print it," he said. "All right?"

"Why not?" she teased. Her tone was more playful than threatening.

"First, it wasn't a date. This is off the record, right?"

She nodded, a trifle too eagerly.

"I know Annette Carlson through a police-related procedure. We happened to meet after my shift was over. She's here on vacation and didn't wish to have dinner alone. She asked me to accompany her. I said I would."

"Are you a bodyguard or what?" she laughed.

"I'm not anything!" he said, finally unnerved. "And let the poor woman vacation on this island without alerting the tourists and the *National Star*. Okay?"

"As a favor to you, Tim," she sang. "Okay."

"Thanks."

"But that means you owe me one."

"A small one."

Andrea Ward smiled and left his office. He watched her go. What was it, he wondered, about Andrea that set his teeth on edge?

And then again that evening, there was one more disturbing incident.

Standing outside her home at dusk, Annette looked up to see—for the third time—the little blond girl in the unfashionable dated summer dress. The girl was standing on the edge of Annette's driveway. Watching her. Very attentively.

Annette smiled.

"Hello?" Annette called from a distance of thirty feet.

The little girl didn't answer. She watched Annette with considerable gravity. Annette began to sense something wrong. She walked toward her.

The little girl stood her ground.

Annette came to her and stooped down. Despite the sunny weather, despite the sundress, the girl had a pallor. She was pretty, but extremely fair.

It surged through Annette that there might be something, well, otherworldly, about the child. So Annette placed a hand on her to be sure.

Solid. Flesh and blood. Cool, but not shimmering. A real person. So it seemed. Thank God for that! Annette was relieved.

"Can't you give me a smile?" Annette asked.

"I'm looking for my parents."

Suddenly serious, Annette answered. "Are you lost?"

"No. I'm looking for my parents. Have you seen them?"

"What's their name?"

"Mommy and Daddy. They were here. I know they were here. Have you seen my parents?"

"What's *your* name?"

"I'm—!"

Then, as if in reaction to a voice unheard by any other ear, the girl turned. She bolted backward and started to run away so quickly that she startled Annette.

"Wait!" Annette called. "I can help you. Come back!"

The girl scooted down Cort Street. Annette stepped into the road and watched her. But the girl grew very small as she moved fifty, seventy-five, a hundred feet down the road. Then she turned a corner and disappeared.

Annette sighed. Pointless to chase. Just one more crazy incident at this location. Just one more thing to wonder about.

Annette telephoned the police department and reported a possible lost child. She gave a very concise description of what she had seen.

Several police cars responded. Every road in the neighborhood was carefully patrolled half a dozen times at minimum.

No child was found that evening. But no child on the island was reported missing. So by nightfall at least, despite the strangeness of the incident, the matter appeared settled. Wherever the little girl had run off to, it could be conjectured that she was back where she belonged.

Nineteen

Late on Friday afternoon, Joe Harris telephoned Annette from New York. Annette took the call in her bedroom minutes after Tim Brooks had stopped by to check on her.

The bedroom was not the best place in the house to converse. Annette found herself standing for much of the call, positioned between a dresser and the bed and gazing out of a window as she spoke.

"What's up, Joe?" she asked after the perfunctory small-talk and greetings.

As was the habit of men who survived a hundred telephone conversations on the average day, Harris moved straight to the point. He had just flown in from Los Angeles. He asked Annette if she had had the opportunity yet to read *Message From Berlin*, the television script which Harris had sent by courier three days earlier.

Annette sighed and admitted that she had not. She also reminded Joe that she didn't care to do television unless the role was extraordinary.

"Annie, honey," Joe Harris said adamantly. "Would Joe Harris *send* this to you if he didn't think it was extraordinary?"

"I suppose you wouldn't, Joe," she said.

"Shame on you, Annie," Harris chided her. His tone was gentle, but this was clearly a reproachful call. The other tip-off was his reference to himself in the third person. It was always a danger signal, always a sign of Joe's personal pique. "You didn't even read Joe's covering letter, did you?" he asked.

"No. I haven't."

There was a silence on Joe Harris' end of the line. Silence meant Joe was midway between irritation and fury, deciding which way to lean.

"Annie?" Joe asked next. He had a way of making some sentences and some requests stand out from others. "I suppose it's none of my God damned business, but I will make it my God damned business. Tell Joe: Are you okay?"

"I'm okay."

"Are you sure?"

"I'm okay, Joe."

"Well, you don't *sound* okay," he said. "And I'm not so sure you're acting okay." He paused. "Are you alone?"

"No."

"Oh." Another pause. "Can anyone hear you talking to me?"

Annette sighed. "Joe, we can speak freely."

"Who's there?"

"A man I know."

"Oh." A longer pause. "Anyone I know?"

"No."

"How could it *not* be?" Harris insisted. "I know everyone on both coasts."

"Joe, it's a man who lives on the island. It's a friend, not a romance. Now, why are you calling?"

"Annie, don't play games. Joe knows you too well. And he resents it if you don't tell him the truth." Harris paused. "Is your boyfriend still out of earshot?"

She sighed again, this time a little more intently. To Joe, nothing could ever be innocent.

Looking downward from the window, Annette happened to see Tim Brooks. He walked on the back lawn, head down as if in deep thought, arms folded behind his back.

"Yes, he's out of earshot. Why?"

There was challenge in her agent's voice. "I want to know

what's wrong with you. Are you in love? Not in love? Depressed? Sick? On drugs? Off drugs? Can't have an orgasm? What the hell is it, Annie? What's going on?"

She was looking downward at Timothy as Harris ranted. Brooks' attention focused on some small object that he had found in the grass. She watched him kneel down to examine it.

"I'm sorry, Joe," she said defensively. "You asked me a question. I gave you an honest answer."

"All right. I know that," Harris said, cooling all the way from the third person back to the first. "And what about you?"

"What *about* me?"

"You've been my client for five years. And never have I known you to not even look at the covering letter to something I've sent to you by express courier. *That's* what about you!"

"I'm sorry, Joe. It won't happen again."

She knew that on the other end of the line, Joe was lighting a cigarette. Annette's gaze drifted to some pieces of her jewelry which she had left carelessly scattered on the top of her dresser.

"Okay," he said finally. "Now that we're on the subject of client misbehavior, and since you haven't hung up on me yet, can I bark at you a little bit more?"

"Bark all you want, Joe," she said.

She fumbled with the telephone cord, stretched it and settled onto a chair. She glanced at the area of the closet where she had seen her first ghost. Then her eyes drifted back out the bedroom window down onto the lawn below. Tim was gone. She saw the small dark reddish clump in the grass that had held his attention. She couldn't tell what it was.

She continued to stare out the window as Joe growled about the importance of Annette Carlson's next project. She listened and watched the progress of an afternoon shadow creep across the lawn. Then her eyes rose and her gaze settled back into the bedroom as she listened to her agent's voice over the wire from New York.

Despite having graduated from both Lawrenceville and Stanford, Harris could wreck immeasurable violence upon the English language. Listening to him, one could have mistaken him for a bouncer from some velvet-roped mob joint in Florida.

Annette tuned back into Harris and was conscious of a question being asked. "You know I'm doing this 'cause I love you, don't you?" Harris inquired. "I'm not doing this for my fifteen percent. My fifteen fucking percent doesn't mean diddly-crap if a client is unhappy. Okay, Annie? We understand that, right?"

"Right," she answered. Alone in the bedroom, she was highly conscious of the sound of her own voice. There was a very slight echo in the woodwork of the antique house. The ear of an actress, finely tuned to even the smallest acoustical quirks, could focus upon it.

"We understand that, Joe. What are you leading up to?"

"Who says I'm leading up to anything?"

"You did. A second ago."

"All right. What's *wrong* with these fucking scripts I've been sending you?"

"I haven't liked any of them enough to want to do them, Joe. It's that simple."

"Okay. Okay, I understand that," he said silkily. "The trouble is, Annette, honey, I can only get you the first look for so long. I'm sending some very good scripts back to producers. Other actresses with half your talent are snapping up the roles you've turned down." He paused. "You're not forgetting how the game works in Los Angeles, are you? Are you sure you haven't been back east just a little too long?"

"Joe, you're back east right now, yourself, aren't you?"

Harris laughed. "So I'm in New York. Baghdad-on-Hudson. Is that such a crime?"

Annette didn't answer.

"Okay, okay! Maybe it is," he allowed, nearing his point. "But, look. Here's what I'm saying, Annie. You've looked at nearly thirty scripts. All of them I screened for you before I sent them. So none of them was real crap. None of them was an insult. But *not one of them* even interested you a little bit?"

He paused and waited.

"Not enough to do, Joe," she said.

"Okay," Harris said flatly. "Again. Joe Harris can handle

that. But that brings us to the script I sent you three days ago. The one you've been kind enough to not even look at yet, much less scan my efforts at a cordial covering letter."

"It's television, Joe. The boob tube."

"Annie. It's not ordinary television. If you'd read my letter, you'd know that. I don't normally call you to push a script. But this time I am. Now, I admit this much to start: the writer is one of my clients and I'm involved in the packaging of this. But can I keep talking?"

Joe was suddenly very serious. Annie said he could keep talking.

"One of the things you and the other clients pay me for, Annie, is to advise you against bad career moves. If you're not careful, you're going to make one."

"What are we talking about, Joe? The television script you sent?" Her eyes went back to the dresser. With a sinking sensation she noticed that one of her favorite necklaces, a gold filigree chain which supported a small gold star, had been inordinantly tangled and knotted.

How do delicate pieces of jewelry tangle and knot themselves? she wondered. She cradled the phone between her shoulder and chin and used two hands to try to work loose the knots in the necklace.

Meanwhile, Joe spoke business.

The script, Harris said, *Message From Berlin*, was a three-part six-hour miniseries being developed for autumn of the following year. It was based on a best-selling novel. The sequences that were not done in a studio in California would be filmed in Washington, New York, London and Berlin.

"This isn't just dumb-assed ordinary television for the peasants out in Nebraska, Annie, honey," Joe Harris said. "This is going to be top-quality television. The money's excellent, the exposure's excellent." He named the director who had already committed himself to the project. He was a man who already owned two Oscars and three Emmys. The producer was top-of-the-line, too. He paid his bills and had never been associated with a disaster.

281

"The lead female role is yours, Annie," Harris said. "They *want* you. You say yes and I can start squeezing the dollars out of them."

"How many dollars?"

"I think they'd pay a quarter of a million to have you aboard," he said softly. "I think they think you'd make the story work and kick them up an extra Nielsen point or two. So I think that's what I could get you. Plus maybe a small part of gross revenues."

Annie was quiet. With all that had transpired in her house over the last weeks, maybe Joe was right. Maybe she hadn't been attentive enough to the scripts she had been reading, or to what her career demanded next.

"It would be a six-week shoot in October and November," he said. "Four in the U.S., two in Europe." He also said that the search for a leading man was down to four names, all of whom were ready to commit to the project if an offer found its way into writing. Annette liked all four names.

So she was listening attentively now.

"The thing is, Annie," he then cautioned, "and this is why I'm calling, they've been doing some sniffing around. They know you don't like television and they know you've rejected more than two dozen scripts. So they've already got their clammy feelers out elsewhere."

"Where's 'elsewhere'?"

Harris named a pair of actresses. Both were good and specialized at television movies. They were logical alternatives to Annette.

"Uh huh," she said.

"Meaning, if their second or third choices come back to them quickly and will work for thirty thousand dollars less up-front, I know these characters, they might come down with a case of preemptive cheapness. See what I mean?"

Annette saw. She promised that she would read the script overnight and give her agent a callback first thing the next morning.

"That's all I'm asking, Annie," Joe Harris said. "That's all I wanted you to understand."

She hung up the telephone. For a moment she wondered what had possessed her to agree to read three hundred sixty pages of script overnight. She sighed. Well, she told herself, she would give it a start. She would know after the first third whether it was any good. Then she could—

A movement through the window caught her eye and distracted her. It was Tim, down below on the lawn, carrying a small shovel from the garage. She couldn't fathom what he was doing. She went downstairs and outside to investigate.

When she walked onto the front lawn, Brooks was intent on his small sad task. He made a shallow hole in the loose soil of the flower garden at the front of the house. Then he returned to the reddish clump which Annette had seen from above.

"See what I'm doing?" he asked.

She didn't. Not until he showed her.

He walked back to the small forlorn object in the grass. Annette drew close enough to see what it was. It was a dead bird, a female cardinal, lying with its wings askew, its head twisted at an impossible angle from its body.

Gingerly, Brooks picked it up with his shovel. "I'm burying the poor thing," he said. "Can't just leave it lying in the grass."

Annette looked at it and grimaced.

"What happened to it?" she asked. "Cat get it?"

"Doesn't look that way," Brooks said without expression. "Its neck is broken." He dropped it into the hole in the garden.

"How does a bird break its neck?" she asked.

Brooks raised his eyes and looked at her, the dirt in place.

"Maybe it flew into the side of the house," he said. "Hit a window. Or something."

She looked at the grave.

Then, with the backside of the blade of the shovel, he pushed dirt upon the body of the slain bird. Annette and Timothy exchanged the same thoughts. But they said nothing.

* * *

Shortly after dinner, Annette picked up her copy of *Message From Berlin* and began to read. She was familiar with the novel upon which the script was based, but she had never read it. The fact was, she had tried to read several books by the same author and had always found the plots too dense, the characterization too shallow and the action unbelievable. Nor did the author have a particularly good prose style, even though he had sold millions of books all over the world. Annette had never been able to finish any of his books. Hence, her initial reluctance to pick up a screenplay based on the same man's work.

But a screenwriter named Jonathan Reed had adapted the book for six hours of television. Reed had taken several liberties with the story. With all of them, his instincts seemed to have been right.

Reed had cut away the overblown prose and had boiled down the plot. The characters were sharply defined from the start, their motivations clear. And they were sympathetic. Annette was hooked from page two.

She read all three scripts. As was frequently the case, Joe Harris was right. This was an excellent piece of popular entertainment—quality television combined with an excellent financial offer. This was a project that would get made, possibly to considerable acclaim.

Yes, she was interested. Damned interested. So interested, that at a few minutes past eleven P.M. the same evening, she went to the phone and called Joe Harris in New York. He was staying at the Hotel Carlyle.

Harris knew no difference between any hour of the day or night when he was busy putting together an entertainment package.

"They're still hot for you, honey," Harris said. "I talked to the producers an hour ago. Told them you were reading the script as we spoke. Did you read it? They want your bod in this project and they want it *v-e-r-y* badly."

"I want to do it, Joe," she said. "Get it for me."

"That's my girl!" Harris exclaimed.

"How '*v-e-r-y* badly' do they want me?" she asked.

"If you'll pardon my French, Annie, they're foaming at their fucking mouths! Look. Tomorrow's Saturday. Fly down. I'll arrange a meeting. Maybe we can start working out the money in the afternoon. That will give the producers a lot more leverage with other parts of the package. It might allow them to raise foreign production money right away." Harris paused. "Plan to stay overnight. I'll book a hotel room at the Carlyle for you. Bring your boyfriend if it makes you happy, don't bring him if it makes you unhappy." The agent paused again. "Jon Reed's in town, too. If you want to talk to him about the script, he's already told me he'd love to meet you. You can choose. Up to you, babe. Whatever."

"Whatever, Joe," she answered.

"Just be here."

"I'll be there."

In sum, it was the type of conversation any actress would kill for. Annette began to enjoy the surge of excitement inherent in becoming a central part of a promising production. Suddenly one of her most pressing problems—what next direction to take professionally—seemed to have solved itself. Now she could make some money, gain some positive visibility and allow herself more time in finding a feature film project. And all with one deft move.

Thank you, Joe Harris! Next time I'll read your covering letter right away!

Then Annette made a final call for the day. She telephoned Detective Brooks at his home, asking if he and the minister wanted to come into the house on Cort Street while she was away. She might be off-island for as much as two days, she explained.

"I still can't find Reverend Osaro," Brooks answered.

"He's not home?"

"We think he might have gone to Boston. Or at least that's what everyone at the church thought. He hasn't come back yet."

"Is that unusual?"

"Maybe not," Brooks said. "He's separated from his wife and

son. He may have gone to see them. Didn't want anyone at the church to know his business. He can be a little private like that." He paused. "The truth is," Brooks said, "I expect him to turn up in a day or two."

"If that's the case," she said, "I'm going to leave you a key."

"You're sure?" Brooks asked.

"I wouldn't offer if I weren't."

"If George doesn't materialize tomorrow do you mind if I have another walk-through by myself?" Brooks asked.

She thought for a moment.

"No. I don't mind," Annette answered. "I'll leave you my agent's number in New York. If anything happens, you can call me there."

He agreed. She said she would leave the key under a large mossy rock in a flower garden beneath the kitchen window.

There was just one other thing, he asked. He wanted her to leave open the two interior doors that were usually locked. The attic and the basement.

She felt a twinge of foreboding when he mentioned those two doors. But she said she would unlock both.

"I would think those places would make you nervous," she said.

"They probably should," he said. "But I'm hoping Reverend Osaro turns up. It's pointless to go through if we don't go through thoroughly. So if you're willing to give me the key, I don't mind."

Annette was willing. So Tim Brooks didn't mind, either.

She hung up and began packing.

Her enthusiasm for this new television undertaking pushed darker thoughts out of her mind. She slept well.

And as if by osmosis, the night at 17 Cort Street passed quietly.

Twenty

The next morning, Tim Brooks drove to Reverend Osaro's home and found it exactly as he had seen it the previous day. Similarly, the minister had not been seen at his church, either.

The voice inside him spoke again.

Osaro is a dead man, Brooks! the voice insisted. *He burns in hell, Timmy! Your friend is burning in hell!*

"Jesus," Brooks muttered.

He's a dead man. Can't you see that?

"Tell me what you want or go away, would you!" Brooks demanded.

Fucking atheistic phony parson! Serves him right! Serves you right, too! You half-baked excuse for a cop!

For an uneasy moment, Brooks suffered in silence.

Could have made something out of yourself. Instead you became a cop!

"I said, 'Tell me what you want or go away,' " said Brooks, louder this time. The voice blithely obeyed, choosing the second alternative and dispersing like a puff of odious smoke.

Brooks drove to the ferry terminal at Steamboat Wharf. When another check of the names of people holding passenger reservations on the most recently departing ferries failed to turn up Osaro's name, Brooks went uneasily to his office.

The person whom Brooks did see that morning was Eddie Lloyd, though not in the flesh. On the television set at the police station, several cops including Lieutenant Agannis stood and watched the noontime news at the courthouse in Hyannis.

There Eddie Lloyd was arraigned for the murder of Beth DiMarco. His parents were present. His lawyer—a local mouthpiece who already appeared to be in over his head—made a statement. Eddie entered a plea of not guilty. Brooks watched the television screen in mounting disgust.

Not guilty. A voice spoke within him again. *Didn't do it. The boy didn't do it.* Different voice this time. More godly. More benevolent. Same voice, different moods? Or was it all just Brooks' subconscious. He wondered.

Brooks picked up a newspaper that lay in the police station. It was that day's edition of the *Hyannis Eagle.* On the lower right half of the front page, Andrea Ward continued her coverage of the Beth DiMarco case.

Something lightly touched his cheek. He swept a hand at the spot to brush it away.

Oh, really? Here we go again, he thought.

Brooks looked closely at his fingertips and found the crushed body of a gnat that had flown against his cheek. There was a dot of blood where the insect had bitten him. At the same time, the irksome inner voice departed.

When the television news switched to another story, Lieutenant Agannis appeared by Brooks' side.

"Timmy, I've lost track. What's on your plate these days?" Agannis asked casually.

Brooks mentioned three cases upon which he had ongoing investigations. Two were burglaries in Madaket. One was an assault case that had taken place outside a bar two nights earlier. Then he mentioned Cort Street.

"What about Cort Street?" Agannis asked.

"More unexplained events," said Brooks.

"What the hell goes on at that place?" Agannis said, lighting an inevitable Marlboro and inhaling deeply. He blew out a long angry cloud. "What are you talking about?

"Nothing you'd believe, Lieutenant."

"I've seen a lot in my life and I've forgotten none of it, Timmy. So try me," Agannis challenged in a low suspicious growl.

288

"How about I try you in your office?" Brooks asked.

"If we must," Agannis answered.

Standing too close to his commanding officer, Brooks' nostrils suffered a joint assault by Old Spice and tobacco-tinged carbon monoxide.

Brooks fell back a pace, then followed the lieutenant into the latter's chamber. Boomer tagged behind them. The license and doggie identification pieces jangled on the Labrador retriever's collar as he loped in pursuit. Love without a leash. It was a human-canine combo—three distinct individuals, eight legs.

Agannis entered his office, pushed the door shut and sat down behind his desk. "So?" Agannis asked. "Start talking, will ya?"

Then, as Boomer settled into the corner on his sad, worn mat, Brooks ran the lieutenant through the sequence of events at 17 Cort Street—from the first apparition to the china cabinet to the battered decapitated doll to Dr. Youmans' X rays.

Agannis listened patiently and puffed one butt after another. His eyes narrowed. He listened carefully. He created enough white smoke to have chosen a new Pope. His brows lifted from time to time, as if he might interrupt with an objection. But he said nothing until Brooks finally finished.

"That's it?" Agannis asked. He snuffed out his most recent cigarette. "That's what all this is about?"

"That's it."

Agannis' finger tapped impatiently on the top of his desk. "You know, deep down, Timmy," the lieutenant said, "I always thought you were a little crazy."

Brooks remained silent, glanced to the ceiling and waited for more.

More arrived quickly.

"Ever see *Hold That Ghost!* with Abbott and Costello?" Agannis asked with exaggerated calmness. But his eyes were alive. Brooks sensed trouble.

"No, sir."

"Well, maybe you should! It would be a whole lot better use of your time than this!"

"Ah, come on, Lieu—"

"Nah, *you* come on! I've never heard such bullshit in my life!" he said. "Women in white. Spirits. Cabinets falling over. Dark forms dispersing before your eyes! Jesus fucking Christ, Timmy! I ought to have your ass on a platter for talking such nonsense."

"There's something strange in that place, Lieutenant."

"Timmy, what did this Hollywood broad do to you? You've lost your brains."

"I'm telling you, I saw something myself. A black—"

"Ah, bullshit!" Agannis snorted again. He rolled his eyes in dismay. His voice rang with such urgency that Boomer was jolted awake from some serious dozing. The dog lifted his head, gazed mournfully at his master, and wagged his tail, thumping it against the office wall as he wagged.

"Before I'd believe any crap like that," Agannis said, "I'd have to see it for myself."

Brooks grinned. "All right," he said. "I'm on my way over to Cort Street right now. So here's your chance."

"Aah, Timmy . . ." Agannis said in disgust.

Agannis sank back in his chair, much of his weight upon the armrests. He looked at his watch and he looked at his detective.

"What is it with you, Timmy? You think I'm as nutty as you are?"

"In the final analysis," Brooks said slowly. "Yes. Maybe." He motioned to the parking lot. "Whose car? Yours or mine?"

The lieutenant stared at his younger peer for several seconds. Then at length, "Mine," Agannis said. "And Boomer comes, too."

The retriever, hearing the word "car," knew enough to get to his feet. The dog shuffled sleepily after the two policemen as they walked outdoors to the parking lot. The sun was bright. Brooks pushed a pair of sunglasses onto his face. Lieutenant Agannis owned a Ford Taurus wagon which was always parked in the same reserved spot on Hicks Street.

That bedeviling voice returned. It spoke to Brooks again. *And what do you think you'll find, my fine moronic friend?* it asked. The voice was impish and shrill.

"Knock it off," Brooks mumbled very softly.

Agannis cast him a glance as they stopped at his car. Then the lieutenant unlocked the vehicle. He opened the left rear door first, allowing Boomer to settle into the back seat. Then the two police officers slipped into the front.

"Just tell me one thing," Agannis said as Brooks buckled himself into his seat on the shotgun side. Agannis, the Marlboro Man, eschewed the belts.

"What's that?"

"You're always mumbling to yourself these days," Agannis said as the car's engine turned over. "Who the hell do you think you're talking to?"

"No one," Brooks answered. He was surprised that Agannis had heard him, much less noticed a pattern of behavior. To Brooks it wasn't even that obvious. It caused him to wonder how long he had been hearing that voice. He couldn't even remember.

The car started to move.

"No one, huh? Yourself, you mean?" Agannis asked. The lieutenant still looked displeased overall by the tide of events.

"Yeah. Myself."

Liar! the voice screamed, mocking him. *Liar! Liar! Liar!*

"Myself," Brooks repeated. "Sure sign of madness, isn't it? Talking to oneself?"

Agannis didn't answer. Instead, he shot Brooks an odd look as they pulled out into traffic. And Boomer punctuated the occasion with a gigantic but dismal yawn.

The key was under the mossy rock in the garden, just as Annette had promised. Brooks found it easily and unlocked the house at 17 Cort Street by the back door. He walked in first. Lieutenant Agannis followed. Boomer sat down stubbornly on the flagstones behind the house. Agannis slapped his thigh and motioned that the retriever could trail along. But the dog stretched out in the sunlight and chose not to follow.

"Just tell me this?" Agannis asked, entering the house behind Brooks. "What are we expecting to find?"

"Don't know," said Brooks. He felt his heart pump a little harder as he stood in the dining room. "Never know in this place."

Agannis looked at him skeptically again. But the lieutenant's doubts were tempered now that he was actually in the afflicted house. Jokes and skepticism did not come as easily, at least not immediately.

But really, there seemed nothing amiss. Someone—Annette presumably—had cut a bouquet of fresh flowers and put them in vases in the living and dining rooms. She had also left some windows open just enough to bring a cooling breeze through the house. The breeze mingled with the scent of the flowers and gave the downstairs of 17 Cort Street a fresh, pure air.

"Want to look around together?" Brooks asked. "Or do we split up?"

"We'll stay together, Timmy," Lieutenant Agannis said. "That way if I see someone marching around with a sheet over his head, I'll know it's not you."

"Very funny," Brooks said. He motioned to the steps. "Let's go upstairs first. We'll work our way to the basement."

"What are we looking for, anyway?" Lieutenant Agannis asked. "Let me know in case I see it, will ya?"

"If you see something, you'll know," said Brooks. "Beyond that, it's more of a sense. A feel. Hell, I don't know either but I wanted a look around."

Lieutenant Agannis shot Brooks another strange look, then followed.

They walked through the first floor, room by room. Then they went upstairs together and looked in each room.

Brooks led. He felt nothing extra anywhere in the house. He had no special sense of anything. No intuition. He wished again that George Osaro—wherever in God's realm he was—could have accompanied them.

They came to the steps to the attic. Brooks looked up the

staircase to the door that was closed at their summit. He hoped that Annette had remembered to leave it unlocked.

"This is the attic," Brooks said. "This is where the dummy got its head torn off."

Agannis grimaced. "I know in what part of a house an attic is located, Timmy," he said. "And I know a dummy when I see one, too. Make that, a couple of dummies."

Brooks let the remark pass. He led his commanding officer up the steps. His hand paused for a moment on the doorknob at the top of the stairs. Brooks looked for the padlock. He found it. Annette had left it undone.

Brooks drew a breath, unlatched the attic door and pushed it. For a moment, Brooks' heart kicked because he could have sworn he felt some resistance to the other side, the type one feels when another hand is on the other side of a doorknob.

But then the door gave way. It moved with a groan at its hinges, but opened easily.

Moments later the two policemen stood in the attic of 17 Cort Street, Brooks more wary than his commander. The chamber was warm, stuffy and stale. Brooks glanced to the windows and saw that Annette had indeed left them partially open. She had bought a small set of screens, in fact, and had positioned them so that air could flow through the room.

"So this is it?" Lieutenant Agannis asked.

Brooks nodded.

The two men poked around for several minutes. Again, they felt nothing. They saw nothing. The room was much as Brooks had seen it the last time, the day he last saw the body of the ventriloquist's dummy, its arm hanging limp, lying beneath a sheet.

"Pretty scary," Lieutenant Agannis said flatly. Clearly, it wasn't.

Brooks lingered for a moment, almost wishing the distant voice, the one he heard within his mind, would beckon him again and give him some sort of clue.

But that voice, he had already learned, knew how to tease

and torment. He knew it would only come when it was unwelcome or wished to mock him. Or when it wanted something.

"I'm getting bored, Timmy," Lieutenant Agannis said.

"All right," Brooks said. "We can go back downstairs."

The two men closed the attic door behind them. They walked down the steps. It was when they arrived on the landing of the second floor that Brooks stopped short.

He had heard something. Movement. A thump. A human voice.

"Wha—?" Agannis began to ask.

Brooks' finger rose to his lips. He shushed his lieutenant, indicating that they should fall silent.

Then they both heard the sounds. A voice murmuring low. A few more thumps. The sound of furniture moving.

Brooks whispered.

"It's downstairs," he said. And it was. It was in the area where the china cabinet had flown off the living room wall. Something was there. As real and demonstrable as day.

Brooks broke a slight sweat. For the first time, a look of concern crossed Agannis' face.

Brooks motioned that the lieutenant should follow.

They moved through the landing of the second floor and went to the stairway that led downstairs. In the living room below them, the sounds continued.

Brooks reached the top of the stairs first, sweat building within his clothing. He took one step onto the top stair, let his foot fall softly and continued.

The voice in the living room was almost discernible now. There continued also the unmistakable sound of furniture moving.

Brooks crept to the bottom step. Agannis remained behind his detective.

Brooks reached the first floor. From where he stood he could see out the screen door at the rear of the house. Boomer lay motionless on the flagstone path, stomach up, neck bent. It suddenly occurred to Brooks that the dog should have barked.

Was Boomer dead? The dog didn't move.

Then there was the sound of music in the living room. Music from a radio. Brooks looked at Agannis, who was directly behind him. Lieutenant Agannis gave a nod.

Instinctively, Brooks placed a hand on his weapon. He advanced two steps and came to the door frame of the living room.

The figure of a man moved among the scattered furniture. The man's head came up with a start and turned when Brooks drew within sight.

Brooks stared. Lieutenant Agannis stared from behind him.

"Timmy? Lieutenant Agannis? What are you guys doing here?"

Brooks felt a tremendous wall of tension collapse within him as he and his lieutenant gazed upon the slightly overweight face and figure of Emmet Hughes, the repairman whom Annette had hired to mend her living room wall.

"Ah, fuck . . ." Lieutenant Agannis said.

"What's the matter?" asked Hughes, ruddy-cheeked and amiable. "Hey, Miss Carlson said I could be in here today. I made this appointment last week. So I came in and went to work. Is that okay?"

On the floor, Hughes' boom box, his constant working companion, played rock from a Boston station. Hughes reached to it and turned down the volume.

Brooks moved his hand from his firearm. His shirt clung to the wetness of his ribs.

"Yeah, it's fine," Brooks said. "Didn't expect you, that's all, Emmet."

"Isn't she home?" Hughes asked.

"No."

Hughes was surprised. "Oh. Well, I saw Boomer out there," Emmet Hughes laughed, pushing a toolbox to one side. "I knew you were here, Lieutenant. Figured Miss Carlson had to be here somewhere, too. Didn't know about Timmy, though." He looked at the two cops for several extra seconds, doubt crossing his mind for the first time. "Nothing wrong is there?"

"No," Agannis said.

"Miss Carlson? She's okay?"

"She went to New York on personal business," Brooks said. "She's fine. More than fine."

Hughes looked relieved.

"Oh. Well, that's good," he said. "Real good. She's a nice lady, you know. Not stuck-up like a lot of them movie people must be."

"Very true, Emmet," Brooks said.

Reflexively, Lieutenant Agannis found his cigarette pack. He drew a smoke and lit it. As Agannis took a long carcinogenic drag, Emmet Hughes moved a chair away from the damaged wall. He also picked up the checkerboard table—the most fragile piece in the room—and moved it to safety near a front window.

"Wow," Hughes finally said, looking for the first time at the full scope of the damage to the wall. The holes were so big that he could practically put his head in them.

"Can you believe this? Something hit through here like an express train," he said.

"It just fell over one night," Brooks said.

Hughes looked at him with a straight expression for a moment. Then he winked. "Yeah. And I'm Nancy Reagan."

"No. Really it did."

"Don't bullshit me, Timmy," Hughes said with no contention at all. "These here moorings got yanked out. This cabinet was bolted to the wall and there was nothing wrong with the hardwood behind it. Look at this. That's impact, Timmy. I'm not giving you any crap about this."

"Is that right?" Brooks said.

"Look, from the force of the destruction, I'd say this wall took a hell of a hit. But there's no impact at all to the other side, is there? So the cabinet got yanked."

"What about impact from within the wall?" Brooks asked.

Hughes looked at the younger man blankly for a moment. "Now where's that going to come from?" he asked. "And where's the momentum going to come from for something like that?"

Brooks shrugged. "Don't know," he admitted. "Dumb idea?"

"Dumb idea," Hughes confirmed. "You said it. I didn't."

Tim Brooks didn't bother to recount his own version of events, as seen from the next room, involving the misty cloudy ominous black form that evolved from the wreckage.

"That's the gospel, Timmy," Hughes said. "Hard to figure what could have happened. I can only tell what *didn't* happen. But, uh, you know these Hollywood people. Probably had six nude starlets hangin' on the china cabinet with six guys pulling at their buns."

"You never know," Brooks said.

"Look here," said Hughes.

Hughes had grown up around housing and its construction. He knew of which he spoke.

"This here's one of the main uprights supporting this building," he said, indicating a large brown timber within the wall. The shattered plaster, missing from the surface, had left it exposed. "These bolts were ripped out so hard that even the main beam suffered damage."

From behind, Agannis watched and listened.

"Damage how severe?" Brooks asked.

"Severe enough for me to have to go downstairs and have a look-see," Hughes said. "It might need to be steadied. It might need some modern support." Hughes shook his head. "Really is hard to figure," he muttered, "what could possibly have been strong enough to wrench them bolts straight out of there?"

Brooks shrugged. "Emmet, you'd know better than I would," he said.

"I'd expect so," Hughes said, starting to smile again. "Seeing's how I'm the contractor and you're the cop." He paused. "Did Miss Carlson leave the cellar door unlocked?" he asked.

"I don't know," Brooks answered. "I haven't checked it yet."

"Hope so," Hughes said.

Brooks went to the kitchen and tried the door. It was open. He reached into the dark staircase that led downward beneath the house, found an electrical switch and turned on some lights.

"Yes, it's open," he called out. "Anyone coming downstairs with me?"

Lieutenant Agannis walked into the kitchen. "You check it out, Timmy," he said patiently. "Call me if you need me."

Brooks hesitated. Then he descended slowly to the basement at 17 Cort Street.

He went down step by step, that sense of foreboding that he had felt once before returning to him as he descended.

The steps were long, narrow and old. They creaked badly. When he arrived on the concrete section of the basement, he stopped.

He looked around. There were numerous overhead pipes which sweated badly and perspired onto the floor. The furnace loomed like a boxcar in the middle of an open space, its aluminum arms and ducts leading to various heating panels throughout the house.

Brooks walked slowly along the concrete. He waited for that internal voice to set itself off again—to tease him, to torment him.

Suddenly he felt something. It was against his cheek. Light and feathery, as gossamer as the touch of a spirit.

He swept at it with his hand and came away with a thick mass of cobweb.

He wiped it off his palm. Against all rational judgment, he found himself anxious to return upstairs.

But he refused to become frightened. He hated to admit it, but he almost sensed that he was close to something.

And that he was being watched.

"Anything here?" Brooks asked aloud.

He paused and waited.

"Anyone got a message for me?"

Silence. No answer. Not even the voice that came from some other dimension in time and space. "Some other universe, one very different from ours," George Osaro might have said.

Brooks grew bolder.

"Scared of me, huh?" he asked, louder still.

Brooks remembered the window shades that had shot skyward in his own home. He waited for a similar phenomenon, never straying too far from his path back to the steps.

But again, no response.

He turned. He walked back to the steps and climbed them.

Was he being watched? Or was he imagining the sensation?

He gained the top of the stairs, turned around and looked back down.

Still, nothing.

He turned off the light and stared down into the darkness. Nothing.

He smiled ruefully. He closed the door and dropped the latch upon it. But he left it unlocked.

Brooks walked back out to the living room. Agannis was sitting on the sofa, smoking and chatting. Emmet Hughes was taking measurements at the points of damage to the wall, returning the police lieutenant's conversation as he worked.

"So you're going to be here by yourself, are you?" Agannis asked.

Hughes grinned affably. "Just me and my radio," he said. "Can't afford no assistant no more."

Agannis nodded.

"Sure you'll be okay?" Brooks asked.

Hughes took it as a strange question. "Why wouldn't I be?" he asked.

Brooks considered an answer. But Lieutenant Agannis stole the initiative.

"No reason on earth you shouldn't be," the lieutenant said. "Aside from the fact that Timmy here thinks there's a ghost in the house."

"A *ghost?*" Hughes looked up from his work. His face, tense and quizzical for a moment, then broke into a broad smile. "Know how many ghost houses I been in on this island?" Hughes asked. "Over the course of thirty years? Know how many?"

"I have no idea," Brooks said.

"Take a guess."

"I couldn't possibly."

"Well, I don't have no idea, either," the repairman said. "Fifty. Eighty. A hundred. It's a real thing around here, isn't it? People move here from New York or Boston and think they should have a ghost." He laughed. "Women mostly, bless 'em. They leave you to work in their house, then they say, 'By the way, if you see something funny, it's just my Aunt Tilly. She's been dead twelve years but she likes to check on things. So just be nice to her and she won't bother you.'"

Agannis grinned, laughed, and tossed the end of his cigarette into the fireplace.

"Know how many ghosts I *seen* in all that time?" Emmet Hughes asked.

He didn't wait for an answer. The repairman held up a hand with his thumb and forefinger connecting to form a circle, indicating none.

"Zero," Hughes said. "Any ghost shows up here while I'm working, I'll shove a T-square up its ass. How's that?"

Brooks nodded hopelessly. Lieutenant Agannis would have loved to have stayed to witness the incident.

"Then I guess you'll be fine," Brooks finally conceded. He motioned to the lieutenant that he was finished and they could leave.

They stepped outside.

Boomer, motionless as a log, suddenly rolled over and came back to his feet. With an unusual whimper, he trotted to his master. Agannis patted the retriever on his head.

"Whatsa matter, fella?" Agannis asked his mastiff. "Bad dreams?"

Without speaking further, they piled back into Lieutenant Agannis' Taurus. Agannis took the wheel and fished in his pocket for the car keys.

"Hope you're satisfied with this bullshit," he said with surprising sullenness. "I even heard you talking down in the basement. Who'd you see down there? Anyone you know?"

Lieutenant Agannis started the car. Brooks didn't answer for a full minute.

"Something funny's happening on this island, Lieutenant,"

Brooks said. "I can't prove it. I can't find it. I'm hard-pressed to demonstrate it. But it's around. Somewhere. I know it is."

"Yeah," Agannis said. He gave Brooks a sidelong glance. "Sure," he said.

They pulled out of the driveway onto Cort Street. An adult on a bicycle whizzed past them the wrong way on the near side of the street. Agannis nearly hit him and never noticed. The bicyclist never looked back.

In the rear seat of the car, Boomer sighed. It was only then, trying to put the visit in perspective, that one small detail of the visit struck Tim Brooks as odd.

Normally, Boomer followed Lieutenant Agannis anywhere. Anywhere and everywhere. Yet the dog had balked at entering the house and had settled instead outside.

Coincidence again?

Or had stumbling, myopic, noisily panting, drooling old Boomer seen something that all three men present had missed?

The first day of Annette Carlson's visit to New York could not have proceeded better.

She met her agent Joe Harris at his office at Seventh Avenue and Fifty-seventh Street. Joe held a corner office in a big plate-glass tower where he shared a suite with his New York associates.

That morning over breakfast at the Regency, Joe had already extorted tentative terms from the producers for *Message From Berlin*. Harris knew when he was holding the best cards. He knew that the producers specifically wanted Annette Carlson for the lead role in their production. He also knew that he would eventually give her to them. But not before, with his velvet-gloved approach, he turned some iron screws.

Harris took Annette to lunch at the Russian Tea Room. He sat in his usual booth, one of the small ones up front where he could face the door, see everyone who came and went, but be overheard by no one. At lunch, Harris went over the terms of their offer. He explained his impending strategy. He figured he could work the producers upward about fifty percent from each of their original numbers.

Annette listened carefully.

"There's just one angle of this that Joe wants you to be aware of, Annie, honey," Harris eventually warned. "I'm going for a quick hit on these negotiations. I want to have an agreement within another twenty-four hours. Forty-eight maximum. I'm telling the producers that we're going elsewhere Monday evening if we don't have a deal by then."

"Why are you doing it that way?" Annette asked, more curious than in disagreement.

"Joe doesn't want to give their tiny minds the opportunity to switch into gear," Harris said. "I'm hitting them real hard for money, both for you and for my writer. They don't need to have the luxury of putting anything in perspective or shopping for other talent. And we sure as hell don't need that complication, either. So over the weekend it's my way or the highway."

Harris merrily sipped an Italian mineral water, his eyes sharp as tacks. "Are you with me?" he asked.

"Why wouldn't I be?"

"Good. Thank you," he said. "Joe will do the rest."

Annette's faith was implicit that Harris would land the best deal possible, without endangering Annette's involvement in the project. She knew that he wouldn't have taken things this far if he weren't brimming with confidence.

After lunch, she walked with Harris back to his office. There her agent introduced her to Jonathan Reed, the writer of the three-part script, who had a two-thirty appointment with Harris. The agent wanted Reed in New York in person to iron out parts of his own participation in the production. This was also another Harris flourish to the deal: all the principles on hand to hash out language with lawyers and initial the eventual deal memorandum.

Reed was a tall, thin, ascetic-looking man, soft spoken and nicely mannered. He stood respectfully when Annette was presented to him. He shook her hand and told her he was honored to meet her. He spoke in a Tidewater drawl and she later learned that he hailed from Virginia. It was Annette's initial impression that he was gay, though she couldn't tell for certain.

"I want you two to develop a good working relationship," Harris said. "Jon, your script will only get better with Annette in a lead role. And Annie, you'll find that parts like this don't just float by every few days. You can't lose doing one of Jon Reed's scripts." He looked back and forth, from one of them to the other. "I see chemistry setting in here."

The remark embarrassed both of them. But Harris was doing his part to encourage the chemistry and cement the deal at the same time.

"Look what Joe Harris has clipped to his date book," Joe Harris said, leading them both to his desk. "And Joe can't use these because he's going to be negotiating for the two of you this evening."

Harris produced a pair of theater tickets which, by no coincidence at all, were to the hottest show in the city, a London import which had opened to tremendous reviews the preceding Friday. The show was in New York for a limited run of six weeks.

"The two of you have to use them," Harris said. "If you don't, I'm going to fall down on the floor and flail, kick and scream until you do."

Neither Jonathan Reed nor Annette could turn down the offer, so Harris could keep a lid on his flailing, kicking and screaming until he met with the producers of *Message From Berlin* again that evening. Harris had a way of riding herd on his clients this way, of making sure that he knew where they were and with whom they were consorting. It would have pleased him to no end if two single clients got married or at least set up housekeeping together. He felt he then had that much more influence over what they did.

"By the time the curtain falls, I may have good news for both of you," Harris said.

"From your lips to God's ears," Reed said. Apparently, he meant it.

Both clients were staying at the Carlyle. So Joe Harris' office arranged for a car and driver to transport them for the evening.

The car stopped for them at six. They went to a small French restaurant for a light pre-theater dinner on West 47th Street. Then the car took them to the Shubert Theater where the London import was playing. As they arrived, a photographer noticed Annette and caught her picture stepping out of the car. It would appear in the *New York Post* the next day, though Jon Reed was misidentified as an actor.

The show was excellent, living up to the acclaim the reviewers had bestowed upon it. The hired car was waiting for them after the show and drove them directly back to the Carlyle.

There were no awkward moments between Jon Reed and Annette. He saw her to her floor and stepped out of the elevator with her. He gave her a chaste good-night kiss on the cheek and said he looked forward to working with her.

The Carlyle's evening elevator man studied his fingernails the entire time. Then Jonathan Reed went to his room and Annette went to hers.

The light on her telephone was flashing when she entered.

She telephoned the desk. There was but one message. It was from Joe Harris. Joe asked that Annette return his call immediately.

She did.

"When Joe promises wonderful news, Joe comes through with wonderful news," he said. "We're all set. Pending your approval, of course."

It was staggering. The best deal of Annette's career, and certainly one of the best ever formulated for an actress in a miniseries. She would receive a guaranteed four hundred thousand dollars for her participation in the movie, plus escalators and residuals that could take the deal to over eight hundred thousand dollars.

"The beauty of it is that now I can go to the film studios, Annie, honey," Harris said, "and tell them that if this is what you get for television, we want ten times that for a feature film."

"*Ten* times, Joe?" she asked.

"Oh, we'll never get it, angel," he said amiably. "But we'll settle for triple that."

She sighed. "Wow," she said.

"Now stay in town and don't get hit by a truck overnight," he said. "I want to execute the deal memo tomorrow and lock up all the signatures by Monday. I don't want to be a pest, but it's very important. Understand?"

"I understand."

"You're going to be a very wealthy lady, Annie," he said. "This is just the first of several big steps for you. And you know what? You deserve it. You're a good person. It couldn't happen to a better client. Except maybe Jon Reed, my most brilliant television writer, who's now on the other line. Can I call you tomorrow? Maybe after ten A.M.?"

"Joe, you can call anytime you want. And you damned well know it."

"Sweet dreams, Annie."

She set down the telephone, almost overwhelmed. Four hundred thousand dollars. Plus escalators. By the end of the year. For a six-week shoot in California and Europe.

She didn't know whether to let out a yelp of joy or tears of happiness. For some reason windfalls were bittersweet. She knew how hard her parents had worked in their lives. And her father had never made more than thirty thousand dollars in a year.

Similarly, moments like these were times when she didn't like to be alone. She would have liked to have been in love with someone enough to share the moment with him. But there wasn't anyone.

For a moment, she thought of Tim Brooks. She felt like talking to him, just for a minute or two. Then she glanced at the hour—it was almost eleven now—and decided it was inappropriate.

Her hotel room was very still. Outside, very distantly, she could hear the low murmur of traffic on upper Madison Avenue.

She thought of calling her father to tell him. Then she decided, no, she would call him just to chat. To say hello. The good news could be conveyed in another call in a few days, after it was official.

She talked to her dad for fifteen minutes. Then, feeling the need to unwind further, Annette put in calls to two girlfriends, one whom she had roomed with in college, another who lived back in California.

Before she knew it, the clock proclaimed midnight. And she was finally growing tired.

She washed and dressed for sleep. Then she slid into the big plush bed in her suite.

The sheets were soft and cool. The room was spacious. She felt alone, but very safe. She settled into bed and thought she would read for a few minutes. But her mind drifted.

For the first time in several hours, she thought back to her house in Nantucket and the troubles within it. Those problems seemed so distant from her perspective of the moment.

So distant. So less threatening.

She wondered whether the solution was obvious.

Just sell the damned place. Walk away from it. Thanks to Jon Reed's writing and Joe Harris' shrewd negotiations, Annette could unload Cort Street quickly and at a loss.

And she would be out of the problem. No more creaking floorboards, female specters in white and ominous dark forms rising from crashed furniture.

God! What was she even doing there? she wondered. Why had she put up with that bizarre little quirk in reality for as long as she had?

Why, when the solution was so clear.

Sell the damned place, take the loss and move on to the next film project. Buy another home somewhere else.

Funny, she thought to herself, how answers sometimes settle into place if only you allow them to.

She turned off the lights of the room. Tonight the darkness was soothing and restful. Annette dozed peacefully and slept without a care in the world.

Twenty-one

As July turned into August, and as the island became increasingly crowded with summer people, more than ghosts haunted Timothy Brooks.

As a professional law enforcement officer, he was in some ways haunted by every case in which he had ever been involved. And by every arrest, every name and every face that had ever passed before him, be it a victim or a perpetrator, a witness or a suspect.

So it was, on an otherwise uneventful Sunday morning when he was attempting to quickly complete his grocery shopping, that he looked up at the deli counter of the Finast and—almost subconsciously at first—found himself staring at a face that he knew he had seen before.

But where?

He couldn't place it, but knew it was recent.

The man he watched wore glasses and had sharp features. Alert intelligent eyes.

The man must have felt himself being watched as he ordered potato salad and salami, for he glanced Tim Brooks' way. He gave Brooks a weak smile and a nod, then ordered a pound of smoked turkey and half a pound of rare roast beef.

Where?

Again, Brooks sensed a karma. He knew the face was important.

The man was joined for an instant by a young girl. Dark

haired and pretty. She asked him something, then vanished into the supermarket again.

Then Brooks placed the face, just as the man was picking up his order from the counter attendant and turning away.

"Doctor Friedman, right?" Brooks asked. "Doctor Richard Friedman if memory serves me correctly."

The man looked back to the detective. His eyes asked questions.

"Why, yes," he answered. He didn't recognize the detective, and, worse, didn't know whether he should.

Yet there was no reason he would.

"I'm sorry," Dr. Friedman said. "Do I—?"

"No. You don't know me," Brooks said. "I'm Detective Timothy Brooks. Nantucket Police Department."

Almost as an afterthought, Brooks reached to his pocket and pulled out his leather ID case. He showed the doctor his shield.

Surprised and apprehensive, Friedman hesitated before he reacted. "Uh oh." he said. "What did I do?"

"Nothing at all, sir. I wonder if I could talk to you for a moment."

"Of course," Friedman said, still confused.

Brooks walked with him to remove him from the proximity of other shoppers. Dr. Friedman's back was then to a display of iceberg lettuce.

"I listened to you at George Osaro's 'spirit night,'" Brooks said. "You were the final speaker. Renovated your house and disturbed some evil spirit, right? The damned thing finally drove you out? Came charging down the steps the day you were leaving?"

"Oh, that?" Friedman said, with a dismal air of recollection. "Yes, that's me. Or at least that was my story. Sometimes I wished that minister had never talked me into coming."

"I wonder if I could ask you a few questions about it?"

The doctor smiled grudgingly. "Everyone else has," he said. "Sometimes I'm not sure which was worse. The haunting of the house or all the follow-up questions."

"I suspect the haunting was," Brooks said with sympathy.

Friedman placed his deli purchases into a shopping cart. "You suspect right," he said. "Anyway, what's on your mind, officer?"

Brooks corrected him politely. It was "detective," not "officer." But he wasn't about to make an issue of it. And at that time, the girl reappeared. Rachel. His daughter. Fourteen.

On closer inspection, Brooks noted, she was a half-sized Friedman, with a similar posture, black hair, glasses and the same bright alert look through her eyes. She was fair skinned and fresh faced, but her pretty eyes were gray, a trait that must have been her mother's, because her father's eyes were brown. There was a section in the rear of Tim Brooks' mind that absorbed such things while the front chambers were busy with other matters.

Dr. Friedman gave his daughter permission to buy some guacamole. Then the girl was gone again.

"I couldn't get your story out of my mind," Brooks began. "It made something of a believer out of me."

"It made one out of me, too," Friedman said, with no amusement at all.

"And everything happened just the way you said it did?" Brooks asked.

The question annoyed the doctor. Brooks was thus quick to explain that he wasn't questioning Friedman's belief in his own tale. Rather, he said, he wondered if there were any details of the haunting upon which the doctor could expand.

There weren't, Richard Friedman said. "And I live for the day when I'm able to legally unload the place."

"Then you still own the house you described?"

"Unfortunately, yes."

Friedman then made immediate and less than loving reference to the bridge loan he was carrying between the first house on the island—the haunted one—and his current one.

"Have you been over to your old house recently?" Brooks asked.

"No. Why?"

"I was just wondering if it was still, well, afflicted."

"Haven't been in it since the day I described," Friedman said. "And I don't care to."

"Mind if I do?"

"Do what?"

"Walk through. Take a look around."

"What for?"

"I'm investigating a similar case on the island. Sometimes," Brooks said steadily, "I hear that when one house ceases to be a problem, another house starts. I was wondering if you still had your tenant."

The doctor sniffed and shook his head. "Who the hell knows?" he asked.

"Maybe we should find out. If we don't see anything," Brooks encouraged, "maybe the word will get around and your place will sell faster. Stranger things have happened."

"Stranger things already have," the doctor said.

Brooks grinned. Rachel reappeared. Her father sent her for two gallons of one-percent milk.

"When did you have in mind?"

"I didn't have anything in mind until I ran into you right now. So, now's as good a time as any, isn't it?"

Friedman thought about it.

"I swore to myself that I'd never set foot in that building again," he said. "And quite frankly, I have no inclination to break that vow."

"You don't have to. *I'll* walk through." Brooks smiled encouragingly. "That way you have nothing to lose, right?"

The doctor didn't answer.

"Still have the key?" Brooks asked. "Or do the real estate brokers have the honor?"

Dr. Friedman's hand disappeared into his pants pocket. "The brokers have a key and I have a key," he said, pulling it out of his pocket. He gave it a final moment's thought.

"I want to take the groceries home and leave my daughter at our new place. No point involving her. I don't even want her to know I'm going near the place. All right?"

"That's fine."

"I can meet you there in thirty minutes. How's that?"

That, too, Tim Brooks said, was fine. Dr. Friedman then gave him the address.

Brooks, who arrived at the agreed-upon time, took a walk around the outside of the house as he waited. The house was a fine piece of property, a good example of 1880s Nantucket-Victorian architecture. The property was well kept, the house freshly painted. From the outside, there was nothing ominous or threatening.

Dr. Friedman arrived in a red BMW convertible, top down, a 325i which appeared to be of approximately a 1987 vintage. Classic rock and roll played loudly from the car. Meat Loaf. "Bat Out Of Hell." Appropriate, Brooks thought. The detective tried not to hold Friedman's mode of transportation against him.

"Hello," the doctor said, arriving and grinning amiably. He spoke above his wall of music. "I was hoping you'd be here."

"Likewise," Brooks answered. The doctor never acknowledged being late. He cut the engine and the backbeat fell as if hit with a bullet. He stepped out of the BMW, left it unlocked in front of the house, and rattled the keys.

"Okay," he said. "Let's get on with this. I still don't know what you're even looking for."

Brooks shrugged. "If I knew," he answered, "I'd tell you."

They walked to the entrance that faced Milk Street. It was set back about fifteen feet from the road. Brooks had the distinct impression that he was pulling the doctor along.

"I'll tell you something, officer," Dr. Friedman said, approaching the front door and starting to loosen up for the first time. "I don't want this to sound bloated or pretentious or self-serving. But I consider myself a man of science and knowledge. Sounds pretentious, doesn't it? But really, I do. You know, medicine. Natural laws. Physical sciences."

"I'm sure you do," Brooks said.

"But here's my point," the doctor said. "My training, when

faced with something unknown, is to consult experts. Or learn what studies have been done into the subject. That's how I'd approach a disease or a symptom that I'd never seen before. And that's how I thought of what I'd witnessed here."

The two men stood at the front door. A cloud passed across the sun and they were abruptly in a shadow.

"I didn't just walk away from this place and try to sell out," Friedman explained. "I approached it intellectually. I tried to apply the written knowledge of the subject—ghosts, I mean, spirits—to what I'd experienced. Am I losing you?"

"No. But I don't know where you're leading me, either."

"To the library at Harvard University. That's where," the doctor said with a smile.

Faced with such a precise location, Brooks frowned. He was finally lost.

"Keep talking, Doctor," Brooks said. "It's just getting interesting."

"Would you call me, Richard?" he asked.

"Sure."

"And what was your name again?"

"Timothy Brooks."

"Timothy," said Friedman, settling on the first name as if Brooks were a child.

"Tim is fine," Brooks said. Absently, the two men exchanged a handshake, accepting the notion that they should speak on familiar terms.

"Now tell me about the Harvard Library," Brooks said.

"Oh, right. Sorry," Friedman said, keeping the key in his hand. "See, Tim, I'm as fascinated by my experience as I am frightened of it. I admit that. Fear and fascination. That's probably not too far from most people's reaction to ghosts and spirits, is it?"

"You're probably pretty close to the mark," Brooks said.

"So I went over to Harvard's library one time when I was in Boston. I spent an afternoon there, looking through some of the more esoteric stuff. Ended up over in the psychology and psychiatric sections. Ever heard of the Eksman Collection?"

The name, which may have been significant elsewhere, rang no bells for Tim Brooks.

"Harvard has a massive collection on the paranormal. The supernatural. Psychic research. You should give it a look. It's called the Eksman Collection. I think some wealthy old alum from nineteen-twenty or something willed the university his collection of stuff. Well, I spent a couple of hours in there reading."

"And?" Brooks asked. "What did you find?"

"All sorts of things. Did you know, for example, that there are perfectly reasonable explanations for all the ghost sightings on Nantucket?"

"Is that a fact?"

"There's one theory that apparitions are part of an electrical process that we don't yet understand in terms of science. Part mental, part atmospheric electricity. The process might be greatly abetted in Nantucket and on other similar islands by the constant presence of humidity in the ground and in the air."

Dr. Friedman firmly held the detective's attention now. He continued to talk. Distantly within the house, something squeaked.

"The water level on the island sits very close to the surface. As for the air itself," Friedman said, shrugging, "well, the fog here is legendary, isn't it? Know where a parallel situation exists?"

"Where?" Brooks asked.

"Ireland. Southwestern coast and several other regions. Sections of Scotland and England, also, the ones which border on the North Sea. And know what? Studies were done revealing that those areas had exactly the same number of ghost stories per capita as we do here."

Brooks managed a wry smile. "Curious," he said. "A good explanation for skeptics, in other words. The vision is in the mind. Not really there."

Richard Friedman nodded.

"Sure," the doctor said. "But I came away with some other interesting points, too," the doctor said. "And intellectually,

313

they're much more substantive. They go a long way to temper the circumstances that I just mentioned."

"What's all that?"

"Did you know that virtually *all* primitive cultures presume the reality of a spirit world parallel to ours? And that reports of ghosts date back as far as history has been recorded? And that purported contacts with spirits, just in the literature of the European languages, number into the millions?"

"I've never made a study of it," Brooks said.

"Maybe you should," the doctor suggested. "There's nothing very new on this planet. Contact with spirits doesn't seem to be very unusual at all. The truth is that two of the great forces of modern civilization—scientific rationalism and the Judeo-Christian religious thought—have both sought to refute the possibility of contact with a spirit world. Other than the ones within traditional religious views, of course." The doctor nodded. "Kind of shakes you up, doesn't it?" he asked. "The theory is that we *should* be able to contact the spirit world. The power is within all of us. But we've lost the skill. Or we repress the mental capability."

"Now that you know all of this," Brooks asked, "what interpretation do you have on what you saw?"

The doctor looked at him. There was a slight pause between them. Friedman took the liberty of filling it.

"My wife, my daughter and I," Dr. Friedman said steadily, "we *know* that we saw a ghost. And as far as I know," he continued, jingling the keys from his pocket, "this ghost is right inside the house here today. Watching. Waiting for us."

Brooks pursed his lips. "Well," he concluded, "we don't want to disappoint it then, do we?" He motioned to the front door.

"Yeah, fine," the doctor said. "Sure. But I'm not going upstairs."

Unable to stall any longer, Friedman turned the key to the front door. The door gave way easily and came wide open with a big silent yawn.

The two men stepped inside, Friedman with obvious apprehension.

They left the front door open and walked to a den on the west side of the first floor. The room was clean, empty and bright. A yellow print wallpaper was still in excellent condition. The only sounds in the house were their footfalls, then their voices.

"We've dropped our asking price from three seventy-five to three twenty-five," Richard Friedman said. "Any number lower than three-two-five and I lose money. Not that I care at this point. I mean, I'd even arrange creative financing if the deal were right. I'd just like to be out of this situation. So would my wife. She's going crazy. Know what I mean?"

Brooks knew.

"Are you married?" Friedman asked.

"No."

"You're lucky. Must be a lot of great tail to chase on this island over the summer."

Brooks turned on the doctor and was ready to be angry. But Friedman was scarcely aware of his offense. Instead, his conversation rambled forward.

The doctor made another reference to the bank and its bridge loan, this one profane. He had added Tuesday evening hours to his medical practice in Boston, he said, just to keep current with what he referred to as "the fucking extortionate financing."

They left the den and followed a corridor that led into an open dining room with a gorgeous old hearth.

"This is the kitchen," Friedman said next as they stepped into it. Clean and modern and spacious, a wall had been removed from what had once been a pantry. Recently renovated. Microwave and work island, as never envisioned by the architects from the 1880s. "I dropped fifteen thousand putting a modern kitchen in," Friedman said. "Opening up the space. Then we took a walk."

The men went into the living room next. Neither spoke.

Brooks looked around and tried to feel something. He couldn't. His overriding sensation was that Dr. Friedman was scrutinizing him.

"Well, it *is* a nice house," Brooks finally offered.

"Thank you. Want to buy it?" he asked with a grin.

"Not on a policeman's salary."

"Ah, yes. Cops don't earn much, do they?"

Brooks let the remark pass. "Plus, I hear the place has a reputation," he said.

"Sure does," the doctor said with a sigh. They stood in the living room, an attractive space with light blue walls. Brooks could understand the love and care that Dr. and Mrs. Friedman had put into the place.

"Well, that's it," Richard Friedman said, standing in the empty living room and pointing toward the landing below the staircase. "You heard what I had to say on 'Spirit Night.' That's where I saw the ghost. He came down the steps right over there. Then he charged over to me. I'm standing where I was standing then. He was where you are now."

Brooks glanced up and looked darkly at the area in question. He walked to the landing at the base of the stairs. It was adjacent to the front door, which remained open. Outside, the air was fresh, the day was sunny. There were voices from people passing on foot.

"I have to ask you this," Brooks said, almost with a tone of apology. "I know you moved out of here, I know your family was frightened. I know you went and did the subsequent research at Harvard. But, tell me, Richard. Is there any chance that this . . ." Brooks searched for the tactful words.

"Didn't happen?"

"Yes."

"No chance at all. My wife and I stood here. We saw it. My daughter saw it. And having done the reading at Harvard, I'm more sure of it than ever. There's something in this house. Or at the very least, there was something when we were here."

Brooks arrived at the base of the steps. He stared upward. The sensation reminded him of gazing up Annette Carlson's attic steps. He turned back and looked at the doctor. Then he peered upstairs again, half expecting some nightmarish, devilish vision to charge down the stairs toward him.

None did. He walked back to Dr. Friedman.

"What's upstairs?" Brooks asked.

Friedman didn't answer.

"It's empty?" Brooks asked.

"There's no furniture there, if that's what you're asking. We cleaned the place out when we moved. Or I should say, the movers took everything out for us."

"Did the movers report anything unusual?"

Friedman shook his head.

"Where was the original trouble spot upstairs?" Brooks asked. "If I remember, you remodeled a room and—"

"It's down the hall to your left. Second doorway. You can't miss it."

"Mind if I have a look?" Brooks asked.

"Be my guest," Friedman said.

"Want to come with me?"

"No."

Brooks smiled. "I didn't expect you to."

Brooks returned to the base of the front steps.

He paused for a second, then he slowly climbed the stairs. Again, he expected some sudden spiritual manifestation as he took step by step.

He reached the halfway point. Did he feel anything? A presence pushing against him, forcing him back down? No. See anything? No, again. In five more seconds he was on the landing at the top of the stairs.

The second floor was more ominous. He heard Dr. Friedman walking in the living room below. Brooks turned and slowly walked down the hallway toward the renovated end of the second floor, the area where the construction had possibly dislodged a resting spirit.

Brooks surprised himself with his own boldness. He glanced in the first room, then arrived at the room that young Rachel had slept in—the room where the Milk Street ghost had first appeared.

The door was partially closed. For some reason, an image of George Osaro flashed before his mind. Brooks reached to the door. He put his hand on the knob. He wondered what horrible thing might lurk on the other side.

He drew a breath.

The thought came to him: George Osaro lying dead. Decapitated, maybe. His brains bashed out. His arms and limbs tied into a playful knot.

Brooks shuddered. The premonition was very strong before him now. He drew another breath and held it. He felt the sweat starting to run off him.

He pushed the door open.

Brooks lowered his eyes, gathered his courage, and looked up, searching quickly through the empty room as he stepped into it.

Nothing. Nothing at all. An empty room like a million others in the world.

"Nothing? Anything?" he asked aloud.

No answer.

His eyes settled upon a closet. That door, too, was partially open. And it was at just the perfect angle so that Brooks couldn't see into it.

His courage faltered.

Osaro is a dead man. Can't you see it?

Was he brave? Or chicken?

He blew out a long breath. He knew that he was psyching himself. Knew it and couldn't stop.

Walk away from that closet?

Or find George hanging there, neck tied to the cross bar, hanging by a belt?

Are you a cop or a coward?

Damn! The internal voice asking him all these questions was his own today. Something had crept within him and given words to all the self-doubts that he had entertained in a lifetime.

Well, what are you? he asked himself. A coward or not?

Brooks crossed the room toward the closet. Before his eyes, the closet door took on an extra dimension. Same shape as a coffin, isn't it? Rectangular, like the lid to a pine box. Or maybe you'd like rosewood!

"Damn it," Brooks said angrily.

He reached to the closet door and yanked it open, expecting the worst—

And found nothing again.

A few wire hangers hung undisturbed, swaying slightly from the vibration of the door. The hangers were where the Friedmans had left them. Right where the movers had missed them.

Brooks exhaled long and deeply. He turned, retraced his steps and walked back downstairs.

He found the front door open. Dr. Friedman was standing outside. He looked relieved when Brooks reappeared in the frame of the front door.

"You told me your dog wanted no part of this place? Am I right?" Brooks asked.

Friedman recalled from the account he had given at Reverend Osaro's church. The dog had avoided the section of the house in which the ghost had first been disturbed.

"Right," he said.

"I wonder if I could borrow the key," Brooks said. "I'll return it later today. I want to bring in another expert."

"If you're thinking of George Osaro," Friedman said, "forget it. He won't come."

"I had another expert in mind," Brooks said. "An individual with an entirely fresh perspective."

"Anyone I know?"

"Doubt it."

"Can you give me a name?"

"It wouldn't mean anything."

Dr. Friedman thought about it, then shrugged.

"Well, why the hell not?" he said. "Look, when you got a three-hundred-seventy-five-thousand-dollar house that you can't sell, nothing's going to get much worse. Set fire to it if you want. It's insured. You'd be doing me a favor."

Brooks looked at him oddly. It recurred to Friedman that he was talking to a policeman.

"Just kidding," the physician said quickly. "You know I'm just joking. Right?"

Brooks nodded. Friedman handed him a key. Brooks thanked him and the two men left the house on Milk Street.

It was early afternoon when Brooks returned. His expert wore a thick black coat and a chain collar and was panting heavily. Brooks had borrowed Boomer from Lieutenant Agannis with the understanding that the Labrador be returned safe and sound within an hour.

Brooks kept the dog on a leash, so he could guide him more securely. Man and beast entered the house on Milk Street without incident. Brooks led the animal through the first floor. The dog's tail wagged. His mouth was open and his tongue hung. He panted.

Brooks prowled through the kitchen and began opening cabinet doors. He found a cracked saucer that had been left behind. It was a garish green and red, clearly a relic of the 1950s, a cucumber-and-tomato design.

Brooks drew some cold water from the tap and served the dog some water. Then Brooks rinsed the saucer and left it in the sink.

Upstairs was a different story.

The dog hesitated on the staircase. Brooks had to tug at the leash to induce the dog to follow. At the top of the steps Boomer wanted to retreat or sit down again.

"Come on, boy," Brooks whispered to the dog. "No one's going to hurt you." As he spoke, Brooks wondered if he betrayed his own fear, his own anxiety, and whether the dog was reacting to that.

The detective tugged on the leash again. Finally, Boomer followed, though the animal wasn't happy. Brooks pulled him down the hall. The house was very still. And with daylight waning and the electricity turned off in the building, there were more nuances and shadings to the second floor.

They reached the door to Rachel's room, the area that had been remodeled. Boomer pulled away. Brooks felt a prickly feeling at the base of his neck. He also suffered from a sense of intrusion, as if he had entered an area where many people had stopped talking and were holding silent.

"Come on," Brooks said to Boomer. "Just come into the room for a few seconds."

But whatever Brooks felt, the Labrador felt, too. The dog pulled sharply on the leash.

"What's the matter, boy?" Brooks asked.

The dog refused to budge. Brooks turned and looked into the empty room. He saw nothing. Yet the feeling on the back of his neck remained.

Were the spirits rising with the approach of night? Did Boomer sense the same thing as he?

Brooks waited for his questions to be answered. He waited for a voice—even *the* voice—to come from somewhere and provide a solution.

But none came.

"Okay, Boomer," he said. "That's enough here."

The dog seemed to understand, because he turned to go.

They went downstairs and piled into Brooks' car, the dog stationed on the passenger side of the two-seater. They drove back toward town, then the dog let out a whimper when Brooks took a turn that led away from the police station and over toward Cort Street. Brooks wondered if the dog knew where they were going.

Brooks pulled his car into the circular driveway before 17 Cort Street. He turned to the dog.

"What's the matter, boy?" Brooks asked. "You've been here before. Nothing happened last time, right?"

Brooks patted Boomer on the head. He took him by the leash and pulled him out of the car. He led him to the back door of the house. The structure was dark, save one light in the downstairs. And there was a small pile of building supplies that Emmet Hughes, who had finished for the day, had left under the rear landing.

Brooks unlocked the house. As he pushed the door open, he experienced a hard yank on the leash.

The Labrador was pulling wildly back from him. Boomer

whimpered and yanked against the collar and the leash. The dog pulled furiously. Brooks had no choice but to back up several paces so that the dog would calm.

"Whoa, whoa," Brooks said. "What's the matter, boy? What's there?"

Boomer knew there was something. And he knew that he didn't like it. Brooks crouched down near him and patted the dog soothingly, under the chin and along the underside of the chest. Yet the dog's body was tense and his canine heart was pounding.

A wind, or something, made the back door open further. Boomer's ears perked, his eyes went alive and he tried to bolt. Brooks stared at the same spot and saw nothing. He heard nothing. He felt nothing.

But the animal recoiled. Brooks held him firmly by the collar. Boomer pulled back again. First, it was as if there was an unseen boundary that the dog didn't care to cross. Then it was as if the unseen boundary—or something unseen—was moving toward him.

Brooks glanced at the doorway again, saw nothing, and looked back to the dog, attempting to steady him. That's when the animal went into a frenzy.

The black fur stood up on his back. Boomer started to snarl, teeth visible beneath curled lips. Brooks looked at the animal incredulously and then felt another deep flash of fear. He found himself staring into animal eyes quite different from any he had seen before. Boomer's gaze beaded upon him. It was wolfish and cunning, gleaming and feral.

Brooks froze. The animal's snarl rose to a bark and the bark to a bite as Boomer snapped with heavy powerful jaws at Brooks' arm. The dog got a piece of him, ripping the sleeve of his shirt, teeth tearing at his skin.

Brooks sprung to his feet and hit the lunging dog with a knee, stunning him. Then as the dog lunged a second time, Brooks chopped at him with the side of his hand. When the dog sprung a third time, Brooks caught him again with a knee, sending the animal sprawling backward and tumbling.

But Boomer achieved what he had wanted. He was free from his handler. He turned his tail between his legs. The fur on his back flattened and receded and the dog, its pride and psyche wounded, retreated, dragging the leash as he slinked toward the car.

Brooks felt a deep aching on his arm, accompanied by something warm and wet flowing down his wrist to his palm. He knew it was blood. The dog had bitten him on the back of the arm, just below the elbow. He stepped away from the house and looked at the wound. Boomer had nailed him with three or four teeth, deeply puncturing his flesh.

Brooks applied pressure to the wound by gripping it with his free hand.

He locked the house again.

He walked back to his car. Boomer—the placid amiable old Boomer—was sitting near the green convertible, as if nothing had happened. Almost apologetically, the dog wagged his tail as Brooks approached.

Brooks leaned down and patted the animal. Then he found the first-aid kit that he always carried in his trunk. He bandaged his wrist and covered the bandage by putting on a windbreaker.

Tim Brooks returned the key to 29 Milk Street to Dr. Friedman. He returned Boomer to Lieutenant Agannis. Then he drove past the parish house of Christ and Holy Trinity and found Reverend Osaro still missing. He then reported to the Emergency Room at the Nantucket Cottage Hospital.

There, as Brooks sat on an examination table, a physician named Peter Shannon used fifteen stitches to close the wounds to Brooks' arm. Luckily, there had been no damage to veins or nerves.

Then Dr. Shannon departed and a nurse applied dressing and fresh bandages. She was a woman in her twenties, with reddish hair and a pretty girlish face. Brooks' eyes settled upon the name tag on her left breast. It said she was Marilyn Blake, R.N., B.S.

Marilyn took several minutes at her task. But as she finished, in the corridor outside there was the sound of something smashing, like a plate being dropped. The abrupt noise—and the nearness of it—made Brooks jump. The nurse jumped as well.

"I don't know what goes on at this place sometimes," she said in mild disgust. "Every once in a while something just falls off a table and crashes."

Brooks' eyes went to the door. Marilyn looked back to her patient.

"Feel okay?" she asked, examining his wrist.

"It's better," Brooks said, moving his forearm, "just from your touch, Marilyn."

The nurse smiled prettily. She blushed and Tim Brooks realized that he was flirting.

Brooks made a fist, then flexed his fingers. "I'll be fine," he said.

"Good. I'll be back in a minute. I want to see if Dr. Shannon is prescribing medication. I'm sure he is. Can you wait here please?"

Brooks said he could. Marilyn left the room and stopped short. There was a broken dish of some sort just outside the door. She made a tisking sound with her tongue, then quickly found a pan and brush. Brooks watched her sweep up the broken shards of china—white with red and green—with quick efficiency.

"You learn to do everything yourself around here," she said absently to Brooks. "Housekeeping staff. Where are they when you need them? You'd wait forever."

Brooks gave her a sympathetic nod. She poured the broken pieces into a waste basket and disappeared again.

In silence, Brooks stared at what she had done. Then, as a realization set in upon him, he bolted to his feet. He moved to the waste basket and reluctantly looked downward, knowing he would confirm his worse suspicions.

He felt a surge in his stomach, like those powerful wings flapping again. He wanted to vomit. The worst part about it was that he was no longer incredulous, no longer surprised.

He didn't even have to reach down to examine the shattered saucer. He recognized its red-and-green tomato-and-cucumber design. It was the same saucer he had filled with water for Boomer at Milk Street.

Brooks went back to the examining table and sat upon it again.

He suppressed a shudder. "Where are you?" he asked aloud.

Very good, my dear swine! At last you can sense my presence!

Brooks, speaking in the empty examining room: "Boomer saw you, didn't he? Even though I didn't, the dog saw you."

And I, him.

"You made him go crazy."

Very easy. A conceit.

"When will *I* see you?"

Soon.

"When will you kill again?"

Even sooner.

"Who will you kill?"

Let us speak of you and the whore-actress. I should think you two might like to go down into the earth in the same box, Timothy. Do tell me your preference before it's too late: Rosewood? Pine?

Brooks ignored the question.

But you lust for her. Admit it. The day will come when you will offer her your phallus.

Loud: "Shut up!"

Losing it, aren't you? I suspect a pine coffin would be best on a policeman's salary. Nothing fancy for a stupid common working man who lusts for a glamorous tart!

Brooks shouted. "Shut the fuck up!"

Insane laughter. Again, from nowhere! Everywhere!

Brooks was on his feet. He slashed at the air with his arms. "Where are you?" he demanded. "*Who* are you!"

The voice came to him next with immense clarity. *Henry Flaherty!*

Brooks froze. "*Who?*"

Silence.

"Come on. Talk to me!"

More silence.

"Were you a person once?"

Still more silence. Ominous and icy.

"Come on!" Brooks finally shouted. "Talk to me, God damn it! Talk to me again!"

The door flew open. Brooks' head turned toward it. He felt a jolt of near panic, intense fear, thinking that the moment of ultimate confrontation was at hand.

But in the doorway were the physician and the young nurse. They stood motionless, having heard his shouts. They stared at their patient. Wordless. Disapproving. Perplexed. Not comprehending.

They were unable to hear the mad symphony that played in Brooks' mind.

Laughter. Insane laughter. From near, from far. From all around, from nowhere.

From the other side of accepted reality. From beyond the boundaries of normal human imagination.

Laughter that rang in Brooks' head until the doctor and nurse very cautiously entered the room and sat down near him.

The laughter eased. Simultaneously, the doctor and nurse methodically explained to him the prescriptions they were giving him to control infection in his wrist. They also described the follow-up treatment that the injuries would dictate.

Brooks said nothing and received their guidance without complaint. But the entire time, Dr. Shannon and Nurse Blake looked at Brooks strangely. And the laughter Brooks heard was only a hollow echo resounding in his own imagination.

Twenty-two

To Tim Brooks, no sight was stranger than George Osaro's white Plymouth van parked in the driveway before the parish house. Brooks spotted it at about seven P.M. on Sunday evening, August 2.

Brooks pulled his own car into Osaro's driveway, studied the minister's house for a second, then cut his engine and jumped out.

He went to the front door of Osaro's home. It was open. An outside screen door was latched. Brooks knocked.

Osaro's voice replied from within. "Who's that?"

"George? Is that you?"

There was a silence and Brooks waited. A few seconds later, the minister appeared from a back room, wearing a T-shirt and a pair of old khakis.

"Hello, Timmy," Osaro said from within. "What's the good word?" Osaro grinned. "Miss me?"

"Well, I was wondering . . ." Brooks said. "Disappeared without a trace. No appointments. No forwarding number . . ."

"Whoa," Osaro said. "Talk to me. Come on in."

"Open this damned door and I will."

"You know, that's three blasphemies in the last twenty seconds, Tim," Osaro said, giving his friend another smile and unlocking the screen door. He opened it. "Three in twenty seconds. You're badly in need of some moral guidance. Religious instruction, maybe."

"Oh, fuck you, Parson," Brooks said, pleased to see George Osaro apparently alive and well. He put his hand on the minister's shoulder as he passed through the front door, almost as if to reassure himself that Osaro was in the flesh.

"That's four times in thirty seconds," Osaro said. "You know, there's a special pyre in hell for the likes of you."

"Is there really?"

"Probably not," said Osaro. He shrugged. "How would I know? I never been there."

Brooks grinned and entered the minister's house. He had been there before many times and the house was more depressing with each visit. Osaro was no one's idea of a great housekeeper. Books and magazines remained stacked on any available surface in the living areas. Osaro's basketball shoes and running equipment, even a torn jersey from Harvard, lay askew on the floor of the front alcove. The furniture was worn, tables were dusty, lamp shades were crooked and a pair of coffee cups sat in the living room, unmoved since before Osaro's disappearance.

Some might have taken all this as an example of a devout nonmaterialist who gave little thought to his surroundings. Brooks saw things differently, sensing an air of need and desolation prevailing over comfort. To Brooks the house had almost—to misuse a term—a spooky atmosphere.

Brooks followed the minister to what passed for a den. Osaro dropped himself into a chair. "Everyone claims to be surprised that I was gone. Didn't know where I was."

"I drove by the church. And I passed by the house several times," Brooks said.

"I'm sure you did. That's what everyone says." Osaro ran his hand through his dark hair. "Did anyone think of *phoning* me at home, however? No-o-o-o. Apparently not. If anyone had, the island's greatest mystery would have been solved."

Osaro reached to an answering machine. He pushed a button. It played a message in his voice, explaining he was going to Boston for three days. It gave a number at which he could be reached.

"Happy?" Osaro asked.

Brooks sighed sheepishly. "No, I never thought to call your home number," he admitted.

"You and everyone else on the island. Next time I'll get an eight hundred number and put it on a billboard out front Jerry Brown style," he said.

"What were you doing in Boston?" Brooks asked.

Osaro looked at his friend for several seconds. Then he yawned. Brooks noticed the minister did indeed look very tired. Or worried. Or depressed. Or some nasty combination of the three creating a pallor that was indicative of something less than robust health.

"Ah, fuck, Timmy," Osaro said. "Why should I talk about it?"

Brooks was preparing a response when Osaro rose. He trudged to the next room in the house, which was the kitchen. He opened the refrigerator and drew out two long-necked beers. A bottle of Budweiser and a bottle of Labatt's.

"What'll it be, copper? Red or blue?" he asked. "I'm out of Kirin or Asahi."

"Blue," Brooks said, meaning Labatt's.

Osaro opened both bottles. Then he lobbed the open bottle into the air in the direction of his friend.

"Think fast," Osaro said.

Brooks was already thinking. The toss of the open beer bottle was one of the endearing customs of the Osaro domicile. The minister had a way of hefting them upright in a manner in which the open top never turned downward. Never, that was, as long as the hands on the receiving end were steady and cleanly picked off the bottle on the fly. In the past there had been some memorable misses, the details of which were immortalized on some of the furniture and walls.

Brooks allowed Osaro to return to the den and fall back into his easy chair.

"So?" Brooks asked.

"So what?" Osaro offered as an answer.

"What were you doing in Boston?"

"Why are you so interested?"

"I'm just asking you as a friend, George," Brooks said. "To tell you the truth, I was worried about you. As a friend. As a policeman. If you don't want to tell me, if it's none of my business, don't feel obliged to answer. Otherwise—"

"Do I look like I'm alive?" Osaro asked.

"Yes."

"Then what's the worry?"

Brooks repeated his original question, plus his concern.

Osaro had already gulped a third of his bottle.

"Ah, I've been suffering, Timmy," he finally answered. "That's where I've been and what I was doing. Suffering."

Brooks said nothing.

"Suffering in my own very personal, private and spiritual way."

Osaro drew another gulp from the Budweiser bottle and slumped down in his chair. Almost as sudden inspiration, he turned and flipped on a tape deck. Grateful Dead. Jerry Garcia. "Ripple."

"I saw that I had a couple of days open on my calendar," Osaro said. "So I tended to some business. Personal and private."

"You went to see your family?"

The estranged husband nodded. There was something very sad in his eyes.

"My wife's seeing a new boyfriend," Osaro explained. "This one's quite serious. Well, our divorce is complete and she's intent on remarrying if this dude asks her."

Osaro spoke sullenly, eyebrows lifted occasionally, as if at any moment he might switch to a more congenial subject. "Her future husband is from Dallas," the minister said. "Been married twice already. If they married, she would move to Texas with her new cowboy and my son."

"And you'd see your son even less than you see him now," Brooks said.

"You got it. Then, as if the personal stuff weren't uplifting enough, I had an appointment face to face with his royal asshole, Steven Albrecht, the bean-brained bishop of Boston."

"How did that go?"

"As expected. He talked. I listened. He screamed. I listened. He ranted. He accused. He bullied. I denied."

Osaro shook his head in disgust and blew out a dispirited breath. "I'm in deep shit here, Timmy," he said. "Brother Bishop would like to transfer me to shark-infested waters off the coast of Bombay. Since he can't do that, he's talking about an imminent reassignment. Oregon, maybe. Northern California."

"Aw, no," Brooks answered. "You'd have to leave here?"

"Or resign from the ministry. The old man says I've muddied up the water here with this spiritualism stuff. Says there's no place for it in his heaven and earth."

"You haven't muddied any water."

"Tell *him* that."

"If you want me to, I will."

"Save your breath. Or your postage stamp. Jesus, the man is on my ass! You can't believe it." Osaro took a long drag of beer, glanced out the window toward his church, then looked back to his friend. "Fact is, apparently some of my own parishioners complained," he said softly and with obvious hurt. "Can you believe that? Anonymous letters." He raised a single eyebrow. "They think I'm 'creepy.' Why didn't they just come to me if they had a problem. Can you tell me that, Timmy?"

Brooks, resentful also, said he had no idea.

"Do you think it's because . . . ?" Osaro began. "You know . . . ?"

"That you're part Japanese?"

"Yes."

"I hope not," Brooks said.

"Then what is it? What is it about me they don't like?"

"George, maybe it's nothing. Maybe it's a generational thing. Most of your parish is older than you are. They were comfortable with your predecessor. You come in with new ideas, a new face, an unusual approach . . . It's just a guess."

"Well, I'm grateful for your friendship and support, Timmy. But, fuck. I suppose I should have expected this from within the congregation. Jesus only had twelve followers and one of them betrayed Him, too."

How much of that was meant as a joke, Brooks couldn't tell.

"This is not without precedence within the church, you know, Tim—the bishop after the renegade cleric for the latter's study of the supernatural. Ever since the Victorian era, spiritualism has been a thorn in the side of the established Christian churches. The leaders of the church have gone to considerable lengths to eradicate it or isolate anyone—I include myself here—who entertains or promulgates any thoughts about it."

"Why is the church so adamant?"

"Which do you wish to hear? The stated reason or the real reason?"

"Try me with both."

"The stated reason is that spiritualism could lead to a return of Devil worship. Or witchcraft. Or paganism. That's why Brother Bishop tries to drop all three on me interchangeably."

"And the *real* reason?" Brooks asked.

"It's just a guess. But there's one theory that's been afoot for more than a hundred and fifty years, since the great wave of spiritualism in the eighteen thirties. The theory is that since Christian orthodoxy and philosophy haven't solved the mysteries of the universe, maybe there's a chance that answers lie in the study of spirits. You can see what a threat *that* is to the established church. So, as I said, rather than allow us to bring a new dimension to Christianity, they seek to expel us. Isolate the idea as well as those heretics who entertain it." He paused. "Again, such as myself."

"Such as yourself," Brooks repeated.

Osaro sipped some more brew.

"But the embarrassment that the Christian churches have had since Victorian times," Osaro mused further, "is the fate of the churchmen who've often been assigned to investigate spiritualism and disprove its merits." Osaro's eyes found Brooks'. "Often, when studying unexplained forces," he said, "the skeptics witnessed events that challenged the system of reason that they had always accepted. And they've ended up as converts to spiritualism." Osaro smiled with the irony and paused. "Such as both of us," Osaro said. "Am I correct?"

"You are correct."

Osaro shook his head. "To me, the existence of spirits around us is clear. Didn't I promise you that you, Tim Brooks, would eventually come to believe?"

"You did."

"And haven't you?"

Brooks nodded.

"Then why can't the old man see it, too? Why does his mind have to be hermetically sealed against any new thought?"

Brooks said nothing.

Osaro finished his beer and set it aside. He continued in a lighter tone.

"Anyway, my transfer, is not effective yet," he said. "The bishop is still brooding upon it. Pontificating, if you'll excuse the metaphor. Or maybe the constipated old bastard is just delaying his announcement in case I'd like to consider it a sword held above my head. You know: I behave. I be good. And I won't get shipped off to live with Bigfoot among the outhouses and rain forests of the Pacific Northwest."

Osaro's eyes narrowed with intrigue. He rambled further.

"God works in strange ways, you know. So between now and the time it's final, maybe we'll get lucky," Osaro said. "Divine intervention. I mean, maybe a truck will jump a curb today on Newbury Street and finish off the senile old cretin. With such a miracle, I do believe the archdiocese might be propelled kicking and screaming into this, the twentieth century."

Osaro managed another distasteful grin. Brooks mustered a similar one in agreement and in response.

"Cheers," said Osaro raising his bottle in salute to his most recent thought. He put his lips to the bottle and tried to drain the last drops from it.

For a second, Osaro held an evil glint in his eye.

"Maybe I should make up a little doll with the bishop's name on it," he suggested. "Stick a few pins in. On the one hand, that would confirm every suspicion he's ever had about me. On the other hand, maybe the voodoo would work. Maybe a curse will befall him and he'll be bitten by a rabid duck some evening."

Brooks smiled again. "Somehow I don't think that's your answer," he advised.

"No," Osaro said. "But what *is* the answer? I'm not into black arts here. I would like nothing more than to define spiritualism and the afterlife in accepted Christian terms." He sighed. "And the old bugger in Boston fights me tooth and nail."

Brooks commiserated.

"Anyway, Timmy," Osaro concluded, "if you're interested in really studying this spiritualist stuff, you ought to make a pilgrimage to Boston, yourself. Harvard Library. Go browse through the—"

"Eksman Collection?" Brooks asked.

"Yes," he answered, surprised. "How did—? Ah! You've been talking to my earnest soulmate, Doctor Friedman."

Brooks nodded.

"Did you go to his home? I should say, his *former* home?"

"I did."

"And? See anything? Feel anything?"

"I took a dog there who didn't want any part of the second floor," Brooks said. "The same dog bit me before he'd let me drag him into Seventeen Cort Street."

Brooks held up his wrist and showed the bandage.

"No shit?" said Osaro with a sly grin. "Which dog?"

"Lieutenant Agannis' Labrador. Boomer."

"Ah, that mutt doesn't like me, either," Osaro said. "But anyway, it sort of figures. Milk Street is a real heavy location. A powerhouse. Is that why you were looking for me, by the way?"

"Not exactly."

"Then what was the reason?"

"Seventeen Cort Street," said Brooks. "I was trying to talk you into walking through the place."

"Oh, Lord. Is there more to that house?"

"Quite a bit."

"Regale me with some anecdotes. Spare no details."

Brooks took several minutes to provide Osaro with both. The minister rose, went to the refrigerator and found another brew as he listened. When he plopped down again he was up to date.

The Grateful Dead tape in the background hit the end of one side and reversed.

"Lord," Osaro repeated with a sigh. "Lord, Lord, Lord." He shook his head.

"And there's one other aspect of this," Brooks added.

"What's that?"

"It talks to me."

Osaro froze and stared. *"What* talks to you?" he asked.

"The Cort Street spirit."

Still staring, "He just sidles up and starts a conversation, this spirit?" Osaro asked. "Or he appears from time to time? Or he comes on your police radio, or what?"

"I hear his voice."

"Out loud?"

"In my head."

"All the time?"

"At times that he chooses. To threaten. To taunt."

For several seconds, Osaro looked away. He considered it. Then he looked back to his friend. "I was hoping when you turned up at the door you just wanted a little basketball," he said.

"Sorry. No such luck."

"Instead, you're describing a full-fledged haunting. Tortured spirit. Unable to rest. The whole damned works."

"I know."

"Shit! And three weeks ago, you didn't even believe, right?"

Brooks answered after a moment. "Right," he affirmed.

"You know what folks usually say about people who hear

voices?" Osaro asked with a certain dismay. "That they need psychiatric intervention."

"I don't hear voices. I hear one very specific voice."

"Man? Woman?"

"Man?"

"I don't suppose he left his name."

"Henry Flaherty."

"What?"

"The last time we conversed, he gave me that name."

"Who the hell is—or *was*—Henry Flaherty?"

"I don't know."

"Have you tried to find out? Tried to trace the name at all?"

"George, the name means nothing. But this voice gets inside my head. I'm getting messages from somewhere. There are times when I even know he's there and I know there's a message coming."

Osaro listened.

"Other times I think I see a dark form. I can never get a good look at it, but I think it's associated with the voice."

"You're lucky that you're telling this to me and not to anyone else," the minister said. "If the police department caught the scent of this, Lieutenant Agannis would have you on Thorazine and off duty on screwball sick leave."

Brooks paused. "Yeah, I know." He hesitated. "I also feel that the DiMarco slaying had something to do with this. So did the boy who drowned at Surfside. Then there are a bunch of smaller, macabre events around the island. The McCloy farm had eighteen ducks strangled. A woman in Madaket had a religious painting desecrated . . ." He paused. "Who knows what's next?"

"Now you're alleging that this spirit is interacting. And violently, to boot. Know how few recorded cases there are of that?" Osaro asked.

"I wouldn't know, George. I only know what I see, hear and feel." He drew a breath. "And I was hoping that you could help me understand it," Brooks said. "That's why I want you to come to Cort Street."

"Ah, Timmy . . ." He shook his head and drained his beer. "You know I'm a sucker for this stuff, don't you? Even after everything I just told you." He looked dispirited. "Is anyone else at Cort Street right now?"

"Annette Carlson is in New York. Emmet Hughes is doing some repair work on the wall in her house. But Emmet should be finished for the day."

Reverend Osaro sighed. "I suppose," he said, "we could take your car. A quick look, know what I mean? Just as a favor to you to take a reading on the place. This is not exactly the most propitious time," he reasoned, "for word to drift back to Boston that—"

"I understand," Brooks said. "Let's get over there now. Before dark."

They took Brooks' car and drove at the time that the sun was setting. In front of them, down a long road bracketed by old trees, there was a crimson western sky rippled with clouds. Once, such a sight had promised Brooks the end of an honest day's work and the advent of an evening's relaxation. Now when he looked at it he saw only the inevitable threat of night.

Brooks wondered whether Osaro read his thoughts telepathetically, for the minister looked at his watch. He, too, was thinking in terms of darkness.

"First week of August," Osaro said. "And already it's noticeable how much earlier it's getting dark. Don't you think?"

"We'll have to hit the roundball courts earlier," Brooks said, trying to maintain both of their spirits. "Tomorrow night, by the way. Let's hit the hoops at six."

"It's a deal." Osaro smiled for the first time.

"Here's the house," Brooks said. He pulled into the semicircle and cut his car's ignition.

They walked to the back door. Brooks found the key where he had left it under the large mossy rock in the garden. When he went to the rear door and unlocked it, his arm ached again where Boomer had bitten him. And once again he encountered the fear of what he had sensed on the other side of the door.

His fear was quickly confirmed. The lock turned against the

key, but the doorknob would not turn. It was as if there were an unseen hand on the other side, holding the knob in place.

Osaro stared at it and the two men exchanged a glance. Then Brooks was again beset by the prickly feeling upon the base of his neck.

"I feel something already," Osaro said softly.

Brooks saw concern on Osaro's face and nearly lost his own nerve to enter. But he fought to be brave. And to move ahead.

"Let me try something," Osaro said softly. "A little psychological warfare."

He placed his own hand on the doorknob along with Brooks'.

The force remained present on the other side, then seemed to dissipate. Resistance faded from the other side and the door opened gently. Brooks pushed it wide open and quickly reached within the house to turn on a light.

Brooks and Osaro stood at the entrance. They both felt something, a presence, pushing past them to flee the house.

For a moment, Osaro seemed shaken. But he, too, brushed his fear aside. "Just stay with it," he said. "Whatever's here, we have to drive it back to its own universe."

Brooks pressed forward. Then the resistance against him was gone. He felt a surge of relief. He looked to his friend.

The minister grinned. "Come on, Timmy," he said. "I think something just left. Maybe for good. Who knows?" He froze for a second. "It's safe to enter. That's the vibration I get." He held for a final split second. Then, "Come on," he said. His voice was relaxed and calm. "Nothing to fear. I promise."

Osaro walked through the house first. Brooks followed him from two or three steps behind. Osaro seemed to proceed with mounting interest, occasionally stopping to sense a room or examine a piece of furniture. Brooks tailed along warily, keeping his thoughts and apprehensions to himself.

They stopped in the living room where Emmet Hughes was reconstructing the wall. They went to the second floor and then with particular caution went through the attic. Brooks reminded Osaro about the incident involving the attic door and the dummy. Osaro nodded thoughtfully and offered nothing. Then they went back downstairs.

In the kitchen, they found the door to the basement open and unlatched.

"What's this? A cellar?" Osaro asked.

Brooks nodded. "Usually it's kept closed."

"Worth a look?" the minister asked.

"Definitely."

They turned on a light and walked down the creaking wooden stairs.

Brooks recalled his own sense of unease about the basement. He also wondered why the door had been left open.

The answer to that question was soon answered as innocently as possible. On the concrete at the foot of the cellar steps, Emmet Hughes had left some measuring devices, note papers and other carpentry tools. Obviously, he envisioned working here as well as in the living room.

Osaro stood by the section of the floor that was earthen. His eyes searched the floor, then the walls. Finally, he glanced overhead. On this task, he looked more like a building inspector than a spiritualist.

"So?" Brooks finally asked.

"Nice old house."

"That's not what I mean."

Osaro smiled. "There's nothing really to get upset about here, Timmy," Osaro said softly. "We'll talk outside."

Brooks was increasingly uncomfortable.

"Unless, of course," Osaro said, "something suddenly leaps out at us and puts its teeth to our throats." He grinned.

"Very funny."

"Just a little joke." His eyes settled upon Brooks. "What's the matter? You're a little jumpy down here."

Brooks folded his arms. "How do you know you're not missing something?" he asked.

"We'll talk outside," Osaro said again.

They turned and started back upstairs. Brooks went first. Three-quarters of the way to the top of the steps, Osaro stopped, looked back down and swept the area with his eyes. Then, eventually, he came into the kitchen.

They closed the door and latched it.

"I've seen enough," Osaro said. "Unless you have something else to show me."

"I do. One thing," Brooks said.

He led his friend back into the living room and to the checkerboard table that sat unobtrusively in a front corner of the chamber.

"Know what this is?" Brooks asked.

"Looks like some scrawny little antique table to me," Osaro said. "Not a bad piece, I suppose," he said, studying it further. "Should I recognize it?"

"Maybe," said Brooks. "Wasn't there a woman in your parish named Helen Ritter?"

Osaro thought for a moment, placing the name. "Of course. A very old, very sweet woman. Died two weeks ago. I used to visit her at Mid Island Convalescent."

"Then you've seen the table before."

Osaro frowned, not understanding.

"Mrs. Ritter willed the table to Annette," Brooks explained. "Wanted her to have it. Did Mrs. Ritter ever tell you what she used to do with it?"

Osaro shrugged. "Keep the business records for a local whorehouse?" he guessed facetiously.

"I'm being serious."

"I would have no way of knowing, Timmy," Osaro said. "What did she use it for?"

"Ever heard of table-turning?"

Osaro looked at Brooks with a stunned expression, one which then changed to surprise. Almost shock. "Oh, shit," he said in a low voice. "No. Really?"

"Anything to it?" Brooks asked. "You're the one with the inside track to the spirit world."

"Old Mrs. Ritter used to turn tables? Is that what you're telling me?" Reverend Osaro shook his head in amazement. "I'll be damned."

"She said she used to turn *that* table," Brooks said. "Used it for successful seances. Talked to dead relatives through it. Did it with her mother and sister when she was much younger."

Osaro was shaking his head. "Dear Mrs. Ritter. A spiritualist," he muttered. "I never realized." He ran his fingers across the rims of the table. The wood was richly colored and almost warm to the eye.

"Mrs. Ritter said she always needed three participants. Three people who believed. Then that table would fly," Brooks said. He waited.

Osaro was forthcoming with nothing.

"Ever heard of stuff like that working?" Brooks asked.

"Oh, yeah," Osaro answered routinely. "Most people discredit it, but I've known cases where it worked. I've heard of people turning tables in houses like this one, where there's been a disturbance."

Brooks drew his friend from the living room and they walked toward the rear door to the house.

"I knew firsthand of a case in Westport, Connecticut, a few years ago," Osaro continued. "A medium turned a table so well that the table danced up the walls of a disturbed house. I knew of another case in Nashua, New Hampshire—I *saw* this one when I was in divinity school—where this West Indian woman could actually levitate a table. Her name was Madame Elvira. Or something like that. Made the table rise a foot off the ground just by putting her fingertips to it."

"Come on," Brooks said. They stepped out of the house. Brooks used the key to lock it.

"I *saw* this one, Tim. It was the scariest thing I ever saw. She called forth a demon in broad daylight. A real bad spirit that had no business in this world. No strings. No mirrors. No fucking tablecloths. The table rose and the spirit came forth."

"What's the point of it?" Brooks asked.

"What do you mean, 'what's the point of it'?"

"Turning tables. What does it accomplish?"

"Arguably," Osaro explained, "you're providing a comfortable conduit for a spirit. If you can call forth whatever spirit is

341

present in a disturbed place, you can address the source of the disturbance. That way, you can put a soul to rest." He paused. "Or at least, that's the theory."

Brooks replaced the key under the mossy rock. There was little outside light left. They walked toward Brooks' car. "You sound dubious," Brooks finally said.

Osaro shrugged.

"Have you ever seen it work?" Brooks asked. "Putting the spirit to rest?"

"It worked in the Westport case. The haunting stopped after two seances. But it didn't work in the New Hampshire case. The seances were followed by a general smashing of windows, plates and furniture about the house. The spirit said it had left its earthly body—died, in other words—in nineteen twelve. Now it enjoyed wandering through a nether world, resisted passing along to the next world and apparently didn't wish to be summoned."

"How did they finally get rid of it?"

"Between you and me?"

"Yes."

"They didn't. The house has had five owners in seven years. And the disturbances continue. They come and go."

Brooks thought about it for a moment, then stopped as they arrived at his car. "So what do you think about it here?"

"About what?"

"Turning Mrs. Ritter's table to see what's in the house."

"You said you needed three believers."

"I got them."

"Who?"

"Annette. Me." He paused. "And——"

"Me? No way!" said Osaro. "Absolutely not."

"Ah, come on, George. You're the god damned expert on this stuff and every time we need you I have to drag you forward."

"So what does that tell you?"

"It tells me that you claim you believe in this stuff, but you're never willing to follow through."

"Just stuff like this," Osaro corrected. "Timmy, this conversation is starting to sound like one we had a few weeks ago. Remember? I told you I didn't want to be involved. And not just because Brother Bishop is on my case."

"Yeah, you told me, but—"

"Well, I'll refresh your mind. This is the occult. This is opening up that window, that crack into one of the other universes, that I warned you about. It may be a very *bad*, very *evil* universe. I always wondered whether Pandora's box was a metaphor for this, written by someone who'd flirted with malevolent spirits."

Brooks grimaced with disappointment.

"You don't know what you're going to contact, Tim. I don't summon up spirits. I try to acknowledge that they're there and deal with them in keeping with my theology. But I'm not going to help summon forth something that I might not be able to control."

"But—"

"There's another reason, too. Turning tables is a highly suggestive procedure. Like faith healing. Or hypnotism. Or like an exorcism. You expect to see. You want to believe. So suddenly you can't even trust your own eyes."

"What's the matter with that?"

"Go look at the literature at Harvard, Timmy," Osaro said. "Make a trip over to Cambridge. When you start to see, sometimes you never stop seeing. When the wrong spirit gets into your mind, sometimes it won't let go."

"I already hear one of them."

"That's because you're letting it control you. Instead of you controlling it."

"What are you talking about?"

In the tree branches above them, there was a rustle.

"I think the spirits are everywhere, Tim. I've told you that many times before. But it's when we finally devoutly decide that, yes, we can believe, that we begin to communicate with them. For some reason you've done that. You've allowed spirits into your mind and—"

"Only *one*," Brooks corrected. "Only one spirit."

"I'm sure there are more. But that's not the point. *This* is: it's your mind, isn't it? Don't let a malevolent force play mental games with you. *You* control it. *You* tell it what it can or can't do. The only reality it has is the one you give it."

"Or other people give it," Brooks said.

"Right."

Osaro eyed his friend. Brooks looked confused, as well as angry.

"I still want to do the table," he said.

Osaro smiled and shook his head.

"There's no need," Osaro answered.

"What do you mean, 'there's no need.' The—"

"It's gone, Timmy."

"What's gone?"

"You were right. There was something in this house. It pushed past us when we opened the door. I suspect it didn't care for my presence."

"Because you're a clergyman?"

"Whatever. The spirit pushed past us and came outside. You felt it, didn't you?"

"I felt something."

Osaro opened his hands and grinned.

"Where did it go?" Brooks asked.

Osaro shrugged. "Heaven. Hell. Cleveland. No way of knowing. It might not turn up anywhere else for a hundred years. Spirits have no sense of time, you know. Time ceases when you're dead."

Brooks stared. "Jesus! You *are* creepy."

"I'm not trying to be. Look. Did I answer your question? You should be pleased, by the way."

Brooks was confused. "You didn't feel anything in there? Anything evil?"

"No."

"Nothing at all?"

Osaro hedged. He pursed his lips.

"Yes, I think there's the spirit of something in there. A

344

woman. Maybe two females. But there are dozens of houses like that on this island. And generally spirits like that don't bother anyone." He thought further. "This house had a light sense. Almost one of warmth. But I didn't grasp anything in the air."

The minister hesitated as if there were more. Then he decided that there was. "There was only one thing that bothered me."

"What was that?"

"Something in the basement. I got some bad, bad sensations down there."

"A spirit? I thought you said—"

"No. Not a spirit," Osaro said. "I think . . . I don't know. It's as if a thought kept trying to form itself in my head but never did take shape. It's as if something happened in that basement once. Something highly traumatic. I think it left an emotional imprint on the place. Ever had the history of the house traced?"

"No."

"You might give that a shot if there are any further spiritual manifestations. Problem is, whatever happened could have occurred two hundred years ago. The imprint would still be there. For those who feel such things, at least. For everyone else," he said, shrugging, "it's just a basement."

Down the road, a car came around the bend. Its headlights cast a pair of long shadows toward them. One of them crossed Osaro's face for a moment and gave it a strange cast.

At the same time, the minister glanced above his head. There was another rustling—a breeze, presumably—above them in the branches of the trees.

"Damn," the minister said.

"What's the matter?"

"It's completely dark. I really wanted to hit some hoops."

"Well, you got a car, I got a car. And they both have electrical systems. Right?"

It took a moment. Then, "Yeah!" Osaro said as if in revelation. "Great idea."

They drove back to the parish house to get the Voyager. Both men changed into sneakers. They drove to the basketball court, positioned their car lights to crisscross the south hoop and played one-on-one till nine thirty.

Brooks won two games: Fifty to forty-two, fifty to forty-four. He was ten for ten in foul shots. Throughout, Brooks noted, there were two games in progress on the court. One played by the human figures. And the second played by shadows—the silhouettes of the two players, cast in long, ominous patterns across the asphalt, jockeying with a shadow ball that loomed large, misshapen and ominous in silhouette as well.

A shadow universe, Brooks thought. A shadow reality. But at the end of Sunday evening, their scores were identical.

Later that night, Brooks slept well. He wanted to believe that the disturbances at Cort Street were at an end. But now, in a new way, he again had trouble believing.

Twenty-three

Emmet Hughes, alone in the house at 17 Cort Street at eight A.M. the following morning, unlatched the door to the basement. He reached into the stairwell and turned on the light. Then the workman trudged downstairs. He carried his radio under one arm and his tool chest in the other hand.

He arrived on the concrete of the basement floor. He glanced in the direction of the furnace, toward the earthen section of the floor. Then, as he set down his equipment, he scanned the ceiling, trying to follow the supporting beams.

He searched for the beam that had been injured when the china cabinet had been torn from the living-room wall. He shined a flashlight at the ceiling and found the timber he wanted.

He moved to the area where the concrete ended and the earth began. He retrieved his radio and turned it on. More classic rock from the mainland.

Using a step stool, Hughes reached to the beam and pushed his hand against it. It gave signs of both age and unsteadiness. He would need to make a brace for it. And, upon further examination of the cross beams beneath the living room, he also concluded that an extra support might be advisable beneath the house.

Hughes set to work with measurements. An hour passed as he examined the construction of the basement. It was then that Hughes started to sense something.

There was first the incident involving a pair of pliers. Hughes distinctly felt that he had set them down behind him while he calculated the weight that an extra iron post would need to support. Yet when he turned to pick them up, they had moved about five feet farther away and were on the seat of an old chair.

Hughes didn't remember placing them there. So who was playing tricks on him? Who, when he was alone in the house, and no one else had come and gone?

At another time a bit later, Hughes was making notes upon a writing pad when the temperature of the entire cellar plummeted strangely. He felt as if he were in a severe draft. But the room was so cold that it almost defied belief. Hughes felt his teeth chatter. He was sure that the temperature had dropped to freezing, before suddenly climbing again.

Inexplicable. Even in an old house. It was as if a gust of arctic air had drifted through.

But it was after the incident involving the air temperature that an even stranger feeling came over Hughes. One of dread. Foreboding. For some reason his focus settled upon the dirt part of the basement floor and the stairs. It was as if he were caught between two strange fields.

Hughes did his best to dismiss it. He adjusted the volume on his radio since the sound kept fading. And he hurried along with his work, anxious to finish as quickly as possible.

Yet the strange feelings persisted for Emmet Hughes. He had the sense that someone, somewhere wanted him out of the basement. And he began to feel someone was observing him.

At first, he checked all the windows. Then his focus returned to the steps. Someone, he felt, was watching him from the steps.

But no one was on the steps. No other living soul was within the house.

He shuddered when he thought of it in those terms.

Strangely, he broke a sweat. Nerves. Another five minutes, he thought, and he would be finished. He pondered the situation. Well, the sooner the better. The basement was rattling his nerves worse than any other place he had worked on in thirty years on Nantucket.

He wondered if he was being crazy, but he had a short list of carpenter's assistants who worked per diem on the island. He made a note that it might be worthwhile to hire one to accompany him tomorrow.

"Ah, that's silly," he said to himself. "Waste of money."

But for Emmet Hughes, what was even sillier was presupposing that there would be a tomorrow. On one day in any man's life, there will not be a tomorrow.

At a few minutes before noon, Hughes was almost finished with his calculations. He looked over his charts on the floor. As he worked, the sound on his radio faded to nothing.

Hughes turned. Why had the sound diminished? he wondered. Batteries. The batteries were worn down, he reasoned. He set back to work when it occurred to him that he had changed the batteries the previous day. A fresh pack. There should have been nothing wrong with them.

Then, suddenly, he was immersed in a feeling of immense dread, a feeling that was both depressing and sickening.

Hughes hurried with his fingers. He wanted to be out of that cellar. He worked rapidly. Then his eyes moved slightly to the side of the paper on which he calculated. There was a shadow forming on the floor—a long, unnatural shadow. Something like a human form, coming into focus from the bottom upward.

Legs, arms, torso, shoulders. . . .

It—whatever it was—was between Hughes and the bare overhead light bulb, the bulb which cast this perplexing silhouette upon the cement floor. Hughes suffered a surge of panic. His fear was so immediate that it almost seemed electric.

And yet, as the shadow filled out, as it came into focus and as there was no denying that there was something—something hideous!—standing behind him, his sense of fear was so great that he didn't dare turn.

Slowly, more and more of the shadow became clear until it was bold and black, cast as firmly along the ground as if it were an actual living human being standing behind him.

Hughes held his pen in one trembling hand. The other hand moved to his tool chest and settled upon an ice pick that he kept for winter work, a sturdy tool with a long, sharp, six-inch blade. It was the sharpest, most lethal instrument in his chest.

He gripped it in his fist.

Yet somehow, like a mouse cornered by a large snake, Emmet Hughes knew that the makeshift weapon would be of no use. Emmet Hughes knew he was going to die. The sense was instinctive. Not something upon which he had time enough to brood.

And he knew he was going to die horribly.

Slowly, he turned.

It was there before him, the supernatural figure that cast the shadow. It made no motion until Emmet Hughes had fully turned to look at it.

Hughes' face paled. He was looking at something that seemed to have risen from Hell itself. Nothing in his past, nothing in his religion, nothing in his set of beliefs or in the experiences of a lifetime could have prepared him.

His face went white with terror. His eyes widened as if they would burst and a scream—like a scream in a nightmare—formed in the depths of his soul, worked its way into his throat, lodged there, caught for several seconds, then worked its way up into the land of the living.

Much as it had for Beth DiMarco in an open field at night.

And for Bruce Markley pulled fiendishly into a current.

A scream that could curdle the blood of humans, yet far from any human ears. A scream that could raise the Devil, if the Devil needed to be—or wanted to be—raised.

Sinking slowly to his knees, Hughes screamed like a hog in a slaughterhouse. He dropped the pen to the ground, raised the ice pick and swiped at the force that menaced him—but his fist and his weapon passed harmlessly through it. He made a desperate attempt to get to his feet and flee.

But the black figure blocked his escape.

When Annette's agent Joe Harris was on the brink of a deal, his normal steely, tenacious, grasping, persistent demeanor was replaced by something much colder, harder and more calculating. Thus it was that Harris was in his office with a secretary by seven-thirty A.M. the Monday morning following Annette's arrival in New York. He was putting into shape a draft of the deal memo for *Message From Berlin*.

By eight forty-five the memo was typed. Harris took a nine o'clock breakfast meeting with the producers. The meeting was at the Sherry Netherland. The producers brought their lawyer, and they and Harris went over the memo phrase by phrase. Onto his draft of the memo, Harris wrote all agreed-upon changes in wording.

But there was little that needed to be changed. The producers were tickled to have Annette as their star, just as they had been pleased to hire Jonathan Reed to write the script six months earlier.

"This proves the old adage," Harris insisted, "that one good Joe Harris client deserves another. Or at least one begets another."

A breakfast meeting over a deal memo was a little early and awkward in the day for humor—particularly Joe's sort—but in this case it was forgiven. That morning, all principals were pleased with the outline of the deal bringing Annette into the project, the freshly squeezed orange juice, the waffles, the bagels, and Joe Harris' sense of humor.

Immediately following breakfast, Joe faxed his copy of the memo—which included his handwritten changes—back to his office. By the time he walked there himself, his secretary had taken the changes and put them on the office computer, amending the original text.

Harris took a printout of the new memo, read it, and found it perfect. He had six copies printed in his office, then sent them by messenger to the producers' attorney's office. There the producers read it. Then they signed it as the messenger waited. A check to Joe Harris, acting as the agent for Annette Carlson, was made out for fifty thousand dollars, Annette's signing fee. The messenger took the check and the executed documents and was on his way.

The Carlyle was the next stop. There Annette received all six copies of the memo. She signed them. One she kept. The rest returned to Harris' office along with the check. Harris would issue Annette her money, less his fifteen percent, within three days. The producers received their copies of the memo later that afternoon.

With all this accomplished, Annette Carlson was officially free to leave Manhattan.

She felt wonderful. She was approaching real affluence for the first time in her life. Her outlook even seemed brighter toward Nantucket and the disturbances in the house she owned.

In the late morning, she walked out of her hotel and went window shopping on Madison Avenue. She walked several blocks uptown, then reversed herself and walked down Madison on the opposite side. In an antique shop, she saw a set of gold-rimmed crystal wineglasses that she liked. She nearly bought them. Then upon further thought, she considered the purchase foolish. Buy new glasses for the house? She was unloading the house, wasn't she? She thanked the clerk in the store, who acted like he had recognized her, and went on her way.

She checked out of the Carlyle shortly after one P.M. and took a taxi to La Guardia. As she rode to the airport, her thoughts from the previous night remained with her.

Okay. It was now an official decision. She would sell the damned house. Take a loss, take a hike, and find another place. So what if she lost ten or twenty thousand dollars? It didn't make much difference. Money wasn't a concern. Safety and happiness were. Best of all, she could hire movers to take her things out of the Cort Street house and put them in storage. She could walk away from that troubling island just that easily.

Only one thing bothered her. The detective in Nantucket. Tim Brooks.

She realized that she held a certain attraction to him. Funny. Here was a relationship that could not possibly work. She could be on the island no more than several weeks a year. He was anchored there. Their worlds were so entirely different. And yet . . .

Well, what was she really thinking about, anyway? They didn't have any sort of real relationship. She trusted him. He helped her. She felt comfortable with him. He believed her when she explained what had gone on in the house.

But beyond that?

She sighed.

Love and romance in the 1990s. Where was it? Hidden away and obstructed by barriers of travel, profession, and risk of terminal disease. Sometimes she wished for a less complicated world, one more similar to the one in which she had grown up. Yet in that world, she reminded herself, there was no room to make four hundred thousand dollars in six weeks filming a television production in Europe and the United States.

She sighed again.

On the Grand Central Parkway, her taxi driver weaved in and out of traffic. But as they neared the airport, Annette's thoughts turned back to more immediate matters.

It relieved her to realize that a solution in Nantucket could be as simple as selling and walking away. Once again, she felt great about life. She began to think about the upcoming production of *Message From Berlin*. Preparations would have to be made for travel. She would have to study her character's role carefully and decide what she wanted to bring to it. There would be days spent on wardrobe and script approval. . . .

Twenty minutes later, Annette checked in for her flight to Nantucket. Her timing was good. Boarding would be in ten minutes. The flight would depart in forty. She sat down in the waiting lounge next to an older couple who were waiting for the same airplane.

Annette pulled a *New York Times* from her travel bag and scanned the headlines on the front pages. Two or three minutes had passed, and she was well into the newspaper, when she heard a gravelly voice next to her.

"Hello," said a man. He had gray hair and a neat mustache.

He wore a seersucker jacket and a regimental tie. "We know you, don't we?"

Annette looked. The man and woman were gazing at her and smiling. An affluent, conservative couple, in their seventies. It took Annette a moment to place them.

"Oh," she said, lowering her paper. "Of course. Mr. and Mrs. Shipley. Right?" she asked.

"Daniel and Martha Shipley," he said, offering his hand. "We met at the closing. At the lawyer's office in Nantucket."

"Yes," Annette said. "Of course."

"This is the young lady who bought our house on Cort Street, Mother," Daniel Shipley said to his wife of forty-six years.

"I *know* that," she scolded her husband. "I recognized her before you did."

"You did not!"

"How are you, dear?" Mrs. Shipley asked, aiming her question directly at Annette. "Still making movies?"

Mrs. Shipley spoke in a booming upper-class bellow that, in previous generations, might have been associated with ear trumpets. When such a voice contained a question like the previous one, it turned at least a dozen nearby heads in the waiting lounge.

"Oh, yes. Of course," Annette answered, speaking softly.

"In New York on work?" Mrs. Shipley asked. "Are you starring in a Broadway play?"

"No. I had to meet a few business people."

"Must be exciting," said Martha Shipley, leaning back, a five-hundred-dollar Donna Karan dress in an orange plastic airport seat.

"Sometimes it's exciting," Annette allowed. "Other times it's very routine. Like any other business."

Mr. Shipley's brown eyes were trained upon Annette—fixed and attentive like a terrier's, never wavering. "I hope you're enjoying our house," Daniel Shipley said. "I know we did. For a long time."

Annette paused and then lied politely. "Oh, yes," she said. "I spend as much time there as possible."

"Well, that's nice," Daniel Shipley said, glancing back to his wife for a moment. "We did, too, didn't we, Mother? Loved the place." Martha Shipley smiled and nodded as if on cue. "It was very much of an island for us. A place of comfort and strength."

"I'm sure it was," Annette answered.

"Bought the house in nineteen fifty-four," Daniel Shipley continued. "Raised our families there during summers. Kids grew up. We grew old. Many wonderful summers, though. Seventeen Cort Street served us very nicely."

"We were always comfortable," Mrs. Shipley said. "We raised our children there." Mrs. Shipley had a way of always adding a detail that had already been covered.

"Well, I'm sure I'll be as pleased as you were," Annette said.

"It's nice to know the house is in good hands," Mrs. Shipley said.

Annette nodded. So did the Shipleys. Annette had the sense that they had by now expended all possible topics of mutual interest.

Mrs. Shipley glanced at her watch. "Where *is* that airplane?" she asked.

"The plane's already here, Mother. It's sitting right out there," Daniel Shipley said, pointing at the ramp. The tail section of a small commuter jet was visible beyond the plate-glass window. "We're just waiting to board."

"Well, when *will* we board? What do you suppose is wrong?"

"Nothing's wrong. But you want them to take on the right amount of fuel, don't you?" Daniel Shipley asked his wife.

"Well, I just think they could start on time."

Daniel Shipley looked to Annette for support. Annette forced another smile.

Mrs. Shipley looked back to her.

"Imagine. Somebody famous is living in our house," Mrs. Shipley said to Annette. "You know, I mentioned your name to my sons. They're grown boys now. In their thirties. One's a lawyer in Denver. The other is in television in New York.

Maybe you know him. He's a videotape technician. Danny Shipley, Jr."

"I'm sorry. I don't know him."

But as she answered, another question was taking shape in Annette's head. Here was the opportunity. She wondered . . .

"I was curious about something," Annette began slowly. Both Shipleys looked at her. "You owned the Cort Street house for thirty-five years?"

"Thirty-six," Mrs. Shipley answered.

"Ever had anything unusual happen in it?"

The Shipleys looked at each other. "A tree fell down during the big hurricane in nineteen ninety-one," Daniel Shipley said. "Huge old oak. Hit the west wall and covered the side lawn. Took a week to clean up."

"That's not the type of thing I mean."

Mrs. Shipley frowned. "What *did* you mean?"

"Oh . . ." Annette didn't want to prime the response. "Unexplained events *inside* the house. Doors that wouldn't stay shut. Furniture that wouldn't stay in place. Noises . . . ?"

Martha Shipley looked surprised at the question and shook her head. She looked to her husband.

"Nothing at all like that," she said.

"I don't remember anything, either," Daniel Shipley added, searching his own memory. "The house was always very restful for us. A place of strength and comfort."

Annette sighed. "I'm sure," she said, withdrawing from this line of conversation. She looked away. Then, almost involuntarily, she questioned further.

"Did you ever think you had a ghost in the house?" Annette asked.

"A ghost?" Mrs. Shipley laughed out loud. "Heavens! That's really quite extraordinary."

Her husband shook his head and a mirthful glint came into his eye. "I don't believe in such things. But I wish we *had* had a ghost on some summer days when we had Mother's in-laws

356

visiting from Tennessee," he said. "Maybe it would have scared the freeloaders out!"

Daniel Shipley immediately caught his receipt for the comment. His wife elbowed him in the ribs. Both laughed.

"No, dear. Nothing at all like that," Mrs. Shipley finally said. Her husband shook his head also, reassuring Annette.

"If there's anything wrong, don't let your imagination run away with you," Martha Shipley counseled wisely. "It's the wind. Or an imbalance in the floorboards. Or simple old-house noises. Expansion and contraction with the changing temperature."

"Of course," Annette said.

It was two minutes before boarding time. Mrs. Shipley started looking for the powder room. Her husband chided her on always waiting till the last moment, then directed her to a nearby door with a picture of a woman on it. Mrs. Shipley gathered her purse, rose and hurried away.

Mr. Shipley remained.

He must have been in a talkative mood that day, or else the memories of those many years that passed at Cort Street put him in a reflective frame of mind. He started speaking about the days when his two sons were young, and how the boys used to walk up to the old Quaker cemetery, the one with flat rolling hills and no tombstones, and fly kites.

"I had a daughter, too," he said, out of the blue. He glanced to where his wife had disappeared. She was nowhere in sight. "My only regret is that the poor little gal never lived to see our house or live in it. She had childhood leukemia."

Mr. Shipley's hand disappeared into his jacket. He found his wallet. He kept speaking.

"You know this was back in the fifties. Back then they couldn't do anything for a disease like that. She died in nineteen fifty-three, our little Sarah. Age seven. We bought the house on Cort Street the following year. Needed to get away for a time. My wife took the little girl dying real hard." He paused. "She'd be a full-grown lady today, of course. Much like yourself. Older though, I'd guess."

Daniel Shipley rummaged methodically through a neat wallet.

"Still think about her sometimes. But I guess she's with God." He riffled through some pictures. He produced shots of his boys first. Then his hand steadied and went still.

"Here's our Sarah," he finally said. And he offered Annette an old black-and-white wallet shot, crinkled and faded, of an adorable little girl in a bathing suit playing by an inflatable pool in some long lost backyard in an America of the 1950s.

She had freckles and a beguiling smile. Almost a little tomboy. She held the end of a hose. In the picture it appeared that she may have just filled her pool. The picture had been taken on Sarah's final summer, her father explained.

Annette's gaze settled upon the photograph. The flash of shock that she felt was inevitable. But she suppressed it. And she didn't say anything.

Nor did she give any indication that she had met the little girl before. The little girl in the party dress that three times had appeared near Cort Street. Or was it Annette's imagination?

No, Annette knew, it wasn't. The conversation replayed itself in Annette's mind.

"Have you seen my parents?"

"Who are your parents?"

"Have you seen my parents?"

"Who are your parents? What's your name?"

Yes, I've seen your parents, Annette thought. And now, little girl, I know why you're keeping a vigil around my house. Looking for Mommy and Daddy, aren't you? But they've moved.

"Miss Carlson?".

Annette was suddenly aware that Daniel Shipley was speaking to her. She had been staring at the photograph so hard that she was barely aware of him.

"Are you all right?" Daniel Shipley asked. He withdrew the photograph and closed his wallet again.

"I'm fine," Annette said, leaning back and steadying herself. "I'm just fine."

He smiled as his wife returned. "You looked strange for a moment," he said.

"No," she assured him, gathering her poise. "I'm all right. I'm fine."

The flight was called. They boarded.

And Annette *was* fine. Or at least, she was composed. She remained so through the short journey back to Nantucket.

Yet certain phrases kept running through her head with alarming frequency. Phrases like . . . must sell and get off this island . . . and . . . so the little girl is a ghost, also . . . and . . . is there any sanity left in this world?

But none of this really pushed her to the breaking point. The latter came when she returned to Cort Street—she looked, but there was no little Sarah maintaining an eerie lonely sentry at the periphery of the property—and stepped inside.

There, at 17 Cort Street, she saw Emmet Hughes' truck in her driveway. There at 17 Cort Street, she found her rear door unlocked. There in the kitchen she found the cellar door un-latched and open.

The light to the basement was on. The radio downstairs was playing faintly.

Annette knocked loudly at the cellar door. She announced that she was home. She called down below.

"Mister Hughes? I'm back from New York. . . ."

No response.

She slowly descended the stairs. And that was when, her feet upon the basement floor, she stepped around the furnace to an angle at which she could see the workman.

And that was when and how she found the late Emmet Hughes, his body contorted and broken, his blood splattered around the basement, his neck snapped and broken, the side of his skull smashed, his arms twisted, his clothing torn. . . .

The most brutal homicide the island would ever see.

His head had been twisted at an obscene angle, but his eyes were open and facing upward—into Annette's. And the expression on his face strongly suggested that if he hadn't met the

Devil himself risen from Hell he might have met something that had broken forth from much the same place.

Annette shrieked until she was senseless and howled with terror until she had raced back up the steps and out into the street and hysterically flagged a passing car, begging, pleading, imploring, that someone summon the police.

Fast!

The carpenter's ice pick had been shoved directly into his skull between the eyes.

Between the eyes and into the brain.

Not that it had even been necessary. The gesture with the ice pick was a macabre mocking touch, one to add a mocking element to the death, a challenge—and for that matter a warning—to any who might choose to oppose the homicidal force in the future.

Twenty-four

"This case is mine."

Tim Brooks spoke softly to his commanding officer as he looked downward at the contorted, twisted face of Emmet Hughes. Lieutenant Agannis stood behind Brooks and stared with equal intensity. Two other detectives from the Nantucket Police Department were already present, as was a sergeant from the State Police barracks. But Brooks had been there first.

Dr. Herbert Youmans knelt over the body, then stood.

"Jesus Christ," the doctor muttered. "Poor Emmet."

Youmans shook his head in disgust. He glanced to Brooks, as if to repeat the question he had asked earlier. Brooks read his thoughts.

Tell me honestly, Timmy. Is there something strange happening on this island?

This time, however, Herbert Youmans didn't give voice to his question. He didn't ask because he already knew. He gave Brooks a second glance and gave Lieutenant Agannis a more hostile one. Then he filled out and signed a certificate pronouncing Emmet Hughes deceased on the spot.

Two medical technicians moved in to prepare the corpse to be moved.

"What do you think, doc?" Brooks said.

Youmans looked from Brooks to Agannis and back again. "You want an honest answer or a polite one?"

"Honest," said Brooks.

"You got one hell of a homicidal maniac loose on this island," he said. "You fellas might want to give some thought to catching him. If you can." His aged but wise eyes shifted back and forth.

Lieutenant Agannis sighed. He was in a white cloud of his own manufacture—halfway through a Marlboro.

"Talk to me, doc," Agannis said.

"This is unofficial. Nothing's official until the postmortem is done. But I think I've been around the corner enough to know what a PM's going to show."

Dr. Youmans looked at the corpse again.

"I've also seen this handiwork before. Compound fractures to arms and legs. Shattered spinal cord at the neck. Severe trauma focused around the occipital bones. Crushed larynx. Hell! You want it in lay terms? Someone tried to rip this man's head off."

He glared back down.

"We've seen it twice before, Lieutenant," Youmans continued. "I showed you those autopsy reports for the girl in the field and the boy in the riptide. I *told* you there was something there that defied coincidence."

He shook his head. Brooks stared at the body, trying to imagine . . .

"And I'm not even a detective," Dr. Youmans said sourly.

"Take it easy, Herb," Lieutenant Agannis growled. It was just the sort of challenge that further rankled Youmans.

"*You* take it easy, Lieutenant! You were quick to start easing me out of this job. Now you got a couple of homicides that don't make sense." His face grew red with indignation. "Maybe if you'd listened to me the first time, Emmet would be alive today."

Brooks placed a hand on the doctor's shoulder. "Okay. That's hindsight, doc," he said soothingly. "The damage is done. Let's see what we can do now."

Youmans muttered softly to himself.

"You and I talked about this once before," Brooks reminded

362

the doctor. "You had this theory. That the DiMarco girl had been lifted up and dropped from a great height."

"That's right."

Agannis frowned and looked at the doctor.

"Judging by my reading of the injuries," Dr. Youmans said, "someone, something, picked her up, maybe fifteen to twenty feet in the air. Then smashed her down on the ground with a tremendous force. I thought the boy in the water got hit every bit as hard, too."

Brooks started to look toward the ceiling in the basement of Cort Street. Agannis and Dr. Youmans followed Brooks' lead. Brooks went to the area above the earthen part of the basement floor and shined a flashlight upward.

"Look at that," he said.

There were blood marks against the beams and water pipes. Brooks cringed. "Looks like Emmet got lofted up as well," he said.

"By who? By what?" Agannis snapped. "Come on! Emmet wasn't Tinkerbell. He weighed over two hundred pounds."

"Well, that tells you something right there then, doesn't it, Bill?" Youmans growled.

"Something very strong was in this basement," Brooks said. "And I'll make you a bet that when we talk to the neighbors we'll hear that they never saw anyone come and go."

Agannis looked at both his best detective and his most experienced medical examiner. He felt confused and disgusted. He said nothing for several seconds.

"More of this ghost bullshit, huh?" Agannis finally murmured. "I'd like to see you take that one to a state prosecutor. You're going to end up in a rubber room. Both of you!"

"I'm just a dumb old island doctor, Lieutenant," Youmans said. "So you can think what you like. But it's my theory that you're not dealing with a human. That's been my theory all along. Your killer's in an open field at night. He's in the water at Surfside. He's in a basement of an old house. He kills but no one sees him. Something's way off base here, Lieutenant."

"Then you tell me," Agannis answered angrily. "Who is it? What is it?"

"I don't know," Dr. Youmans said with residual bitterness. "Anyone seen a trained ape around the island?"

"What's that supposed to mean?" Agannis asked.

Brooks caught the allusion and explained it. The same one that Youmans had made once before. Poe. *Murder in the Rue Morgue*. The trained ape with superhuman powers.

"I can't comprehend the strength with which this perpetrator works," the doctor said. "Or, for that matter, the insanity. The violence of it." He looked back down to the body. "Poor Emmet," he said again. "I bet he barely understood what was happening to him."

"All right, Doctor," Agannis finally conceded. "What are we talking about? If you got a theory, tell it to me, will ya?"

"I don't have a theory. That's not my job," said Youmans. "I tell you how they got killed. *You* find out who. Or *what*."

Agannis dropped the butt of his cigarette and nervously squashed it with his foot. Seconds later, he lit another. "Timmy?" he asked. "Any bright ideas?"

"I told you my theories about this house," Brooks said. "I know it sounds absurd. I know this is something that none of us ever expected to deal with. But . . ."

He motioned to the body of the repairman.

Agannis glanced around. The other cops avoided his gaze. "Isn't anybody sane on this island anymore?" he asked.

"I'll be back in a minute," Brooks said. "Excuse me."

Outside the house, on a picnic bench on the back lawn, Brooks found the two people he was looking for.

George Osaro sat next to Annette. They were speaking in low tones, the minister comforting the tearful woman who had discovered the body.

Annette looked up to Tim Brooks.

"I should never have let him work in that house," Annette said. "I knew there was a problem."

"It's not your fault," Brooks said, sitting down on the other side of her. His placed a hand on hers. "You knew there were disturbances in the house. But you had no way of knowing something like this would happen."

She looked him in the eye. "I should have," she said. "I should have known. Something's in there. Something that doesn't want the rest of us invading its space."

In the distance, Boomer lounged on a grassy area beneath a tree.

"I felt so good when I came back to this island this morning," Annette said. "I figured I had everything worked out in my mind. This house. My future." She paused and stared at the house. "Now this."

"If it's anyone's fault, it's mine," Reverend Osaro said. "Whatever's in there, I missed it."

Annette looked to him. "You what?"

"I walked George through while you were in New York," Brooks said. "As I said I would. I haven't even had time to tell you."

"Oh," she said.

"How the hell did you miss it?" Brooks asked. "For years you've been telling me: 'I can go into a disturbed place and feel things. I know if there's something there.' Now we have the main event here, George. And you missed it?"

"Simple explanation."

"I'm waiting," Brooks said.

"The spirit wasn't there when we went in. That's what we felt push past us when we entered. The spirit is feral. Its focus may be upon this house, but it moves around the island." He paused. "Have you sensed it anywhere else?" Osaro asked.

Brooks told him about the incident at the hospital. And at his own cottage. And possibly even at the Friedman residence at Milk Street.

"That proves what I'm saying," Osaro said. "It moves. It avoided me. That's going to make everything that much more difficult."

Brooks grimaced. So did Annette.

"Want my further analysis of this, Tim?" Osaro asked very soberly.

"I'd love it."

"We're dealing with a malevolent haunting," Osaro said. "A very evil one. Something, some tormented soul, some spirit, for some reason, is trying to break loose from a very bad universe."

Tim Brooks and Annette Carlson looked at the minister as if this were a routine straightforward suggestion.

"What's a 'very bad universe'?" Annette asked. "Purgatory? Hell?"

"I don't know whether those are the names you'd want to use. I don't even know how many universes there are. I only know there's more than a few after this one."

Brooks watched the house as he listened. The body of Emmet Hughes was carried from it. Around front, a crowd of the curious had already gathered. Two or three reporters, all local, had penetrated the police lines and were asking questions.

Inwardly, Brooks groaned.

"Call it what you want to call it," Osaro said. "But it comes from some place parallel to our universe. But much more evil. Much more malevolent. What we're dealing with is like a demon. This is like a possession, but in the case of a malevolent haunting, it's the house that's possessed."

"You're the expert," Brooks said. "How do we get rid of it before it takes another life?"

"I can only guess. There's no book of rules."

"Try me with some ideas," Brooks said, losing his patience. He looked up in time to see a photographer snapping a picture of him, Annette and Osaro. Brooks removed his hand from hers.

"I'm speculating. But I think this spirit has willed itself back into this world," Osaro said. "What was that name you had?" he asked Brooks.

"Henry Flaherty."

Annette frowned in confusion. Brooks explained that the name had come to him telepathically, which made her look even more confused.

"The spirit has done what it has done with a purpose," Osaro reasoned. "When it comes back, it makes itself known for a reason. It wants something. Give it what it wants. Or eliminate its reason to be in turmoil, and maybe—maybe—we can be rid of it."

"So what's so difficult about that?" Brooks asked.

"It depends on what it wants," Osaro said. "Suppose it wants someone's soul. Yours. Annette's. Mine. Ready to give that away? Or lives? Suppose it wants more lives."

"This is finally starting to sound insane," Brooks muttered. "I've half a mind to take a walk on all your theories and start looking for a flesh-and-blood killer."

"You'd be wasting your time, Timmy," Osaro said. "And you know it. You saw the same things I did. In fact, you've seen more. And you hear the voice. You're the only one who hears the voice. So you know what we're dealing with."

"What voice?" Annette asked.

Brooks explained. For several seconds, they sat beside each other in silence. Annette stared off into the distance.

"But if we *do* give this spirit what it wants, allow it to rest," she asked. "Will it leave me alone? Will it leave my house?"

Osaro opened his hands and closed them again. "No telling. But judging by previous incidents, the chances may be good. In fact, that's probably our best—"

"All right then," she finally said. "Let's go looking for our spirit. Communicate. All three of us. Find out what he wants and give it to him."

"Great. How?" Osaro asked.

"We'll use the checkerboard table."

Osaro stared at her. "What are you talking about?" Osaro asked anxiously. "A seance?"

"Yes. Just like Mrs. Ritter used to do. 'Come forth, any spirit in our home!' That's why she left me her table. Isn't it clear? She knew this was going to happen."

She looked at the two men who flanked her. "But we need three people at the table. Three who believe."

Tim looked at her and tried to summon up his courage, wondering again if he would ever have any when he needed it.

367

Osaro looked even less enthusiastic, but waited for Brooks to answer first.

Waited, because perhaps Osaro *knew* how Brooks would answer.

"Jesus," Brooks said. "I don't know." Something fearful was pounding in his stomach. Once again a challenge was before him. And once again, terror surged.

"Why not?" she asked.

"I don't know . . ." He looked at Osaro, who said nothing. He looked back to Annette and saw the disappointment in her eyes. That, and the sudden comprehension that he might be—

A coward!

The voice shrieked at him so intensely that it jarred him. And for a moment, Brooks wondered if George Osaro had heard it, too. The minister seemed to jump slightly and looked around as well.

"All right," Brooks said. "I'll do it."

Won't work, my craven friend! I won't come to your party. But I'll send my friends. We'll put you and the girl in the earth with Hughes.

Go away, Brooks thought in return. Willpower. Like Osaro had said. Not now. We'll converse later. Go!

The voice fell silent. Brooks felt eyes upon him. He wondered from where a ghost was watching him. His eyes drifted to Osaro and settled upon him.

"Tim!" Osaro snapped.

Brooks looked at his friend, not knowing whether Osaro had heard something, disagreed with something, or read his thoughts.

"What?" Brooks answered.

"You're going to ask me to be the third. I can tell."

"That's correct."

"I can't do it."

"Why?"

"It's an occult practice. It could cost me my position with the church here. And, more importantly, God knows what we might summon forth."

"Are we going to wait until someone else gets killed?" Brooks asked.

"Summon up a whole legion of malevolent spirits, Tim," Osaro said calmly, "and you'll end up evacuating this island."

"George, sometimes I think you're creepy. The rest of the time I think you're crazy."

"Think what you want," Osaro said, standing. "But if I fly a table with you, I'm signing my own ticket out of this parish. I'm not yet ready to do that."

Annette sighed. Brooks met Osaro's refusal with both relief and disappointment.

"Is there anything more I can do here right now?" Osaro asked. "If not, I have to get back to my church." He looked first to Annette, then to his friend.

Annette shook her head. "I'll be all right," she said. "Thank you."

"It's okay, George," Brooks said. "You can go."

They watched him leave. On the bench behind the house at 17 Cort Street, Brooks looked to the shaken woman sitting near him. He moved to her and carefully placed an arm around her shoulders. She leaned her weight toward him and lay her head against him.

"I have the worst impression," she said, "that this will never end. That we'll never get control over what's going on here."

He tried to reassure her, but there was little that he could say. To make any promise, he knew, would be to tell her a lie. And he wondered, deep down he wondered, if someone else could be the third at the checkerboard table. And if they could really make the table turn.

In the days that followed, the island was alive with rumors.

Dr. Herbert Youmans performed the autopsy on Emmet Hughes at the Nantucket Hospital. Nothing in the laboratory results detracted from his initial suspicion, linking the killing of Hughes to the deaths of Mary Elizabeth DiMarco and Bruce Markley.

The findings posed many mysteries beyond that of the killer's identity. As Tim Brooks had suspected, no one had been seen going in or out of 17 Cort Street during the time surrounding Hughes' murder. So how had a killer come and gone? How had it also happened that there were obvious parallels with the DiMarco slaying, and yet young Eddie Lloyd, the officially accused suspect in the first place, remained in jail? His family was unable to make the $500,000 bail.

What about fingerprints, also? And how about palm prints? The police wondered. The newspapers in Nantucket and on Cape Cod inquired. The only prints on the ice pick that had been driven into Hughes' head had been his own. Yet it was outside the realm of reality that he could have committed that act upon himself. This point alone was enough to keep Lieutenant Agannis up at night.

Thinking. Pondering. And staring out his window into the darkness of two summer nights.

Suppose . . . Agannis kept thinking to himself. Suppose Detective Brooks' supernatural theories carried even the remotest semblance of weight. He shuddered. Bill Agannis was a man in his late fifties and had witnessed his own share of inexplicable events over his lifetime. But there had never *ever* been anything quite like this.

For Agannis, here was the worst of all possible worlds. To deny that there was a supernatural angle to the killing—or killings—was to suggest that a human killer was loose on the island. But to accept the Brooks theory was to suggest something even more chilling . . . and to risk the outbreak of hysteria among the residents—summer and year round—of the island.

Once again, there had never been anything quite like this. Nor had there ever been a series of crimes that so urgently begged for a solution.

For her part, Annette Carlson tried to behave as rationally as possible under the circumstances. She scheduled a follow-up appointment with her head doctor in Boston. And she made a point not to go into the Cort Street house by herself.

Over the course of two days, the rumor had traveled around

370

the island that the murder of Hughes had pathological overtones. Rumors, half-baked tales and outright falsehoods had all
fed upon each other. The word "witchcraft" had even been
mentioned in some quarters. A shark at one of the local beaches
might have caused less alarm. It was the first thing that summer
tourists, arriving from off-island, wanted to know about.

And worse for Annette, some of the local people began to
mention to reporters that the slaying had been in the cellar of
a movie star's home. So by the following weekend the movie
star had been identified. It was a matter of time before the
tabloid press, and subsequently the mainstream American
press, would catch the story.

Annette dreaded it.

She thought of returning to California. But she initially rejected that. Her behavior would only appear *more* scandalous if
she fled the East, she reasoned. And further, she kept hoping
that Tim Brooks could find a third person to sit at the checkerboard table.

Come forth any spirit in our home!

Hell. She knew there were all sorts of spirits. And she wanted
to reclaim her home from the more unruly of them. To reclaim
the house she had purchased, would be to reclaim part of her
life. And who would buy it now anyway, following a murder
and the ensuing rumors?

Tim Brooks. Well, he at least was a bright spot in her life, she
reasoned.

She spent as much time as she could with him. He consoled
her. He looked after her. He spoke to her with kindness when
she thought she was again going crazy. And if he felt any fear
of the situation, she could not pick it up from his behavior.

She moved out of Cort Street and took a pair of rooms at a
guest house on Ash Street as she decided what to do. And
whenever she went into her house at Cort Street to retrieve
something, Tim came with her.

The inevitable—in terms of Annette Carlson and Timothy
Brooks—occurred on August tenth, exactly one week after the
death of Emmet Hughes. And it was the same day as the first

371

reports hit the national newspapers and magazines that Annette's "summer home"—this was what the press called it—
had been the scene of a homicide.

Tim and Annette had spent much of the evening together.

They had dined in a quiet corner of a restaurant called 21
Federal Street, a table upstairs away from the view of others.
Afterward, they drove down to Cisco beach and walked together—half a mile down the shore, half a mile back—listening
to the soothing crash of the waves.

He held her hand as they walked. And in a new sense, both
Annette and Timothy tried to decide: Was this really happening? Was a romance imposing itself upon danger, upon tragedy,
upon the other conflicts of their lives?

They soon knew the answer. Both of them.

When he mentioned something about taking her back to her
guest house, she demurred at first. She did not wish, she said,
to be alone.

"You can flop overnight at my place," he offered. "If an
actress doesn't mind staying with a cop again."

"This actress doesn't mind," she said. "This actress would
like to."

She stopped and stood in front of him, facing him. And
suddenly the pretension of their respective stations in life were
no longer there. They were simply a man and a woman, enjoying being with each other. *Wanting* to be with each other. Not
wishing to be away from each other.

His hands slowly went to her waist. She did nothing to
discourage him. On the contrary, her lips came forward and
met his. There was urgency within the kiss, as there frequently
is when love is settling in for a long stay. There was even more
urgency in the second kiss and the lengthy embrace that followed. And by this time, little question remained about the
course of the rest of the evening.

Timothy drove her back to the guest house. He waited outside as she went upstairs to pack a few things for overnight.
They drove to his cottage. He put some music on his CD

player, found two brandy snifters in his bar and poured a pair of cognacs.

They sat by each other on a sofa for several minutes. They savored the cognac and told each other funny stories about their very different pasts. Like mature adults, they worried that if they became lovers something might change between them, some barrier might rise, some conflict evolve. They looked for little men waving danger flags, but didn't see any.

So, in the end, they each decided that really, when it came right down to it, there was no reason not to do what they both wished to do.

So they rose and went to the next room. Playfully, they undressed each other. Passionately, when they were fully naked, they fell into each other's arms. And that easily, they went to bed together and made love for the first time.

Afterward, his arm around her bare shoulders, they talked for a long time until sleep, like a good friend, arrived to claim them both.

At a few minutes past two in the morning, Tim realized that he was awake. Annette slept beside him, her leg still against his. Her breathing was delicate and even. He looked at her in the dim light of the room and softly kissed her cheek. She did not awaken.

Then he rose. He silently left Annette's side and walked from the room.

He closed the bedroom door behind him and turned on a hallway light.

The house was still and quiet. What had caused him to come awake? He wondered for a moment if *it* was there. The presence. He thought of speaking aloud to it, but decided not to.

He walked to his kitchen. He turned on the light.

He realized that he had developed a new mannerism, always scanning a room when he walked into it. The black ghost had changed his life in so many ways large and small, obvious and subtle.

He went to the refrigerator and uncapped a bottle of beer. He sat down at his kitchen table.

He looked out a window into the night. He thought of the beautiful woman sleeping in the next room. He wondered what it would be like to share a bed with Annette for the rest of his life.

He smiled to himself. No, no use deluding himself, he decided. An affair was one thing. Love and a long relationship was something else. Who knew how many lovers she had or how casually she took them? A man a month? One a year? Two a week?

Normal in Hollywood—socially accepted behavior—was not the same as normal in eastern Massachusetts. What a joke. He was flattered that she would spend one night with him. Tomorrow morning, he figured as he sipped his beer, she would very civilly and very sweetly apologize for her mistake, explain how nothing possibly could ever work out between them and break the relationship off as suddenly as it had begun.

And all this, probably with good reason.

Something made him think of Heather Gold, his lover during his days in Chicago, lying naked next to him, taking the occasional and contemplative puff on a reefer after—as she so elegantly used to phrase it—"banging his brains out."

Yes, Heather. Heather from seven years ago. As in, "Permanent relationships suck. Better start screwing some new people."

He wondered where Heather was that night, as he seated himself at his small Formica kitchen table, on the lookout for a ghost, a new and unexpected lover in his bed in the next room. He wondered how many new people Heather had screwed in seven years—double figures surely, but *where* in double figures?—and he further wondered what had even made him think of her.

And then he knew why: The casualness of her physical relationships. I'm tired of sex with you and so now I'll try someone else. Changing partners was like putting on a different shirt. No big deal. And that was what was gnawing at him. One of the things, anyway. He expected, when dawn's cruel light came through the window, for Annette Carlson to have much the same attitude.

Which would have been fine, he further understood. Fine, except for the fact that—damn it to hell!—she was out of his class, out of his league, out of his world, and he was falling in love with her.

Damn it again.

His thoughts drifted. My, how they drifted in the sleepy consciousness of a new day's earliest hours. They drifted like a corked bottle on an easy, distant tide. A bottle bearing a message.

From whom? To whom?

He didn't know.

"Can't see that far," he said aloud.

He tried to sense if the ghost was present. He could almost tell now when it was or when it wasn't.

Osaro's words echoed. "I can go into a disturbed place and tell if there's something there."

Dr. Friedman's learned ruminations echoed as well.

". . . we SHOULD be able to contact the spirit world. But we've lost the skill. Or we've repressed the mental capability."

Well, there was nothing repressed within his psyche anymore. Any skill that mankind had bred out through societal evolution, Timothy Brooks had reacquired within the last weeks.

And as for disturbed places, hell. His mind was a disturbed place. And it would remain so until somehow this ghost business was resolved.

He sipped some cold beer. He sipped a second time. His mind continued to crank forward. He continued to stare into the nighttime darkness.

For most of his life, he had always believed that death was one's earthly end. Heaven? Hell? Whatever followed was a matter of faith. Or a matter of philosophical conjecture. He had had loved ones die and never once had he sensed their presence in an earthly return. Never once had he received a message from beyond. . . .

Beyond what? The grave? The reality that he accepted? The universe as defined by modern Western thought?

So what that Christ had purportedly brought Lazarus back from the dead? It was a nice reassuring story. Comforting. But wasn't it much like the loaves and the fishes and the sun stopping in the sky during creation? Wasn't it something that no rational, thinking person really accepted literally?

But now what could he believe? The unbelievable? That human souls could shoot around like invisible bullets or float like little clouds through walls, in and out of the consciousness of others, into and out of sight?

Like ghosts?

What could he believe, indeed? As his friend George Osaro had asked, how many realities were there? One? Three? Six million? Were they good? Evil? Some of each?

How could a human mind ever fathom what was really out there? And how could a small-town policeman, hunched over a bottle of beer at several minutes before three in the morning, hope to master any of this?

It would be enough just to survive.

Then, as his thoughts began to return to the room that he was in, he was aware of a certain sensation. It was something new. Nothing he had never known before. But it formed an intellectual link.

"Uh, oh," he said aloud.

The more he stared out the window and into the darkness, the more the darkness took shape. What had once been solid black was now merely dark. And he could see within it.

He could see the shape of his lawn furniture. He could see his car parked in the driveway. Faintly, on this overcast night, he could see the contours of trees and shrubs.

But now he sensed something more. And at last when his eyes drifted deeply into the darkness and—with a flash—he came upon an upright figure that was foreign to his front yard.

"Oh, fuck," he said softly. Yes, he had been right.

He knew what it was. Tall. Black within the darkness, the amorphous human shape. He had the sense of his eyes spiraling as he kept focused on it.

Arms . . . legs . . . torso . . .

Then the voice. *So! You finally fornicated with her.*

Brooks didn't respond.

Succulent body, yes? I've watched her dress and undress many times at Cort Street.

"But *I* became her lover. Not you."

No matter. When I am ready, I will force her to take me in her mouth. FORCE HER. Do you understand?

"There are some things you will never do," Brooks whispered. "And that is one of them."

There followed a brief silence, as if the malevolent spirit were taken aback. And when it spoke again, it was more sardonic. Arch. Belligerent.

And don't think for a moment that you satisfied her, however, Timothy. You couldn't satisfy anyone. Yourself. Your father. The imagined god of your church. A woman.

Brooks glanced away and sipped more beer.

I hope the whore-actress has left her legs apart. I may wish to ride her tonight, too.

"I'm not listening to you," Brooks said aloud.

But of course you are! We are conversing now!

"What I mean is," said Brooks, "I hear you. But I am not listening."

You have no choice but to listen. I come from the other side of life. You will have to hear me. There was a pause. *I have many, many ways of arresting your attention.*

Abruptly, through the wall, Brooks was assaulted by a foul smell. It was a horrible stench. Brooks tried to place it. It was like . . . an overflowing sewer. It was like . . .

"Is that you?" Brooks asked, recoiling very slightly. The smell was like . . .

Merely one of my tricks. A present for you. Now that you've shot your foul sperm into her busy furrow, you can both rot in the same coffin.

Oh, Jesus! That was it!

The smell was like decaying flesh. The memory flashed back from his days on the police department in San Jose. The trips to the morgue. The medical examiner's office. The stenching bodies found in car trunks, brains perforated by bullets . . . the filthy reeking winos and drug addicts, lying in back alleys and cheap hotel rooms, dead for days in urine-soaked excrement-stained pants. . . .

The worst part of being a policeman. Notifying their relatives, if they had any. Hoping, when you found a body like that, that they *didn't* have any relatives.

Buried together, it taunted again. *That's how the two of you will stink.*

As quickly as it had materialized, the revolting stench was gone.

Do I have your attention again?

Brooks fingered the beer bottle. He feigned confidence, although the spirit had again slashed right through to one of his most private fears and frailties.

With horror, he began to realize: sometimes his adversary could read his mind.

Brooks lifted his gaze. He looked back to the night beyond his window. He wasn't absolutely certain, but he thought the dark figure had drifted closer. Now it was about twenty feet beyond his window. Close enough, he assumed, to pass through a wall if it wished to.

Pass through the walls of his home and confront him.

He felt like standing up and screaming. Then running. Dear God! At what point did he come to accept that something like this could really happen?

You must give me your attention, it insisted. Angry this time.

Brooks maintained his ground. He sat at his table. His moist fingers toyed with the lip of the beer bottle.

"I don't have to do anything," Brooks answered.

No? It mocked him.

Now Brooks was certain. It *had* drifted closer.

"I have a new weapon," Brooks said.

A weapon for what?

378

"To use against you."

And what would that be?

"Free will. Thought transference. My mind against what remains of yours. Willpower."

Laughter. Then, *No match there! Whatever are you talking about, my most feeble friend?*

"My clergyman advised me," Brooks whispered.

The same old perceived threat. *George Osaro is a dead man. Don't you understand that?*

"Willpower," Brooks repeated. "My intellect against yours. I would compare it to the action of a magnet in deflecting a compass needle," Brooks said.

I'm going to fuck the lady in your bed.

"You will stay out there in the night and in the darkness," Brooks said. "I do not will you within my home tonight."

The policeman's hands were soaked with sweat. More sweat rolled down his ribs from his armpits. How, he wondered, was he able to just *sit* there with this thing . . . this creature . . . this odious, vicious presence moving closer and—

Your will has little to do with it.

"It has quite a lot to do with it," Brooks answered. "I've learned this much. You can only exist when some small part of my mind allows you to exist."

But you KNOW I exist, the voice croaked with glee. *You can no longer EVER deny my existence. Therefore—*

"But I do not allow you within my home tonight."

I will enter and—

"I do not allow you within my home tonight," Brooks repeated. His voice was firm, clear and calm. He turned and watched. But already the form showed signs of dissipating in the darkness.

Fool!

Brooks looked away from it.

Fool! It screamed again. *I am leaving of MY will. And you and I will not be finished until the earth has received you.*

But the specter receded as Brooks glanced back to it.

Fool! Fool! Fool! I will be doubly avenged.

The shadow withdrew into the night until it was gone.

For a moment, Brooks waited, wondering if his calculation was wrong and that the spirit would materialize beside him. Or jolt to life behind him. Or flash into view in the hallway when he turned the corner.

Or be lurking in a closet in the dark bedroom when he returned to it. Lurking, and waiting until he was comfortably in bed before it—

But there was no sign of it.

No Henry Flaherty.

Just as when he could now sense when it was present, he could now sense when he was safe.

A final time for good measure: "Not within my home tonight," he whispered again. He exhaled long and deeply.

He looked away from the window. He finished his beer. He put the bottle in the sink, turned and left the kitchen, flipping the light off when he passed.

He walked through the unlit living room and through the door to the bedroom. He slid into bed.

In the silence, in the darkness. He looked around the room. Nothing.

"Tim?" Annette asked sleepily.

"Hmmm?"

She moved to him. She held him. She was a magnificent lover. "Where did you go?" she asked.

"Just for something to drink," he answered.

She sleepily pressed her breasts to him and snuggled close. Her body was warm, as was his against her.

"I was having a bad dream," she said. "It was horrible."

There was a small lamp by the bed. He turned it on. A twenty-five-watt bulb threw light across the room.

"Nothing to be scared of," he said. "Not tonight."

She sat up, her back against the pillow. She sighed in relief.

"A bad dream about the two of us?" he asked.

"Yes. How did—?"

"Ignore it," he advised. "Don't let it control your mind. Let your mind control it."

"But I kept hearing this horrible phrase. About the earth receiving us. Together. Buried together." She shuddered. "I don't want to be dead, Tim. I want to live happily for a long time."

"You will," he said. It was the type of promise one instinctively makes in the middle of the night. He leaned to her and kissed her on the forehead. Then on the lips.

"Know something?" she asked. "Right now I don't even want to go do my next film. The one for television. I want to stay with you."

"I'm flattered." He kissed her again.

"Maybe you can come to Europe with me. Or California."

It was a silly time of the morning, a time for the ideas borne of passion to prevail over common sense.

"That would be nice," he said, agreeing without agreeing. "Real nice."

He turned off the light. Their bodies found each other again.

"You're gorgeous," she said to him. She kissed him on the upper neck, just below the ear. "And I'm a very horny lady tonight. Haven't had you-know-what for a long time. Think you can make a horny lady happy again?"

"I think I'd like to try," he answered.

Her palm slid deftly across the muscles of his lower abdomen. Then downward. She giggled when her hand arrived at its destination.

"*Try?*" she teased. "You bad boy. You're all hard and waiting for me already."

"I thought you'd never notice."

He took her tightly in his arms and kissed her with a passion that neither of them had known for years. And they made love for the second time that evening.

Twenty-five

Andrea Ward appeared as a shadow might, silently and late the next afternoon. She stood at the door to Detective Brooks' office and knocked twice.

Brooks raised his eyes.

"Hello, Andrea," he said flatly. "What took you so long?"

"What a greeting! Aren't you glad to see me?"

"Not when you're carrying a pad and pencil." He smiled when he said it. She smiled back and kept the pad and pencil handy.

"What's a woman to do when she's so unwelcome?" she asked.

"She probably walks in, sits down, makes herself at home and starts asking questions," Brooks answered.

Andrea walked in, sat down and made herself at home. She turned to a fresh page on her notepad and laid it across her lap.

"So?" she asked.

"So what, Andrea?"

"I've got the story of the year, Tim," she said. "And I want you to confirm it for me."

He grimaced. "I might not be able to."

"What a story. Love, death. Murder. Mystery. The occult. Am I getting warm?"

He ran a hand over his eyes. "What's your story?" he asked.

"A young man named Eddie Lloyd is arrested for murder on Nantucket. But after he's charged, and while he is off the island, a similar murder occurs. Maybe two, if you count the Canadian boy down at Surfside. No real suspects. So the local police department—encompassing you, I believe, Tim—turn to the occult to try to find a solution. Or, and I may be stretching it here, sane heads within the police department actually suspect that there may be a supernatural aspect to the murders. What do you say, Tim? Am I close?"

"Is that your whole story? Where's the love?"

She grinned. "I'll get to that presently."

"Get to it now."

Her eyes fastened upon his.

"Well, this is more of a social note than a crime report. But," she intoned, "are you denying that you've spent a night or two with a very famous lady from the West Coast?"

"Oh, come on, Andrea. Give me a break."

"That part's true, too, isn't it?"

He thought for a moment. "You're shameless, aren't you?"

"I try to be."

"Well, what you're asking about is my own personal business. You can write what you want, but I'm not talking to you about what I do on my own time."

"I'll keep that part out of the paper, if you'll give me a confirmation on the first part."

"Sounds like you've got most of a confirmed story, anyway," he said. "Who did you talk to?"

"Everybody in sight, Tim. Doctor Youmans. Lieutenant Agannis. The medical technicians who carted out Emmet Hughes' body. One of the state cops who was standing around listening to you." She smiled. "Even got a few vague words out of the island's spiritualist guru, Reverend Osaro."

"So?"

"What's going on, Tim? Are you running a homicide investigation or acting out plots for 'The Twilight Zone'?"

"What are you implying?"

"Tell me, how did you ever get so good at answering questions with questions?"

"Why do you ask me that?"

"Are you planning a seance, Tim? In connection with this case?"

"Who told you that?"

"I've heard you are. Are you?"

"Do I look like a seance type?"

"I have my ways of finding out, Tim." She paused, triumphant. "And you just confirmed almost all of my story for me."

He leaned back in his chair and shrugged. "Print what you want. But I didn't confirm anything."

"Come on, Tim. . . . Toss me a little something good."

He sighed. "Andrea," he said. "Try to act with some responsibility. You print a story like this, involving a murder case, maybe two murder cases, a clergyman and a seance, and this island is going to have every reporter in North America, print and electronic, on it. The place will be a zoo."

She smiled sweetly. "All the more people to buy the *Eagle* as they're passing through the area."

Brooks gazed at Andrea for several seconds, considering her and her inevitable involvement in the case. He weighed some options and moved quickly to a decision.

"Close the door," he said.

"Why?"

"Close it and you'll find out."

She hesitated.

"Don't close it and you'll never find out," he teased. "No loss to me."

"All right," Andrea said. She rose, leaned on the door and pushed it. Brooks waited till it clattered shut.

"You don't write anything till I tell you that it's okay," he said. "That's the deal. Break that agreement and you'll never see any cooperation out of this office again."

She raised her hand like a girl scout, two fingers up, thumb folded. "On my honor," she said.

"I *do* have a suspect," he said.

"That's not what Lieutenant Agannis says."

"Okay. Don't believe me," he said.

"No, no. Keep talking."

"I even have a name. But you can't print it."

"Can you tell me?"

"I *want* to tell you. You can't repeat it. But you can help me investigate." He assessed her. "Yes?"

"Yes," she answered.

"Henry Flaherty," Brooks said.

"Who's he?"

Brooks shrugged. "My suspect. Or maybe a link to the suspect. The name ties into the case some way."

"How do you know that?"

"It just kind of came to me."

"Oh, come on."

"Trust me, Andrea. I know. And I can't give you a source."

She thought about it for a moment. She was jotting in her notepad.

"This is where you come in, Andrea. I gave you the tip. Now, don't take this too personally, but I consider you nosy, pushy and aggressive."

She stopped writing and glanced up. He kept talking.

"All in a complimentary sense, to be sure," Brooks continued. She smiled. He did, too.

"So you do some digging for me, Andrea. Figure out where I can find Henry Flaherty or how I can identify him, and I'll give you the whole story. Top to bottom. Every bizarre piece of it."

"All this for identifying 'Henry Flaherty' for you?"

"Yup. As long as you're first."

"All right," she said. "It's a deal. It's a *great* deal."

"I know."

Her fingernail polish was the color of a fire engine. Considering how fast her fingers moved across her note pad, the color was more than justified.

"When you check the name out, you might dig through some newspaper archives," Brooks suggested. "Marriages. Deaths. Check everything. I've done the same on the island. And can't find anything."

He watched her write.

"Don't be afraid to dig back too far. Many years."

"Like how many? Five? Ten?"

"Stay in this century," he said.

She stopped writing again and looked up.

"What?" she asked.

"I'm looking for someone who may have been dead for a long time."

"This is for real?"

"This is for real."

"So you're looking for a ghost?"

"I'm looking for a link to my current case. Just find me the right Henry Flaherty, Andrea, and everything else should drop into place. I'll explain it then. Okay?"

She went back to her pad. "What can I print, meantime?" she asked.

"Well, anything you want. But cut out the occult stuff. Cut out the seance. If anything comes of the latter, you'll have the story first." He paused. She seemed to be receiving his request and viewing it as reasonable.

"And cut out the alleged romance between any aforementioned police officer and any unnamed actress. Please?"

" 'Alleged?' "

"That's part of the deal, Andrea. Take it or leave it."

"Aw, Timmy. You cut the heart out of my work sometimes."

"Sorry."

She stared at him for several seconds. "So you really *are* sleeping with a glamorous movie star?" she finally said.

"Andrea . . ."

"Lucky girl," she said. "When she's finished with you, I'll be happy to pick up where she left off."

She rose and blew him a kiss. "Henry Flaherty," she said aloud. "I'll be back in touch." Then she departed.

Brooks stood alone on the basketball court in the dying light of day. He had already waited for George Osaro for fifteen minutes. He had worked up a good sweat on his own, alternately making and missing shots from the three point line.

He moved to the free throw line and sank five in a row. Still no George.

He retrieved the ball, returned to the foul line and sank four more. Then another two. That made eleven.

His personal best was thirty-one. Oh, he reasoned, why couldn't the rest of life be like foul shooting? He was up to seventeen straight when he heard the cranky wheezing engine of George Osaro's Voyager pull into the driveway of the high school and rumble toward the court.

Brooks hit three more. He was at twenty.

"Where the hell you been?" Brooks called as Osaro stepped out of his van.

Osaro made an indecipherable gesture with his hands.

"I'm going for twenty-one straight," Brooks shouted. "Can't miss tonight."

"Yeah?" Osaro called back. He walked slowly toward the court.

"Yeah!"

"I can make you miss, Timmy," Osaro shouted back. "Just by thinking about it."

"Bull!"

Brooks returned to the foul line. He aimed carefully, just as he had the twenty previous shots. He stuck his tongue out at his friend, who stood and watched, arms folded.

Brooks shot.

The ball hit the front rim, bounced erratically, and fell away from the hoop. The bounce was so unusual that Brooks stared at it for a second, not believing his eyes, wondering if it had hit something in the air.

"Better luck next time, bubba," Osaro said, striding toward his friend.

The ball rolled to a corner of the court and stopped. So much for Brooks' streak.

"I have to think that my streak would still be going if you hadn't arrived," Brooks said.

Osaro's spirits seemed low. "I have to think you might be right," the minister said.

Brooks picked up the ball and tossed it to the minister. Osaro swished two gems back-to-back from the left side corner. They were so neat and clean that they were almost out of character.

"Where did those come from?" Brooks asked.

"Divine intervention," Osaro said, meaning it, Brooks supposed, as a joke. "And couldn't we all use some?" He returned the ball to Brooks.

Osaro began to remove his sweatshirt.

"Have a bad day?" Brooks asked.

"No thanks. I just had one."

Brooks hit a jump shot. Osaro took the ball and sank an easy toss from underneath.

"I'm serious," Brooks said.

"Horrible day," Osaro answered. "I got my transfer."

Brooks stopped short. He turned. "What?"

"I got my transfer."

"So quickly?"

"Effective in thirty days. The bishop wants me to join a parish in Oregon before the end of summer." He grimaced. Brooks stared at him in disbelief.

"It's all the usual bullshit from the bishop, Timmy: 'The need is great. You must go where your calling leads you. You must bring your skills to new places and open new human hearts.' What drivel! He just wants me out of his face."

Brooks cursed low and bounced the ball hard on the asphalt. "I can't believe it, George. How can they do that to you?" He shook his head.

"I suppose you could say I was looking for it," Osaro said. "And if you look for something, you often find it. Don't you?"

The sun was setting in a screaming pink and orange beyond the tall trees that ringed the court. In the distance, there were shouts from a softball game upon a nearby field contained by goalposts.

"On the other hand, I can't believe he really did this to me. I like this parish, Tim. I like this island. And I'm finished here."

There was little Brooks could say. He felt as sorrowful as if someone had died.

"But there *is* an upside," Osaro said. "For you, I mean. One good will come of this."

"I can't imagine. What's that?"

"Well," Osaro said, picking up the basketball, "now I don't have to *worry* about being transferred, because I've *been* transferred. See? The Bugger of Boston has fired his only shot. He's already shipped me out of his bailiwick, so there's not much more he can do."

"So?"

"It means I can be as spiritualist as I want for the remainder of my time on this island, Timmy. So we can fly Miss Annette's checkerboard table. We can go spirit hunting all we want at Seventeen Cort Street and we can summon up Uncle Satan himself if we see fit."

Brooks looked at his friend strangely.

"Just kidding about that," Osaro said. "But we can fly the table. Look for your Henry Flaherty. You still game?"

"Yes."

"What about Miss Carlson?"

"She'll do it."

Brooks felt his own apprehension suddenly start to build.

"Then tomorrow?" Osaro asked. "In the evening. After it's dark. That will be the best time."

The next day was out, Brooks said. Annette was going to Boston to see Dr. Rossling again. And she had asked him to accompany her. As it was his day off, he had agreed. He had his own tasks in mind for Boston.

"Thursday, then?" Osaro asked.

"Thursday. The thirteenth."

"In the evening," Osaro said. "That's when the spirits rise. With darkness. Get a good night's sleep the day before. Sometimes these things can take hours. If contact is made."

Osaro looked at his friend.

"And in this case," he said, "I expect contact."

Brooks nodded. He turned with the basketball, twenty-five

feet from the bucket, and lofted it toward the hoop without taking aim.

Perfect arc. Straight through the hoop.

Brooks later remembered the thought that shot through his mind when the ball zipped through the hoop:

Enjoy this one. Remember it. For this would be the last truly great shot for a long, long time.

Part Three
Purgation

*—Everything that has being
has being in the flesh.*
D.H. LAWRENCE

Twenty-six

While Annette Carlson kept her second appointment with Dr. Gary Rossling elsewhere in Cambridge, Massachusetts, Tim Brooks sat in a quiet corner of the Lowenstein wing of the Harvard University Library. He plodded through the books, academic papers and pamphlets that he had assembled on the long reference table.

It was eleven A.M. on Wednesday morning. He sat, as he had for the last two hours, poring through oblique and sometimes baffling writings drawn from the Eksman Collection of Paranormal Psychic Studies.

He sought facts in a field where theories were plentiful and facts were as elusive as phantoms themselves. He tried to draw analogies out of case studies, psychiatric transcripts, exhibits and files. Even out of the occasional police report. Anything that would lend him a deeper insight into what was happening on Nantucket Island.

Having traveled to the mainland by air with Annette that morning, Brooks had set to work comparing the experiences of other men and women to his own. He sought conclusions that no rational man or woman—which he had been just a few short weeks earlier—would normally choose to believe.

Theory: The "poltergeist effect." Several articles conjectured whether poltergeists were the spirits of the dead or some other disembodied entity. A predominant number of poltergeist cases involved children with preexisting psychiatric problems. All the

393

papers Brooks read rejected the theories surrounding disembodied spirits. The most popular option, the most prevalent interpretation of the "poltergeist effect," suggested the existence of "spontaneous psychokenisis" of an electromagnetic field that human science does not yet understand. The field can move furniture, break windows, or make small objects move of apparently their own accord.

Facts, Brooks demanded. What were the *facts?*

Fact: The crash of the china cabinet at 17 Cort Street was a much more powerful manifestation than any incident described in any paper before him. It was one thing for a pencil to fly loose from a table. Quite another for an eight hundred-pound cabinet—he had carefully calculated the weight—to rip loose from solid moorings anchored in wood.

Theory: Poltergeist manifestations, it was noted, often accompanied a young girl passing through puberty. Therefore, poltergeist manifestations may be presumed to carry sexual overtones.

Fact: No such circumstances were relevant in the case of 17 Cort Street. Yes, a woman was involved. But not a teenager. And if there were any sexual overtones at the outset of the haunting, Brooks did not know them.

Brooks noted the mention of psychiatric disturbance. He recalled that Annette had previously mentioned mental problems. And she was in fact at a psychiatric evaluation that day, he reminded himself.

Cause and effect? Effect and cause? Or simply coincidence?

He set his poltergeist pamphlets aside. He looked through several volumes about purported ghosts and hauntings.

Brooks found a volume titled *American Hauntings,* written by Edgar Dunphy, an American psychic researcher, in 1973. Dunphy had been on the faculty at Harvard. Brooks scanned several cases—contemporary and historical—that Dunphy had investigated. Some were laughable. Others were chilling.

Eventually, Brooks' attention settled upon a case in Hydesville, New York, a small town outside of Rochester. The year was 1871 and the focus of the case was a small farmhouse inhabited by a Methodist minister named William Bay, his wife and four children, who were new to the Hydesville community.

In late March of that year, a few weeks after the Bays had moved in, the entire Bay family was kept awake by a strange series of rappings that appeared to have no point of origin. The rappings continued for several weeks, usually at nightfall, often around bedtime. Failing to find any other explanation for the noises, the Bays concluded that they had a ghost.

Mrs. Bay gathered her family around her in the bedroom one April evening. Determined to ask the "ghost" a question that no one outside the family could answer, she inquired the ages of her children.

The "ghost" proceeded to successively rap the correct ages of all four Bay daughters. Chillingly, it also included five final raps to denote the age of a Bay son, the most recently born, who had died of influenza two years earlier at the age of three.

"Are you a Christian human being making these raps?" Reverend Bay asked.

There was no answer.

"Are you a spirit?"

A sharp knock, much closer than the previous ones, came in return.

On subsequent evenings, the Bays summoned their neighbors to record the haunting and act as witnesses. Half of the neighbors were terrified. The other half were skeptical. In response to further questioning, the spirit revealed that his name was Abraham Warren, a peddler who had been murdered in the house before the Civil War. The spirit went on to reveal that he had been shot in the head by a local citizen and that his body had been buried in the cellar of the structure. His spirit had been unable to rest as a result.

The story caused a sensation. Older members of the community remembered the peddler and recalled his abrupt and inexplicable disappearance while passing through their community. Visitors flocked to the house. The rappings continued. Accounts of the "haunting" swept through the northeastern

United States and were picked up by the mainstream newspapers in Boston and New York.

Later in the spring, sentiment arose to verify the Bay family's story. A team of townsmen plus Reverend Bay thus set to work with shovels one day in the basement of Bay's house.

They dug.

At a depth of two and a half feet, they encountered water and had to stop. But when they returned in July, a drier season, and proceeded further, they found a series of heavy oak planks five feet below the earthen floor of the basement.

Below the planks, there were a few bones and a few books, both badly disintegrated.

Intriguing, but inconclusive.

Years passed. The Bay sisters, knowing a good thing when they were on to it, claimed to have developed their skills at communicating with the dead. Inevitably, they became professional mediums. They traveled to different parts of the country and around the globe, going into darkened rooms with strangers and—for very modest fees—offering their skills at conversing with spirits.

The eldest, Clara Bay, was the most famous and renowned of the sisters, as well as the most skilled. She became the most famous medium of her generation. And it was she who popularized the act of turning tables.

Brooks read with fascination.

It was said that Clara Bay could levitate human beings as well as tables. "Table Moving," she called her art, and her notoriety at it preceded her to Europe. The English press lampooned her and her alleged talent. The *Times* of London proclaimed her "a fraud" and denounced her art of table-turning as "a craze of the ignorant American masses, not much different from tribal rites of dusky savages in Africa."

"English audiences," sniffed the Newcastle *Guardian*, "are too sensible and educated to fall for this low-minded sham of an act."

Oh, really?

In London, according to more than two hundred witnesses,

Clara Bay became one of the most famous women in the city when she levitated a "possessed" child ten feet out of a fourth-floor window of the Hyde Park Hotel. Eventually she performed her magic—or whatever her skill was—before Queen Victoria and Prince Albert, both of whom concluded that Clara Bay was "convincing" and "beyond trickery." Beyond a doubt, Brooks concluded as he read, Clara Bay was either endowed with a supernatural talent or was an early-day master of illusion, a nineteenth-century Harry Houdini in skirts.

All of this resulted in the great craze of table-turning of the 1880s and 1890s across the United States and England. Clara Bay's fame was worldwide. Amateur attempts at table-turning followed, some with possible success, the rest with evident chicanery. The table-turning craze lasted some two decades, after which time, Clara Bay, as well as her sisters, retired in financial comfort.

As the trend faded, skepticism about table-turning grew—accompanied not coincidentally by a revival of Protestant fundamentalism in North America. The entire movement was in disfavor by 1900. Clara Bay died in 1901.

Then in 1904, a lengthy book was published on Clara Bay, denouncing Miss Clara and her sisters as catty little charlatans. Said the author:

> No evidence of any burial in the Bay residence was ever found, nor even the existence of the Yankee peddler said to have been murdered. Nor is there any reason to believe that Clara Bay ever lifted a table without the canny use of hidden strings or called forth a single soul.

The book was written by a self-ordained Baptist minister, a man, naturally, and published in New Orleans by a Christian publishing house. It attained a wide circulation and was serialized in many newspapers.

There the matter rested until 1918, when the old Bay home in Hydesville collapsed from age and rot. As carpenters took away parts of the old dwelling to make way for a new structure, it was discovered that the old Bay house had two cellar walls. A real one and a fake one. Between the two was found, in a remarkably good state of preservation, the skeleton of a man with a bullet hole in the temple. With him was a peddler's tin box bearing the name of Abraham Warren. Experts of the World War I era deduced that Warren appeared to have been murdered in the 1850s, at least a few years before Clara Bay's birth.

Brooks drew back from his reading and rubbed his eyes, still trying to decide what he could make of the Clara Bay case. Did it give credibility to the art of turning tables? Or had the Bays somehow known of the body in their basement and hatched out profitable careers as clever fakes?

Then again, how could the Bays have even known about the murder of the peddler, being new to the Hydesville community? And if the skeleton of Abraham Warren was intended to have been their proof of legitimacy, why had they never raised it themselves?

Brooks sighed. Interpretations of events in this field were like turning a kaleidoscope, ever opening onto complicated new vistas and arrangements.

He went for coffee. He consumed a large cup. Black. Then he found and opened a book titled *The Ghosts of Pennsylvania*. He browsed through.

This book, like the one before it, came with good academic credentials. Its author was Dr. Frederick Mann, a retired professor of the humanities at the University of Pennsylvania. The author didn't shy away from his controversial subject. He offered readers "close to a hundred"—ninety-seven in point of fact—case studies of ghosts that were said to be "well documented, witnessed and scientifically investigated."

The work had been published in 1966 and Brooks found himself quickly absorbed with it.

Dr. Mann made the traditional "spiritualistic hypothesis," about ghosts, concluding that such visions, such manifestations are, like poltergeists, the spirits of the dead. He went on to note differences, however.

Poltergeists interact with the living world via the movement of objects and then can be contacted through mediums. Yet of the many cases of ghosts presented, the ghosts appear, but do not appear to have interacted with their witnesses. They behave as if they were a part of a film image projected into a room.

This gave rise to the theory that certain apparitions were no more than a "recording" upon the physical surroundings of a room or place. The examples were given of haunted houses in which some horrible tragedy or trauma took place many years earlier. The hypothesis held that the original tragedy had imprinted itself on the place through the intensity of the emotions of those who originally experienced it. In persons capable of picking up such impressions—here Brooks thought of George Osaro—a certain hallucinatory effect resulted. The author wrote,

> This theory accounts for the feeling one has upon entering certain chambers in a house, that there is a paranormal or supernatural presence within, though it remains invisible to normal senses.

Here Brooks again thought of George Osaro. But he also thought of himself and Annette, and the very definite feelings they had entering certain rooms.

And then again there was Boomer, with his wet, suspicious canine nose, who wanted no part of certain places and people.

Brooks followed closely. Dr. Mann set forth several cases which he claimed would support his eventual conclusions that ghosts, as discarnate spirits of the dead, existed.

Typical was the case of a graduate student named Al Dawger at the same university who in May 1953, when he was about to exit a comrade's room in the Birthday House dormitory, stopped short when he saw a man in a tweed suit and overcoat enter Room 313. Dawger assumed that the well-dressed man was either a faculty member or a parent and said nothing as they passed.

Two days later, encountering the friend at a political science lecture, Dawger inquired what the visitor had wanted. The friend denied that anyone had come into the room as Dawger had departed. It then struck the student that a breeze of frigid air—icy cold, frosty as mortality—had followed the man in tweed.

Over the course of the next several months, it emerged that others had witnessed the man as well, only to have him disappear through walls as abruptly as he appeared. It was only then, after Dawger's initial inquiry, that those on the floor realized that they were party to a haunting.

It was a benevolent haunting, perhaps, but a haunting nonetheless.

The ghost was eventually identified, in theory at least, as one Professor Harold Pepper, a historian who had visited Europe following World War II and died in Naples during the great cholera outbreak of 1949, never to return to the university. He died leaving unfinished the last few years of his life's study on the Italian Renaissance.

Dr. Harold, the boys called him. Over several years, sightings on the third floor of the Birthday House dormitory became quite common, almost to the point where it was an initiation ritual. You weren't really a resident of Birthday House until you had "met the professor." Some young men who "met the professor" were so terrified that they requested transfers to other locations. The university, understanding that some sort of problem existed, granted all requests.

Whether or not the ghost interacted with the living seemed to be a moot point, or rather one of interpretation of action and events. Several dozen students, over the course of six years, did see the ghost, however. To a man, they all recalled that Dr. Harold looked and sounded "like an ordinary, solid, normal human being."

No transparent limbs, no shimmering. Upon viewing, the ghost was indistinguishable from any other human being, right up until the moments when he would walk through a solid wall. The university students were emphatic. Dr. Harold was made of sterner stuff than one's preconceived notion of a misty translucent spook.

So consider that if this is the nature of our university's ghost, wrote Dr. Mann, it is very possible that many of us have seen ghosts many times. But as ghosts can pass for ordinary living people, we remain unaware of this. How many of the strangers we pass each day on the street may be stranger than we could ever imagine?

"Dr. Harold" hung around the University of Pennsylvania until one of his teaching assistants finished his body of research. Once that was done, the ghost disappeared, satisfied that his earthly commitment was finally complete, and moving on apparently to wherever he went next.

All of which, Brooks brooded, reflected only obliquely on the events of Cort Street. Speculation about the electromagnetic energy caused by a sexually aroused young girl might—if the point were stretched and if a certain disbelief were suspended—just *might* explain how a few bottles could fly off shelves or how a book could jump off a shelf.

But they didn't answer Brooks' most pressing questions—as a policeman, or as a friend, concerned with Annette.

How had Mary Elizabeth DiMarco, Bruce Markley and Emmet Hughes all died? *Why* had they died? What manifestation of the supernatural or unconscious mind could be tied to them?

Brooks felt himself more baffled than when he had begun. He began to move more quickly through the material that remained before him.

He glanced at something called *The Spirits' Book* which had been published more than a hundred twenty years earlier. The author, a Frenchman writing in English, argued that man was a "fourfold being," consisting of body, aura, intelligence and spiritual soul. The purpose of existence on earth was to allow the spiritual soul to evolve toward perfection, and upon earthly death the spirits were said to wander in a nether region, then eventually be reincarnated on earth or in another region of existence.

Brooks rolled his eyes.

The book had been a best-seller in 1866. The author founded an influential spiritualist movement in Europe after its publication and went more deeply into the tenets of reincarnation. He promised his audience that eventually he would prove his theories dramatically by returning to earth and identifying himself after his death.

He died in 1872. In the six score years that had followed, Brooks noted, he had not been heard from. Yet.

Brooks sighed. A glance at his watch showed that it was past noon. Annette would be finishing with Dr. Rossling near this time. They were to meet for lunch at two o'clock. Brooks went back to his reading.

He found a paper by William James, the philosopher, who was converted to believe in spiritualism by a medium named Mrs. Leonore Kachner. He found a pamphlet by Carl Jung, the Swiss psychiatrist, and founder of analytic psychiatry, expressing his privately held views that "the metaphysic phenomena can be better explained by the hypothesis of spirits than by the peculiarities of the unconscious." Then he found an article of 1970 detailing the final months of the life of Bishop James Pike, the American Episcopalian bishop, who died in the Judean desert searching in vain for the spirit of his son, with whom he had said he had communicated.

On Brooks' watch, one thirty arrived. He closed his final book.

Facts, he asked himself again. What were the facts?

He had read of more than two dozen hauntings. Yet none bore much extra light on Cort Street.

Parallels. Where were they?

Theory: Places that had ghosts—or poltergeists—were places where usually some extreme trauma had taken place. Or the ghosts themselves sprang from individuals who had suffered violent deaths. Or extra heartbreak. Or extreme sadness. Therefore, there always seemed to be an extreme emotional input into the situation surrounding a restless spirit. That was the one constant that seemed to have evolved from everything he had read.

Fact: Three deaths on Nantucket were probably attributable to the Cort Street haunting. On the back of an envelope, Brooks sketched a map of the island. The field in which Beth DiMarco died was about a hundred yards from 17 Cort Street. The shore at Surfside was about five miles away.

Brooks drew a lopsided triangle on the map, linking the three places. He wondered: Was there another way to link them? One buried in the history of the island? One touching upon tragic or traumatic events?

He saw none.

But he couldn't shake the idea. In terms of trauma, in terms of some long-hidden event, something horrible in the past, mustn't there have been *something* linking the places?

He called up the name of a man about whom he knew nothing.

Henry Flaherty.

"Where are you, Henry?" Brooks whispered aloud. His voice carried so well in the library that someone in an adjoining study cubicle glanced his way, then looked back down to his work. "Come on. Talk to me."

Henry didn't answer, though. Henry wasn't in the mood to issue responses. Then again, this time he probably wasn't present.

Then Brooks' rational mind flitted off on a completely unrelated track, one so obvious that he shuddered over not having explored it earlier. Maybe there was an earthly explanation for all three deaths on the island. And maybe only two were related.

Might not he have been more prudent to canvas house to house following the deaths of DiMarco and Hughes? Might not it have been wiser to look for a human being all along?

Might not there be some human killer lurking on the island? Whatever happened to an old-fashioned concept like that?

For some reason it was Dr. Youmans' voice that then repeated upon him. "You're an educated sort of young swine for a policeman. Ever read Poe's *Murder in the Rue Morgue*?" And there Timothy Brooks was again, stuck with the supernatural.

Shortly before two o'clock, Brooks returned every item he had accessed. He felt more confused than when he had started the day. What had he accomplished? By his own calculation, damned little.

His head was lowered in mild dejection as he wandered out of the library and into Harvard Yard. It was a clear August day and he felt like walking a few blocks. He did, strolling toward Dr. Rossling's office. It was halfway in that direction that a mild epiphany overtook him.

One additional small truth emerged from all he had read that morning, one which would grow as time passed. He thought back on the frequently seen ghost of Dr. Harold Pepper at the University of Pennsylvania.

A few of the phrases came back to him. A few of the things that the witnesses to the Philadelphia ghost had noted.

The ghost of Dr. Pepper had looked and sounded "like an ordinary, solid, normal human being." No transparent angles, no shimmering. The ghost was indistinguishable from a normal human being.

Brooks felt a surge of understanding. And shock. And fear.

So consider that if this is the nature of our university's ghost,

he recalled Dr. Mann writing,

it is very possible that many of us have seen ghosts many times. But as ghosts can pass for ordinary living people, we remain unaware of this. How many of the strangers we pass each day on the street may be stranger than we could ever imagine?

Brooks stared ahead of him for several seconds. He wondered whether the truth itself was like a ghost: obvious, yet shocking, so blatant that it is difficult to believe even when it is clear and out in the open.

He met Annette at Dr. Rossling's office twenty minutes later. They had lunch at a small French bistro on the fringe of the Harvard campus. She spoke well of the psychiatrist and said she would visit him again. But she had not yet set a date for a third appointment.

"You seem quiet," she finally said to him over coffee.

"I *am* quiet," he said. "If you'd been reading about ghosts and discarnate spirits for four hours, you'd be quiet, too."

She smiled. "I suppose I would."

"I'm sorry," he said. "I'm just turning over everything I've been reading. I went through an enormous amount of material."

"Find anything?"

"I'm still thinking about it," he answered. "Still thinking."

They went from the restaurant to the airport and arrived back in Nantucket by four-thirty in the afternoon.

Slowly, the spirit rose after dark from the earth beneath 17 Cort Street. It passed through the stone basement walls of Annette's old house and emerged into the shadows of the aged trees on her front lawn.

There was a breeze that evening. The presence drifted to the street before Annette's house.

It rested almost invisibly beside an elm tree on Main Street. To anyone who did not look that carefully, it appeared like any other shadow. It floated a few feet from the ground. No one saw it.

A pair of teenage girls wandered up Main Street. The girls giggled, in a conversation about their boyfriends. One cracked a large bubble from her gum and both laughed. A car passed. The spectre followed the girls for a full block—in life, it had been drawn to girls early in their sexual prime—and then let them go.

Night. Blackness. Dark. Perfect for a restless unhappy animus to wander. It drifted across the old Quaker cemetery, the grave-yard without the tombstones. Other spirits rumbled on this land, normally imperceptible to the living who passed. It was aware of a murmur of other spirits—some angry, some sad, some displaced, others passing through. It was like dozens of little wisps of smoke or steam flitting across the surface of the world, cast about by every slight breeze.

Dozens here. Dozens there. How many were there across the earthly surface of the planet? The same number—as Reverend Osaro might have paraphrased in his sickening divinity school way—as could dance on the head of a pin?

A car passed, radio blaring, a college boy and girl. On the island for the summer.

Care for some terror, young lady? Care for a night you will never forget?

The shadow passed through a red brick wall through the courtyard of a two-million-dollar mansion. It drifted through a parking lot for the supermarket and then across an open meadow.

Several minutes later, like a little dark cloud it neared the green Miata parked in the driveway before Tim Brooks' house.

It loitered outside. It formulated itself, then defined itself. It gained mass and it divided, summoning up its own sense of willpower.

Then it passed through the outer walls of Brooks' home. It loomed in the hallway beyond his bedroom.

It could hear voices. A man and a woman.

Annette. Timothy.

They couldn't hear him. It kept its thoughts—its impulses, particularly the hideous homicidal ones—to itself. It cast a long shadow in the hallway just outside their bedroom door.

But neither Annette nor Timothy looked to see it.

They were lying on his bed. Undressed again. Naked. Kissing. Caressing. Exploring each other. Making love.

Their actions, their fulfillment of their physical affection, made it very angry.

One of the lovers reached to the bedside lamp and extinguished it. The spirit passed through the wall. The lovers were so busy with each other that they didn't even see it when it came through to the other side and took a position in the corner of their bedroom.

Watching them.

Brooks didn't even *sense* it. Not now, anyway. Not while the policeman was indulging in the carnal satisfactions that the woman offered him.

The lovers were visible in the moonlight from outside.

The man held the woman very close to him. He kissed her lips and breasts as his hand slowly caressed her legs. His mouth moved downward from her breasts.

She moved and toyed with him, heightening his passion and his urgency.

The shadow loomed near the bed. Still the lovers were unmindful.

I will kill them both! Right now. Pine coffin? Or rosewood? One coffin for the two of you! Nothing you can do to stop me! I'll smash your heads in! Rip your necks off! You don't even know I'm here, you—!

Tim Brooks broke away from the woman he loved. He whirled in the bed and lunged for the bedside light. He turned it on and bolted upright in stark terror.

Annette, shocked and alarmed, abruptly sat up.

With a speed that has no measurement in time, the spirit withdrew directly through the wall.

"Timmy?" she asked. "What the—?"

He looked all over the room.

Brooks had felt . . . was *certain* that . . .

"Timmy. Talk to me, honey," she said. "What is it?"

He settled back. Apprehensively.

"I don't know," he said. "I thought. . . . Just for a second I felt something."

He did not have to tell her what he meant. She knew what the something was.

She scanned the room. Her fear subsided when she didn't see anything. And when he didn't see anything, either.

She placed her hands on his strong shoulders. She pressed

her bare breasts to his back and held him. She kissed him on the side of the neck.

"I know *I* felt something," she said, trying to cheer him. Yet some residual fear remained.

"I want to make certain," he said. He kissed her to comfort her. "Okay?"

"Okay. Make certain."

He rose from the bed. Naked, he turned the corner from his bedroom. He walked down the hall. Again, he sensed something. He had a very faint sense of—

Yes, it was there! But he couldn't find it. Couldn't place it. Wasn't sure if his sense was real, was on the mark, or if his imagination was running wild thanks to the morning's reading at the library.

He turned on the light in his living room. Nothing.

He examined the doors. Locked. Untouched.

The kitchen. Quiet and empty.

He turned on the outside lights and scanned. All he saw were an array of summer moths, fluttering upward toward the lights in their crazy suicidal patterns.

Still . . .

He sighed. This must be what it's like, he thought, to go slowly crazy. Searching for something that rational minds claim does not exist. Insisting that something is there when no one else can see or feel it. . . .

"Not in my house tonight," he whispered aloud to the ghost. "I do not will you into my house tonight."

No answer.

Brooks gave up.

He returned to the bedroom. Annie was there waiting. She had pulled a pale blue sheet up over her. The sheet was up to her chin, but it left one leg and one breast uncovered to his view. Much better than chasing a malevolent ghost.

"I want to leave the light on," he said, settling in next to her. "Okay?"

"Mmmm. Okay," she murmured. "Now. Where were you?"

He pulled away the sheet. He found just the spot, kissing just to the left of her navel. "I believe I was right here," he whispered.

"Exactly," she agreed.

The light stayed on. They made love and fell asleep with their bodies intertwined, the sheets and covers fallen away.

It was in the middle of the night when they were dozing soundly that the spirit rose again.

In the twenty-five-watt light of the bedroom, the tall, ominous figure cast a shadow across the lovers. It moved close to the bed, gliding as if on rollers. The aura of malevolence, the mood of homicide, moving gently with it.

In sleep, they were indeed a beautiful couple. The shadow liked the woman in particular. It inclined toward her and touched her on the lips.

In sleep, her hand moved and brushed at its touch.

The phantom turned its attention to the man. The man made the spirit very angry, satisfied lover as he was to such a gorgeous woman. A blow to the man's exposed genitals would be amusing. Twist them the way he had twisted the necks of the other three victims. Crunch them.

Its touch hovered above Brooks' groin, ready to smash downward and twist.

Or maybe just get on with it. Kill them both here and now in their postorgasmic sleep. . . .

But the presence desisted in the light of a wonderful new notion.

Too easy to send them to death together.

The spirit soared. It would kill only one of them. They were so much in love, this actress and this policeman! What would be more painful than if one lived and one died? Oh, what terror he would soon bring to every living soul on Nantucket!

What misery!

Exquisite! Exquis—!

Tim Brooks' eyes flashed open and he bolted upright in bed. Sweat poured from his brow.

God! What a horrible feeling!

The first thing he did was look at the woman sleeping next

to him. Yes, she was breathing. Evenly and beautifully. He sighed in relief.

He placed a protective arm on her. In response, she snuggled closer to him.

The second thing Brooks did was move his eye around the room.

But there was nothing he could see.

As quickly as Brooks' eyes had opened, the phantom had vanished.

Twenty-seven

"How much is it worth to you," Andrea asked with a smile. "I mean, if I told you who Henry Flaherty was, what would you do for me?"

Detective Brooks looked up from his desk. Andrea stood in the doorway to his office, a familiar position these days. She was wearing a short summer dress that was far too young for her and, to Tim Brooks' fatigued eyes, she looked terrific in it. Andrea also knew how to read a man's gaze.

"What?" he asked, leaning back in his chair.

"First things first," Andrea Ward of the *Hyannis Eagle* said. "May I come in?"

"Sure. If you don't mind hard-backed wooden chairs." He motioned to one at the side of his desk.

"I probably should, but I don't," Andrea said. She sauntered in and sat down, positioning herself across from him as provocatively as possible. Vintage Andrea: incessant banter, flirting around the point, coupled with body language that was as subtle as a punch in the nose.

It had already been a memorable Thursday morning for the Nantucket Police Department, not to mention the county prosecutor. Influenced by the fact that the attendant details of the Hughes murder had resembled that of the DiMarco murder, Eddie Lloyd's bail had been reduced by eighty percent. His family had quickly posted a bond, secured by the equity in their home. Eddie had been released.

What troubled Tim Brooks much more, however, was the laboratory report on the ice pick that had been planted in the center of Emmet Hughes' forehead. The only fingerprints found were Hughes' own, leading to any of three dead ends, none of them terribly plausible.

Hughes had stabbed himself in the brain while in the process of wringing his own neck. Or second, the pick had flown through the air of its own accord and then had slammed into the front of his skull. Or third, a human killer, equipped with surgical gloves and whom no one—*no one*—had seen come or go, had done the deed.

Brooks knew better. But now, shortly after ten A.M., it was Andrea's turn to contribute to his morning.

"I already told you," Timothy said, taking up her inquiry. "I'd give you the full scoop on the story. What have you got for me?"

"Come on, Timmy," she teased. "There must be something better than *that*. How important is this Henry Flaherty to you?"

"Enough to throttle you if you don't tell me what you have."

"Just throttle?" she asked.

"Just throttle."

"That answers my other question. I guess you and Annette Carlson are still an item."

He sighed dismally. Two of the national tabloids had picked up the scent of a story on Nantucket. One had run a picture of 17 Cort Street and pronounced it the site of an "occult murder." The other had run a similar story, but also included the "scoop" that "film-sexpot Annette Carlson" was "hiding from the police" and "bedding down with a local fireman." Meanwhile, both papers had reporters on the island. Neither could locate Annette and neither were allowing facts to deter them from a good story.

Brooks held Andrea in a long, cold, impatient gaze. That was her cue.

"I have *a* Henry Flaherty for you, Timmy," she said. "I don't know if it's your man. Been dead for . . ." She hunched her shoulders. "Well, that's part of the mystery. No one knows how long he's been dead. I *assume* he's dead. Born in eighteen ninety, which would make him the same age as President Eisenhower. A hundred and three years old. Well, most people that age *are* dead, Timmy, even if you can't prove it."

He leaned forward.

"So who is he? Or who *was* he?"

She smiled, crossed her legs dramatically, and explained.

By spending a day cruising through old newspaper clippings, telephone directories, tax listings, birth and death certificates, and police records, Andrea had found him a handful of males named Henry Flaherty. Four, in fact. One was six-years-old and currently enrolled in the Hyannis public school system. Another had operated a Chevrolet dealership in Hyannis for thirty years and was living in comfortable retirement in Florida. Andrea had even called and chatted with the man.

Another Henry Flaherty had been a librarian on Martha's Vineyard since 1978. "Very quiet, very pleasant man," Andrea said. He was still employed at the public library in Edgartown, if Brooks wished to talk to him. "But somehow," Andrea said, "I don't think he fits the profile of what you're looking for."

"Probably not," Brooks conceded. "So who's the fourth?"

"He was a New York theatrical producer in the nineteen twenties," Andrea said. "Had some very successful shows. Not the top ones of the day, but close to it. Made a lot of money in his time and left quite a fortune, more than a million dollars, when he was declared dead in nineteen thirty-five."

Brooks knew enough to hang on Andrea's tantalizing phraseology. " '*Declared* dead'?" he asked.

"After being missing for seven years. The legal limit."

Part of Brooks' mind was taking in the new information as Andrea presented it. The other part was trying to put in order what had already been received.

"Okay. Here are the odd spins," Andrea said. "This Henry was last seen on Nantucket Island in nineteen twenty-eight. Disappeared here. Rumor had it that he met with some sort of foul play. There were several accounts that he was murdered. But he may have committed suicide." She paused. "Big search

413

for him at the time since he was an important theater man. But, as I said, no one ever found him." She pursed her lips. "Tragic."

"Was it?"

She sighed. "Had all the elements of a good trashy novel," said Andrea, who'd never been able to sell her own mediocre trashy novel. "See, Henry was married to this pretty young girl named Mabel Mack. Great name, huh? Double M's. I've always liked double M's. Mabel was his wife and one of his stars. But she drowned on this island."

"When?"

"Nineteen twenty-eight."

"Is that established? Her body was found?"

"Go over to town hall and check Nantucket's own death records. Or take my word for it because I was already there. She went down in the tide off Surfside Beach," Andrea said. "Same as—"

"Bruce Markley."

Brooks froze for a moment.

"That's right," she said. "Interesting geometry, isn't it?"

Andrea, as a reporter, had a religion similar to Brooks' as a detective: when investigating a case, neither believed in the existence of coincidence.

"Put the story in chronological order, Andrea," Brooks asked, now possessed with a newly found sense of indulgence. "Tell me what you know from the start."

Among many other things, Andrea was a quick study. She had a sheaf of notes and never consulted them. But she poured forth the official version of long-dead events. Much of it was rumor and another chunk of it was innuendo, reported in the local press at the time. Andrea had ferreted this much out of the libraries and police records, but had also obtained a few more tidbits by fax from the theater library at New York's Lincoln Center. Henry, after all, having been a producer, and Mabel Mack, his wife, having been an actress, both had entries.

Flaherty had been a Horatio Alger story of the ragtime and

World War I era, but somewhere along the line his tale had taken a dark turn and spun out of control.

He was an immigrant from Ireland who had traveled to New York from Cork in 1908 and set up shop as a professional stage comedian. He worked as the straight half of a "Double Irish" vaudeville act called Kearns & Flaherty. But a few days after a violent argument in 1912, Flaherty became a monologuist and the popular Ed Kearns was dead.

There was a trial. Ed Kearns was an old-timer in New York and the Broadway scuttlebut had it that Flaherty had murdered him in the latter's Greenwich Village home. There was a high-profile trial but a jury failed to convict. Amid scandal, Flaherty continued his career.

This career, according to the lengthy write-ups he received when he turned up missing in 1928, was surprisingly successful. The fact that he had ducked a murder conviction gave him something of a novelty as an act. This didn't help in New York where the many friends of the late Ed Kearns refused to book him. But on tour across the rest of the United States, his appearance fee tripled.

On top of this, Flaherty was apparently quite a good performer for several years. He saved his money. And his success on the legitimate boards bankrolled him for a move into stage production. There again, he succeeded.

Flaherty took traveling shows to the Catskills, Philadelphia and Boston, before returning them to New York. He met with still more success. He also met a nineteen-year-old girl named Mabel Mack in September 1924, when she auditioned for one of his productions.

Flaherty knew how to go after what he wanted. He wanted young Mabel. They were married in January of the following year.

Thereafter, details in the press were both sketchy and contradictory. Mabel enjoyed success in Flaherty's shows, but the producer himself was seen around New York with far too many other beautiful young things to suggest monogamy by both parties to the marriage.

Obviously trouble, serious trouble, brewed around this point.

Andrea smiled like the Cheshire cat. "Is this getting close to your mark at all?" she asked.

"I don't know. Maybe."

In the middle of all of this, something dawned on Tim Brooks, something buried in his subconscious which made him listen all the more intently.

He remembered Annette's account of her first encounter with a ghost. He remembered that she said she had been dreaming about a woman on a stage . . . dancing to a syncopated ragtime beat . . . lost somewhere between the present and the 1920s. . . .

"Then I'll nudge things a little closer," Andrea said. "I've been digging through your own police department's records. Ever cruise through the year nineteen twenty-eight, Tim?"

He shook his head.

"Try it sometime. It'll make for interesting reading if you like characters named Henry Flaherty."

"Come on, Andrea," he said. "Get to it."

She winked.

Back in 1928, she revealed, the producer Henry Flaherty had come to Nantucket with a small acting company. He put on some summer productions in Siasconset, the town at the other end of the island. His wife Mabel Mack headlined.

But one evening in July, out at Surfside, Mabel marched into the surf fully clad in her stage clothes. Or at least that was what witnesses said. It was also what the coroner agreed.

"They called it a suicide. Death by drowning. But her friends told reporters that she was depressed. Disconsolate. About what?" Andrea asked, immediately answering her own question with a shrug. "No one at the time ever revealed what the problem was. Not in anything I could find. And I doubt if there's anyone alive anymore who'd know."

In his mind, Brooks felt the pieces of the puzzle busily moving around, trying to take shape one second, failing to fit the next.

"No," he found himself thinking, "no one's alive who would know, but—"

"The thing was, Tim," Andrea Ward continued, "Mabel was a pretty popular girl. I don't mean promiscuous. I mean popular. Lots of friends. On Broadway. On the theater circuits. And apparently here. On this island. So who made her so depressed? Who made her so miserable with life that she would march into the sea?"

"We both know," Brooks deduced. "But you tell me."

"Cherchez l'homme," she said. "It's always a man, isn't it? Most of the other actors held Henry responsible. As did everyone who loved Mabel. Well, here's where the story ends, Tim, because two days later, *he* disappeared. Henry Flaherty. The police at the time thought he had fled the island. But there was no record of him having left. Needless to say, an investigation followed here on Nantucket. He was never found. Nor was his body. Seven years later, in nineteen thirty-five, he was declared legally dead." She paused. "And that was the last time Henry Flaherty figured directly into anything theatrical or otherwise."

Andrea smiled. "So? What do you think? Like it? Does it help?"

"I like it," he admitted. "You did well." He paused. "What about this 'Mabel Mack'? Was that a stage name? 'Mack' sounds like it might have been truncated from something else. Did you happen to notice a real name?"

Andrea hadn't noticed and the question propelled her back into her clippings. She couldn't find an answer.

"Why do you ask?" Andrea inquired, looking up. "Got an angle?"

"Maybe."

"Good," she said. "Then maybe you can tie it into the final footnote to the story."

"What's that?"

Across Brooks' desk she handed a copy of a clipping that had been sent to her from the theater library in New York. This item was datelined 1955 and, while it dealt with an unsubstantiated tale, lent a possible explanation to Henry Flaherty's demise.

His demise and more.

A terminally ill actor named Kenny Carkner, dying in a film industry nursing home in southern California, spun forth a strange tale two days before his death at age eighty-one. It was the type of conscience-clearing tale frequently spun on deathbeds.

Mr. Carkner recalled working the straw hat theater circuits in the summer in the East before the Great Depression. And he remembered falling in for a two-week stand with some other actors whom he didn't know very well at an island theater in Massachusetts.

And he had heard a story that had always stayed with him.

There had been this young actress married to an older producer, the account went. "A mean old Harp from County Cork," recalled the actor, an Irishman himself. The producer's physical and mental abuse of his wife—he both beat her and flagrantly cheated on her—had driven her deeply to depression. But only when she had fallen in love with another man, sought a divorce, and had been denied it by her outraged husband, had she totally despaired.

It was then, according to the tale the old man had told, that young Mabel Mack, walked into the surf and committed suicide.

Brooks followed the deathbed tale into its final paragraphs.

A bunch of the other actors got good and drunk following Mabel's death, he said, and were set to exact their revenge upon the producer, whose name the dying actor didn't recall three decades after the fact. They dragged him out to a field at gunpoint, the story went, intent on beating him.

A struggle followed. The gun was fired. The producer was dead and no one was really sorry about it.

But thereupon, the story took a final ghoulish turn, something that separated it from the normal amateurish homicide. It was a touch that seemed to have meant little to anyone—other than lovers of the macabre—across the years until now.

Panicked by what they had done, the actors made an effort to conceal their crime. They disposed of the producer's corpse somewhere on the island. But just in case it were ever found, they wanted to make it impossible to identify.

"One of the actors had worked as a butcher as a young man," the dying thespian said. "So it was a simple matter, I was told. They decapitated the corpse before getting rid of it. They buried the head under a local house."

Brooks stared at this, the monstrosity of it all sinking in as he finished reading. Apparently there had been some token investigation of the old man's tale in 1955, when it was first told. But no one had found anything and, with all the principals long dead, no one had shown much enthusiasm for investigating further. Nor were there any specifics or, for that matter, any proof that the tale was anything more than a good creepy yarn.

But Tim Brooks raised his eyes. He knew differently.

Mabel Mack and Henry Flaherty. A suicidal actress and a decapitated corpse. The perfect companion pieces for a tall, angry, malevolent, headless vision.

For several seconds there was silence in the room. Brooks stared at Andrea. She smiled.

"Well?" she asked eventually. "How did I do?"

"Great. Up until the end."

"Hell. What did I miss?"

"That was *almost* the last time Henry figured into anything," Brooks said, recalling her closing remark. "It was the last time until a month ago. That's when Beth DiMarco died in the field past the cemetery. And that's when Henry Flaherty came back to this island."

Andrea looked at him blankly for several seconds.

"Didn't get you," she finally said. She looked down again at her notes. "Remember? I said he'd be a hundred and three years old. And that's if they didn't chop his—"

"Got your pad and pencil?"

She did.

"You can't print it yet," he said. "But in case I don't live to the end of this case, here's the story."

And then he told her.

419

Two hours later, Brooks fit into place another piece of the puzzle.

He telephoned New York and found a young researcher at the theater library at Lincoln Center. The researcher was kind enough to go to her files and look at the earliest entries for the long-deceased music hall ingenue who performed under the name of Mabel Mack.

As Brooks suspected, "Mack" was a stage name. The actress had been born with the less memorable and less stage-worthy moniker of Irma May Myers.

The significance of this might have escaped most people. And, for many years, it had. But armed with this, Brooks walked over to the Nantucket Town Hall, intent on reconciling the town's death records with his own suspicions.

It did not take long. The proof was as fresh as the death certificate of Mrs. Helen Ritter, the longtime schoolteacher on the island.

Myers was Helen Ritter's maiden name, too. Irma May, or Mabel Mack, had been Mrs. Ritter's older sister. Henry, the much despised Henry, had been her brother-in-law, and old Helen might have spoken volumes about the whole thing, had only anyone induced her to speak in the many years before her death.

But no one had ever asked.

Twenty-eight

It was ten P.M. on the evening of the thirteenth when Annette placed the checkerboard table in the center of the living-room floor. There remained the breaks in the wall which Emmet Hughes had tried to repair. That area of the room was kept clear, upon Reverend Osaro's advice. The rest of the furniture was pushed to the side. The carpet had been left in the center of the room.

"Draw the shades," Osaro said. "That's a very important part. Draw the shades."

If a seance was going to work at all, he suggested, it needed all the help it could get.

By quarter past the hour the room had been "dressed" for the ceremony. Annette stood near the hearth, watching Timothy and the minister steady the table upon the carpet. Three old wooden chairs were chosen from the contents of the house and were placed by the table.

"Annie?" Tim asked. "Where do you want to sit?"

She looked as if she didn't want to sit at all. But she steadied her nerves.

"Nearest the door," she said with a jittery laugh. Tim and the minister smiled. She could have that place, they said. Annie was the first to sit down.

Brooks drew a deep breath and sat down next; he faced the door that led to the rear of the house. Annie's hands were already on the bare wooden table, her pulse pounding rapidly.

421

Tim was seated next to her and placed a hand on hers for a moment.

"Does the room have to be absolutely dark?" she asked. "Or can we . . . ?"

"We can have a small amount of light," Reverend Osaro said. "But spirits don't like lights, remember. So success can be contingent upon darkness."

He paused.

"Crazy as it sounds, you'd be surprised how well you can see once your eyes get used to the blackness," he explained. "And spirits also provide their own illumination, too."

"Yeah," Annette said, still nervous.

Brooks' gaze settled upon the candle that had stood on the checkerboard table. "Let's try it with a candle first," he said. "And see what happens."

Osaro protested mildly, but said they could try it if they felt more comfortable that way.

Osaro closed the doors and the windows. He drew the shades. He snipped much of the existing wick off the candle so that the flame would burn very low. He set the candle on a side table. When he turned off the room lights, the shadows from the small single light in the room threw a series of macabre shadows across the walls.

Osaro sat down at the table. "Now," he said. "Everyone relax. Try to breathe deeply and settle yourself. Close your eyes if it makes it easier. Put yourself in a receptive frame of mind. Tell yourself that you wish to converse with a spirit. Make this room a friendly receptive place for the soul of a departed person to come forth."

Several seconds passed.

"Oh, yes," Osaro said, recalling. "And rest your hands on the table. Don't worry about fingertips or the edges of the table. Just rest. Allow yourself to drift a little, if you can."

Annette did as instructed. Brooks did, too. Each closed both eyes and tried to imagine the presence of spirits coming forth in the room. Each, however, found it difficult to keep both eyes closed.

Annette peeked. Brooks peeked also and caught Annette peeking. He winked at her and suddenly they both laughed lightly.

"Don't horse around," Osaro counseled softly. "We must try to be serious. Otherwise this won't work."

The smiles eased from the faces of Timothy and Annette. They became aware of noise beyond the house. The occasional sound of a car passing. Very distantly the voices of two people walking by. Once there was a small lonely aircraft overhead. Nothing else.

"I got to tell you, George," Brooks said quietly. "I'm starting to feel like a jerk."

Osaro didn't answer. Brooks opened his eyes very slightly. He saw the minister's face possessed with an expression that he didn't understand. He knew it was one of peace and tranquility because there was nothing upsetting about it. But his friend seemed to have entered some sort of light trace. His lips were moving very slightly, as if to invoke a prayer or communicate on a higher level with a presence that Brooks could not yet see.

Annette's eyes opened and she saw this, also. She looked at Tim Brooks for reassurance. He gave it with a nod.

"Do as I do," Osaro said in a very low voice.

The minister's hands glided to a fresh position on the table. Flat with palms down. Fingers very slightly spread apart.

Annette's hands assumed the same position. So did Brooks'. Then Osaro took a deep breath, held it for several seconds, and appeared to sink deeper into his state of concentration.

Then his hands made another movement. He slid his palms to the edges of the table and pushed them to where they touched the person next to him on each side. On his left, his palm touched Annette's hand. On his right it pressed against Timothy's.

Brooks nodded. He extended his hand to his right and he and Annette made the same link on the other side of the table.

"Good," Osaro whispered, seeming to speak as if he were asleep. "Very good. Now wait."

The wait was several minutes. The flame of the candle

danced and flickered. Once, with a mutual flash of terror, Annette and Timothy thought that it had danced so low that it would extinguish itself.

But still it burned, bravely and boldly.

"Is there a spirit present?" Reverend Osaro asked softly.

There was no answer.

"Is there a troubled spirit present?" he asked again after half a minute.

Again, nothing, though distantly in the building there was a creak in a floorboard.

"We wish to speak with whatever spirit is in this house," the minister repeated after a longer wait.

Annette and Tim held a silence, their eyes open now and alert, vigilant, anxious and expectant.

Many minutes went by.

"What do we do, George?" Brooks finally asked. "No one's dialing our number."

Several seconds later, the question settled into Osaro's mind. "What the hell do you think we do, you dumb-assed cop?" he answered genially. "You shut up and we wait."

"Yes, sir," Brooks said with mock respect.

Osaro's answer lopped off some of the tension in the room. Brooks winked at Annette and the actress allowed herself a slight schoolgirl smile.

Then a door opened.

"Don't look!" Osaro snapped, his own eyes remaining shut. "If it passes in your line of vision, you can look! But don't turn! Don't stare!"

The door was the one that led to the rear of the house, to the kitchen and to the cellar. The latch of the knob mechanism rattled and the old hinges creaked.

Brooks was facing it. He stared despite the minister's warning. His own eyes were wide. There was nothing there. Just a door that had opened of its own will.

Or to an unseen hand.

Brooks had closed the door himself. He knew he had shut it securely.

Oh, God in Heaven! he thought to himself. This is not really happening.

He had come here with expectations of success. Yet nothing had prepared him for being face to face with that window that Osaro had once mentioned.

The window into the next reality. Or some other reality. Or some dark unknown place where there are no maps and no points of reference.

Just an abyss.

Then the door closed. The room was very still. Even the flame of the candle didn't move.

Annette's damp jittery hand found its way onto Tim's. Brooks gave it a squeeze, madly rallied his own courage and then returned their hands to the edge of the table. Deep down inside, he had the urge to flee.

He conquered it. For the moment.

"Is someone there?" Osaro asked softly. "Is there a spirit in this room?"

There was a long, dreadful pause. Annette dared not breathe. Brooks stared straight ahead. Somewhere in the room there was a sound, like a small footfall. Brooks felt his heart in his throat. Couldn't anyone see how frightened he was? Why did Annette turn to him for strength when he himself was ready to—

He drew a deep breath and steadied himself again. He waited to feel a set of cold steel hands upon his neck, creeping up from behind him, squeezing and—

"A child," said Osaro very softly. His face broke into a lovely smile. "A beautiful little girl."

"What?" Brooks asked, speaking quietly, too.

Osaro didn't answer.

Brooks and Annette glanced toward each other. Then they were jolted so hard that together they felt they'd leap through the roof.

But they didn't. They kept their hands together on the table, linked and touching, as they were suddenly aware of the figure of a little girl a few feet behind them.

She didn't speak aloud. But they knew what she was saying. They heard her within their heads, the same way that Brooks had heard the greater more evil spirit.

"Have you seen my parents?"

Did they imagine it? Or did they feel the checkerboard table give a tremor, too?

Annette felt her heart pound and thunder. Her hands were soaking wet on the table.

The little girl's voice was plaintive. Pleading.

"Have you seen my parents?"

Annette drew a breath. "I've seen your parents," Annette whispered.

Not understanding, Brooks turned to Annette.

Annette looked straight ahead, as Osaro had instructed.

"Where are my parents?" asked the ghost of Sarah Shipley.

"Your parents don't live here anymore," Annette said. "Your parents moved to Vestal Street." Annette remembered the Shipleys' number and gave it.

"I miss my parents," the little girl communicated next.

Annette nodded. For her, there was an aura of disbelief upon this, too.

The table shuddered beneath their palms. Annette and Timothy looked toward it. When they looked back to where the little girl had stood, she was gone.

They looked in each direction. Almost imperceptibly, the table had a slight quiver to it now, almost like a heartbeat. For a split second, Brooks thought he saw something out of the corner of his eye flit by—like the little girl moving quickly. But when he looked, it was gone.

Or it had never been there at all.

Many minutes passed. Reverend Osaro instructed Annette and Tim to relax, almost as if they were trying to go to sleep.

"Close your eyes. Think of someone you love who has passed over to the next world," Osaro said, his gentle Asian lilt very apparent in his invocation. "Create a loving climate for a spirit to visit. Attempt to communicate. . . ."

Several more minutes passed.

"Tell your legs to relax. Then your arms. Your body. Your mind. Feel yourself tumble gently into a friendly world where you will meet the spirits halfway."

Brooks opened his eyes a crack. There was no movement in the room. Osaro remained stationary. So did Annette. The candle still flickered.

Then the table rose.

It rose very slightly. Only an inch or two above the ground. But both Annette and Tim Brooks knew it was elevated, for when they pushed hard upon it there was give to it. An off-balance wobble. They knew it was no longer on the floor.

"Don't press. Don't offer resistance," George Osaro whispered. "You'll discourage a visit . . ."

Osaro's eyes remained shut. His hands were firm.

The movement of the table was stunning. Unlike any feeling either of them had ever experienced before. It was akin to the shock one might feel when, thinking one is alone while groping through a dark room, one presses up against another body.

Across the room, the doorknob moved again. And again the door opened. It opened wider this time and Brooks, who was seated across from it, was aware immediately of a white presence on the other side.

"Don't stare. Again, don't stare," Osaro repeated. "Make our friends feel welcome." He paused. "Is there a spirit present?"

There was.

Brooks stared, anyway. This figure was translucent. It was white and a woman and Brooks felt his body swept with goose bumps when he recognized Mary Beth DiMarco.

She was young and pretty, but obviously very sad. Brooks had the feeling of looking directly into the dead woman's eyes, though later Annette would report the same sensation. In any case, Mary Beth was crying.

Brooks glanced at Osaro. The clergyman's expression was one of sadness, too. It seemed to match the mood of the ghost.

The table gave another tremor.

"You shouldn't be dead, should you, child?" Osaro asked.

"Something horrible has happened in the universe. It was not yet your rightful time."

Brooks and Annette watched as the figure nodded her head.

"Your hour will soon come to enter Heaven," Osaro said. "Why are you here?"

The girl put a hand to her face. She cried. Brooks thought he could hear her. Very low. Very subliminal. The distant sound of a young woman sobbing. Now that he knew what it sounded like, he wondered if he had heard it before in other places of abject human cruelty.

"What is unsettled?" Osaro asked.

She communicated. "Eddie."

"Eddie didn't hurt you?" Osaro asked.

The ghost of Mary Beth DiMarco stared at the only policeman present. It should have been scary. But strangely, there was nothing fearful about this apparition. There was almost something reassuring about her.

"Eddie would never have hurt me."

Brooks barely drew a breath. He nodded slowly. The table wobbled and lowered. But it never touched the floor.

The figure of Mary Beth DiMarco receded. Not that it moved. It just faded until it wasn't there. And simultaneously, a new shadow swept the room, thrown by the light of the small candle.

Reverend Osaro opened his eyes. He appeared surprised by this third visitation. Annette and Timothy moved their heads almost in unison.

Mrs. Ritter was standing near them. She was steady and solid. Nothing shimmering or translucent.

"Poor dears. Poor all of them. Poor all of you, too," Mrs. Ritter said, raising her eyes and scanning the assemblage at the table. *Her* table.

"Why are you here, Mrs. Ritter?" Brooks whispered.

"Same as last time. To warn you. To warn you." In death, she repeated herself much as she had in life.

"About what?" Annette and Tim asked together.

"Henry," she said. "He's mean and crazy. Always was. Always was. Not a decent man." She smiled cryptically and gave a little laugh.

She looked to Brooks, then to Annette. "I'm pleased to see the two of you together," she said. "Of course, I *knew*. One look at the two of you and I *knew*."

She raised her fingers to her lips and moistened them. Then she turned, reached her hand to the candle and blithely put her fingers to the flame.

She held her fingers to the fire for several seconds. Brooks could see this very clearly. She smiled as if this were great mischief.

She looked back to the three figures at the table. "Be very careful of Henry Flaherty," she said. "He's caused so much misery. Don't let him cause more for you."

A final smile. A motherly, protective one.

Mrs. Ritter's white fingers moved further against the burning wick. Then she arbitrarily snuffed it and the room went completely dark.

Annette gasped. Brooks put a hand on her shoulder to keep her in place. Somehow they all knew that Mrs. Ritter had departed with the candlelight.

"Remain still," Osaro said. "This might be the moment."

Brooks spoke. "For what?"

"For Henry. That's the spirit we want, isn't it? Henry Flaherty!"

Brooks felt his heart thunder. He guided his hand back down to the table. Annette's stayed next to his.

They passed several minutes midway between heightened anxiety and overt fear.

"Be very careful of Henry Flaherty. He's already caused so much misery."

It was not the first time Mrs. Ritter's words had held wisdom. Nor did he need an introduction to what he thought of as the elusive black presence.

He waited. It occurred to him that he and Annette might be killed, so, as he waited, he began to will that they would not be.

He knew she was doing the same thing. Only perhaps with her, it was prayer.

Gradually, his eyes grew accustomed to the darkness. He could see vague features within the room. The lamps against the walls. The chairs. The contour of the old hearth.

He waited, conscious of his own heartbeat. Somewhere distantly in the house there was another of the maddening creaks. He was aware of Annette next to him and Osaro on the other side. Their hands remained joined.

"Come to us, Henry," the minister said. "Come to us and share in the holy peace of Our Savior, Jesus Christ."

Osaro paused. The room remained silent. Many more minutes passed. Brooks lost track of time. He suddenly felt greatly fatigued and almost like he was ready to sleep. But the minister roused him when he invoked another prayer.

"As the Apostle Paul said in his Epistle to the Romans, 'The night is far spent, the day is at hand: let us therefore cast off the works of darkness, and let us put on the armor of light.'"

Nothing again. In the dark, the table gave a very short quake, as if something might be starting to happen. But then it settled and became very still, its four legs firmly on the underlying carpet.

"We wish you to come forth, Henry," the minister urged in a kindly voice. "We wish you to share with us your worldly pain, your eternity of troubles, your panoply of tears, so that we might help you ease them."

More time. More nothing. Osaro asked Annette and Tim to attempt to will the spirit of Henry Flaherty into the chamber.

They both tried. The result was the same. Gradually, Brooks was aware that Osaro was coming out of his meditative state. The minister's body fidgeted. His hands flinched.

"Damn," he finally whispered. "We can't get him."

Osaro made this pronouncement so banally that it sounded as if he were talking about someone receiving a telephone call.

Osaro drew his hands away from the table. Brooks was aware of movement by the minister, though he remained in his chair. Then suddenly there was a flash in the darkness. Both Annette and Timothy recoiled until they realized that Osaro had lit a match.

The minister rose and relit the candle. He moved through the room with no fear whatsoever and, for a fleeting second as the wick of the candle took the flame from the match, almost looked like a shimmering presence, himself.

But then that odd vision was gone. Osaro blew out the match and sat down again. He lay his hands on the table, more casually this time, and didn't touch his partners.

"A few more minutes," he said quietly. The mood in the room was broken now. "I don't think we're going to get anything, but we'll wait a little longer."

They waited and Osaro was proven correct. Nothing further. Eventually, the minister asked Annette to turn on the room lights. When they did, the living room looked very ordinary again, even with all the furniture other than the checkerboard table pushed against the walls.

A small wave of relaxation washed around the room, a tiny descent into boredom.

The seance was over.

Half an hour later, they closed the house at 17 Cort Street and walked outside.

"What's it doing, George?" Brooks asked. "Why won't it come forth?"

"'It'?"

"Henry. The spirit we want," Brooks said.

"He—or 'it'—is royally jerking us around," Osaro answered. "It doesn't *want* to come forth."

"I thought it had to. I thought we were drawing it forth with the opportunity to communicate."

"Not necessarily," Osaro said moodily. He watched Annette lock her house. Brooks held a flashlight for her so that she could turn her keys properly.

"These things have their own will," Osaro explained, continuing. "Do I need to remind you? It's nothing more than their will that brings them here. Their spirit *is* their will. That's what makes them so difficult to battle. It's all they have to fight with."

"I want it to come forth," Brooks said again.

"Then you have to make it want to," Osaro said. "That's really the only solution. It will do only what it wants to do."

Annette completed locking the house. Brooks turned off the flashlight.

"What if it's not here?" Brooks asked, looking at the house as Annette stepped away from it. Annette had left a small lamp glowing on each floor. "What if Henry's not in this house anymore? What if the ghost is somewhere else?"

"He's here," Osaro said flatly. "I can feel it. His presence is so strong that he's stirred up every other spirit in the place. Even the little Shipley girl."

They turned toward where they had left their cars in front of the house. They walked several paces in the night air. A mosquito buzzed Annette. She slapped at it.

"Then what if we *can't* draw this particular spirit forth?" Brooks asked.

"There's always a way," Osaro said. "Has to be. Otherwise the spirit wouldn't be wandering. Otherwise it would have passed on. Something's holding it in this world. We have to find out what. Then we can summon it very easily."

"Does *it* know that?" Brooks asked with evident sarcasm.

Osaro shrugged. "If it didn't know already, it probably knows that now."

"Why?"

"I'm sure it's listening to us," Osaro said routinely. "You don't think it's not curious what we're about, do you?"

Brooks felt the surge of anxiety again. That feeling in his stomach. Behind his neck. For a half second, he thought something touched his cheek.

"God," Annette said softly.

Brooks touched his cheek and took her hand.

He waited. He waited to hear the spirit's voice within his head. But it wasn't forthcoming.

Where *is* Henry's spirit? Brooks wondered. Ten feet behind me? Lying in a graveyard? Hurtling through infinity?

Brooks led Annette from the house to the circular driveway. His mind churned, trying to fit all events and theories into a neat scheme where no neat scheme seemed possible.

A pair of mosquitoes buzzed him. He waved them off. Another buzzed Annette. She slapped at it.

"Rather than provide a feast for flying insects," he said to Annette, "why don't you go ahead to the car. I'll be there in a minute."

"Okay," she said.

She jogged ahead to the Miata. Brooks and Osaro walked slowly behind her, out of earshot.

"I think Henry's ghost was in my house last night," Brooks said. "I thought I felt its presence."

Osaro received this with several seconds of reflection. "You're getting very good at that skill, aren't you?" Osaro asked. "This sense of when a ghost is present."

Brooks looked at his friend in the shadows. "Very," he said. "Maybe too good."

"What's that mean?" Osaro asked.

"It's not the most comfortable skill to have," Brooks said. "Unsettling. Much the way you described it yourself the day we had a talk outside your church."

"Ah, yes," Osaro said, remembering.

They walked slowly, insects not withstanding. "I read this one paper over at the Eksman Collection at Harvard," Brooks began. "I found this particularly intriguing. This one psychic researcher, I forget his name, postulated that many ghosts walk the face of the earth. But they look so routine and so normal that no one even perceives them as ghosts. Very flesh and blood."

Osaro grinned. "I guess that lets me out," he joked. "The 'routine and normal' part."

"But what do you think about that theory?" Brooks asked.

"I don't know, Timmy," Osaro mused. "That one's a little like the old saw about the tree falling in the woods, isn't it? 'If

433

a tree falls and no one is there to hear it, does it make a sound?' No way to prove it or disprove it." He paused. "And why do you ask *me?*" he inquired. "Who the hell else might be a ghost around here? Bill Agannis? Gelman and Rodzienko." He laughed. "Boomer? That would be a novel development, wouldn't it?"

Brooks smiled. "I just wondered about your thoughts."

Osaro shrugged. "Those *are* my thoughts," he concluded.

It was a beautiful night. Nearly full moon and a billion stars. A breeze from the ocean. Much like the previous evening when Henry took a ride on the island breezes and landed at Brooks' home.

Tim watched Annette settle into his car. She put the top up. He slapped at another mosquito. They all seemed to pursue him while ignoring the minister. More divine intervention?

"I would think that your Henry is your most pressing problem," Osaro said, shifting the discussion. "And he doesn't fit that category of behavior at all, does he? Solid, I mean. He's very obviously a spirit from what you and Annette tell me."

"That's right."

Osaro nodded. "One deals with spirits accordingly," Osaro said.

They stopped outside the two vehicles. The Voyager had a new dent in its rear fender. A souvenir of the minister's most recent trip to Boston, Brooks guessed.

"How do I get him out of my house, George?" Brooks finally asked, turning very serious. "You're the expert on this. I want to end this haunting before I wake up dead or find Annette dead beside me."

"Why do you think that could happen?"

"I think it's what's next. Unless we dispose of Henry some way. Soon."

Osaro looked deeply concerned. He blew out a breath.

"We'll do another seance and try to summon him," the clergyman said. "Similarly, we also have to create a situation where we *make* him come forth by holding the key to whatever disturbs him."

To Brooks it sounded almost hopeless. He sighed. "That's all, huh?" he asked. "How in hell do we do that?"

Osaro saw how forlorn his friend looked. He rapped him confidently on the arm.

"Buck up," Osaro said. "Sometimes these things resolve very quickly. Have to be positive, you know. A lot of this is will-power, remember. Yours against the spirit's."

"Isn't that something of a mismatch?" Brooks asked.

"Maybe," Osaro allowed. "But until this is over we don't know who's got the stronger hand. Follow?"

"No."

"Then don't worry about it. We'll go after Henry again tomorrow. The more you believe in what you're doing the easier it becomes."

"But—"

"See you tomorrow," Osaro said.

He tapped Tim Brooks on the shoulder again and climbed into his van. Brooks watched as the minister turned over the engine of the car. The Voyager lurched into gear and pulled out onto the street.

Brooks watched him go, then slid into the Miata with Annette.

For several seconds, Brooks sat without starting his car. He stared at the road.

"What did you think?" he finally asked Annette.

"Scary," was the only word she could find.

"Think we really saw what we both think we saw?" he asked. "Or were we under some bizarre form of hypnosis? Or did we see only what we wanted to see?"

She leaned on him, her arm on his shoulder. "Tim, three people are dead on this island. That's no one's form of hypnosis. Nor is it anyone's self-delusion."

"Yeah," he answered in a toneless voice. "You're right."

But already a sickening notion was upon him. It seemed so neat and obvious that he wondered why it had taken so long to take form—even if it flew in the face of all the new supernatural reasoning that emerged from the last few weeks:

Was George Osaro a pathological murderer and liar? For reasons that only he knew, he had assaulted the college girl, caused the Canadian boy to drown, then murdered Emmet Hughes. Motivation? Where was it? Oh. Sure. Three inexplicable ghostly murders lent credibility to all this spirit stuff he was always pushing. An endless and multifaceted pattern of deceit.

Brooks toyed again with running Osaro's name through the FBI files. Just for fun. Just to see what rose to the surface. Well, this theory was a damned bit more rational than some of the others he had been working on about George in the last few hours.

Then he was deeply ashamed of himself for casting suspicion upon his closest friend. Proof of what stress can do to a man's reason, he told himself.

"Timmy . . . ? You falling asleep or what?"

Annette's yawning voice drew him back into reality, into the car where he sat with her.

"Do you realize what time it is?" she asked.

"I don't know. Midnight?"

"Guess again."

He glanced at the car's clock and was as surprised as she had been when she noticed moments earlier. It was twelve minutes past two in the morning.

"Two twelve! Can that be right?" he asked.

"We must have been in there for four hours," she said. "Didn't seem that way, did it?"

"No. It didn't."

What had they been doing? Drifting in and out of some other reality to summon the spirits? Brooks' sense of time was out of kilter. But so were a lot of other things.

They drove back to his house.

Annette slept right away, lying close to him.

Warily, Brooks remained awake for as long as possible. Toward three A.M. he finally drifted off.

But the rest of the night passed without incident.

Twenty-nine

Friday the fourteenth of August marked the third weekend in the summer's final month. The island was crowded and busy, but already some summer residents were making preparations for closing their houses for the year. At the same time, the final wave of two-week vacationers hit the island, predominantly people from New York or Boston who would stay until Labor Day.

The weather no longer had the clear crispness of June or the glowing warmth of July. Mid-August turned sticky and humid and hazy muggy days turned into foggy damp evenings.

But the day gave every early indication of passing peacefully. George Osaro spent the day at his church, putting his papers and personal belongings in order. The end of the month would close his tenure at Christ and Holy Trinity and he was taking the first steps of easing himself out. His departure date was advancing steadily.

Annette went back into her house alone for two hours in the afternoon to retrieve some clothes, books and scripts. The time passed uneventfully. Similarly, Timothy Brooks had a quiet shift on duty.

In the evening, Annette and Timothy dined out, again visiting 21 Federal Street, in their opinion the island's finest restaurant. They sat at a table downstairs this time, both ordered scallops with a ginger sauce and they split a bottle of sparkling white wine. To Annette's delight, no one recognized her.

Afterward, they took a walk together on Straight Wharf, watching one ferry pull into the harbor and another pull out. Across the harbor to the east, adjacent to the Coast Guard station, the red beacon of the Brant Point lighthouse flashed. As a haze remained on the water, its horn sounded, also.

Then they walked back to where Timothy had parked his car on India Street. Annette and Timothy climbed into his Miata. There was a low mist on the island and Brooks drove steadily through it to arrive at his home.

He and Annette went inside.

She showered and readied herself for bed. Brooks had only been home for ten minutes when the telephone rang. He made the mistake of answering it.

"Brooks?" boomed the voice on the other end.

Brooks recognized the lieutenant's voice.

"Yes?" he answered.

"Don't you ever wear your fucking beeper when you're off duty?"

Brooks grimaced.

"Normally, yes. Tonight, no. I—"

"I'm at the airport," Lieutenant Agannis said. "Get the hell out here right away, will ya."

"What's going on?"

"This is your fucking case, Brooks, God damn it! Just get here fast!"

"Yes, sir."

On the other end of the line, Bill Agannis set down the phone. Brooks set down his and turned.

"Tim? What is it?"

Annette had slipped into a nightgown and wrapped herself in a robe.

"I don't know," Brooks said. "The lieutenant just requested the honor of my presence at the airport. Obviously there's a problem. Of some sort."

He went to her and kissed her.

"I've got to get out there fast," he said. He turned away and began to look for a jacket. Late evenings at the airport could turn very cool.

She watched him. "Can I go with you?" she asked.

"Think it's a good idea?" he asked. "You'd probably be safer here."

He found a blue windbreaker and pulled it on. He strapped his pistol into his ankle holster and took his badge from the top of the dresser. When he turned she was standing very still, very quietly watching him.

He hated to go. Something about leaving her bothered him. Something that made him apprehensive.

"If it were up to me, fine. Come on along," he said. "But it just wouldn't *look* right if you turned up with me. Know what I mean?"

She nodded.

"Keep the doors locked till I get back. Okay?"

"Okay."

He went to her a second time and kissed her again, harder and more passionately than before. "If I'm late," he said, "just go to sleep. I'll slide in next to you when I get back."

"Okay," she said.

He went to his car and turned the ignition. The engine leaped to life. His car lights went on and sent a long beam across his lawn. He backed out of the driveway and onto the main road. In the corner of his eye, he saw her silhouette at the window, pulling closed the shade of the living room.

The airport was no more than three miles away, but Brooks drove quickly. Somehow he knew.

"This is your case," the lieutenant had said. Well, Brooks had more than a dozen cases on his desk, but only one that would bring his irritable chain-smoking commander to the airport at an hour before midnight.

Only one that really mattered.

His car hugged the night road. There was virtually no traffic. He had an image of himself, as he shifted gears and as the car moved through the smooth darkness, as an undergraduate oarsman skulling on a river.

He took the curves of the road with authority, tapping the brake when he needed to, holding his foot steady on the accelerator at the same time, daring not to take a second longer in transit than was necessary.

Lieutenant Agannis' words echoed. "Get the hell out here right away." And, "It's your case, God damn it!"

As he drove, he thought of Annette, left behind and alone, and he thought of how he felt about her. He thought, as his car cut through the night, how long it had been since he had fallen really, truly, madly in love with someone.

And then a bittersweet feeling took over him as something that he perceived as reality set in and told him that he was being a fool of the highest order. How could he ever think that this relationship could lead to anything except disappointment?

He was a town cop on the way to a nighttime emergency. Nothing more. Nothing less.

A cat—or something—darted across the road. Brooks hit his brake and swerved slightly. Whatever it had been, there was no sickening crunch under the tires. He had missed it.

He exhaled, calmed himself, and cut his speed.

Then the road ahead was brighter and, not that he didn't know the route, the signs indicated the turns to the airport. He made the final turn into the parking lot and less than a minute later pulled up beside a pair of fire engines, their sirens off but red beacon lights flashing on each.

The crew of one engine was already assembling itself to leave. The other crew lagged behind. Whatever crisis had befallen, it was almost over and appeared under control.

All except the aftermath.

Brooks parked his car and locked it. He passed a pair of firefighters. Brooks knew them both.

"You guys have some action?" he asked.

"Had to hose a runway," one answered. "No big deal."

"A New England Airways jet overshot and spun," the second man said. "The big one from New York. It's still out there if you want a look."

The detective didn't ask for a further elaboration. He knew one would come soon enough from another source.

There was a uniformed policewoman in the lobby of the airport's main terminal. As soon as Brooks entered the waiting room the policewoman saw him and, with a nod of her head, indicated that Lieutenant Agannis was in a private room in the adjacent administrative building.

Brooks stepped outside. He gazed at the tarmac. The jet from New York, a DC-9, and one of the stars of the small New England Airways fleet, was sitting with its nose thirty feet from the walls of the terminal. It had skidded badly and had nearly crashed into the terminal.

Brooks cringed. The yellow wing lights on the jet still flashed and a team of firemen from Engine Two were making sure any fuel spill had been sanded or washed before the big bird could back up.

Brooks cringed again. Then he went to the administrative building next door.

Lieutenant Agannis, his expression grave, turned and looked at Brooks as the latter entered a New England Airways office. There was a man sitting on a chair, greatly shaken, his face white. He was balding and about forty and wore the uniform of New England Airways. A name plate proclaimed him as Capt. Alan Jensen.

Brooks surmised quickly that it was his jet that was still on the runway. A moment later, Brooks realized that there was a second uniformed person standing to one side. Martin Hendricks, lean, angular and twenty-five years old. Brooks knew Hendricks but not Jensen.

Pilot and copilot.

Hendricks gave Brooks a curt nod of recognition. He didn't say anything. He, too, looked shaken.

Brooks looked at the situation and couldn't completely read it, aside from the fact that there had obviously been trouble with—or aboard—an aircraft.

Bill Agannis was an unhappy guy. He skipped any formal greeting. "How many unsolved deaths do we have on this island right now, Timmy?" the lieutenant quietly asked, looking Brooks in the eye.

"In my opinion? Three," Brooks answered.

"We nearly had fifty-one more. Sit down and listen to this."

Brooks chose to stand.

Jensen turned toward the detective and spoke.

"All of a sudden there was something on the runway when we were completing our landing pattern," Captain Jensen said. "I saw it. Marty saw it. There was something there. We didn't imagine it."

Martin Hendricks nodded to confirm.

" 'Something'?" Brooks asked, already with an inkling.

Jensen picked up the narrative. They—the pilot and copilot—had had a routine evening flight from New York, leaving La Guardia at 8:40. At takeoff, the night had been clear with a high cloud ceiling. Perfect summer flying weather. No incident. No problem. They had forty-seven passengers on board, plus two flight attendants to pass out the soft drinks and peanuts.

"We were coming into Nantucket eight minutes ahead of our SAT," Captain Jensen said. "That's Scheduled Arrival Time. The flight was a cream puff all the way. We took a routine approach and had head winds of less than five knots. Came in from the southwest, figured we'd be on the blocks smooth as silk." He paused. "That's when we saw him," Jensen said.

"Saw who?"

Brooks searched both Jensen and Hendricks. Lieutenant Agannis looked like he was cast in granite.

"We saw what looked like a figure of a man standing in our path," Martin Hendricks said. "I know this sounds nuts. But both Al and I saw the same thing."

"Real tall," said Captain Jensen. "Maybe six feet ten. Maybe seven feet."

"See the thing is, though," Hendricks said as Brooks' eyes darted back and forth between them, "he didn't really have any *features*. It was as if he were just this giant upright *shadow*. See what I'm saying? And he was pitch black."

Brooks felt those sensations again at the back of his neck. The icy hands. The tingle. The surge of cold fear. It coupled with the fearful sensation in his gut.

"A human figure without a head," said the pilot.

A frightful silence held the room. Jensen's gaze grabbed Brooks' and arrested it.

"Go ahead. Tell me I'm crazy. Tell me I hallucinated," Jensen said, anger rising to his defense. "And I'll tell you *you're* crazy and that I know what I saw."

"We both saw it," Hendricks repeated. "The figure of a man about seven feet tall. Black like a shadow. Standing right in our path as we brought our equipment down. And no head."

Agannis pondered and looked befuddled. A frown lingered. Brooks felt a horrible extra thump in his heart.

"I'm not here to tell you that you're crazy or not crazy," Brooks said. "What happened next?"

Jensen chewed on his lower lip for a second. "Well, I don't think we had much reaction time. Maybe a second and a half. Two seconds maximum, between the time we saw the figure and the time we would intersect at his location."

"We were still airborne," Hendricks added helpfully. "Eighty feet and descending."

"I put the aircraft into an evasive maneuver," the pilot said. "Turned the throttle back, pulled the rudder starboard, lifted the wing flaps. Standard procedure for evasion if there's an obstacle on the runway."

"And?" Brooks asked. He gave each a sidelong glance.

"The aircraft didn't react fast enough. I say we hit him. Or went right through him," Captain Jensen said. "The figure, the shadow, whatever was there, never moved. It held its position. Almost daring us. I saw it clear as day as we . . . we . . ."

"We hit him," Copilot Hendricks affirmed softly. "Went right through him. Could not possibly have missed him."

"And your plane skidded?"

"*After,*" Hendricks said. "After the impact. Or the nonimpact. We skidded westward across the tarmac. Reaction to the starboard thrust with the rudder. We took about an eighty-

443

degree spinout, traveled two hundred meters toward the arrival terminal. I was scared we'd tip a wing and tumble, in which case we would have bought the farm, baby." He shook his head adamantly.

"The runway was slick from humidity," Hendricks added. "Almost always is on evenings in August. Felt like we were on fucking ice." He paused. "But, of course, we weren't."

"Managed to pull it up and straighten out the nose," Jensen said. "But you can see where we ended up," he concluded, alluding not so subtly to the aircraft's position near the south wall of the terminal.

"Let's just say the passengers didn't have far to walk to the baggage claim area," said Hendricks.

Jensen blew out a breath.

"First thing we did was look back to that spot on the runway," said Jensen. "Well, I knew exactly where it was. No one there when we looked. No impact. No sign of anything."

"Control tower was watching the whole thing," Hendricks said. "They never saw anything out there. Radar didn't give us an inkling, either."

"They think we're crazy," Hendricks said. "Control tower thinks we misread our approach vector and now we're spinning fairy tales to cover our ass."

"So we got a spinout and an 'Incident Report' to write up," said Jensen. "We know what we saw, the tower says we're nuts and there's no corroboration on the tarmac. See our problem?"

Brooks nodded.

Hendricks looked to Jensen. "Tell him about the flash," he reminded the pilot.

"Oh, yeah," Alan Jensen said. "That wasn't even the least of it."

"A flash?" Brooks asked.

"It happened right at the moment when I think our plane passed through"—he searched for an appropriate term—"whatever was out there. We both experienced a flash of brightness. Real fast. Tenth of a second. Maybe faster."

"Woods, trees and ocean," Hendricks said softly.

Brooks looked back and forth. Agannis, who had obviously heard this already, looked sourly downward. "Come again?" Brooks asked.

"Woods, trees and ocean," Jensen said. "We were talking about it afterward, wondering what the flash had been. We both had a split-second image of woods, trees and ocean. Very bright. Like some location on the shore of this island on an intensely clear summer day."

"And that's what *you* saw, too?" Brooks asked Hendricks.

The copilot nodded. There was silence all around until Captain Jensen broke it.

"Anyway, Bill Agannis here said to call you," Jensen said. "Said you might be able to help. Or lend some insight. Or that what we saw might help you."

Brooks thought about it.

"When you write the report," Brooks said, "tell what you saw. You're not the first on the island. What more can you do other than relate it as it happened?"

Brooks looked at his commander. He was finished.

"That's it, boys," Agannis said to the two flyers. "I wanted Detective Brooks to hear this. You can get on with whatever you have to do next."

The pilot and copilot thanked Agannis. Brooks thanked them for recounting their story.

Agannis walked Brooks into the lobby of the administrative building. The lieutenant's mood built as he walked.

"All right, Brooks," he said with a sigh. "I don't know what's happening on this island, so I don't know what to do about it. I only know we nearly had a catastrophe out there thanks to something that sane, reasonable people claim doesn't exist."

He stopped. "You're telling me there's a ghost on this island right? Some crazy homicidal spook that gets off on killing people?" The lieutenant held his detective in his gaze. "Look me in the eye and tell me that you believe this is genuine."

Brooks looked him in the eye. "I'm *convinced* this is genuine," he answered softly. "More convinced than ever."

Agannis shook his head slowly. "Judas Priest," he muttered.

He looked back up to Brooks. "All right. Tell me what you're doing now, will ya? About this ghost of yours?"

"I've organized a series of seances," Brooks answered. "We're attempting to contact whatever spirit is involved and resolve its problem. If we're lucky, that should resolve the haunting on the island."

"What if we're not lucky?"

Brooks didn't answer.

Agannis gave it a long, hard and thoughtful consideration. "Judas Priest," he muttered again. "I can't believe I'm hearing this."

"Believe it," Brooks said.

"Well, a solution can't come too soon," Lieutenant Agannis answered. "Good luck with it. Someone's got to do something. A little more bad luck and we would have had a few dozen people dead out here. Know what I mean? Last thing we need is a few dozen more ghosts."

"Ever heard of anyone on the island named Henry Flaherty?" Brooks asked.

Agannis looked very thoughtful for a moment. He lit a cigarette and shook his head. "No. Who is he?"

"I think he's our malevolent spirit," Brooks said. "That's who we're trying to rouse."

Brooks left Lieutenant Agannis in the administrative building and walked to his car. One of the fire engines was gone from the parking lot. The other was boarding its crew. It pulled out of the lot—several of the firefighters waved to Brooks as they passed—as the detective was unlocking his car.

Brooks was alone in the parking lot. Almost.

The funny thing about Henry Flaherty was that he liked to drift past at the least expected moments, not when summoned up from the earth.

Brooks could feel it coming. A sudden intense weight in the night air. Then something coiled and thickening. Surrounding him. Preparing to crush him if it wanted to.

Powerful. But growing stronger. . . .

Brooks pulled the key out and opened the car door. Then he held perfectly still.

His eyes were cast downward. His heart skipped when he caught sight of something—a shadow? an image?—in the reflection of the car's side mirror. It was dark and not far to the side of him.

"You're here, aren't you?" Brooks said.

I'm here.

"What do you want?"

The woman I watched you fuck. So lovely!

Brooks' anger began to build past his fear.

He held the car door at an angle and saw part of the shadow, part of the darkness—part of the ghost!—again in the mirror. He made a decision. He would turn slowly toward his enemy and look squarely at it. And no matter what he saw, he wouldn't flinch. He wouldn't collapse in horror.

He wouldn't run.

"What do you want?" Brooks asked.

The woman I watched you fuck. So lovely!

The moment was at hand. Brooks turned and slowly raised his eyes unto the terror that beset him.

There was nothing there. Thinking he had miscalculated the angle of the reflection, feeling his heart thunder, he jerked his head sharply in the opposite direction.

Nothing there, either.

You look for me in all the wrong places, Timothy, the spirit said. Mocking. Deprecating.

"I asked you what you wanted."

And I told you.

Brooks thought. "My woman."

Cowardly scum! Not there to protect her late this evening when I called again!

The most horrible possibility of all was upon Brooks: Mary Beth DiMarco . . . Bruce Markley . . . Emmet Hughes . . .

And Annette Carlson . . . !

I killed her while you were dicking around at the airport, Brooks. Fucked

447

her, then killed her! Do handle the funeral arrangements with great good taste!

The voice exploded into a wall of shrill laughter.

A fearful, sickening sensation possessed Brooks. He threw himself into the car and smashed the key into the ignition. The car sprung to life and Brooks threw the auto into gear so fast that he ground them.

The tires erupted from the asphalt with a screeching sound.

Drive safely, you ineffectual failure!

Brooks drove at a mad speed down the road that led from the airport. He slid through the first stop sign and floored the accelerator, moving down the road that ran back toward town. He took the proper turn that led him out toward the center of the island, and passing on a double line, roared past another auto at a speed in excess of sixty.

The other driver blasted an indignant horn at him.

He waited for someone else from his own police department to flag him for speeding.

He hit a straightaway on the Milestone Road that led to the center of the island. His headlights cut into a cottony mist that lay across the highway.

He pressed the accelerator harder. The car hugged the road and cut through night.

The thought raged within him: *Maybe* he would not be too late. *Maybe* the spirit would have been unsuccessful. *Maybe* he would arrive in time to prevent Annette's murder.

Ahead, in the cones of lights that his car threw into the darkness, something caught his attention. In the middle of the highway there stood a human figure.

Brooks slammed his brake. At first the vision came to him as a teenage boy in a sweatshirt, shorts and carrying a basketball, a hallucinatory image of himself.

Then his tires squealed and in a time frame of milliseconds he realized that to avoid the boy he would have to turn the wheel and skid off the road and into the trees.

But his mind was ahead of his physical reactions. He stared down the image and recognized the hallucination as what it was. It dissembled before his eyes and took another more evil shape, a shape that was meant to be his last image before a crash.

A tall, black, human form. Arms extended like a beckoning death. No head.

The ghost again. Henry Flaherty. A masterful deathly game of enticement and illusion, life and mortality.

Brooks turned the wheel back into the road and released the brake.

The car tore toward the spot where the ghost stood on the highway. The blackness of the specter was as big as night itself and Brooks heard an involuntary scream in his own throat. The ghost yielded no ground and Brooks' sports car hurtled directly through it—

And then Brooks, too, experienced the flash that the pilots had spoken of. It happened in a time frame almost too small to measure. Intense brightness. The same woods, trees and ocean; all forming a brilliantly clear picture in his mind—

Then the brightness was gone and the car, like an aircraft cutting through a cloud, broke free from the other side of the black image.

Brooks' heart pounded as if it would fail. His hands were wet on the steering wheel. But all he could think of again was Annette and how the malevolent spirit would have surely by now taken her life and mutilated her body.

And why? Brooks wanted to know. Why Annette? Why someone he had so recently come to love?

Brooks took a final turn off the Milestone Road, continued another six hundred yards and saw his house at the end of the driveway. He turned into it. The lights were the way he had left them.

He cut his ignition and leaped from his car. He ran to the front door. It was locked. He fumbled with the keys and finally pushed the right one in the slot.

Too late!

The door opened. He burst in.

"Annette? Annie?" he yelled. "ANNIE!"

No answer. He turned toward the bedroom and ran.

He arrived at the bedroom door and stopped short when he saw her lying there.

She was on the bed, semiclad, much in the way he had left her. But she was in a three-quarters sitting-up position, a pillow behind her, a magazine open and discarded to one side. But she was slumped to the right, her head at an odd angle facing away from him, looking for all the world like she had been strangled on that very spot.

"Annie!" he yelled a final time, his voice breaking. He raced into the room and to the bed, terror in his heart unlike any he had ever known.

"Oh, God . . . ! Oh, God . . . !"

He ran to her side and put his hands on her. One hand went to a shoulder and propped up her head. Another hand went to her wrist. He shook her.

Her body was warm.

"Annie . . . Come on . . ." He almost cried.

His hand on her wrist found a pulse beat. A strong one. Her eyes flickered.

Then her eyes came open.

"Oh, God . . ." he said, almost incredulous. "Thank God!"

"Tim?" She blinked slowly awake. "Oh, Tim. You're back. What time is it?"

"It doesn't matter."

He held her and hugged her.

"Oh, Christ!" he said, gaining control of himself. "It doesn't matter what time it is."

She pulled from him slightly. "Hey? What's all this affection?" she asked. "Not that I mind."

"I was afraid . . ." He caught himself. "I don't know. I felt bad that I'd left you alone," he lied. "I thought you might be in danger."

She laughed. He released her.

"I tried to wait up for you," Annette said. "I was reading and fell asleep. What's the matter? Don't you think I'm safe here?"

450

"I don't know whether there's any safe place on the island," he said. "Not while Henry's loose."

A strange look crossed her face. "Oh," she said. "Henry! Something strange *did* happen," she said.

"What?"

She described it. A few minutes after Tim had left, she said, she had been overcome with fatigue. So she'd climbed into bed, intent on waiting for him to return.

For a while she had read a magazine, but found herself nodding off. Thereupon, Annette said, obviously a dream took hold of her. A frightening one at the end of which Tim careened off the road in his car and crashed into a row of trees.

"I dreamed you were dead," she said. "I dreamed that you and I were separated by death. Yours. I tell you, Timmy. This stuff is getting to me."

She paused. She thought of her mother's death following her winning of the Academy Award. She thought of David McIntyre dying in an airplane crash in Santa Barbara just when she had started to put her life together. She thought of all this and did not wish to go through it again.

"Maybe you and I should just get out of here," Annette said. "Come back to California with me. Travel to Europe with me. Why not? Leave here until it's safe to come back."

But he was already shaking his head, reminding her that he lived there, held a job on the island and had responsibilities there.

Running away from them wasn't going to solve anything, he suggested. Deep down, she knew it, too.

"Henry would only follow us," he said. "We have to deal with him here. Put an end to him here."

Brooks looked around the room, in case Henry was present to hear. He didn't sense him.

After several minutes, Tim undressed and crawled into bed with Annette. She moved close to him and when they slept, they slept in each other's arms.

They left the light on. There were no visitors that night, and no more bad dreams. The next morning was overcast and rainy, but both Annette and Timothy were grateful when it dawned.

On Saturday afternoon in the church office, Reverend Osaro put a few of the previous evening's events in perspective.

"Henry is playing psychological games with you, Tim," Osaro said. "When a spirit communicates, it will weave lies within a larger fabric of truth. The good spirits do this as well as the evil ones."

"But why?" Brooks asked. He sat across the desk from the pastor, same as he had on other earlier occasions.

"Spirits do this to weaken your will. And they do it because it's your will they're fighting," Osaro said. "If they leave you in a weakened position, they're that much more at an advantage."

Brooks was still on edge from the previous night. It seemed to him that the tension within him was mounting, as well as the stakes. An airplane had nearly skidded into the town terminal. . . . And he had been foolish enough to leave Annette alone and vulnerable.

The ghost could have done anything it had wanted at that time. In the back of his mind, Brooks wondered if it was the ghost's ambition to eventually carry out its threat. Only he wanted to do it later than sooner. Was toying with the enemy part of the game?

Osaro expanded. "The spirit knew he hadn't killed Annette and he knew he wasn't going to. Not just then," the pastor said. "But he wanted to terrify you. He wanted to have you experience the terror of losing someone you loved and blaming yourself for it having happened."

Brooks thought back to other occasions and another apparent lie. *Osaro is a dead man.*

"He used to tell me that you were dead, too," Brooks said. "During those days you disappeared from the island."

Osaro raised his eyebrows. "Did he now?" The minister slowly managed a laugh.

Brooks nodded.

" 'Dead' as in 'already dead'?" the minister asked wryly, "or 'dead' as in 'soon to be deceased'? There's a difference, you know."

"He really didn't elaborate."

Osaro pinched himself to indicate that he was solid. Flesh and blood solid. "Well, I suppose that supports my above theory," he said. "A clever mingling of fact with fantasy."

Brooks remained agonized. "But I still don't get it," Brooks said again. Outside, the morning cloudiness had given way to a day of rain. "I mean, what does it *want?*" Brooks demanded again. "Why does Henry bedevil me? And why is it walking our earth, anyway?"

"What Henry wants, Timmy?" Osaro asked with a shake of the head. "I still don't know that. What most spirits want is to pass comfortably into the next world, with all business finished on this plane." He shrugged. "But something is preventing it from doing that. Something unfinished. As to why it's bothering *you* . . ."

The minister let go with a deep sigh. A troubled look crossed his face.

"Yeah? What?" Brooks asked.

"Well, I think I may have come up with an answer on that," he said. He waited.

"Well? Let's hear it."

"I used to think that Seventeen Cort Street was the focus of this haunting. And it may have been at the beginning. But if it was at the beginning, I don't think it is any longer."

"Then what is?"

"It's *you*. You're the focus now."

"*Me!* Why me?"

"Something you've done. Or something you're doing. Or some place that you are. Some action or actions of yours have intersected with the spirit's reason to be back here."

Brooks turned the thought over and took it under advisement. "Is that right?" He pondered for a moment.

Osaro shrugged. "It's only my theory," he said. "Or, I should say, another part of my larger theory."

"I have a few theories, too," Brooks announced casually. "Want to hear?"

"Sure." Osaro leaned back. His pipe, unsmoked for days, lay in the ashtray on his desk. He fingered the lip of it, down near the teeth marks.

"I think Henry tried to kill me last night," Brooks said. "And I suspect he'll try again if I give him the chance."

"Tell me about last night first," Osaro said, obviously concerned. He rubbed his tired eyes with his hands. "What happened?"

"When I was speeding home from the airport," Brooks said. "Henry put illusions in the road. Two of them. The first was an image of myself. My first instinct was to swerve. Would have taken me straight into the trees."

"Uh huh."

"That was followed by the ghost itself," Brooks said. "Appeared at half a second's notice. I held the road again and drove right through it."

"Be careful next time," Osaro said. "The next individual Henry might place in the road may well be real. This world real. Know what I mean?"

"I know."

"Why do you think he'll do something again?" Osaro asked.

"I think that's part of his plan. Kill me or kill Annette. I think one of us is next."

"Again, why?"

"He's focused on us, isn't he?" Brooks asked. "You just said that, yourself."

Osaro allowed the point.

"But that's not what I wanted to ask you," Brooks said. "There's something else."

Osaro waited.

"When I drove through the ghost I felt something very bright," Brooks said. "Like a flash. For maybe a tenth of a second it was as if I'd intersected with some feeling or some emotion that I'd never known before." Brooks paused. "The

New England Airways pilot and the copilot had the same sensation when their aircraft cut through Henry's ghost, also."

"Uh huh."

"Well, what's that all about?" Brooks asked.

"What are you asking me for?" Osaro's tone was subdued.

"You're the expert, George. You seem to be tuned into things that most people don't even know exist. And I want to know everything I can about whatever it is I'm fighting."

The minister looked at his friend and nodded silently. "Do you remember from one of our previous talks, we discussed different planes of reality? I asked you how many there might be. And I said that we had no way of knowing how many there were but that occasionally we catch a glimpse of one."

"Yes."

"Most people aren't astute enough to recognize it, Tim. But you may have."

Brooks thought about it as Osaro held him in view.

"What about *entering* it?" Brooks asked.

"Tim—!"

"I asked you a question."

"And you're pushing this awfully far for someone who didn't even *believe* five weeks ago." The minister pulled back. "Trying to enter it is probably not a very good idea. How do you know you'll ever get out?"

"Would the plane be mental or physical?"

"My guess is it would be mostly mental. Or spiritual, actually. Physical perhaps in a way that is unlike what we accept as physical."

Brooks thought about it for several seconds. The minister's gaze was upon him the entire time.

"It seems to me that the flash point came right when my body intersected with the spirit's presence," Brooks said. "But I was moving very fast at the time. So were the pilots. Suppose I'd remained stationary?" he asked. "Would I have entered Henry's plane?"

"Tim," Osaro said in an anxious tone. "Don't get ideas. Did

455

·you hear what I just asked? If you get into that plane, and I'm not saying you could, how do you know you'll ever get out?"

"I don't know that I would," Brooks said.

"Well, then . . . ? Behave with some common sense."

"See the thing is, George," Brooks said slowly, "I've learned an awful lot about this in the last few weeks. From Henry. And from listening to and watching you."

Taking it as a compliment, the minister tried to dismiss it.

"If Henry's going to try to take one of us—Annette or me— I'd prefer he try to take me. That's my thinking. See, I think I might be able to beat him."

Osaro leaned forward. "And know what I think, copper?" he said in his friendliest voice. "I think you've finally lost your marbles. You're really talking nutty now."

Brooks stood.

"Thanks, George," Brooks said. "You've answered all my questions. When's the next seance?"

"Tomorrow. Sunday night. I want to do it on the Sabbath. That's if you can stay out of trouble between now and then."

"Perfect. I'll be ready."

The detective turned and went toward the door.

"Timmy?" Osaro called after him.

Brooks turned.

"I'm your friend, right?"

"Right."

"Then listen to me. Don't do anything crazy. Really. All right? Don't fuck around with weird stuff you don't know about. Okay?"

Brooks smiled. "George, this whole thing is crazy. How could I do anything that doesn't fit in with what's already happened?"

"I don't know," Osaro warned. "But I'm reading your mind and I don't like what I see. So just don't. Okay?"

Brooks smiled, offered no promises and departed.

Thirty

That night, Brooks stayed up late. He waited until Annette had settled in to bed and drifted off to sleep. He watched television. Then he read a book until midnight had passed and one A.M. had arrived.

At that late hour, when his house was very still, he opened the front door and stepped out into the night. He was already quite tired, but carried a bottle of beer in his hand. Moral support. Fear made him thirsty, so why not a Heinekin to address this weakness of will?

He sat down on the front-door step. He looked up at the stars. It was a brilliant night. The more he stared at the sky, the more stars faded into his view.

Millions of them. Then millions more gradually coming into focus. He thought back to when he was a child and his parents told him that certain stars represented "heavenly bodies." That train of thought brought him to concepts of Heaven—obsolete and otherwise.

Which brought him again to notions of the afterlife. And Henry Flaherty. Evil Henry Flaherty.

Brooks lowered his gaze. He waited. He sipped from the bottle of beer.

"I'm ready for you, Henry," Brooks finally said aloud. "I'm waiting for you if you have the nerve."

There was virtual silence all around him. A cricket chirped

somewhere, then stopped. Many seconds later, Brooks heard the sound of a car shifting gears on a distant road.

He waited some more.

Still nothing.

Henry liked to play games, Brooks knew. Typical ghost games. Or poltergeist games: Now I'm here, now I'm not. I'll materialize when I want, not when you want. My rules not yours.

"Lose your nerve, Henry?" Brooks asked. "Not interested in us anymore?"

Brooks leaned back against the door to his home. He took another swig of beer.

"Come on, you filthy murderous old spirit," he said, almost taunting. "You know you're no match for me. Show yourself."

But nothing immediately happened.

Brooks fixed his resolve. He was ready to dedicate some time on this evening to confronting the pernicious spirit of Henry Flaherty. Brooks knew what he wanted to do. Where he wanted to go.

He leaned back against the door and settled himself. Beneath the stars, he closed his eyes. He would will Henry's spirit forward, that's what he would do. He would draw him forth.

Many more minutes passed. His eyelids grew heavy. The moon had passed above the branches on the horizon and was now above the trees. Brooks closed his eyes again.

He did not know how many minutes had passed when he became aware of Henry's presence. He knew only that the feeling was upon him. A gradual tension building in the air around him. An unnatural stillness. Then a very low subliminal pulsing.

I'm here.

Brooks leaned forward and opened his eyes, first a crack, then completely. He scanned. Then he realized that, yes, he was looking right at it. Henry was in front of him. Tall and black, obscured as ever in the shadows of night, never affording him a good look.

Not till I'm ready to take someone under the earth, the presence communicated.

"What?"

You don't get a good look until I'm ready to take you under the earth, Henry repeated.

"So you can read my thoughts?"

Your thoughts are obvious.

"Then here's one you should already know. You will never take me," Brooks said.

I take whomever I wish.

"You can't even touch me," Brooks said.

Why are you daring me?

"If you know everything," Brooks taunted, "you shouldn't have to ask."

There was silence. The spirit moved closer, almost cautiously. It obviously sensed a change in Brooks' attitude. Brooks felt his heart race even faster. He kept his eyes downcast. He was afraid that if he raised them and looked directly at this thing, terror would grip him and his courage would fail.

Obviously, the spirit sensed a tremor of fear, for it moved ever closer. Brooks was aware of the thickening of the pressure around him. It was as if he had been enclosed in a bag. The presence was stuffy. Oppressive.

The detective kept his eyes lowered. He was aware that the ghost was directly before him now, just before the front step of the house. Maybe a yard away. Then closer. It was like a solid black shadow, erect and standing before him. It must have been, Brooks thought to himself, at this close distance that Henry killed—

Yes, it was from this distance. All three of them.

No! Brooks dismissed the idea.

"I'm ready," Brooks said to rally himself.

For what?

Brooks sprang forward and hurtled his body into the dark specter. He felt the bright flash that Captain Jensen and Copilot Hendricks had described. It was the same flash that Brooks had felt on the Milestone Road the last time they intersected.

Brooks endured an overbearing weight, as if a giant hand was around his ribs, forcing the air out of him.

He struggled to remain standing. He fought to stay upright. The illumination from the flash remained with him and then the pressure around him eased.

He wondered if he was dying. He recalled the brightness experienced by people who had described near-death experiences, but then he felt something else, a sense of release, a sense of arrival somewhere, as clear as stepping off a boat onto solid ground.

And the brightness around him began to come into focus. He had a sense of ease and liberation. He felt himself set down in pleasant familiar surroundings.

Woods, trees and ocean. He was there! Or at least he thought he was! With relief, he knew he had passed into Henry's plane.

"What are you doing here?" Henry asked.

There was a human standing near him. Not a black shadowy specter, but a human figure. Brooks took this to be Henry. It communicated like Henry. But even though Brooks stared directly at it, he could never have later described it. There was something vague about it, something ephemeral, some incomprehensible quality that prevented Brooks from focusing too carefully upon it.

"I've come to confront you," Brooks said.

"Over what?"

"Why are you still walking the earth?"

"It is my choice to do so."

"You have no right to take lives."

"I will do what I want. I took lives when I was on the earth. I've taken them after I left. I will take yours, too."

"You want no eternal peace? You don't wish your spirit to pass completely on to the next plane?"

Henry didn't answer.

As the landscape came sharply into focus, Brooks was aware of where he was. He was in the open field near the old Quaker cemetery on Nantucket, the field a few hundred yards from

Annette's house. Henry stood on the spot where Mary Beth DiMarco's body had been found.

"Why are we here?" Brooks asked.

Henry laughed. Still, Brooks had the sense of trying to see Henry's human features. But he remained unable.

"You don't like it here?" Henry asked.

"It's a place of extreme unhappiness."

"That's true. But all the world is."

Brooks looked again and Mary Beth's tormented body was before him, face twisted in its death agony.

"Not for me," Brooks said, lifting his eyes. This agitated the spirit.

"Would you prefer to be somewhere else?" Henry asked.

They were instantly transported into darkness, as if on cue. They were out of the sunlight and into a dank place. Brooks recognized it. He was in the cellar beneath 17 Cort Street.

"Another place of misery," said Henry.

Emmet Hughes' battered body appeared. Neck broken. Ice pick in the front of the brain. The body still moving in its death agony. Brooks suppressed a cringe.

"Your beautiful world," said the spirit.

"And Surfside?" Brooks asked.

"Ah! The Canadian boy."

"And many years earlier, your wife," Brooks said. "Mabel Mack. You drove her to her death."

"Liar! She took her own life!"

"You caused her such pain that she killed herself. What about your one-time partner? Edward Kearns? Murdered him, I suppose."

Again, Henry was angry. "You want death? I'll show you death!"

They were transported again, this time to a hilly cemetery that Brooks recognized as being in the center of Nantucket Island. It was a breezy peaceful place, overlooking the town and the ocean, not far from the old windmill.

The day was sunny, but Brooks had a sense of standing alone at a funeral. The spirit waved its arm and Brooks saw a coffin.

The coffin was open. Annette lay in it. Very still. Very beautiful. Quite dead.

Brooks shuddered.

"As you prefer," Henry promised. "Tomorrow's misery."

Then the coffin was gone and the ghost showed Brooks a new image, one of Brooks himself, kneeling at Annette's tombstone. In prayer. In tears.

"I don't believe you," Brooks said.

"You will soon."

"You've lied before," Brooks said. "So I assume you are lying now."

"No," Henry said. "This is your future."

"I understand you now," Brooks answered. "In life you were a bitter, homicidal man. You caused death and misery. Returning to our plane after your death, you do the same."

Henry listened.

"Your pretense is that the agony of your death unsettled your spirit. You walk our earth to redress your execution."

Brooks paused.

"Your decapitation," Brooks said. "The torment your body addresses is the torment of your spirit. But what shines through is the meanness of your own soul, just as it was when you lived. Your fate was horrendous. But you brought it upon yourself."

For the first time, the ghost turned its head toward Brooks. There were no features on Henry's face. Just plain flesh. Brooks drew a breath and held steady before this horror.

"And this fate of yours," Henry communicated, turning away again. "It is inescapable. Your lover will perish, same as the others."

Somehow by "the others," Brooks knew who he meant. Mary Beth DiMarco. Bruce Markley. Emmet Hughes.

"The others believed you could kill them," Brooks said. "I'm not so sure. If I don't allow you, I don't think you can."

"Wrong!" Henry Flaherty ranted, growing angrier. "Wrong! Wrong! So wrong!"

"I'm planning to live a long happy life with the woman I love," Brooks said.

Henry screamed profanely. "I didn't! So you won't!" he roared. "You will do as I dictate."

"No," Brooks said.

"*She* believes I can take her," Henry howled. "So I *can!* And I *will!*"

"I'm leaving."

"You won't!" Henry swore.

"My will," Brooks said, "is stronger than yours."

"This is what your will is worth." The ghost reached to the dirt and picked up a penny. He shoved it into Brooks' palm. Brooks closed his fist on the coin and spat contemptuously at Henry.

The world started to spin.

Brooks had the sense of Henry's spirit howling with rage. But he had the further sensation of the entire vision brightening until he could no longer see it. Then it began fading.

More spinning. The sensation was dizzying. Brooks knew he was on a trip and hoped it was back to his own world. He hoped he was still alive and not a spirit, himself. But he was hurtling somewhere and couldn't be sure.

Back to life?

Onward to death?

He felt something on his arm and took it to be the grip of the ghost. Psychological as well as tactile. A heavy pull. He fought with it, yanking his elbow away from whatever was touching him.

Then he saw the grave—Annette's grave—growing larger before him. And beneath the new tombstone, the ground opened before his eyes, earth spreading itself to the side by its own accord.

The grave beckoned. It welcomed him. It almost rose to meet him.

"I'm leaving," Brooks said steadily.

"You're staying. You can sleep in the rosewood box with the woman. Your flesh rotting with hers for eternity. We'll nail the lid on nice and tight."

In blackness, Brooks thought again, "I'm leaving. I don't want this. I'm leaving."

Brooks pulled mightily. He turned his eyes from Henry's spirit. He had the sense of spinning, then falling, then flying. He was nowhere, sailing and tumbling through more blackness. The sinking sensation was upon him again, and then there was another vision.

Annette.

Alive and terrified! In the hands of Henry. The killer's spirit was dragging her down into the earth. Into a cold, lonely death.

"Tim!" she cried out. "Tim! Tim! Tim!"

But he was motionless as he watched this. He tried to move his body but was rooted to his position.

"Tim!" she said again. "Come on, Tim! Wake up! Move! Move!" Something shook him. A hand. An arm.

He tried mightily and shook himself. Then there was another flash as he left the ghost's plane.

His body pitched forward and came awake. His eyes opened but he was in darkness.

He was on the front step of his house again.

His heart pounded. Sweat poured off him. Then his heart jumped again at the figure next to him.

"Tim!"

A woman's voice. Annette. Shaking him. Waking him.

"What are you doing out here?" she said.

He realized where he was, where Henry had returned him. Or had he never left?

"I couldn't sleep," he explained. His heart still raced.

"Fine place to go if you can't sleep," she said. "The front steps, huh?"

Blearily, he asked, "What time is it?"

"Past two," she said. Annette sat down next to him, pulling her nightgown close to her. He looked at her. Even when tired and sleepy, at two A.M. in the morning, she was very beautiful.

He put an arm around her. He lightly kissed the side of her face, a kiss as delicate as a fine lace.

"What are you *really* doing out here?" she asked. "Looking for Henry? The ghost?"

He nodded.

"See him?"

"Maybe."

"How would you know?"

He thought about it. "I think I just invaded Henry's air space," Brooks joked.

"Find out anything?"

"He's not as tough as we think."

"Ha! I wish I could believe that."

"We're still together aren't we? He hasn't been able to touch us, has he?"

"Tim, he's taken over my house and we live in terror. He's winning!"

"He's about to lose," he said. "He *will* lose."

She sighed. "You're so confident. I wish I could believe you."

"Believe me," he said. He was aware that his left hand remained in a fist. He opened it and there was a coin in his palm. A warm penny caked with bits of dirt.

From his pocket? From the earth outside his home? Or from the old cemetery? The date on the coin was 1928.

Annette peered out into the darkness of the night. "Sometimes I feel myself slipping," she said. "Back into the mental traps that I was stuck in a few years ago. You know. Depressed. Unable to cope with anything. What is all this except an assault on our sanity?" She paused. "If this keeps up I'll be back in the loony bin before you know it. That, or worse."

"It's not going to happen, Annie," he said. "Henry can be reduced to something small and mean. He's vulnerable."

"Tim, he's killed three—"

"That was before we understood him. He's like any other murder suspect. Small and mean. And vulnerable," he repeated. "I know how to attack him."

She sighed. "I hope you're right," she said.

"Come on," he said, raising her up with him as he stood. "Back to bed. Tonight we sleep."

He allowed her to walk inside first. For a moment, Brooks stood on his front step and scanned the darkness around his house. He felt something low and brooding nearby and thought he saw a shadow move within a larger shadow.

But he glared at it defiantly. Then he turned his back on it, went inside and locked the door.

Thirty-one

On Sunday evening at 17 Cort Street, Annette pushed the furniture out of the way and Osaro set the checkerboard table in the center of the living room. Tim Brooks arranged three chairs around the table and waited for the other two principals to be ready.

Annette drew the shades. Osaro lit the candle in the pewter candlestick and set it on a side table. All other lights were extinguished. Then they sat down, the three of them, joined hands on the edge of the table and hoped.

It was past ten P.M. The night began slowly.

Reverend Osaro said a prayer at the beginning. Their six hands remained in position on the edge of the table. Many minutes passed. Annette kept her eyes closed. Osaro tried to move himself into the near trance that had succeeded the first night. Brooks remained alert, his eyes open much of the time, waiting, watching the flickering of the candle cast strange images upon the living-room wall.

There was a creak to the floor in the kitchen. But nothing more. An hour passed.

The door to the room never opened. The room and the night were silent as a granite vault beneath the surface of the earth. Then the table gave a very slight tremble.

George Osaro spoke for the first time in an hour. "Something's happening," he whispered.

Brooks was staring directly at it. Annette opened her eyes and saw it, too. Helen Ritter, or at least a shimmering white image of her, stood in the corner of her living room.

"Hello, Helen," Brooks said.

The ghost of the woman didn't say anything. But it became more visible. It conveyed the feeling that she accepted their welcome.

Brooks felt his hands sweat involuntarily. Annette felt her pulse quicken. Her hand reassured itself next to Timothy's.

"We're very sorry about Mabel," Brooks said. "All those years ago." He paused. "We never knew."

"A beautiful young thing," she said. "My dear sister. It was she who first came to warn you, Miss Annette."

"Are you reunited now?" Brooks asked.

"I've seen her," Mrs. Ritter said. "Her soul is content."

"But yours is not," Brooks guessed.

There was no response. Brooks took it to be an affirmation.

"They did something terrible to him, didn't they, Helen?"

The specter faded slightly.

"What does he want, Helen?" Brooks asked.

The specter shook her head, as if she didn't know. Or couldn't say.

"No, you must tell us," Brooks said. "We must know for peace in this world."

"I cannot tell," she said.

"Then why do *you* still wander this world?" George Osaro asked. "You know yourself that something is unsettled. Something terrible."

"Many terrible things."

"Then you must trust us," Osaro said. "As you trusted us before death, you must trust us after death."

Before their eyes, before they could beg her not to, the woman's spirit faded from view. They were greatly relieved seconds later when she reappeared on the opposite side of the room.

"Henry wants what anyone would want," Mrs. Ritter said softly. "No matter what he says. What could any soul want?"

"Eternal peace," Osaro asked. "Peace with the Creator."

She nodded.

"They did something terrible to him, didn't they, Helen?" Brooks asked.

The specter faded again. And now Brooks knew how dangerous the subject was. How horrible.

"You must tell us," Brooks said.

"I mustn't."

"Please, Mrs. Ritter," Annette said. "Our happiness, our lives depend on it."

Her eyes, though yellowish and ghostly now, seemed kindly. She looked closer to the next world than this one.

"They killed him, didn't they?" Brooks asked.

Silence.

"The rumor was all over the island," Brooks tried slowly. "Henry had done many horrible things to Mabel. Made the poor girl miserable. Wrecked her life. Drove her to suicide. So the actors came out one night and took Henry to a field. Am I right?"

Mrs. Ritter's image faded and drifted, as if the story disturbed her. But she didn't disappear.

"They shot him," Brooks said. "And they buried him?"

In the room, from somewhere, there was the sound of a human moaning. Annette felt her entire body crawl with goose bumps when she heard it. Brooks was jolted, too.

"But they were afraid that his body might be found. So they did something to the body, didn't they? They did something so that the body, if found, couldn't immediately be identified. It's all right, Mrs. Ritter. We know what they did. We understand."

Brooks paused.

"They cut his head off," Brooks said simply. "There. Let's all admit it now. It was many, many years ago."

Annette felt her flesh crawl a second time.

"My sister was a lovely young woman," Mrs. Ritter said. "Henry made her very unhappy. He saw many other young women. Incessant other women. It wasn't fair to Mabel."

"And did Mabel meet someone else?" Brooks asked.

Mrs. Ritter nodded.

"And she wanted out of the marriage?"

Mrs. Ritter nodded again.

"And Henry held her. Wouldn't give her a divorce?"

Mrs. Ritter nodded a third time. "And in time, the man Mabel loved married another. Mabel felt very much alone. So she walked into the sea."

"And this was in the year nineteen twenty-eight?" Brooks asked.

The ghost nodded.

"And you were familiar with this house back then, Mrs. Ritter. You feel that you check on it because you helped part of the evidence be hidden."

"This was my sister's house," she said. "From nineteen twenty-four until nineteen twenty-eight. As a little girl, I used to visit . . ."

"In a way, you're still guarding your sister's house, aren't you? Keeping an eye on the evidence, even though Henry has returned."

Through the darkened room, past the flicker of the candle-light, Brooks thought he saw the nuance of a nod from Mrs. Ritter.

"But wouldn't you like your peace, too? Wouldn't you like to pass on to the next world and be finished in this one?"

The image of the old woman drifted through the room. It came softly toward the table. One arm reached out. Brooks stared directly at it. He allowed the ghost to reach to him.

Spectral fingers touched his cheek. He would never *ever* forget the feeling. Warm. Gossamer. Again, almost like a spider's web, but more ethereal.

"You're very kind," she said.

Then she did something that she hadn't done before. More than words, she conveyed an image. Brooks saw her standing on the plot of ground where Beth DiMarco had been killed. When that vision faded, Brooks realized that she was then standing on the earthen patch within the cellar below them. Later, both Annette and Osaro recalled seeing the same visions.

And then the specter was back in the room with them.

Mrs. Ritter addressed Annette. "He's a very wise young man, this policeman," she said. "He will take good care of you."

Mrs. Ritter glided before Timothy Brooks. "There was no gun," she said. "Only a sword. The actor who had been a butcher, he was my husband. And he only had a sword. They made Henry kneel, as if to ask for forgiveness. I remember. It was a night with a full moon and Henry begged and begged, for the first time in anyone's memory." She paused. "And then they executed him." Many seconds passed. "Henry deserved it," Mrs. Ritter said evenly. "An evil man deserved an evil fate."

Brooks absorbed this in all of its horror. He kept his eyes on the ghost. Mrs. Ritter's spirit glided backward from him.

Then the image receded. "You know all you need to. And you know what to do. So now I can go, thank you very much."

Wordlessly, they watched her vanish.

All three participants in the seance remained at the table. There was no easing of tension. None, because as soon as Mrs. Ritter was gone, they felt the air thicken in the room.

They felt the unseen grip, the growing thickening and pulsing of the air. A sense of murder and death. All three had experienced it enough to recognize it.

"Come on," Brooks finally said. "Come on, Henry. Let's have you right out here!"

They waited for several minutes. But then, finally, there was a gut-wrenching stench in the room. Foul. Putrid. This combined with an oppressive thickening of the atmosphere. Worse than they had encountered at any previous seance.

Annette felt like she would vomit. She didn't. She moved her hand on top of Brooks' and held on. Brooks squeezed her hand to reassure her.

The candle wavered.

The pressure increased heavily in the room.

Suddenly there was a loud banging. It seemed to shake the entire house. A clap of thunder could not have sounded more dramatically. And they heard, they thought they heard, the sound of a woman screaming, a terrifying death being played out in infinity.

Mabel Mack? Pulled under the waves to her earthly destruction?

Beth DiMarco? Murdered in a field?

Helen Ritter? Encountering Henry's homicidal fury?

It was almost too intense. Annette made a motion to stand and flee. Brooks held her and shook his head.

"No! We stay!" he said.

The foul smell worsened. It was the odor of decomposing animal flesh.

"He's challenging our will," Reverend Osaro said with concern. "Henry's putting up a fierce opposition to what we want to do."

Again, Annette suppressed a feeling of sickness. To Brooks, the feeling was more one of physical challenge. The pressure in the room dropped so low that he felt as if something was trying to push him out.

Another loud bang. It came from everywhere and was much closer this time. It was as loud as the time that the china cabinet had collapsed.

"We will not leave, Henry," Brooks said. "You will come to us."

One of the window shades shot up with a loud clap. Then the other. Both Annette and Tim felt a surge of panic in their chests. Henry was *that* close! And that furious! But still they stood their ground. Still, they would not move.

"Stay, stay, stay," Osaro urged. He reached again for prayer, his eyes closed, his face lifted.

" 'Now it is high time to awake out of sleep; for now is our salvation nearer than we believed.' " St. Paul.

Subliminally, there was the sound of a man groaning. Then distantly screaming. The cries gave the impression of great torment, great agony, being played out.

" 'Be not deceived,' " Reverend Osaro continued softly. " 'God is not mocked. For whatever a man soweth, he also shall reap.' " St. Paul for a second time.

Then a bloodcurdling scream. It sounded like it was in the

room with them. And there followed the sound of something falling to the mud.

. . . like a head lopped off with a sword. . . .

Then the shadows shifted in the room. The flame of the candle moved.

"Tim!" Annette screamed.

He saw it, too. His eyes went as wide with fear. They were as incredulousness as hers.

The candlestick had levitated. It was a foot off the side table, hovering in the air.

Never—*never!*—in his life had Brooks held such fear within him. Never had he so violently wrestled with the gripping desire to stand and flee.

But he couldn't. Flee and his battle of wills was lost. Flee and Annette may be lost as well. Flee, and everything he now wanted in life was left behind.

Instead, he stared. The candlestick—with the candle still burning—floated in the room.

"Go to hell, Henry!" Brooks intoned softly. "Go back to hell and stay there!"

You are terrified, Brooks! Admit that you're terrified!

"Show yourself, Henry. If you dare."

Annette's eyes were frozen upon the candlestick.

Words. A voice speaking. Rising from the night. Osaro again. Another scripture.

" '. . . for we wrestle not against flesh and blood, but against powers, against rulers of the darkness of this world, against wickedness in high places . . .' "

The flame danced and grew.

" '. . . take unto you the whole armor of God, and ye may be able to withstand all evil and all night . . .' "

The candlestick whirled in the air. The candle fell to the floor and burned faintly. Above it, from a distance of six feet, the pewter stick flew directly at Tim Brooks. He ducked his head to one side, but only enough to escape the full force of the thrown object. The candlestick glanced hard off his left temple and fell to the floor.

Brooks, dazed and hurting, stared at the void near the closed door.

"I'm not moving, Henry. I won't go," he said.

He felt a trickle on the side of his head.

Warm. Wet.

Blood flowed slowly down from an open cut where the candlestick had hit him. Annette looked to him in horror.

Brooks turned and picked up the candlestick. Annette picked up the candle. Carefully, Brooks put the two back together. The flame, never dying, was born again.

"You're winning," Osaro said softly. "Hold on."

The stench returned and grew foul again. The three at the table held their hands together. There was another bang. This one sounded as if it came from beneath the table, as if the floor was collapsing.

As if it were about to fall through.

It didn't.

Then the nature of the stench changed. Suddenly Annette, Timothy and George Osaro involuntarily recoiled.

Before them on the table, stacked high, were the eighteen slaughtered white ducks. Corpses rotting. Crawling with lice. Eye sockets hollow. Festering and stinking, advanced in their decomposition.

Somehow, all three seated at the table managed to hold their places.

"Take them away, Henry," Osaro said softly. "And present yourself, not a metaphor for your soul." He paused. "You will not have another chance. We will hold no more seances."

But the image of the slain ducks faded upon the table. Then the stench receded, as did the oppressive atmosphere in the room.

Then there was a final, tumultuous bang within the house. It was as if they were seated directly below a clap of thunder. Everything shook. The flame of the candle spasmed wildly and nearly died. From other rooms came the sound of small falling objects, dislodged from tables.

But Brooks could sense the easing of the tension. He knew

that Henry had withdrawn. Several minutes passed. The room seemed cooler. The air less stagnant. Almost fresh again.

A tangible wave of relaxation went around. Osaro opened his eyes.

He withdrew his hands. He announced what all three knew.

"Henry's gone," the pastor said. "He's fired his best shots. He's displayed his anger." He sighed. "We have the offensive now." He turned toward Brooks. "Are you certain you don't want one more seance?" he asked. "Tomorrow we could probably coax him forth."

Brooks gazed at the minister.

"I don't think we have to," Brooks said.

"What?"

"We won't need another seance," Brooks said. "I think it's clear why he's here. I think it's clear why he can't rest."

"Is it?" Osaro asked, almost as a challenge.

"Yes. Can you perform a standard Christian burial?"

"Of course. If you have a body. Or some remains."

"Got a few shovels in your garage?"

"Sure, but—"

Annette curled her lip.

"Then we're almost home," Brooks said. He rose from the table and turned on an electric light. The room again seemed very mundane, very ordinary. Just another room in an old house with a queer little checkerboard table at its center.

He opened a window to let in a fresh breeze.

"I'd say, another twenty-four hours," Brooks said. "And I'm pretty confident about it."

Reverend Osaro stared at him, saying nothing.

Fifteen minutes later, they stood outside as Annette locked the house. Osaro then allowed her to walk ahead to the cars before sharing a final thought for the evening. He had been doing some thinking, too, Brooks learned.

"You might remember something," the pastor said slowly. "From one of our conversations? Or maybe it was from one of your readings at the Eksman Collection. Extreme trauma, extreme psychological duress will sometimes result in a haunting. Do you recall that point?"

Brooks remembered it. He believed that he had read it, and Reverend Osaro had mentioned it, too. "Of course," he answered.

The minister exhaled slowly.

"I once read in a psychological study," he mused, "that the human brain can stay alive for maybe five to ten seconds after separation from the rest of the body. The brain continues to work until the lack of new blood makes it stop."

Brooks listened. "So?"

"Well, this is just a thought, Tim, albeit a little bit of a grisly one. What could cause greater psychological distress than that? If Henry's head was chopped off while he was still alive, he had five to ten seconds to brood upon the psychological anguish of his execution. And his particular sort of execution."

Brooks waited, trying to envision the anguish. He couldn't. It was incomprehensible. Something out of the days of guillotines.

"Well, in terms of psychological agony, in terms of a spirit imprinting on an area," Osaro continued calmly, "I can't think of anything much more hideous. Can you?"

Brooks couldn't.

"I'm surprised that we haven't been haunted by this for seventy-five years on this island." He laughed. "Then again, maybe we have been."

"No," Brooks said. "Someone triggered it."

"Who? How?"

"Someone brought a happy, healthy, loving relationship to this island and dropped it right down on Henry's remains. It was the type of relationship Henry might always have wanted, but never had. That, literally right on top of his mutilated corpse and . . . well, use your imagination."

"But who are you talking about?"

Brooks clapped his hand on his friend's shoulder.

"That's how I know where his grave is," Brooks said. "See you tomorrow," he said. "And bring a Bible."

Thirty-two

On Monday morning, in the bedroom on the second floor at 17 Cort Street, Henry was waiting.

How foolish these living people were. Thinking they could defeat him. Thinking they *had* defeated him. What idiots! Like those people who had cut his head off years ago. Each of them, in their separate times and places, had died a horrible death.

Well, so would one of these two—Annette Carlson or Timothy Brooks. Henry would draw the big chasm of death between them. How dare they enjoy the type of relationship that he had never had?

Maybe the man's will was very strong, Henry reasoned, and maybe he had proven difficult in a confrontation. But these people knew nothing about how events could be manipulated. There were ways of bringing about a death without directly causing it.

Wonderful ways.

Annette's footsteps sounded on the stairs leading to the bedroom. Henry recognized her steps.

She arrived on the landing outside. Henry withdrew into the wall as Annette entered her bedroom.

Busily, Annette went to her dresser. She opened drawers and pulled out clothing. For a few moments, Henry drifted into the room and hovered directly behind her as she leaned over. He was close enough to easily touch her, had he decided to. To caress her neck. Her cheeks. Her lips. Sometimes Henry reasoned that he loved Annette, too, and causing her death would bring her closer to him.

She turned abruptly and he slipped out of her line of sight.

Annette paused for a moment and froze, as if he had moved not quite fast enough and she had caught the movement of a shadow.

"What's there?" she asked. "Anything there?"

She looked very worried. But Henry was out of view and did nothing to attract her attention.

She leaned over again, which was perfect. She was looking for a pair of shoes. She reached under the bed, thrusting her hand way back and—

Perfect again. She found it! Oh, Glory, Henry thought! She had found it already!

"What the—?" Annette asked.

The strange metal object clanked against the floor. Annette pulled out the big heavy bed that had been there since the previous tenants.

"Good God," Annette muttered in both consternation and amusement. She reached down and picked up an old steel sword in its sheath. The sword was magnificently preserved, she discovered when she pulled it out. Clean and sharp.

Annette looked at it with fascination and wonder, mixed with a little shock.

No one ever cleaned behind the bed, Henry conveyed. *It's been there for years. Everyone has missed it.*

He saw the thought successfully arrive within Annette's head. And she took it for her own.

Perfect, Henry reasoned again. Perfect again.

Annette lay the sword on the bed and went about her business. Henry drifted downward through the house.

Annette found all the items she had come to the house for and departed.

No more than six hundred yards away, in the open field where Beth DiMarco had died, a local building contractor used a small steam shovel to break the surface of the earth. The gasoline-powered shovel clawed up an area twenty by twenty feet. Then, carefully, a team of auxiliary police officers with spades, rakes and hand shovels prowled deeper into the earth.

Two hours came and went. Then three. Noon arrived and passed. The excavation occurred directly below where Mary Beth had huddled into a sleeping bag with her boyfriend . . . and died before the next morning.

Toward three-thirty in the afternoon, Brooks' shovel struck wood. At first he thought he'd hit a long box—a makeshift coffin—and he was certain that he had found the bones—some of them, anyway—of Henry Flaherty. But the wood, when he and another policeman moved it, turned out to be a rotting dresser top abandoned many years earlier. They pulled it out of the earth and kept digging.

More time passed. More work went into the dig. They were four feet beneath the earth's surface when they hit what they wanted, even though they didn't recognize it at first.

One of the diggers, a woman, came upon a long strip of discarded canvas, rolled up and about eight feet in length. It obstructed her shovel and she asked for help pulling it out of the ground. It was only when Brooks saw it coming up, saw its length and shape, that he dropped his own shovel and walked over.

"Want to unroll it?" he offered.

The female volunteer shook her head. She passed on the honor.

"Someone give me a hand with it," Brooks said next.

Someone did.

They pulled the canvas to a bare plot of grass. Brooks took the lead in unrolling it. Whatever the contents of the canvas, it had acquired earth and water over the years. It wasn't pretty. Brooks pushed away the dirt and the package took a shape. He found that it had been tied in three places, which told him immediately that this wasn't something that had been simply thrown into a hole. It definitely had contained something when it went into the ground.

Brooks cut the ropes and started to bend back the canvas. Several of the auxiliaries gathered around. Others preferred not to. The scent of tobacco smoke that wafted to Brooks as he dug deeper into the canvas came from Lieutenant Agannis, who watched without speaking.

Mostly dirt, as Brooks unwrapped the final layer. He pushed his hands through the soil. Through the rot. Then he found bones.

The human skeleton contained in the bag was not immediately recognizable as one. Brooks saw no fragments of clothing and assumed that those who executed Henry Flaherty would indeed have removed anything as identifiable as a suit or a shirt or a belt. If they'd gone to the trouble to remove Henry's head, then surely they would have removed his clothing.

The bones were in a pile within the canvas and not at all a disorderly pile, considering that they had rested there for nearly three-quarters of a century. Something important, of course, was missing.

"Jesus fucking Christ," intoned Agannis. "So that's him, huh? That's the missing man? From nineteen twenty-eight?"

"That's his bones," Brooks said. "One part of him, in other words. And, if you look, you'll see that this collection is incomplete."

"Yeah. No head."

"No head."

Some of the diggers jockeyed for a closer look. Others wanted no look at all.

"Do we keep searching here?" Agannis asked. "Timmy, this is your party. You call the shots."

"We can give the place a tumble before we fill the earth in again," Brooks said. "But I think I know of another location that's going to be more promising." He paused without explaining. "Do you have any objection if we get him buried again right away?" Brooks asked.

"Me? Why should I?"

"I've got George Osaro waiting. We've acquired a coffin. I

think," Brooks said respectfully, "that we should get on with it as soon as possible. Before nightfall."

Agannis looked at him strangely. "Well, it is a body, I suppose," Agannis said on second thought. "We got the normal procedures."

"Want to take a chance of another airplane spinning out?" Brooks asked.

"No."

"Then let's move on it right away."

The remains were removed by police van to the hospital office of Dr. Herbert Youmans. The medical examiner pronounced "John Doe" dead. It was one of the doctor's easier findings.

"This, uh, ties in to all this funny business that's been going on?" Youmans asked Brooks.

"Remember our talk the day you were fishing?" Brooks asked. "You mentioned two different worlds existing inches apart from each other?"

Youmans nodded.

"Someday I'll tell you all about it," Brooks said. "You'll be fascinated."

"I'm sure," the doctor answered.

For all of Henry's inquiries about rosewood as opposed to pine, he drew the latter. A simple pine coffin had been purchased for his remains and delivered to Reverend Osaro's church that afternoon. Grave diggers had readied a spot in the far corner of the big cemetery that overlooked the windmill. The spot gave Brooks some pause. It was the same plot in which he had stood when he invaded Henry's plane. Henry would be buried—if he was successfully buried—in the spot that his spirit had designated for Annette.

It was six in the evening when Brooks used Annette's key to unlock the back door of 17 Cort Street. He wished to proceed by himself. He locked the door behind him and turned on no lights on the main floor.

Brooks opened the door to the basement and flicked on the cellar lights. He carried a shovel in one hand and a canvas bag in the other. He looked down the cellar steps and felt the aura of menace before him.

He waited to hear the voice of Henry Flaherty. But the voice didn't come.

Brooks walked down the steps and stood on the cement floor. He looked to the spot where Emmet Hughes' body had been discovered and he cringed. This place still had a deathly aura to it. And yet, Brooks knew he had only one good method of purging the house.

Bury Henry. All of him. In a cemetery where his spirit could rest.

Brooks moved across the cellar floor. He looked around and tried to sense the presence of whatever spirits were there. Specifically, Henry's. He couldn't find him.

Brooks turned his attention to the earthen section of the basement floor. There was little doubt in his mind that Henry's skull had been planted there by those who executed him.

Mrs. Ritter had indicated as much. Or at least her spirit had.

Brooks pushed the shovel into the dirt. The dirt had a high clay content and was very damp. He turned over one shovel full of it. Subliminally, he thought he heard a distant groan. Or a warning. Or an admonition to go. Then there was another as he pulled up a second bunch of earth and clay. But he kept working. The digging was slow, the ground resistant.

Through the one high window in the cellar he could see daylight dying. Evening turned to night. Brooks worked carefully. He went down and searched a foot at a time, then another six inches, then another six after that.

When, he wondered, would he find it?

He continued to work well into evening, unaware of the long dark shadow that lurked occasionally behind him. Every few minutes, Brooks would feel something, turn and look.

But each time, Henry had vanished at the moment Brooks turned and scanned. Henry had it all worked out for this day. No one would lay him to rest quite so easily.

Brooks continued to dig. He found nothing. Above him the cellar door slowly moved closed, guided by a dark but unseen hand.

It latched securely and Brooks remained unaware. Then the door locked.

Annette was annoyed. She had removed two shopping bags filled with items that she needed from 17 Cort Street. She had carefully packed the bags, so she thought, and took them to Brooks' cottage. Then, that evening when she opened them, two pieces of jewelry were missing. So was a blouse.

She would have to go back. Yet she was certain she had put them in the bag. She shook her head and wondered how she could have been so unmindful.

Brooks was in the cellar digging when she arrived. He never heard her. And as he had walked over from the nearby field, there was no car for her to see.

She unlocked the door from the outside and walked upstairs.

The house was still creepy at night. Annette wished to be in and out as quickly as possible. She went to her bedroom and prowled for the missing objects. Where could they be? How had she failed to take them?

She found the jewelry on the floor, both pieces. And the blouse? It was right in plain sight, draped over a chair.

Annette felt a little spasm of fear. Who was playing tricks on her? Her mind began to work overtime. Her imagination.

Henry, invisible, stood behind her.

Nothing to fear. Just take your items and calmly leave.

Where were these thoughts coming from? Well, at least they were reassuring.

"Damn," she said. When she examined the blouse she noticed that there was some soil on one sleeve. Almost like a handprint. She sat down on the bed, next to the sword, and tried to brush the soil away.

In the basement, Brooks recoiled.

"Oh, Christ!" he said.

He had what he wanted—and what repelled him most—both at the same time. He had found Henry Flaherty's skull.

It had been buried with nothing around it, just thrown into the earth five feet beneath the house. Brooks felt the urge to vomit and suppressed it. He had seen worse, much worse, in contemporary times in San Jose. But there was something particularly macabre about this.

Brooks suppressed a shudder. Wearing rubber gloves now, he reached into the earth around the head. He worked the dirt away from it. He cupped his fingers around it and gently pulled.

Behind him, a long, dark shadow was apparent, not far from the master switch to the electricity for 17 Cort Street.

Brooks loosened the skull from where it had rested for nearly sixty-five years. He gently eased it upward. It came loose from the ground.

There had been a heavy amount of slaked lime in the soil beneath the house. Probably a gardener had once used this area to dump discarded chemicals.

Lime would have eaten into the flesh and skull and destroyed it. Slaked lime worked differently. It acted as a preservative. Some of the hair remained on Henry's head. Bits of the skin. The teeth were intact. The face—Henry's face—was recognizable. . . .

Upstairs, a terrible thought was upon Annette. *Another demon! Rising from your basement! You must defend yourself!*

She looked up, alarmed. Oh, these thoughts! What was getting into her head? What demon?

Brooks unraveled a set of newspapers. He lay the head out. He could barely bring himself to look at it. He raised his eyes to the window in the cellar. There was a moon, but night had long since fallen.

He looked back to the head. He gazed at the sunken eye sockets and seemed to be held by them for several seconds. It was the last image that Brooks saw.

The power in the house went out. And something in the dark threw up a fistful of dirt into Brooks' face and eyes.

He cursed violently and stood. His eyes burned. He couldn't

see his enemy, but he knew who it was. He slashed at the darkness with his arm. One thought overrode all others. He wanted to get out of the house.

Upstairs, Annette was almost beset with panic. She stood and uttered a short startled scream when the lights failed. But the voice reassured her.

No, no, no! it said. *Nothing to fear. Heaven and all Goodness is with you! But you must slay the demon!*

She didn't know what that meant. Then two other thoughts were upon her. The demon in the basement. And the sword on her bed.

She reached to the sword and unsheathed it, hardly knowing what she was doing. Her heart kicked in her chest.

Yes. That is good! Bring the sword!

The inner voice guided her and reassured her. Then she heard the thumping downstairs. Her heart kicked even harder.

Go downstairs. Bring your weapon. Defend your home from evil and you will be rid of it forever.

She hesitated.

You know what you have to do!

Downstairs, Brooks had found his way to the top of the cellar steps. His eyes burned. He had hit his head on a low beam in crossing the cellar. He banged at the door.

He wondered how it had closed. Then he knew. He hit it with his fist, trying to dislodge it. He didn't scream or yell. He knew it would be pointless.

Above, Annette heard this all the more clearly. The cellar again! The focal point for all the terror in her home. Her courage rallied. Yes, indeed. She would do what the guiding voice told her. This time, she would exorcise her own demons.

Slowly, with the sword in her hands, she descended the stairs from the second floor to the main.

The knocking remained at the cellar door. The thumping.

The demon! the voice within her said. *You must decapitate it like the last one.*

Yes, Annette thought. Surely the voice was telling her what to do. It wouldn't be pleasant. But surely providence had sent her the sword for exactly this purpose. At least kill it. Don't let it loose.

On the other side of the cellar door, Tim Brooks had lost his patience. No one was home. No one was within earshot. He hit at the door repeatedly to try to get it to move. It budged only barely. But he was convinced he could knock it open. He would have to put his shoulder to it. He would have to knock it through.

On tiptoes, terrified, Annette came into her kitchen, holding the sword aloft. Holding it in an upright position so that she could slash downward upon whatever was in the cellar.

God, it was terrifying, she thought. She wished Tim were present to do this for her. She stood not far from where the demon banged upward at the cellar door. It was trying to break through. In the darkness. She could barely see.

She opened her mouth to scream at it.

No! the voice cautioned. *No! Silence on your part! Don't warn it!*

The voice was right. She held silent, all except for the pounding of her heart. It had practically risen to her throat now.

A large form will come through the door in seconds, the voice told her. *It will resemble a human. But it will be low. Bent over. Bestial. Strike down on it. A savage blow to the back of the neck with the blade. As hard as you can! As hard as you have ever hit anything in your life!*

"Oh, God," she prayed. "Give me the force. Give me the force to hit it accurately."

Don't fear, the voice told her. *I will guide your blade. I will see that it finds the demon's neck. And I will give you the strength to kill with one blow.*

From within, Brooks continued to put his shoulder to the door. He hit it hard. The door nearly left its hinges. One or two more blows, he reasoned. One or two more hard hits and he'd be through!

Don't fear, Annette. You will slay him! You will kill him! In moments, he will be dead on your floor!

Brooks pounded the door. One hinge came loose. Fantastic! Finally! The old woodwork was giving way in this infernal house.

Be ready, dear! Strike from behind its neck. Then for good measure plunge the blade into his heart when he falls.

Annette poised herself by the side of the door. As soon as it opened . . . as soon as any body hurtled through . . .

She raised the sword high above her head. She held it with all her strength, ready to slash downward in the darkness. Ready to defend her home with every ounce of anger she could muster.

Brooks hit the door and it flew from its hinges. The woodwork crashed forward into the kitchen. Brooks drew a breath. He saw light from the kitchen window and—

A scream! A primal hideous scream! A woman's cry of terror filled the air and Brooks turned away from it as the sword came down inches in front of him.

Annette's body lunged forward, following the sword. His eyes still smarted, but he could see that much. She raised the sword again and he burst forward, knocking the weapon from her hand, screaming her name.

"Annie! Annie! Annie!"

She cried hysterically until she realized that the arms around her, the force restraining her, was a human one. Not an alien one. Not a ghostly one.

She collapsed into tears, almost fainting. He held her tightly for several minutes until calm approached again.

"I nearly killed you," she cried. "I'm sorry. Can you ever forgive me. I nearly killed you!"

"You weren't even close," he said, trying to coax a reassuring smile from her. Another mingling of a lie with truth.

Once she was steady, Brooks washed the lime from his eyes. He wanted her to go on ahead to the cemetery. He asked her to walk to the adjacent field and pick up his Miata.

"I don't even want this thing in my car," Brooks explained.

"This thing" was Henry's head. Brooks would carry it over himself. Right away.

She shuddered. She pulled his car keys from his pocket and went to the Miata. She climbed in, turned on the ignition and drove. After she was gone, Brooks went back downstairs and retrieved the skull.

Brooks would never be able to describe it, but there was something horrible, something beautiful and something therapeutic about the walk.

He walked in the moonlight, the human head in his gloved hands. A funeral cortege of one. He stared straight ahead. He prayed that he would encounter no one who saw what he carried. It was a scene out of all Halloweens, a nightmare for all midnights.

He walked steadily. Henry was in his mind the whole time, cursing vehemently.

I'll have you slain yet. I'll haunt you till you burn in hell, Brooks. I'll see that woman drown. I'll see her crushed by a truck.

"I'm not listening," Brooks answered. Truly, he could lie as well as Henry. Every word from the spirit, every threat, rang home. The moon cast a million shadows through the branches of trees and every one—as he walked with Henry's head toward the cemetery—was in the shape of a small demon.

Brooks turned a final corner and walked through the gates of the graveyard. In the moonlight, up ahead, on the crest of a hill, he saw his own car parked. Annette stood next to it.

Reverend Osaro was there, as were four men to help lower the casket.

The head seemed to move in his hand. Brooks refused to look down. It had an animation of its own now. The final illusion of Henry's spirit, the final desperate, horrible trick to attempt to cause him to panic.

But Brooks wouldn't. He held his ground.

He was halfway up the walkway now, halfway to where the grave was located. A breeze riffled through his hair.

Henry's voice came from just below Brooks' hand now, speaking as if it came from the aged skull.

As if the mouth moved . . .

As if the long-dead eyes saw and shined . . .

As if the ears heard and the nose smelled . . .

You'll burn in Hell, Brooks. I'll see to it that you burn in Hell. I'll see that a million other devils come forth and torment you every day of your life. I'll see to it that your days and nights are laced with tragedy and failure, that your body is plagued with cancers, that your children die young, that—

"You can't do anything," Brooks said. "I won't let you. You're nothing without fear."

Brooks arrived at the grave site. Reverend Osaro looked quizzically at him. Then he lowered his eyes slightly and looked—for only one second—at the grisly thing that Tim Brooks carried in his hands.

"Couldn't you at least have used a shopping bag?" Osaro asked.

"That way he couldn't have said anything."

In Brooks' mind, Henry was still cursing violently, vehemently and profanely.

Osaro looked around. "I don't hear anything," he said.

Brooks shrugged. Henry was screaming into his soul.

"Me neither," Brooks said.

Brooks went to the coffin. Carefully, he laid the head at the top of the skeleton. Then he stepped back. The other members of the funeral team came forward and closed the lid. Then they stood back.

Henry's cries were muffled, then silent.

Osaro held his Bible in his hands. He might have read but didn't need to.

St. Paul a final time.

" 'I will arise and go to my Father, and I will say unto Him, Father, I have sinned against Heaven and before Thee, And I am no more worthy to be called Thy son: make me as one of thy servants.' "

The ceremony took place over five minutes. Then the casket was lowered. Brooks wasn't sure but he thought he heard a terrible long hissing sigh as the casket went down and the earth received it.

Annette must have heard it, too. Or perhaps she sensed it, for she tightly gripped Brooks' hand. In the moonlight, they could see quite well. They saw the casket settle on the floor of the grave. Then the grave diggers reached for shovels.

Brooks held one, too. He stayed with Annette until the grave was filled in and complete.

It was at that time that a wave of exhaustion overtook them both. Emotional and physical. They climbed into the car.

"It's over," he said. "It's over."

They drove back to his place and slept more soundly than either of them had in months—since the very peaceful days that they could barely remember, back before the death of Mary Elizabeth DiMarco.

Then again, that was way back when they didn't even know each other.

Part Four
Epilogue

Faith is the substance of things hoped
for, the evidence of things not seen.
THE EPISTLE OF PAUL TO THE HEBREWS

We walk by faith, not by sight.
THE SECOND EPISTLE OF PAUL
TO THE CORINTHIANS

Thirty-three

Over the remainder of August, Annette Carlson reclaimed her home at 17 Cort Street.

She reclaimed it slowly at first. Spending an hour every day there, then two hours, then more. Eventually she worked up the nerve to spend an evening. Next a night with Tim. Then two nights. By then the spell—if that's what it had been—was broken.

The old house still gave an eerie creak occasionally, but there were no more sightings, no more strange otherworldly appearances. As a conduit from one plane of reality into the next, the place had fallen fallow.

It was as if a mood had been lifted, an unseen grip released. Whatever force had been in control of 17 Cort Street held it no longer. The house, in fact, became a charming, comfortable place for her, one where she enjoyed being and one which she hated to leave.

The charges against Eddie Lloyd for the murder of Mary Beth DiMarco were eventually dropped. Lack of evidence. Though the case remained officially open, the Nantucket police considered it solved. Andrea Ward even wrote a long series about the case for her paper. Her editor cut much of it, not believing it could actually be true. Eventually, Andrea resigned. She would try the story as a book, if only a publisher would believe her.

George Osaro soon departed Nantucket, also, though, in his

usual manner, nothing could have occurred in a straightforward fashion.

On August 31, two weeks after the burial of Henry Flaherty's remains, George appeared to begin his goodbyes. He was leaving a week early for his new parish in Oregon, he explained. And he was doing it as he saw fit.

He distributed small trinkets to friends and parishioners, tokens by which to remember him and his Spiritual Nantucket soirees. He had also left his Voyager at the church, having signed the title to the car over to the parish.

"It's my small gift," he said to the gray-haired ladies who volunteered at Christ and Holy Trinity, dismissing his own generosity. "I'm tired of paying the frigging insurance and I don't think the filthy old heap will be able to drag its ass across the entire country, anyway."

George rolled his eyes. Then he winked.

The ladies blinked.

"So how *are* you getting to Oregon?" Brooks eventually asked.

"It's a big country," Osaro answered. "I thought I'd see it close up."

He showed Brooks a new pair of hiking shoes and his battered backpack, the latter crammed with a few changes of clothing and a Bible. George was planning to hoof it across the country and had every intention of traveling light. "Material possessions are really a damned chore anyway," he explained. He was nothing if not unorthodox. But for a spiritual man he was consistent.

Annette gave him a kiss shortly in advance of his departure. There were the inevitable awkward moments when the pastor seemed to waver about going. But then George Andrew Osaro rallied his spirit and promised he would remain in contact.

At four o'clock on the overcast afternoon of September first, George said his final goodbye at the police station. Tim Brooks embraced his friend and told him he'd miss him. Then George turned and left without looking back. Simple as that. From a window, Brooks watched the minister walk to the ferry terminal. He thought of all the suspicions he had ever entertained about George and he weighed the many theories about ghosts that he had unearthed in the Eksman Collection at Harvard. Yet Brooks felt a lump in his throat and a deep sorrow as he watched his friend depart.

Labor Day passed, and with it, summer. The island was left to its year-round population, plus a few who felt that the glory of autumn is Nantucket's most beautiful season. But in the end, September was a time of departure, a time of things coming to an end, a marking of the passage of one more season from the life of every human.

Annette began to assemble many of her things first for the journey back to California for preproduction, then for the voyage to Europe. *Message From Berlin* was going to happen. And there was work to be done.

Brooks had some vacation time coming and Bill Agannis agreed that he could take it toward the latter half of October and early November. Tentative plans were made by Brooks to travel to Europe to visit Annette on her set. She insisted that he come.

At first he had demurred, muttering something idiotic about it "not being right" or it being "kind of awkward." He also knew that the cheap-shot press would have a field day with their relationship.

"But I love you," she told him. "I don't give a damn what anyone writes in the press and I'm going to cry if I lose you."

He realized that he felt much the same way, and told her so in those words. So he agreed to come.

"Plus if I get a free week we can drive from Italy up to Paris, all by our lonesomes," she whispered in his ear at one point. "We can stay in these sexy little guest houses along the way."

He applied for a passport renewal immediately.

In the best sense of everything, he felt like he was twenty years old again, with a bold, wonderful life stretched out before him. Better yet, after the experience with George and Henry, he would never fear anything again in his life.

Even death.

495

Then a week after Labor Day, Annette locked up her house and flew to California. Like George Osaro, she said she'd stay in close touch.

Annie did. She and Brooks exchanged brief calls each evening for no other reason than to hear each other's voice. It was a bittersweet way to maintain a relationship, full of frustrations and insecurities. But looked at from another angle, knowing there was someone in the world whom one loved that greatly and would soon see again, it was a soaring wonderful addition to each of their lives.

It was more, however, than anyone heard from George Osaro.

Not a word came from George. Not a letter. Not even a postcard as he traveled his unorthodox path across the United States.

The darker side of Brooks' psyche took over and he began to imagine what dire fate might have befallen a single, boyish-looking Japanese-American traversing the continent on foot. Or, for that matter, exactly what plane of which universe had George dropped into? So Timothy Brooks, ever the detective, ever concerned about people he cared for, took it upon himself to find out.

He wrote to the parish in Oregon to which Osaro claimed he had been assigned. Ten days later, Brooks' letter was returned. The destination was nonexistent, though on checking, Brooks had used the exact address that Osaro had provided him.

So Brooks picked up the telephone and tried to call. The parish named had no listing. And when Brooks pursued the matter and dialed all the Lutheran parishes in Salem, none had heard of a George Osaro. None was even expecting a new pastor.

Brooks took the matter to Lieutenant Agannis one slow morning in late September. Agannis sat behind his desk, shrouded as always in his cloud of tobacco smoke, and ruminated upon yet another elusive point of police work.

"So what are you asking me for, Timmy?" Agannis asked.

"Well, I think all of us on this island owe George a little

something. We never would have put Henry to rest without him. So I'd like to make sure George is at least safe."

Agannis moaned. First he had been asked to believe in ghosts. Now he was being asked for an extra hit on the town's staggering treasury. "You talking about *traveling expenses,* kid?"

"Yes, sir."

Agannis whistled low and pondered the point for a moment. In the corner of the office, Boomer glanced up at the invocation of Osaro's name. Then, as if even the dog knew George was gone, Boomer exuded a gigantic yawn.

"I guess we can label this a 'Missing Person,' can't we?" Agannis concluded. "What do you need?"

"Maybe a week."

"Ouch! Take it before I change my mind."

Brooks smiled gratefully and stood. "Thanks," he said.

"Get out of my God damned sight, will ya?"

"Yes, sir."

Two mornings later, Brooks found himself sitting in the office of Stephen Kerrigan Albrecht, the Lutheran bishop of Boston. Bishop Albrecht was late arriving from another meeting.

As Brooks waited, his head swam. He recalled the many times that he had sat in Reverend Osaro's much smaller rectory office in Nantucket. And he recalled also the profanity-laced conversations on the subject of this very bishop.

At ten minutes after two, Bishop Albrecht rolled into the room. The bishop was not at all what Brooks had expected. He was a genial gray-haired man, immaculately dressed in a dark blue suit, trim and patrician, with friendly, kindly eyes. He had an easy manner and greeted Brooks warmly.

"From Nantucket, are you?" the bishop inquired after excusing his tardiness. "I used to summer there myself. How are things on Nantucket?"

"Overall, just fine," Brooks said. "A bit quiet after the summer, sir. Mercifully."

"I'm sure. Lovely little patch of the world," the bishop said. " 'The Old Gray Lady of the Sea.' Isn't that what they call the island?"

"Yes, sir."

"You're so lucky to live and work there. I understand the island is particularly beautiful in the autumn."

"It can be."

"Please sit," the bishop offered.

Both men sat.

"My wife and I were hoping to sail over to Nantucket with friends this past summer," the bishop began. "But, well, you know how things are, Sergeant. We never did have the time."

Brooks was not a sergeant and doubted that he ever would be. But, yes, he knew how things were.

"Maybe next year," the bishop said.

"That would be nice," Brooks said. "If you have a moment, come by police headquarters and say hello."

"I'll do that," the bishop said indulgently. "That's very thoughtful of you." He paused. "Now, tell me. What can I do for you today? Is this personal business or professional?"

"A little of both. Mostly personal."

The bishop waited.

"I've been trying to get in touch with one George Andrew Osaro. Formerly of your parish in Nantucket."

"Ah, yes. George . . ." The bishop nodded, though his voice tailed off inconclusively.

"Apparently, I have the wrong address. I was wondering if you might—"

"You and me both," the bishop said, still nodding. He laughed slightly.

"What?"

"I've been trying to contact him, too," the bishop said. "When I heard that you were from Nantucket, I was hoping that you might have come with a message. Or that you might be able to help me. Seems I have the wrong address for him."

"But George was transferred."

"That's right."

"Through your archdiocese."

"That's right."

"Then surely you must have the address in Oregon that—"

"Oh, but he never reported," the bishop said.

Brooks was stunned for a moment. Then, "But he gave me . . ."

Brooks' voice trailed off in astonishment. The bishop picked up the silence.

"George has left the ministry," the bishop said with evident regret. "It came as an absolute shock to me. I received his letter, oh, just five or six days ago. Postmarked somewhere in Illinois. I've been trying to contact him since. We never knew he was even considering a resignation. And needless to say, we would have attempted to change his mind. Or offer him a sabbatical if he desired one. He's a fine, fine pastor."

Brooks, thoroughly confused, still said nothing.

"I really didn't understand what was going on with George," the bishop continued sadly. "He was doing an excellent job in Nantucket. And I heard he was popular. Well liked. Then he wrote to me early in late July requesting an immediate transfer for personal reasons. We spoke a few times. George didn't choose to share with me his problems, which I can understand, though I wished I'd been able to help."

"Wait a minute," Brooks asked. "You're telling me that George Osaro *requested* a transfer?"

"Why, yes. Didn't you know?"

"With all due respect, Bishop. . . . You're certain of that?"

The bishop chuckled. "I certainly am. Everything goes through my office. I'd know."

"I knew George had *received* a transfer. But he never said he had asked for it. In fact, quite the contrary."

Now the bishop showed some confusion. He shrugged. "Why else would we have given him one? We don't move people who are doing a good job unless they have a specific skill that is urgently needed elsewhere. And even then, we would never *order* a move. The church is not like that today. So there was no reason to relocate a kindly soul such as George."

"I'm quite confused by this," Brooks said.

"Likewise."

"George said that his 'Spiritual Nantucket' nights had created some disfavor within the church hierarchy," Brooks said, trying a new angle.

"Really?" the bishop frowned. "With whom? Specifically?"

"Specifically, your office, sir. With you."

Bishop Albrecht frowned. "You must be mistaken. No one here objected to George sitting around spinning a few ghost stories for the summer crowd. Fact is, I thought it was a crackling good idea, myself. Exploration of the human spirit," he said with enthusiasm. "The levels of God's love and reach. I *adore* a good ghost yarn as much as the next man, and I have nothing at all against new ideas or the exploration of the human spirit. I'm sorry I was never able to attend."

The bishop studied his visitor. "Son," he finally said, "you look completely baffled."

"I am."

"Don't be." He paused. His eyes narrowed. His voice softened to a more confidential tone. "George isn't in any sort of trouble, is he? With the police or anything? If he is, the archdiocese would be happy to help the situation in any way."

"No, sir. He's not in any trouble."

"Then why are you looking for him?"

"It's a matter of personal concern more than anything."

"Then you really *are* here more on personal business than professional?"

"Yes, sir. As I stated earlier."

There was something sly in the bishop's eyes. And there was an unsaid something upon which he was deciding whether or not to touch.

"I rather knew this would happen someday. George just disappearing," the bishop finally began. "I'm just sorry that the day has finally come."

He hedged with anything further.

Brooks nudged him. "Anything you could tell me that would help . . ." Brooks suggested.

The bishop sighed. "In terms of George's comings and goings," Bishop Albrecht said, "this isn't the first time George has presented us with a bit of a mystery."

"How do you mean?"

"In confidence? Between us?" The bishop's gaze traveled to the door, which was closed.

"Of course," said Brooks.

"We never really *did* know George's full background," the bishop said in a hushed voice. "You see, he was always sort of a special case. He came to the divinity school without the normal academic credentials. Oh, he very much had the intellectual qualifications. No question about that. Lightning intellect. Well, you know. You knew him. But he hadn't the years of formal study. Quite frankly, I'm not sure I *ever* learned where he spent his late teens and early twenties."

"I thought he went to some little liberal arts college out in California," Brooks said.

Bishop Albrecht was already shaking his head. "George was from western Massachusetts," the bishop said. "After he was ordained, for some reason something came up, and his background was reexamined. Turns out that very little that he had told us was true. Liberal arts school. Driving a cab in Montana. Whatever other fictions he was spinning."

"A clever mixture of lies and truth?" Brooks offered.

"Well, yes," Albrecht said with no malice whatsoever. "You could describe it exactly as that." He sighed. "I'm afraid that *did* offend *some* people. Certain members of the administration of the church here wished to revoke his ordination. And not without good reason." He pursed his lips in thought. "I must confess: I was George's main proponent. His advocate. His chevalier. He was so good, so perfectly suited to the clergy, that I felt very deeply that an extreme exception had to be made for him." He paused. "And, of course, one was. Otherwise we would have deprived ourselves of a unique individual."

"What are you telling me?" Brooks asked. "That he fabricated much of his background?"

"Well, yes," the bishop nodded as if it weren't unusual. "Just about everything," he said, "except for the fact that he was born George Andrew Osaro in Pittsfield, Massachusetts in nineteen

501

sixty-one. His mother still lives there." Bishop Albrecht paused. "You can take it from there, I suppose."

"Pittsfield, huh?"

"Pittsfield. Other end of the state. Out by the New York border. Lovely scenery this time of year."

"Same last name? His mother?"

The bishop stolidly spelled it out. "O-S-A-R-O," he said. "A name with a certain geometry. Almost spells the same thing backward as forward, doesn't it?"

The bishop smiled.

"Almost," Brooks answered.

"Almost," Bishop Albrecht agreed.

"Thank you, sir," Brooks said. He rose and made a move toward the door.

"Oh, Sergeant?" the cleric said with a smile.

Brooks waited.

"If you happen to see George," he said with a strange cast to his voice, "*do* tell him that any fence can be mended. He can come back whenever he wants." The bishop winked. "I'm inclined to believe in spirits myself."

"I'll tell him exactly that," Brooks said.

"Thank you. Drive safely."

The next stop of the day was in the Boston suburb of Framingham. It was an address that Brooks had brought with him from the island, having carefully memorized it.

In that town, he found himself in front of a small, depressingly ordinary tract house in the early afternoon. There were broken toys on the front lawn and two cars in the short driveway. The garage door was up and the interior of the garage seemed to be filled with packing cartons and broken pieces of furniture.

There were two cars in the driveway, one a rusting green Toyota from the early 1980s. That one carried a Massachusetts registration. Its companion was something from the Ford Motor Company and was both more recent and more muscular. It bore a Texas license plate and—to Brooks' careful eye—an expired registration sticker.

Across the street a woman with a scarf around her rollered hair was walking a dog and staring at Brooks and his exotic wheels.

Brooks went to the front door and rapped. Someone should give a course in the police academy, Brooks thought idly, on how to go to a front door and rap.

He heard some movement from within but there was no response. He knocked a second time. Then the door opened a crack, held firmly by a chain. A small female body—a pale girlish woman in a stained sweatshirt and very short cutoff jeans—stood on the other side.

"Yes?" she asked. Two cautious but bleary eyes assessed him.

He recognized her. "Carol Ann?" he asked, kindly and patiently.

"Who are you?" Her tone was defensive.

"We met a few times on Nantucket," Brooks said. "I'm Tim Brooks. Used to play basketball with your husband."

The chain didn't move. Neither did Carol Ann. Nor was there any welcome or flash of recognition. "Yeah?" she asked. "What do you want?"

"I wish to speak with you for a moment," Brooks said pleasantly, "preferably without a door between us. How would you feel about opening up?"

Her eyes flickered past his shoulder to peer across the lawn, seeking, Brooks reasoned, to establish that he was alone. Then she looked him over a second time and finally arrived at a very unenthusiastic decision.

"Yeah. I sort of remember you," she said flatly.

The door closed again, then opened partway. She kept one hand on it and did not ask him in.

Four years had passed since he'd last seen George Osaro's wife. On this day, her face registered at least twice this. Her hair was pulled back and there were gray streaks in it. For a fleeting disturbing moment, Brooks saw himself again as a much younger man in San Jose, working undercover, and presenting himself at a hundred such doorways, each one as hostile and uncooperative as the next or the last.

"What is it?" she asked without emotion. "George? Is that it? Something happen to him? He die?"

"I don't know," Brooks said. "He told me he set off across the country. I was wondering if you—"

"I haven't heard from him. Don't expect to," she said. Behind her, a shaggy calico cat sauntered across a tattered carpet. Beyond that, there was a living room. The decor and arrangement of furniture called to mind an explosion in a junk shop.

"I thought he kept in touch," Brooks said.

"Why would he?"

"He frequently told me he did."

"He lied. He lied all the time. About everything. What would he want with me?"

"You have a son for one thing. I was under the impression he paid child support."

"It's not his child, which he's damned well aware of. And he doesn't support it," Carol Ann said angrily. "*I* do. And if you want to know the fucking truth, we were never married, either. Not legally."

"I see." Brooks groped along. She had come a long way since taking up with George and posing as the minister's wife. "Well, would you have any idea—?"

"Carol . . . ?" a male voice called. "Who you talkin' to?"

From behind, from the next room, appeared a tall, barefoot man with a short gray-black beard. He brought with him the attractively blended scents of tobacco, sweat, marijuana and oil paints. He wore dirty jeans and no shirt. Brooks took him to be her Texan, or, as he remembered George labeling him, "her cowboy."

Tex stopped short when he saw that they had company.

Carol Ann turned and cut him off just as fast. "I got a visitor, Bobby. This gent here's a policeman. Looking for George Osaro."

Two and a half sentences. Enough to pull a tight shroud across Texas Bobby's friendliness.

Carol Ann turned back to her visitor.

"I haven't seen George," she said. "I won't see George. I

moved out years ago and haven't heard from him since. He's out of my life. I don't know what you're doing here."

"He never came to see you?"

"Why would he?"

"I got your address from his files."

She shrugged belligerently. "I can't help what he writes in his damned address book," she snarled.

Philosophically, she had a point.

"Anything else?" she asked icily. Her hand was anxious to push the door shut.

"Nope," Brooks said. "That's it. Other than the fact that you ought to get that car registration renewed."

"Yeah," she said. "When we got the bread."

She closed the door without another word. But by then Brooks had enough, too. So he offered no goodbye either, and slipped back into his car. Across the street, the woman in the scarf turned and resumed walking her mutt.

Returned to the solace and comfort of his Miata, Brooks found the route that led him to Interstate 90. He threw his car into its highest gear and drove westward across the state. He stopped for a fast high-carbohydrate lunch at some anonymous take-out joint and wasted as little time in transit as possible. He sensed an inner urgency to all of this, even though rationality suggested that there wasn't any.

On the less congested sections of the westbound Massachusetts Turnpike, he frequently found himself doing a steady eighty miles per hour. Once, through the farm country west of Springfield, the needle of his speedometer tickled eighty-five. And in an event that was not unrelated to this number, when he flew past Woronoco in the west central part of the state, he found himself looking at a red flashing light of the Massachusetts State Police in his rearview mirror.

A state trooper with reflector sunglasses and a Third Reich mentality stepped out of an unmarked car. But Brooks' identification as a Nantucket town cop and his explanation that he was on what he termed "urgent official business" let him off with a smile and a warning. This was not, of course, until after his license and shield number were run through the computers of the state gendarmerie.

Tim Brooks arrived in Pittsfield at a few minutes before six in the evening and soon found himself rapping on his second front door of the day.

George Osaro's mother was a gracious, small-framed woman who answered the door promptly. Trustingly, she invited him inside as soon as Timothy Brooks identified himself. She insisted in fluent but not-quite-perfect English that first he take his shoes off and that second he join her for a cup of tea.

Brooks did both.

As she brewed tea for the two of them, he sat in the neat living room in a modest cottage. He established that he was the only one in the house besides George's mother. The room was furnished with some modern pieces and some handsome antiques, a curious blend of Americana and Japan.

Mrs. Osaro returned with a warm smile, never asking Brooks' reason for the visit. She served tea. Both sipped.

"I hope you don't mind," Brooks began, "but I came to ask you a few questions about your son."

"Which son? There are three."

"George Andrew?" he asked.

A very slight pause. She waited. "Yes? You go ahead, please?"

"I realize that this might be a bit painful for you, Mrs. Osaro," Brooks said. "But can you tell me. . . . When did George die?"

"That was nineteen seventy-seven," she said. "September seventeen of that year. Yes." There seemed to be no pain. That, or it had eased over a decade and a half.

"You want to know how he die?" she asked. Her accent was delicate like her son's.

"If you care to tell me," Brooks said.

"He was attempting to meet God through the use of mescaline," she said. "Or peyote. Or are they the same?"

"They're similar."

506

"He take an overdose," she said very routinely. "Met God, all right, didn't he?"

"I suppose he did," Brooks agreed. He had absolutely no idea what nuance she had intended to her response.

Mrs. Osaro smiled.

Brooks noticed some pictures on a desk in the corner. He asked if he could take a look and if she would be kind enough to tell him about them. Again, she was more than gracious.

Her other two sons were still alive and had families, she said. One was living in Boston, the other in New York. The son in Boston had an American wife, the other had married a pretty Japanese girl. Mrs. Osaro was a proud grandmother four times over and revealed portraits of the handsome, affluent families headed by her two living boys.

She also showed him a photograph of her and her late parents when they were young in Hawaii in the 1920s. And there was also a much more recent portrait of George's father, a sturdy handsome man who looked much like George, taken in 1982, a year before his death.

Tim Brooks expected her mood to darken over when the topic inevitably shifted to her deceased son. But it didn't.

She said that from his boyhood he had always been a bit of a mystic, influenced greatly by Eastern writings as well as theology. She said that it was always his goal to join the American clergy and bring an Eastern sense of the mystical and the spiritual to those badly in need of it. His mission, she said, was always to watch over people. To bring them together. To help his fellow man in matters that defied normal means of assistance.

Brooks listened to all of this with a feeling that goose bumps should have been crawling up and down his spine. But none were. None were, because this was much as he had suspected, little by little, for several weeks. Suspected, but never quite able to completely believe until this moment.

George had also been, Mrs. Osaro related, a pretty good athlete for a boy of small stature.

"Did he play basketball?" Brooks asked.

507

She laughed. "Georgie love basketball," she said with enthusiasm. "And he play very well against the bigger and stronger ones."

"I'm sure of that," Brooks said.

She led him across the room and showed Brooks a trophy George had won in the eighth grade. Most valuable player on his junior high team.

She put the trophy down and walked back toward where they had sat.

"Funny thing is," she said, "that I always use to worry about him. Somehow knew George would do something crazy like that. Kill himself. And know what he'd say to me? He'd say that he had seen the other side. Said there was another beautiful world out there and that he was going to travel between it. And he said he'd have his way of communicating back to me. Sending messages. Have people come by and tell me he's fine. Just to let me know that his spirit was out there."

"Uh huh," Brooks said.

"So your visit today doesn't come as shock. Doesn't upset me. Just reassures, I guess you say. Know what I mean?"

Brooks knew.

"Sit back down," she said very routinely. "Have some more tea."

Brooks sat. "Well, he *is* fine," Brooks said.

"Oh, I know," Mrs. Osaro said very casually. "I sense him all the time, too."

As more days passed, as a cold October arrived, and as the dark shadow of all preceding events withdrew, the more Timothy Brooks puzzled over what had happened. And the more he puzzled, the more he was beset by the many contradictions he had witnessed.

He at first tried to see events within traditional Christian terms. But this eventually struck him as too sparse, too narrow, and he tried to add spiritualist shadings with maybe even a little Eastern touch sprinkled in.

The same as George Osaro might have done. Or at least, the same as George's spirit might have put forth.

Contradictions. And of course questions. Including the largest question of all. Where did life end? What were the levels of reality?

He could hear his friend again. "How many levels are there, Tim? One. Two. Six million. And what are the levels of each?"

And, "Once you've accepted that the paranormal exists, you can accept anything that follows."

And so on.

Brooks could even hear the ghost of Henry Flaherty, reduced to a harmless echo now: *George Osaro is a dead man!* Well, yes. He had been all along. Another clever mingling of lies and truth.

And yet to another degree, none of the answers that took shape for Tim Brooks would ever approach the answers he had held a few weeks earlier. He would never walk past a cemetery in the same way. He would never attend a church service, act as a pall bearer, or enter a dark, creaking house in the same way, either.

Life. Resurrection. Hope. Salvation. All the abstracts took on new meaning. Yet in some ways they weren't abstracts at all.

Some of this, some of his suspicions, some of what he most fervently held, came to fruition on the evening of October sixth that same year.

Tim Brooks was on the high school basketball court and a sense of loneliness was upon him.

He stood by himself, a solitary figure in the twilight. He had just passed another birthday and, he reasoned, had marked a point in his life midway between birth and death.

He hit a jump shot from the top of the key. He sank two from beyond the three point line.

Then he moved to the foul line, that small patch of the world where he had always reigned.

He shot and missed.

He retrieved the ball, shot and missed again.

Then he missed a third time. Extraordinary.

He returned to the foul line and missed four more consecutive shots. He watched each one, its arc perfectly true until the end when each shot found some way to land awkwardly on the rim of the basket and fall free—as if cleared by an invisible hand.

Brooks stared at what had happened right before his eyes.

"Goaltending!" he said aloud.

He went back to the line and shot again. Nothing would fall. Thirteen misses in a row. Then sixteen. Never in his life . . .

He thought. He smiled.

"Damn you!" he said aloud.

He turned. In the few rays that remained of daylight, he saw, he thought he saw—no, afterward he was *sure* that he had seen—the figure of a small man watching him from the grove of trees that bordered the parking lot.

He took a step toward it and the vision proved misty. But at the same time, he was aware that a car was coming.

He glanced at the car. A rental. At least one diehard tourist left over from the summer, he reasoned.

Then he glanced back at the man in the shadows. The figure did not recede. In fact, it moved slightly. And far from fear— Brooks did not think he would fear anything again in his life— he felt a sense of comfort. A sense of well-being.

He took a step closer and thought he recognized—

The car pulled up near the court. Its horn gave a honk. But Brooks ignored it, stepping to the edge of the court. He then looked back to the grove of trees.

He called out. "George . . . ? I see you, George!"

But this time no one was there. Yet he had this sense these days, this *sense* that he had picked up from a dear friend. Why, he could often go into a disturbed place or a paranormal situation and—

The car pulled as close to him as it could. The window rolled down on the passenger side.

"Hey, you big hunky dumb cop!" called out a familiar female voice. "Did you forget what I look like?"

The recognition was upon him. He stared.

"Annie?"

"Get in the car, you jerk! I'm on my way to Paris! How much time do you think I have?"

He tossed the basketball toward the car window. This shot went straight through. Perfect. Swish.

She laughed, then knocked the ball into the back seat so that she could hug him long and hard when he jumped in.

He had no idea how much time she had. But it turned out to be five days, a Thursday through a Monday, en route to Europe for her movie.

Five days, and since Massachusetts lay on the path between Los Angeles and Italy . . . sort of . . . if you bent the airline routes a little . . .

This time they drove back to Cort Street. They re-opened the house and put logs in the fireplace. They braced themselves against the chill of autumn. And they found new charm to Annie's home.

It was a warm, inviting place now, filled with happiness, good times and cheer. And as the years subsequently passed, as Annie and Timothy grew older together, it was difficult to imagine that 17 Cort Street hadn't been that way forever.